The Resurrected Holmes

The Resurrected Holmes

NEW CASES FROM THE NOTES OF

John H. Watson, M.D.

Completed by Divers Hands &
Edited by Marvin Kaye

with an introduction and rubrics
by J. Adrian Fillmore,
Gadshill Adjunct, Parker College

ST. MARTIN'S PRESS ✖ NEW YORK

THE RESURRECTED HOLMES. Copyright © 1996 by Marvin Kaye. All rights reserved. Printed in the United States of America. No part of this book may be used or reproduced in any manner whatsoever without written permission except in the case of brief quotations embodied in critical articles or reviews. For information, address St. Martin's Press, 175 Fifth Avenue, New York, NY 10010.

Library of Congress Cataloging-in-Publication Data

The resurrected Holmes : new cases from the notes of John H. Watson, M.D. / completed by divers hands & edited by Marvin Kaye ; with an introduction and rubrics by J. Adrian Fillmore.—1st ed.
        p.   cm.
    ISBN 0-312-14037-1
    1. Holmes, Sherlock (Fictitious character)—Fiction.   2. Detective and mystery stories, American.   3. Detective and mystery stories, English.   4. Private investigators—England—Fiction.   I. Kaye, Marvin.
PS648.D4R47   1995
813'.0108351—dc20   95-41626
                                                                CIP

Copyright page continues on page 336

First Edition: March 1996

10 9 8 7 6 5 4 3 2 1

To
Otto Penzler
Mystery editor par excellence
and guiding genius of Manhattan's mystery mecca,
The Mysterious Bookshop,
and to A. C. D.
This form of . . . flattery?

Contents

Foreword

This is the most unusual book I have ever edited.

It offers fifteen new stories about Sherlock Holmes—but there all similarity ends between *The Resurrected Holmes* and other Holmesian collections (with the single exception of my own 1994 anthology, *The Game Is Afoot,* which included a "trial balloon" for the present volume: "The Sinister Cheesecake," ostensibly penned by the unlikely "Craig Shaw Gardner," but generally attributed to Damon Runyon).

IMPORTANT—Before enjoying the serendipitous pleasures of *The Resurrected Holmes,* readers are urged to read the brief introductory essay, "The Resurrection of Sherlock Holmes," by the distinguished Gadshill Adjunct of English literature at Pennsylvania's small, but exclusive Parker College, J. Adrian Fillmore.

—MARVIN KAYE
New York City
July 1995

The Resurrection of Sherlock Holmes

If you love the Sherlock Holmes adventures (and if you don't, someone behind you is probably waiting impatiently for you to put this book back on the shelf!), like me you have sorely lamented the fact that The Great Detective's best friend, coadventurer and erstwhile roommate John H. Watson, M.D., only wrote sixty of them.

Like me, you have also surely dreamed about visiting the bank vaults of Cox & Company, London, to peep into the battered tin dispatch-box that Dr. Watson stored there. This legendary container was crammed full of notes for over sixty additional Sherlock Holmes cases that, for various reasons, Watson never got around to writing. For the past half-century, this seemed to be a forlorn dream, for Cox & Company was destroyed during a World War II Nazi bombing raid.

But now, fifty years later, the truth can at last be told—Dr. Watson's unpublished records have survived!

WAIT! Before you wolf down the stories in the rest of this book there's something *even more amazing* to tell you about them . . .

Near the end of World War I, Watson inexplicably disappeared from public life. After an appropriate interval, his one living relative petitioned the English courts, which declared Watson legally dead.

The decision caused great dismay when it was learned that Watson died intestate. Certain personages of wealth and power feared a public auction of the dispatch-box that Watson had more than once mentioned in print. It held secrets that Mycroft Holmes once called "my brother Sherlock's insurance policy."

Influence was brought to bear and a staggering amount of cash was spent to prevent the tin time bomb from being sold to just anyone. Finally, a private sale was arranged to a well-known Philadelphia book collector on the condition that the lid be kept on the dispatch-box, figuratively if not literally, for a minimum of five decades.

This collector, whom we will call Mr. R., was true to his word, though naturally he was elated when the box at last arrived, and naturally he wasted no time examining his priceless literary treasure. Only there was a rude awakening in store for him, one that most any professional writer or editor could have predicted . . .

For Dr. Watson's unadorned notes, though models of clarity, are disappointing to read. Inevitably, they lack the spellbinding narrative gifts that he applied to his bald workshop entries to transfigure them into legitimate parts of our beloved Holmesian Canon.

Fortunately, Mr. R. had plenty of time, money and determination. With great secrecy, the collector negotiated with some of the world's most noted authors to turn Watson's notes into full-blooded Sherlock Holmes adventures. He offered generous fees for their efforts.*

For nearly fifty years, Mr. R. appealed to established writers and promising newcomers alike. Not all accepted his commission, of course, but even a partial roster of those he petitioned reads like a veritable ABC of western literature, including both Conrad Aiken

---

*Average: $5,000 per story. Exceptionally famous authors got more, as they were commissioned to create works-for-hire, with all rights purchased in perpetuity. One enfant terrible designated in the records as H. E. asked for $50,000, which Mr. R. actually agreed to. But he changed his mind when the arrogant youth swore at him on the telephone for refusing to honor H. E.'s demand for advance payment.

and his daughter Joan, Edgar Rice Burroughs, Raymond Chandler, Theodore Dreiser, Helen Eustis, F. Scott Fitzgerald, Graham Greene, Ernest Hemingway, Michael Innes, James Joyce, Eric Knight, Ring Lardner, A. Merritt, Vladimir Nabokov, John O'Hara, Leo Perutz, Ellery Queen, Bertrand Russell, Rex Stout, Dylan Thomas, Leon Uris, Kurt Vonnegut, Edith Wharton, W. B. Yeats, Eugeny Zamyatin.

Mr. R. stipulated that writers must suppress their own narrative styles and thematic concerns, except insofar as each could choose the Holmes escapade he or she liked best. He insisted they strive for as close an approximation of Dr. Watson's voice as humanly possible. But pastiche is an exacting art. Some succeeded, most of them did not.

When Mr. R. died in 1991, his last wish was that his family release the best of the Watsonian redactions he bought. His estate approached St. Martin's Press, which invited me to select and edit fifteen stories from Mr. R.'s collection, and to write prefatory notes for each. To this end, Mr. R.'s descendants patiently endured endless nitpicking interviews, allowed me to examine Mr. R.'s financial ledgers and canceled checks, and also to sift through his voluminous, cryptic journals in order to prepare my notes.

While the identity of the authors Mr. R. commissioned remains a matter of opinion, I trust the style of each story speaks for itself.

Readers, rejoice! The long embargo has been lifted and Sherlock Holmes lives again. Though legal reasons require us to assign each story two bylines, one real, one obviously false, remember the *real* author is John H. Watson, M.D. . . . as seen through a glass darkly.

—J. Adrian Fillmore
Gadshill Adjunct for English literature
Parker College (PA)

Literary
"Ghosts"

While searching for authors to build Dr. Watson's notes into complete Sherlock Holmes adventures, "Mr. R.," the Philadelphia book collector, tried to enlist some of the most important names in literature. The response was spotty; those who did agree either were already enthusiastic Holmes fans, or just plain strapped for cash. Thus, in the total mix of Mr. R.'s inventory, "mainstream" writers are outnumbered three to one by genre specialists like those in this volume's two remaining sections. This is regretful, since Mr. R.'s "stars" were mostly successful in sacrificing their own styles for a genuine Watsonian tone.

*In "The Five Orange Pips," we are told that 1887 furnished Sherlock Holmes "with a long series of cases, of greater or less interest," one of them involving "the Amateur Mendicant Society, who held a luxurious club in the lower vault of a furniture warehouse." This untold story was the first commissioned by Mr. R., who inscribed "HGW" in the "Recipient" column of his ledger of payments. This suggests H. G. WELLS (1866– 1946), England's prolific author of mainstream and genre fiction (*The Invisible Man, The Time Machine, The War of the Worlds, *etc.), as does the story's lean, sinewy style, in some ways similar to short fiction written by Watson's literary representative, Arthur Conan Doyle. Only the end of the story does not ring true, a fact I attribute to the fact that H. G. Wells was a Socialist.—*JAF

The Adventure of the Amateur Mendicant Society

BY *"JOHN GREGORY BETANCOURT"*
(ASCRIBED TO H. G. WELLS)

As I have written previously, my first years sharing lodgings with Mr. Sherlock Holmes were among the most interesting of my life. Of all his cases—both public and private—which took place during this period, there remains one in particular of which I have hesitated to write until this time. Despite an ingenious resolution—and to my mind a wholeheartedly satisfactory one—contrived by my friend, the bizarre nature of this affair has made me reluctant to place it before a general readership. However, I feel the time has come to lay forth the facts concerning Mr. Oliver Pendleton-Smythe and the most unusual organization to which he belonged.

My notebook places our first meeting with Mr. Pendleton-Smythe, if meeting it can be called, at Tuesday the 24th of April, 1887. We had just concluded a rather sensitive investigation (of which I am still not at liberty to write), and Holmes's great mind had begun to turn inexorably inward. I feared he might once more take up experimentation with opiates to satiate his need for constant mental stimulation.

So it was that I felt great relief when Mrs. Hudson announced that a man—a very insistent man who refused to give his name—was at the door to see Mr. Holmes.

"Dark overcoat, hat pulled low across his forehead, and carrying a black walking stick?" Holmes asked without looking up from his chair.

"Why, yes!" exclaimed Mrs. Watson. "How ever did you know?"

Holmes made a deprecating gesture. "He has been standing across the street staring up at our windows for more than an hour. Of course I noticed when I went to light my pipe, and I marked him again when I stood to get a book just a moment ago."

"What else do you know about him?" I asked, lowering my copy of the *Morning Post*.

"Merely that he is an army colonel recently retired from service in Africa. He is a man of no small means, although without formal title or estates."

"His stance," I mused, "would surely tell you that he is a military man, and the wood of his walking stick might well indicate that he has seen service in Africa, as well might his clothes. But how could you deduce his rank when he's not in uniform?"

"The same way I know his name is Colonel Oliver Pendleton-Smythe," Holmes said.

I threw down the *Morning Post* with a snort of disgust. "Dash it all, you know the fellow!"

"Not true." Holmes nodded toward the newspaper. "You should pay more attention to the matters before you."

I glanced down at the *Morning Post,* which had fallen open to reveal a line drawing of a man in uniform. MISSING: COLONEL OLIVER PENDLETON-SMYTHE, said the headline. I stared at the picture, then up at Holmes's face.

"Will you see him, sir?" asked Mrs. Hudson.

"Not tonight," said Holmes. "Tell Colonel Pendelton-Smythe—and do use his full name, although he will doubtlessly bluster and deny it—that I will see him at nine o'clock sharp tomorrow morning. Not one second sooner and not one second later. If he asks, tell him I am concluding up another important case and cannot be disturbed." He returned his gaze to his book.

"Very good, sir," she said, and shaking her head she closed the door.

The second the latch clicked, Holmes leaped to his feet. Gathering up his coat and hat, he motioned for me to do likewise. "Make haste, Watson," he said. "We must follow the colonel back to his den!"

"Den?" I demanded. I threw on my own coat and accompanied him down the back stairs at breakneck pace. "What do you mean by 'den'? Is he another Moriarty?"

"Please!" Holmes put up one hand for silence and eased open the door. Pendleton-Smythe was striding briskly up Baker Street, swinging his walking stick angrily, as though it were a machete. We both slipped out and Holmes closed the door behind us. Then together we crossed the street and proceeded surreptitiously after the colonel. He seemed to be heading toward the river.

"What is this affair about?" I asked as I hurried after Holmes.

"Mr. Pendleton-Smythe, had you bothered to read that article in the *Morning Post,* disappeared two days ago. Foul play was suspected. In the fireplace of his London home police inspectors found several scraps of paper, but little could be made out except one phrase: 'Amateur Mendicant Society.' What do you make of it?"

"A mendicant is a beggar, I believe—"

"True!"

"But a whole society of amateur beggars? And for a retired army colonel to be involved in them! It boggles the mind."

"I suspect," said Holmes, "that modern views of beggary have colored your thoughts on this matter. Mendicants have been, at various times and in various cultures, both revered and despised. I suspect this is another name for the Secret Mendicant Society, a network of spies which is—or was, at any rate—quite real and much older than you realize. Its roots stretched back to the Roman Empire and as far abroad as Russia, India, and Egypt."

"You think it still exists, then?" I asked.

"I thought it had died out a generation ago in Europe, but it seems to have surfaced once more. I have heard hints in the last few years, Watson, that lead me to suspect it has become an instrument of evil."

"And Pendleton-Smythe—"

"Another Professor Moriarty, pulling the strings of this society for his own personal gain? Fortunately, no. He is, I believe, a pawn in a much larger game, although only a few squares on the board are yet visible to me. More than that I cannot say until I have questioned Pendleton-Smythe."

"What do these 'amateur mendicants' do? Are they beggars or not?"

"Quickly!" Holmes said, pulling me behind a stopped Hansom cab. "He's turning!"

Pendleton-Smythe had stopped before a small rooming house. As we peered out at him, he paused on the steps to look left then right, but did not see us. He entered the building and shut the door behind himself.

"Interesting," Holmes said. "But it confirms my theory."

"That he's a beggar?" I asked, feeling a little annoyed for all the rushing about. "If so, he is surely a well-lodged one."

"Pendleton-Smythe has gone into hiding out of fear for his life. Why else would a man who owns a house choose to rent a room in such shabby surroundings as these?"

"Are we to question him here, then?" I asked.

He paused, lips pursed, deep in thought. After a minute I cleared my throat.

"No, Watson," he said, turning back toward Baker Street. "I think that can wait until tomorrow. I have much to do first."

The next morning Holmes knocked loudly on my door until, bleary eyed, I called, "What is it, Holmes?"

"It's half past six," he said. "Mrs. Hudson has the kettle on and breakfast will be ready at seven sharp."

"For heaven's sake," I said, sitting up. "Tell me, why have you awakened me so early?"

"We have an appointment!"

"Appointment?" I asked, still cloudy. I rose and opened the door. "Ah. Pendleton-Smythe and his amateur beggars, I assume. But that's not until nine o'clock sharp—you said so yourself!"

"Exactly!" He had a fevered look to his eye and I knew he'd been up most of the night working on the mysterious colonel's case—although what the actual nature of the case was, I still hadn't a clue. Yet Holmes seemed to place singular importance on it.

When I had shaved and dressed, I emerged to find an excellent repast set out for us by Mrs. Hudson. Holmes had barely touched his plate. He was rummaging through stacks of old newspapers strewn across the floor and every flat surface of the room.

"Here it is!" he cried.

"What?" I asked, helping myself to tea, toast, and orange marmalade.

"A pattern is emerging," he said softly. "I believe I have all the pieces now. But how do they fit?"

"Explain it to me," I said.

He held up one hand. "Precisely what I intend to do, Watson. Your clarity of thought may be what I need right now." He cleared his throat. "In 1852, Oliver Pendleton-Smythe and six of his schoolmates were expelled from Eton. They were involved in some scandal, the nature of which I have yet to ascertain—official reports tend to be vague on that sort of matter."

"Rightfully so," I murmured.

"Young Pendleton-Smythe found himself shipped off to South Africa after six months of knocking about London, and there his career proved unexceptional. When at last he retired and returned to London, taking charge of his family's house, things seemed to go well for him. He announced his betrothal to Dame Edith Stuart, which you may also remember from the society pages."

"A step up for an army colonel," I commented.

"I suspect she may have been involved in the Eton scandal, but that is mere conjecture at this point," Holmes said. "Yes, to all appearances it is a step up for him. However, two weeks later he broke off the engagement, and the next day—three days ago, in fact—he disappeared."

"Until he showed up on our doorstep."

"Just so."

"Where does this Amateur Beggar Society fit in?" I asked.

"The Secret Mendicant Society, as it is more properly called, was part of a network of spies set up by the Emperor Constantine. The Roman Empire had more than its share of beggars, and Constantine realized they heard and saw more than anyone gave them credit for. Originally, noble-born members of the Society would dress as beggars and go forth to collect news and information, which then made its way back through the network to Constantine himself.

"The next few emperors made little use of Constantine's beggars, but oddly enough the Society seems to have established itself more strongly than ever rather than collapsing, as one might have expected. It developed its own set of rites and rituals. One faction in India splintered off and became affiliated with the Thuggee, of whom you may be familiar."

"Indeed," I said, "I have heard of those devils."

Holmes nodded. "Sometime in the Middle Ages they seemed to disappear. However, in 1821 a condemned man mentioned them in his last statement. Since then I've found two other mentions of the Secret Mendicant Society, the first being a satirical cartoon from *Punch* dated 1832, which refers to them as a rival to the Free Masons as if everyone had heard of them, and the second being the scrap of paper found in Colonel Pendleton-Smythe's house."

"So where does the colonel fit in?"

"I was just getting to that," Holmes said. "Of the six chums expelled from Eton, I have been able to trace the movements of three. All three died in recent weeks under mysterious circumstances. What does this tell you?"

"That the colonel is next on the list to be killed?"

"Precisely, Watson. Or so it would seem."

"You have reason to believe otherwise?"

"Ha! You see right through me, Watson. It seems distinctly odd to me that this rash of murders should coincide with Pendleton-Smythe's return from Africa."

"Indeed, it does seem odd," I agreed. "But perhaps there are other circumstances at work here. You won't know that until you speak with the colonel himself." I looked at my watch. "It's only half an hour until our appointment."

"Time," said Holmes, "for us to be on our way."

I stared at him in bewildered consternation. "You'll have Pendleton-Smythe convinced you don't want to see him if you keep to this course!"

"Rather," he said, "I am endeavoring to make sure the meeting does take place. Your coat, Watson! We'll either meet him on the street on his way here—or if, as I suspect, he intends to skip our meeting since he was recognized yesterday, we will meet him at his rooming house!"

I grabbed my coat and hat and followed him once more out to the street.

We did not, of course, meet Pendleton-Smythe in the street; Holmes always did have a knack for second-guessing other people's actions. When we arrived at the rooming house, we found a stout gray-haired woman who I took to be the landlady sweeping the steps.

"Excuse me," Holmes said briskly, "I wish to ask after one of your tenants—a military man with a slight limp, dark coat, dark hat. I have a letter he dropped last night and I wish to return it to him."

"You'd mean Mr. Smith," she said. "Give it here, I'll hand it to him when he's up." She held out her hand.

"Is he in, then?" Holmes asked.

"Here now, who are you?" she said, regarding us both suspiciously and hefting her broom to bar our way.

I hastened to add, "This is Mr. Sherlock Holmes, and we must speak to your Mr. Smith. It's very urgent."

"Mr. Holmes? Why didn't you say so, gents? 'Course I've heard of you, Mr. Holmes. Who hasn't, round these parts? Come in, come in, I'm forgetting my manners." She lowered the broom and moved toward the front door. "I'm Mrs. Nellie Coram, sir, and I own this establishment. Mr. Smith's room is on the second floor. I'll just pop up and see if he'll come down."

"If you don't mind," Holmes said, "I think we'd better come upstairs with you."

"Oh, is he a slippery one, then?" she said. "I thought he might be, but he paid me a fortnight's rent in advance, and I can't afford to be too nosy, business being what it is these days."

"He is not a criminal," Holmes said. "He is a client. But it is urgent that I speak with him immediately."

She laid a finger alongside her nose and gave him a broad wink, but said no more. She led us in at once, up a broad flight of steps to a well-scrubbed second-floor hallway. She turned right, went down a narrow passage to a closed door, and there she knocked twice. A gruff whisper came in answer almost immediately: "Who is it?"

"Nellie Coram," the landlady said. "I have two visitors for you, Mr. Smith."

The door opened a crack, and I saw a single piercing blue eye regard Holmes and me for a second. "Come in," said the voice, stronger now, and its owner moved back and opened the door for us.

Holmes and I went in. I looked around and saw a small but tidy room: bed, washstand, armoire, and a single straight-backed chair by the window. A copy of the *Times* lay open on the bed.

Pendleton-Smythe closed the door before Mrs. Coram could join us, and I heard a muffled "Humph" from the other side of the door and the sound of her footsteps as she returned to her tasks downstairs. The colonel himself was a man of medium height and strong build, with iron gray hair, blue eyes, and a small moustache. He wore dark blue pants, a white pinstripe shirt, and a blue vest. But it was the service revolver in his hand that most drew my attention. Pendleton-Smythe held it pointed straight at Holmes and me.

"What do you want?" he barked. "Who are you?"

Holmes, who had already taken in the room with a single glanced, crossed to the window and parted the drapes. "Rather," he said, "I should ask what *you* want, Colonel. I am here to keep our appointment. I am Sherlock Holmes, and this is my colleague, Dr. John Watson."

Holmes turned and stared at Pendleton-Smythe, and after a second the colonel lowered his revolver. His hands were shaking, I saw, and I steadied his arm for a second.

"I am glad to have you here, Mr. Holmes," he said. Nervously he crossed to the bed and sat down, tossing the revolver beside him. He cradled his head in his hands, ran his fingers through his hair, and took a deep breath. "Truly, I am at wit's end. I don't know if you can help me, but if any man in England can, it's you. Your presence here is proof enough of your remarkable abilities."

Holmes sat in the straight chair, steepled his fingers, crossed his legs, and said, "Begin at Eton, with your involvement in the Amateur Mendicant Society."

He started violently. "You know about that, too? How is it possible?"

"Then he's right," I said, "and the Amateur Mendicant Society *is* involved?"

"Yes—yes, damn them!"

"My methods are my own," Holmes said. "Please start at the beginning. Leave out no detail, no matter how small. I can assure you of our utmost discretion in this and all matters."

I sat on the bed beside the colonel. Suddenly he looked like a very tired, very old man. "You'll feel better," I told him. "They say confession is good for the soul."

He took a deep breath, then began.

Everything started with one of my professors, Dr. Jason Attenborough. He taught second year Latin as well as classical history, and one day after class, six of us stayed late to ask about the Secret Mendicant Society, which he had mentioned in passing in that afternoon's lecture. It was thrilling in its own way, the idea of spies among the ancient Romans, but we found it hard to believe any noble-born person could possible pass as a beggar. Dr. Attenborough said it was not only possible, it had happened for several centuries.

Later, at a pub, almost as a dare, the six of us agreed to try it ourselves. It seemed like a rum lot of fun, and after a few rounds at the Slaughtered Lamb, we set out to give it a go.

We went first to a rag merchant—he was closed, but we

pounded on his door until he opened for us—and from him we purchased suitable disreputable clothing. Dressing ourselves as we imagined beggars might, we smeared soot on our faces and set out to see what news and pennies we could gather. It was a foolish sort of game, rather stupid really, and the prime foolishness came when we decided to visit Picadilly Circus to see what sort of reception we got. We were pretty well potted by this time, you see, so anything sounded like fun.

Suffice it to say, we terrorized several old women into giving us pennies and were promptly arrested for our trouble. The next day, after being ransomed home by disbelieving parents, we were summoned to the Dean's office and informed that our activities had disgraced the school. In short, our presence was no longer desired. The news was devastating to us and our families.

That's where things should have ended. We should have quietly bought our way into other schools, or vanished into military life, or simply retired to family businesses—there were many choices available. However, that night, as we gathered one last time in the Slaughtered Lamb, Dr. Attenborough joined us. He was not consoling or apologetic. Rather, he was ebullient.

He asked what we had learned as beggars—and we hadn't learned a thing, really—but as he led us through the lesson (for that's what it was to him), we could see that we had gone to the wrong section of the city, spoken to the wrong people, done all the wrong things. Beggars have their place in our society, as you know, and we had stepped outside their domain. That's where we had gone wrong.

As he had done in his lecture hall, he inspired us that night with his speech. He persuaded us that we should go out again—and this time he went with us.

Dressed once more as beggars, we ventured into the sordid, dark places near the docks, where such as we had never dared go at night. Using the Roman system as a model, he showed us what we had done wrong—and how we could do it right.

We listened at the right windows. We lurked outside sailors' taverns and heard their coarse, drunken gossip. And suddenly we began to understand how the Secret Mendicant Society had worked so admirably well. Wine loosens men's tongues, and much could be gleaned from attentive listening. For who pays attention to beggars, even among the dregs of our society?

There were a dozen ship's captains who we could have turned in for smuggling, a handful of murders we could have solved, stolen cargoes that could have been recovered with just a word in the right ear at Scotland Yard.

We did none of that. It was petty. But we were young and foolish, and Dr. Attenborough did nothing but encourage us in our foolishness. Oh, he was a masterful speaker. He could convince you night was day and white was black, if he wanted to. And suddenly he wanted very much to have us working for him. We would be a new Secret Mendicant Society—or, as we chaps liked to call it, an Amateur Mendicant Society. Dabbling, yes, that was a gentleman's way. It was a game to us. As long as we pretended it was a schoolyard lark, it wasn't really a dirty deal.

I regret to say I took full part in the Amateur Mendicant Society's spying over the following six months. I learned the truth from dishonest men, turned the information over to Dr. Attenborough, and he pursued matters from there. What, exactly, he did with the information I can only guess—extortion, blackmail, possibly even worse. However, I do know that suddenly he had a lot of money, and he paid us handsomely for our work. He bought an abandoned warehouse and had a posh gentleman's club outfitted in the basement—though, of course, there were no servants, nobody who could break our secret circle. Later he leased the warehouse out for furniture storage.

I was not the first to break the circle. Dickie Clarke was. He told me one evening that he had enlisted in the army. His father had used his influence to get him a commission, and he was off to India. "I'm through with soiling my hands with this nonsense," he told me. "I've had enough. Come with me, Oliver. It's not too late." I was shocked, and I refused—to my lasting shame.

When Attenborough found out, he had an absolute fit—he threw things, screamed obscenities, smashed a whole set of dishes against the wall. Then and there I realized I had made a mistake. I had made a pact with a madman. I had to escape.

The next day I, too, enlisted. I've been away for nineteen years—I never came back, not even on leave, for fear of what Dr. Attenborough might do if he found out. He was that violent.

I had stayed in touch with Dickie Clarke all through his campaigns and my own, and when he wrote from London to tell me Attenborough was dead, I thought it would be safe to return home. I planned to write my memoirs, you see.

Only two weeks ago Dickie died. Murdered—I'm sure of it! And then I noticed people, strangers dressed as beggars, loitering near my house, watching me, noting my movements as I had once noted the movements of others. To escape, I simply walked out of my home one day, took a series of cabs until I was certain I hadn't been followed, and haven't been back since.

Sherlock Holmes nodded slowly when Pendleton-Smythe finished. "A most interesting story," he said. "But why would the Amateur Mendicant Society want you dead? Are you certain there isn't something more?"

He raised his head, back stiff. "Sir, I assure you, I have told you everything. As for why—isn't that obvious? Because I know too much. They killed old Dickie, and now they're going to kill me!"

"What of the four others from Eton? What happened to them?"

"The others?" He blinked. "I—I really don't know. I haven't heard from or spoken to any of them in years. I hope they had the good sense to get out and not come back. Heavens above, I certainly wish I hadn't!"

"Quite so," said Holmes. He rose. "Stay here, Colonel. I think you will be safe in Mrs. Coram's care for the time being. I must look into a few matters, and then we will talk again."

"So you will take my case?" he asked eagerly.

"Most decidedly." Holmes inclined his head. "I'm certain I'll be able to help. One last thing. What was the address of the warehouse Attenborough owned?"

"Forty-two Kerin Street," he said.

As we headed back toward Baker Street, Holmes seemed in a particularly good mood, smiling and whistling bits of a violin concerto I'd heard him playing earlier that week.

"Well, what is it?" I finally demanded.

"Don't you see, Watson?" he said. "There can only be one answer. We have run into a classic case of two identical organizations colliding. It's nothing short of a trade war between rival groups of beggar-spies."

"You mean there's a real Secret Mendicant Society still at large?"

"The very thing!"

"How is it possible? How could they have survived all these years with nobody knowing about them?"

"Some people *can* keep secrets," he said.

"It's fantastic!"

"Grant me this conjecture. Imagine, if you will, that the real Secret Mendicant Society has just become aware of its rival, the Amateur Mendicant Society. They have thrived in the shadows for centuries. They have a network of informants in place. It's not hard to see how the two would come face to face eventually, as the Amateur Society expanded into the Secret Society's established territory. Of course, the Secret Mendicant Society could not possibly allow a rival to poach on their grounds. What could they possibly do but strike out in retaliation?"

"Attenborough and Clarke and the others—"

"Exactly! They have systematically eliminated the amateurs. I would imagine they are now in occupation of the secret club under the old furniture warehouse, where Attenborough's records would have been stored. And those records would have led them, inexorably, to the two Amateurs who got away—Dickie, who they killed at once, and our client, who they have not yet managed to assassinate."

"Ingenious," I said.

"But now Col. Pendleton-Smythe is in more danger than he believes. He is the last link to the old Amateur Mendicant Society, so it should be a simple matter to—"

Holmes drew up short. Across the street from 221 Baker Street, on the front steps of another house, a raggedly dressed old man with a three-day growth of beard sat as if resting from a long walk.

"He's one of them," I said softly.

Holmes regarded me as though shocked by my revelation. "Watson, must you be so suspicious? Surely that poor unfortunate is catching his second wind. His presence is merest coincidence." I caught the amused gleam in his eye, though.

"I thought you didn't believe in coincidences," I said.

"Ye-es." He drew out the word, then turned and continued on toward our front door at a more leisurely pace. "Let us assume," he said, "that you are right. What shall we do with the devil? Run him off? Have him locked up by Lestrade?"

"That would surely tip our hand," I said. "Rather, let us try to misdirect him."

"You're learning, Watson, you're learning." We reached our house; he opened the door. "I trust you have a plan?"

"I was rather hoping you did," I admitted.

"As a matter of fact, I do," he said. "But I'm going to need your help . . ."

Two hours later, I stood in the drawing room shaking my head. The man before me—thick lips, stubbled chin, rat's nest of chestnut colored hair—bore not the slightest resemblance to my friend. His flare for the dramatic as well as a masterly skill for disguises would have borne him well in the theatre, I thought. I found the transformation remarkable.

"Are you sure this is wise?" I asked.

"Wise?" he said. "Decidedly not. But will it work? I profoundly hope so. Check the window, will you?"

I lifted the drape. "The beggar has gone."

"Oh, there are surely other watchers," he said. "They have turned to me as the logical one to whom Col. Pendleton-Smythe would go for help." He studied his new features in a looking glass, adjusted one bushy eyebrow, then looked up at me for approval.

"Your own brother wouldn't recognize you," I told him.

"Excellent." He folded up his makeup kit, then I followed him to the back door. He slipped out quietly while I began to count.

When I reached a hundred, I went out the front door, turned purposefully, and headed for the bank. I had no real business there; however, it was as good a destination as any for my purpose—which was to serve as a decoy while Holmes observed those who observed me.

I saw no one as I went about my business, and in due course I returned to our lodgings in exactly the same professional manner. When Holmes did not at once show himself, I knew his plan had been successful; he was now trailing a member of the Secret Mendicant Society.

I had a leisurely tea, then set off to find Inspector Lestrade. He was, as usual, hard at work at his desk. I handed him a note from Sherlock Holmes, which said:

Lestrade—

Come at once to 42 Kerin Street with a dozen of your men. There is a murderer to be had as well as evidence of blackmail and other nefarious deeds.

Sherlock Holmes

Lestrade's eyes widened as he read the note, and a second later he was on his way out the door shouting for assistance.

I accompanied him, and by the time we reached 42 Kerin Street—a crumbling old brick warehouse—he had fifteen men as an entourage. They would have kicked the door in, but a raggedly dressed man with bushy eyebrows reached out and opened it for them: it wasn't so much as latched. Without a glance at the disguised Sherlock Holmes, Lestrade and his men rushed in.

Holmes and I strolled at a more leisurely pace back toward a busier street where we might catch a cab home. He began removing his makeup and slowly the man I knew emerged.

"How did it go?" I asked.

"There were a few tense moments," he said, "but I handled things sufficiently well, I believe."

"Tell me everything," I said.

"For your journals, perhaps?"

"Exactly so."

"Very well. As you headed down the street looking quite purposeful, an elderly gentleman out for a midday stroll suddenly altered his course after you. He was well dressed, not a beggar by appearance or demeanor, so I took this to mean he was now watching us. I overtook him, grasped him firmly by the arm, and identified myself to him.

" 'I am pleased to make your acquaintance, sir,' he said. 'I believe we may have business to discuss.'

" 'Exactly so,' I told him. 'Are you at liberty to speak for the whole Society, or must we report to your superiors?'

" 'Come with me,' he said, and he led me to a quiet building on Harley Street. I had been there once before on business with the Foreign Office, but I showed no sign of surprise; indeed, this piece of the puzzle seemed to fit admirably well.

"He took me upstairs to see a rear admiral whose name I agreed not to divulge, and there the whole truth of the Secret Mendicant Society became apparent to me."

I said, "They no longer work for Rome. They work for us."

"Quite right, Watson," Holmes said. "This rear admiral took me into their confidence, since they have a file on me and know I can be trusted. The organization of the Secret Mendicant Society was once quite remarkable, though it seems near its end. Their membership is small and, as far as I can tell, consists largely of septuagenarians or older. The times have changed so much that beggary is dying out; modern spies have much more efficient means of political espionage . . . for that is the current goal of the Secret Mendicant Society."

"But what about the murders!" I exclaimed. "Surely not even the Foreign Office would—"

"Not only would they, they did. Politics is becoming less and less a gentleman's game, my dear Watson. For the security of our great country, nothing is above the law for them—laws that must govern the common man, such as you or me—or even poor Pendleton-Smythe."

"So there is nothing you can do to help the colonel," I said bitterly.

"The admiral and I rapidly reached an arrangement," Holmes said, "when I explained what I had done with you and Lestrade. With Scotland Yard about to close in on the headquarters of the Amateur Mendicant Society, there was nothing he could do but agree with me that the Amateurs must be exposed. The publicity surrounding them will camouflage the activities of the real Secret Mendicant Society and allow Pendleton-Smythe the luxury of living out the rest of his days in peace. He, for one, never for an instant suspected the Secret Mendicant Society actually existed. That is his salvation."

"It would seem, then," I said, "that everything has sorted itself out remarkably well."

"I, for one, find it far from satisfactory."

"What will Lestrade find?"

"He will uncover the records of the Amateur Mendicant Society, which reveal their wrongdoings in excruciating detail. Their specialty was blackmail and extortion, as we had surmised. Their records will be doctored to include, I dare say, the full catalog of murders by Dr. Attenborough, as he desperately tried to maintain control of a crumbling criminal empire. The newspapers will, I am certain, find much scandalous material in it—and the colonel will have little choice but to deny his participation and suppress that part of his memoirs, should he still choose to write them. All the Foreign Service wants, at this point, is to maintain the Secret Mendicant Society's anonymity while contributing whatever small gains it can to the war effort."

"You're fortunate they didn't try to kill you," I commented.

"I believe the admiral considered it. However, I do make my own small contributions to the Foreign Office, as you well know. You might say we have friends in common."

"Your brother for one," I said.

"Just so," he said.

"Then we have reached a successful resolution to the case— after a fashion."

"After a fashion," Holmes agreed, "although I find it impossible to condone what the Foreign Office and the Secret Mendicant Society have done. It makes me wonder if a superior form of government might not be the answer, one where the working man is protected—indeed, empowered!—by his system of self-rule."

"Indeed?" I said. "You sound like you've been reading Marx and Engels."

My good comrade Holmes said, "Karl Marx's *Das Kapital* is quite remarkable. I take it you have not had a chance to read it."

"Not yet," I admitted.

"Remind me to loan it to you. I think you would benefit from it enormously."

"I will do that," I told him.

"But first let us pay a visit to Col. Pendleton-Smythe. I'm sure he'll want to hear the good news."

Although THEODORE DREISER *(1871–1945) wrote such important American novels as* An American Tragedy, Sister Carrie, The Genius, Jennie Gerhardt *and the Frank Cowperwood trilogy, to my knowledge no critic ever complimented his style. Even his friend H. L. Mencken had qualms about Dreiser's sense of structure, and students of twisted syntax shudder at an infamous sentence that begins with "The" followed immediately by a comma! "Victor Lynch the Forger," while undeniably diverting, is a bit like observing Sherlock Holmes through a window rimed with frost.—JAF*

Victor Lynch the Forger

BY "TERRY McGARRY"
(ASCRIBED TO THEODORE DREISER)

That the sole purview of Mr. Sherlock Holmes was logic, and at no time did he venture personally into the mysterious and shadowy realm of the heart, by no means rendered void of irony—even, if one may say it, tragedy—the myriad adventures which I shared with him. Indeed, the human element was ever present in his cases. But at times his intellect, with its scientific bent, was, however expert in the art of deduction, capable of unraveling only actions, and not the tortuous trail of passions precipitating them.

One incident illustrative of this crept upon us in increments; its first indications dawning at breakfast one winter's morning, as snow drifted down to blanket the great city enfolding Baker Street.

Holmes, lounging in purple dressing-gown and worn slippers, exclaimed over the *Daily Telegraph*, "Hullo, here it is again. A queer thing, this."

I roused myself from my immersion in the rival *Morning Post*, knowing well my friend's ability to ferret out the more interesting articles, his collection of which might almost be classified as obsessive.

Holmes creased the paper into several folds and handed it to me, denoting with a finger a notice in the agony column thus displayed.

THE PAST IS BUT AN HISTORIATED INITIAL (it said). SEEK OUT THE HANGED MAN. GILT WILL OUT, AND THE BOOK OF HOURS HAS SCANT PAGES LEFT.

"Cryptic, to be sure, but that is not in itself unusual," I ventured, mystified as to his interest. "I take it this has appeared before?"

"Each morning for a month now."

"Obviously the person who took the ad wishes to contact someone else without furnishing information to the casual peruser," I said, and then added a further thought: "And has perhaps only a vague idea of when the other will arrive in London."

Holmes took up his after-breakfast pipe. "Obviously. But why? It perks my interest, Watson. Something tells me we shall be involved in this before the day is out—though whether the case comes to me or I go to it, I would not hazard to guess."

A delicate knock on the outer door, an exchange of words in feminine tones, and quick, light steps ascending the stair caused us both to look up.

"Perhaps speculation will prove unnecessary," Holmes said with wry anticipation, echoing my own thoughts as he set his pipe down unlit.

A woman swept into the sitting-room on a current of chill air, her cheeks as red as the froth of hair that her hat could not restrain, her eyes all emerald sparkle. She wore a creamy lambswool coat over an ivory dress, a wintry vision that one suspected would be lost in the snowscape outside.

"Mr. Holmes?" she began. As we rose to our feet, she took a moment to dab daintily at her nose with a monogrammed lavender handkerchief; the motion caused a locket at her throat to gleam in the gaslight. "I'd never be bothering you at such an hour, sir, if it weren't something of great importance. My name's Anne Gibney—"

"From County Westmeath, if my ears do not deceive me. I see from your locket that your maiden name began with a *K,* and you are staying at the St. Pancras, which furnishes the most delightful shade of scented handkerchief."

Although unquestionably anxious about the matter that had brought her here, Mrs. Gibney seemed not at all nonplussed by Holmes's evidently accurate appraisal of her origins and situation; rather, she favored the gloves she was now removing with a slight smile—a quirk of the mouth, really—as if she had expected this keen acumen and was not disappointed. We saw her seated and offered her tea, of which she took but a small sip before launching into a description of her dilemma: a husband missing overnight, suspicious behavior preceding the unexplained absence, love letters sent from England—written in her husband's hand, which she intercepted but maintained he could not have written—never followed by the expected threat of blackmail.

Holmes listened attentively at first, but a few sentences into her speech his interest flagged, and before she had finished he got up abruptly and halted her delivery with a wave of his hand. "Forgive me, madame, but I will be of no help to you. Pray waste no more breath."

Her slim eyebrows arched in surprise over what I myself perceived with some discomfort to be uncalled-for rudeness.

"Really, sir?" she said, her tone icier than the cobblestoned street below. "Even where I come from we've heard of your considerable skills. Maybe you think the task too difficult, or your price too dear?"

"Tracking an errant spouse is, I'm afraid, not my bailiwick," Holmes said—taking, this time, more care in his speech, I was relieved to note.

"But you make it sound as if he's after having an affair, and he's not, I'm dead sure of it, sir; I'd stake my life on it. Harry would never stray from me. I know it in my bones. I don't know who wrote those letters, but it was never him, and I can't imagine what they're after if it isn't money. Something else is amiss, something terrible will happen—oh, God, that it hasn't happened already! I must find him before trouble does!"

"You say you have followed him unobserved," Holmes said. "You say he merely stops at auction houses, art galleries, his customary places of business. I am not persuaded that there is anything amiss. No doubt he met up with associates and spent a dreary night haggling over contractual matters."

"But he won't tell me why he wanted to come here!" she cried—as if she had had this very conversation with herself, in the confines of her own thoughts, and had been unable to assuage her own fears. " 'I needn't worry myself about it,' says he. Always in the past he has been open with me on business matters, answering any question I put to him! But from the outset he didn't want me along on this trip. And the letters . . . Oh, it is all so confusing."

Holmes proved immune to her entreaties. "My dear Mrs. Gibney, there is simply nothing I can do for you, save urge you to confront Mr. Gibney with the letters and have out with it. I have pressing matters to attend to. I wish you luck and a pleasant visit here in London. Now, good day."

It seemed to me that frustration, even desperation, were the source of the tears that now glistened in her eyes, rather than offense at his abrupt tone. But she blinked three times, composed herself admirably, and took her leave of us. If Holmes heard her small, pathetic murmurs as she exited—"What shall I do now? What *can* I do?"—he gave no sign, merely picking up the paper again and resuming his examination of the cryptic advertisement; it being the only pressing matter of his of which I was aware.

"You might have been more sympathetic," I said, still moved by the young woman's distrait condition, and surprised at Holmes, who was, I knew, a kind man, ever ready to lend aid where he could.

"Sympathy would have served no purpose. The letters are no doubt his, sent by the mistress's husband in an attempt to put a stop to the affair, or by the mistress to ruin the marriage; there is nothing so complex at work here as a Charles Augustus Milverton. The truth is right under her nose. There is no mystery to solve."

Before I could speak further—to me the case's lack of challenge was far outweighed by the lady's personal distress—he leapt from the chair in a characteristic but nonetheless startling burst of energy. "I must dress and go down to the *Telegraph*'s offices. Would you be so good as to remain here, Watson, in the event that someone calls with a problem more germane?"

It came to me then that this was wishful thinking on his part; that he was afflicted with one of his periodical dearths of activity, and only the thorniest tangle would suffice. Loath to dissuade him from even a manufactured puzzle, lest he seek less savory mental occupation, I acquiesced.

When he had gone, I took up the *Post* again and resumed the article therein about the ongoing sale at Sotheby's of Sir Thomas Phillips' lifetime collection of manuscripts—sixty thousand in all, the disposition of which would presumably take years. The art world is an odd place, I mused, thinking of this art dealer Harry Gibney, whose affairs we had so narrowly avoided being embroiled in; but my reverie was cut short by a second caller.

Holmes's intuition of an oncoming case turned out to have merit. He returned from his news-office foray to find me entertaining Inspector Leland Barney, who, owing to the weather and his own consternation, had accepted a small brandy and was warming his robust frame at the hearth.

"Ah-hah!" Holmes cried. "Inspector, you are welcome here,

although your news of a murder at Number Five Aylsley Street is unfortunate indeed."

The inspector's jaw dropped noticeably. "How . . . ? We've been keeping the newshounds off it all night! I swore they'd bollixed my investigations for the last time!"

"I've got a four-wheeler waiting to take us there; I came round only to pick up Watson, as it was on my way. Your presence is a fortuitous bonus, as you may now fill in the details while we travel."

We donned scarves and overcoats and tramped through the thickening snow out to the carriage. Once installed within, the Inspector, rubbing his craggy features from either fatigue or bafflement, began to speak.

"Man was run through with a poker. Landlady thinks he was some kind of writer; looks more to me like he was a chemist, or a madman . . . or a witch. Judging by the state of his flat, robbery can be ruled out—not much worth stealing there, nor ever was, from the look of it. Not even a scrap of extra clothes. A few old books and papers seem to be all the possessions he had, that and—well, you'll have to see it, I can't make heads nor tails of it. Landlady found him when she went to tidy up. Surprised her no end, since she swears he left the building hours before, just as she was returning, and he never came back in. Body must have been there awhile; fireplace was stone cold."

"If he was as poor as you say, perhaps he had nothing to burn," I suggested.

The Inspector shrugged. "Hearth's brimful of ashes. He burned something sometime, if only some of those old books. At any rate, we're at a loss. The only clue we have is a set of initials—V. E. L.—carved into the mantel."

"Had he any identification?" Holmes asked, somewhat acerbically, as the victim's name was customarily the first information given in such circumstances.

Inspector Barney scratched his head. "That's just it. He had papers bearing several names, none of them the one he gave the landlady, none of them with the initials V. E. L. He had clearly paid to have them forged."

"You say there are books. Are any of them inscribed?"

The Inspector's puzzled expression was testament to his not having looked.

Holmes asked no further questions, but occupied the rest of the journey gazing out at the drifting whiteness, a contemplative half-frown on his narrow face.

The address proved to be a dilapidated clapboard edifice, much neglected, in a downtrodden neighborhood prettified only slightly by the kindness of concealing snow. Holmes sprang from the carriage, his pace scarcely hindered by the recognition of a reporter, who endeavored to draw information from him by shouting, "It is a murder, then, if you're here, isn't it, Mr. Holmes?" Holmes gave neither confirmation nor denial, brushing by the persistent young whelp with a clipped, "My dear fellow, you will simply have to wait for your answer."

Inside, the building was dim and redolent of stale smoke, old food, and despondency. Yellowish-brown wallpaper lined the halls, and a narrow stair, creaking under the descending weight of the constable whom Barney had left in charge, led up to the second- and third-story flats.

A brief interview with the horrified landlady—a beefy, small-eyed woman, small of stature—yielded no information the Inspector hadn't already imparted. "A man goes out, then turns up dead somewhere he wasn't! Who'd believe it? And in my own house! And the rent not paid!"

Holmes gave the stairs a cursory examination, muttering about policemen's boots tracking slush over the evidence, and then requested that the constable show him the victim's lodgings. I excused myself to the landlady and, with Barney, followed close at his heels.

The room, on the third floor, was a chill tomb indeed for the poor fellow who met his end there, bare of all ornamentation and furnishings except for a stained mattress, a chair, and a rickety table, the latter covered with an astounding miscellany of papers, jars, bits of wood, dried roots, feathers, stones, and books. Other books, with leather or wooden covers, lay in haphazard piles on the floor; objects had been strewn everywhere, as if in a mad rage, or a struggle. The place smelled faintly of turpentine, and other substances I could not quite put my finger on. Gas had not been laid on in the building; a lantern, low on kerosene and wick alike, had toppled onto the threadbare carpet, and it seemed amazing that this sepulchre had not become a funeral pyre.

The body lay next to the cold hearth, the murder weapon a grisly protrusion from its sternum; he had been a tall man, once strong, but poverty, it seemed, had sapped his vitality long before his violent demise. He had but a shabby, sooty tweed suit for his shroud, and his eyes, a grey as pale as the winter sky without, were still open, frozen in their first glimpse of the hereafter, their last sight of what had clearly been a hard life on this earth.

My work in Afghanistan with the wounded, my experience of the hardships of war, had not prepared me as well as one might think for my association with Holmes. We had intimate connection with so much evil and sadness, seeing always their tragic results. Murder, arson, bribery, corruption, false witness of every imaginable sort (and some unimaginable). . . . My heart went out to the victims, dead and survivors alike—for even if we could bring them justice, we could not undo their pain or loss. As a medical man, my impulse was to heal, and at times, I must admit, I wearied of the irreparable. And this poor wretch, lying dead in the squalor that served as home, could never be healed. I found myself possessed of a cloying sadness, and could not shake it off.

Perhaps Holmes sensed my unusual melancholy. He had been engaged in a feverish stalking about the room, bent at the waist to inspect books, papers, the faint marks of shoes, the ashes in the fireplace, the body itself—particularly its fingers, which had an odd greenish tint; he had sniffed pots and jars and examined the hodge-podge of odd articles. But now he straightened and, piercing me with a look sharper than the poker embedded in the corpse, said, "He was a forger, Watson, an excellent one. No doubt he once made a considerable income from it; his clothing, though much worn with age and hard use, was at the outset of high quality. Something led to his reduced circumstances, compelling him to scrape by, forging bank drafts and contracts, mundane labors that could have brought him but a pittance. See here, how he has torn several of them up; probably he also burned some. But look at this."

He handed me a cracked, leatherbound book. I opened it, and gasped: within were pages of the most precious, aged vellum, inscribed with Latin words in ancient lettering, the initials il-luminated with intricate pictures of beasts, landscapes, human fig-ures, some gilt-embossed; around the borders twined ivy leaves, blossoms, interlaced animal forms, ribbons and braids of brilliant hue. It was a work of art.

"A Book of Hours," Holmes informed me, "from sometime in the thirteenth century, I would guess."

"This must be extraordinarily valuable! Are the others of the same age and quality? Perhaps he meant to sell them . . ."

I paused, and the glint in Holmes's eye told me that he had long ago made the connection that was only dimly beginning to form in my own mind.

"Forgeries, Watson, no more genuine than these shredded contracts. See the pens on the table, and the contents of the pots? Pigments ground from malachite and copper and madder root and such. The woody marbles steeping with iron nails in the jam jar on the windowsill are oak gall, and will be ink in a few days—our man was a stickler for authenticity."

"Is *that* what they are! By God, I'd thought them toad's eyes!" exclaimed the Inspector, but he fell quiet at a sour look from Holmes, who continued:

"The pigments were bound with egg albumen, which would account for the fragments of eggshell in the carpet. The stone slab and agate muller were for grinding. At any rate, many of the codices were burned in the fire; this sort of ash, and the soot on the body's garments, could only have been made by leather, parchment, pigment—and linen and wool." He leaned down and extracted from the pile of ashes a bit of cloth, which, when he presented it to me, proved to be a scrap of clothier's label.

"Does it match the victim's coat?" I asked.

He shook his head. "But both are of Irish manufacture, the best tweed from that region. I begin to think," he said, his tone taking on a regretful note, "that I sent our first caller away far too hastily this morning. I should have trusted my instinct—she was part of this all along."

"Not the murderer, surely, but—her husband?" I scarcely refrained from uttering the man's name, sensing that I should hear Holmes out before I spoke prematurely.

"We have found our advertiser, Watson, as I discovered at the *Telegraph* when I claimed to seek the Hanged Man. But I was not the first to enquire there. Someone else, the intended contact, found him yesterday, with these results."

"What about the initials in the mantel there?" asked Inspector Barney.

Holmes had barely seemed to give it a glance, but he said, "Recently done, no doubt with that small knife on the hearthstone there. See how the blond wood shows through, undarkened by age or smoke. V. E. L. is one of our men."

"Who are they, then?" the Inspector burst out, unable to contain himself any longer. "Let's make an arrest and get to the bottom of this straightaway!"

Holmes shook his head, heavy brows drawn down. "There are still several factors which do not fit. I shall contact you tomorrow, sir, with the results of my further enquiries. Until then, I will vouchsafe only this: it is unlikely a murder was done here. You can tell your young newshound as much, if you wish; perhaps then he will leave you alone. And now you must excuse me, for I have calls to make and a telegram to send before the hour grows too late."

It is as I suspected," Holmes said after tipping the boy who had brought him a return telegram, and reading it. "This is from the coroner's office in Galway City. Our victim, Mr. Victor Lynch, has died before—ten years ago, in Galway, where the Lynch family has been prominent for centuries."

"Then you must have the wrong name," I said. I was examining one of the books we had removed, with the Inspector's permission, from the scene of the crime: its inscription read, TO MY GENTLE ANNIE, WITH AFFECTION, VICTOR LYNCH, and I had been mulling over whether the gift had ever been presented, and if so, had then been returned—and whether Annie was, as seemed at once most likely and most coincidental, our own visitor Mrs. Anne Gibney. "The initials in the mantel are the same, and the signature in this book, but the man had forged many identities for himself—"

"And his own death certificate. Whatever drove him from his homeland in ruin, it was serious enough to impel him to fabricate his own demise. His self-given appellation is the key: one of Lynch's fifteenth-century ancestors was condemned by his own father, the Mayor of Galway, for murder, but was so popular thereabouts that none of the townsfolk would execute him. His father, feeling justice must be done, hanged the boy himself. It is all in the commonplace book." He gestured at the shelf behind him, which housed his voluminous scrapbook collections of ephemera.

"A sad tale. It makes one wonder about the origins of the term in America."

"Perhaps the vigilante William Lynch was a distant relation. It might bear research, for one of an etymological bent. But the task at hand is less scholarly. Would you mind very much, Watson, running that volume down—no, not the one with the personal inscription, the other, yes—to Potterdon's and seeing what their art appraiser has to say about it? I have an errand of my own which may last well into the evening, whereupon we will meet back here and see if the three strands with which we have been presented today haven't woven together like the finest Irish tweed."

What I found out at the appraiser's was that some forgers—most often posthumously—had of late acquired more fame than many original painters, their works becoming collectors' items of some value. The appraiser offered me an astonishing sum for the sample codice I showed him, and was quite disappointed when I would not part with it. "A Victor Lynch!" he exclaimed. "See here, in the historiated initial, the little curlicues—we believe they were meant to be nooses in the shape of a script *v* and *e* and *l,* and they were the artist's signature, as it were, macabre as that may seem."

"Whatever happened to this Lynch?" I enquired.

"Oh, he died years ago, of an illness, when his manuscripts were discovered to be phony—he'd tried to flog one too many, an inferior work, done, we suspect, when he was already ailing. It was recognized as a fake straight off. We'd thought almost all his works were in a private collection, that of a Mr. Kenny in Ireland. Lucky for him his daughter married an art dealer, who was able to persuade the art world of the value of these works in and of themselves. In fact, the dealer himself is here in London. . . . Ah, no matter. I don't suppose you'd reconsider, if I offered you an additional ten pounds? Twenty?"

I shook my head absently, feeling the solution to this mystery loom immediately closer. Once I had verified that the name of the visiting art dealer was Harry Gibney, I hurried back to Baker Street to share my new knowledge with Holmes, but he had not yet returned, and after a light supper I sat by the fire, dreaming over the picture-filled pages. Regarded through a filter of warmth and fatigue, they gave one the sense of peering past jungle vines into sunlit stained-glass windows, a poetic, soporific effect. There was nothing counterfeit about their beauty.

Once again, my reverie was interrupted, by the third caller of the day. "I've come about the matter of the forger," said the slouching Irishman who entered—a coachman or hostler, by the scruffy look of him, his mud-encrusted boots and damp, horsy odor.

"Well, you may sit down and wait for Mr. Holmes to return," I began—and then took a second look, having noted, out of the corner of my eye, a strange twinkle in his. "You've done it again!" I exclaimed, as Holmes resumed his natural, upright posture and doffed the tweed cap of his costume.

But he did not indulge his actor's delight overlong. "I have spent an informative, if trying, evening in the coach house of the St. Pancras," he told me, investigating the platters that held the cooling remains of supper. "Mrs. Gibney spent the evening out, and upon her return engaged a carriage for tomorrow morning at half nine. Unless I miss my guess, she has been to see her husband, and she will return to his hiding-place tomorrow, to bring him traveling clothes and money, perhaps even to convey him to the station—a ferry leaves from Holyhead tomorrow night, and he will want to be on the noon train. We will intercept him well before that."

"You did not attempt to speak with her? Or ascertain the address from the driver?"

Holmes speared a cold carrot and shook his head. "She was canny enough to have the driver deliver her within walking distance only of her destination, where she met him again an hour later, having given no indication of where she'd been. And circumstances have changed drastically; she will no longer wish our involvement, and is undoubtedly relieved that I sent her away so precipitously, much as I myself rue it."

"I believe her maiden name, as you noted from the pendant on her necklace this morning, did start with a *K,*" I said, "for

Kenny," and I told him what I had learned at the appraiser's. He smiled in satisfaction, his deductions apparently borne out.

"The picture is slowly but steadily filled in," he said, "as by a painter's brush. There are layers of forgery here, unparalleled by such banalities as banknotes and contracts. All that is left is to find out why—and whether murder, or a tragic accident, led to the sad end we witnessed this morning."

Unable to maintain interest in the food, he retired to clean up and thence to his chemical corner, to immerse himself in some organic puzzlement as he was wont to do when in need of distraction or a clear head. I looked in on him there before retiring, and he said, "It is as I suspected, Watson. I took the liberty of borrowing a couple of the jars from Lynch's flat, and have been testing the substances they contained. Bisulphide of tin, lead antimonate, mercuric sulphide . . . the list goes on. The man was using authentic medieval pigments, several of which were deadly poison, quick or slow-acting, and I noticed traces of one of the latter on his fingertips today. The death certificate he forged for himself in Galway was but a prognostication; a similar illness would have overtaken him sooner or later in any event. I wonder if he knew it? 'The Book of Hours has scant pages left' . . ."

It should have made no difference, but it seemed to me that the thoughts of the dead man were more real to Holmes in this state than those of the living, whatever role they played. "Perhaps Harry Gibney will enlighten us," I said.

"Oh, I am counting on it," Holmes replied, but his expression was strangely pensive, as if my earlier melancholy, like a slow-acting poison, had gradually affected him over the intervening hours. "There is much to make one wonder, isn't there, Watson?" he asked; this time I knew the question was rhetorical, and held my peace. "That perhaps a man is only this—" He picked up a beaker of some volatile substance. "—the sum of the chemistry on which his very physical form relies? Perhaps we collide with the randomness of Brownian motion, mere molecules in a vast, collective sea.

Perhaps our motives themselves are born of the passionate chemistries of our own minds and hearts, the precise elements which are the study of physicians such as yourself. One might precipitate human motivations as I do these acids, these bases—might one not?"

I did not know what to say. I had never considered human interaction in this microscopic light. But before I could manufacture some reply, he was released by whatever mood had taken him, and applied himself with renewed vigor to the experiment at hand, leaving me to my own perturbed sleep.

W e arrived at the St. Pancras at precisely 9:20, saw Anne Kenny Gibney enter her prearranged four-wheeler, and followed it to the East End, disembarking our own hansom a block behind her, so as to follow unobserved. Clutching a valise in one hand and her cloak to her throat with the other, she made her way determinedly to a shabby inn, only a step above the lodgings in which Victor Lynch had died—like water seeking its own level, I thought uncharitably. A modest sum conferred upon the innkeeper secured us the room number, and upon knocking, Holmes was quick to announce our names and the fact that we were unaccompanied by any constabulary.

"Oh, Harry, I'm so sorry!" Mrs. Gibney cried as she admitted us. "I did take care, I swear I did!"

Harry Gibney stood near the bed, on which was laid out the valise carrying his fresh clothes; he had been in the process of changing, and his garb was now an odd study in contrasts, with shiny shoes, neat brown gaiters, and well-cut pearl-grey trousers topped by a ragged tweed jacket the twin of Victor Lynch's. He laid a hat on the back of an overstuffed chair as we entered. He was a tall man, wiry of build, a slimmer version of the dead man we had seen the previous morning, as if whatever travails they had shared had molded them into similar creatures. He passed a hand wearily over his face, which was deeply graven by his ordeal, but embraced his wife comfortingly with the other arm. "It's not your fault, love," he said gently. Then he looked at Holmes. "How did you ever . . . ?"

Mrs. Gibney gave a strangled cry. "It was me, you see, it *is* my fault," she insisted. "I should have told you. I was so confused . . . I approached Mr. Holmes, I know it was thick of me, but I was afraid you were in danger, afraid to ask you about the letters . . ."

Gibney was clearly baffled, but his bewilderment twisted quickly into suspicion. "What letters? Did he write you? Did Lynch write to you from London? What did he want?"

"Perhaps we should all have a seat," I suggested before tempers could rise further, "and attempt to straighten all of this out."

Gibney hesitated, unwilling to relinquish his mounting anger; then he seemed to deflate, and sank into the ragged chair as if gravity had become too much for him to bear.

"They were letters from *you*," his wife said, sitting on the corner of the bed, which creaked under her insubstantial weight. A tear slid down her cheek and nestled in the drab coverlet. "They were love letters to some woman here. They were in your handwriting. I'd know your hand anywhere. But I knew you couldn't have been . . . wouldn't . . . would never . . ."

To the surprise of, I believe, everyone in the room, Harry Gibney began to laugh, great, hoarse gusts of laughter that wracked his frame and subsided at last into something nearly a sob. "Oh, Annie, my sweet Annie. No wonder you insisted on coming here! To find my English lover, was it? The letters were from him, not me. He can imitate anyone, anything. He is the best forger . . . he was the best forger . . . who ever lived."

"*Who?*" Anne cried.

"Victor Lynch," said Holmes.

Anne drew a startled breath—apparently she had known the man, or at least his name. But when she said nothing, and Gibney merely nodded, Holmes went on, "Perhaps he wished your wife to confront you with these letters, as a cruel message to draw you to London, so that you would see his advertisements. I assume he held some malice toward you—perhaps because you profited from his works?—and hoped vengefully to sour your marriage."

"Malice," Gibney echoed hollowly. "Yes, you're right on that count. But it wasn't the letters that drew me—she never told me of them. I was surprised to see his ads; I thought somehow he'd known, known I'd come eventually, come looking for him. . . . And I deserved his malice. This is no one's fault but my own."

"Did you murder Victor Lynch?" Holmes asked quietly.

Gibney looked up, startled, as if he had forgotten why he intended to flee London. "Murder? Why, of course not. I came here to find him, to give him money, to make up for things, like. I wanted to make amends, though nothing could make up for it all. I knew he had saved some of his work; when it never appeared on the market, I realized he didn't know how things had changed. I came here to tell him what it was worth, tell him to sell it. And give him some money. And leave." He buried his head in shaking hands, overcome by the consequences of his guilt-inspired visit.

"It might be better if you start at the beginning," Holmes prompted carefully.

The man seemed to pull himself bodily back from collapse; he gathered himself, nodded, and began. "I was a lowly clerk in a Dublin auction house, barely scraping by, when one of Victor's illuminated manuscripts came into my hands, a lovely psalter. It was masterful work—more than just using original materials, he had aged the leaves somehow, damaged some, removed some, so that it would look like an authentic find. I saw at once that it was a fake—I prided myself on my eye, and I was frustrated that I hadn't advanced farther than I had in the firm. But I also knew an opportunity when I saw one. I wanted to better myself, and why not? So I sold it, through the firm, my first commission, and contacted him for more. In the meantime, Ryan Kenny—Anne's father—had seen the first one, and asked if there were any others. He assumed that some vault had been opened somewhere, or some private collection unearthed, and as the years passed he made it his goal to collect them all." He laughed again, a short, harsh bark. "The experts came up with theories, about a cleric in a Galway monastery, secreting work away. It was a monumental hoax, but everyone was so keen to believe it, it took on a life of its own. They accepted the seller's desire to remain anonymous. It seemed so easy, so very easy."

Anne's eyes were wide as she listened; this couple had kept many secrets from each other, however faithful they had been to their other wedding vows.

"What spoiled the arrangement?" Holmes asked, body canted forward—I suspected that he had developed a fascination for this Victor Lynch, and wanted to understand the entirety of his story.

"Anne," Gibney said wryly, reaching for her hand to soften the revelation. "I had met her through my dealings with her father, and we had fallen in love. But one day Victor came to my offices in Dublin—he rarely delivered his work himself, to avoid the association, but he had grown suspicious of go-betweens. And that very day, Anne and her father were visiting. They met, and Victor professed to be charmed by Anne, though it was really her father's holdings that enchanted him. He was the black sheep of some famous Galway family, you see, and his position had rankled him for years, for he felt his artistic talents were not admired as they ought to be." Gibney's voice dropped a register, tinged with old bitterness. "He began to court her, and I was left in the dust—a clerk was no match for Galway aristocracy."

Anne took up the story, almost as if she had to measure her own place in this somehow, articulate it for herself. "He asked my father for my hand, and my father agreed. I had no choice—I loved Harry, but my father wouldn't hear of the match. We should have eloped . . . we should have just run away, none of this would have happened . . ."

"It's spilled milk now," Harry said softly. "For us—for a

while—it worked out all right in the end. Till now, anyway. Well, what happened was this. I was beside myself with rage—I had rescued Lynch's finances, bleeding Anne's family of funds in the process, and the whole thing was so backwards, it drove me mad. And so I made a forgery of my own. A bad copy of one of Lynch's leaves I had been holding. I knew enough of his work, his methods, to make it recognizable as his, and I wanted it to be substandard. I presented the forgery to my firm, saying that it had come from the same source as the others, but that this one made the others suspect, and what should I do? Well, it ruined Lynch, all right. They examined all the others with a jaundiced eye, and suddenly the flaws jumped out, the historical inconsistencies, small as they were. It was a scandal. It went to the courts, and he had to make what restitution he could to the family—which wasn't much, as he had gotten back into debt—and needless to say the engagement was off. Anne stuck by me during the bad time, because of course my firm let me go, even though they had been as duped as everyone else. They said it was my fault the fakes had come on the market, and they were right, but being condemned for stupidity was better than jail, as I saw it." He paused, eyes focused inward, ruminating, no doubt, on swallowed pride.

"But you turned it around," I put in, remembering what the appraiser had said. "You created a market for the forgeries themselves, as works of art."

Gibney nodded. "Yes, but—well, he had left by then. He came to see me, on his way to England. Said he'd faked his own death to avoid prison, forged the death certificate and all, and now he had to run away. He threatened to kill me, for ruining him. But he didn't have the stomach for it, and he left in disgust, saying he'd do better here, he'd show me."

He reached back for the hat on the back of the chair, as if taking it up might remind him that his own escape, reversing the course of Victor Lynch's flight from Ireland, was still possible. But he continued, "I'd lost track of the right and the wrong of it by then. Men prey on men, I told myself. That's the way of it, I said. It was eat or be eaten. If I hadn't done what I did, Lynch would never have profited; and if I hadn't done what I did, he would have taken Anne from me. Competition's the way of the world, and may the best man win—sometimes it's one, sometimes the other. That's what I told myself. And I saw no harm in doing well by his work. He'd made his own money from it, and looked to make more in London; why shouldn't I, as well? Why shouldn't I? And so I talked up the forgeries, told everyone how they really were artwork, after all. That the artist was dead made it that much more attractive. Mr. Kenny took a chance and let me put one on the market, and it sold, and then the collection was worth something again, which pleased Mr. Kenny. I had redeemed myself, regained my reputation—rebuilt it, really, from nothing; I started my own firm, and I married Anne. And we lived well."

"And then you thought better of it," I prompted, for he had once again lapsed into tortured silence.

Gibney wrung his hat in his hand the way a fellow will who has only cheap felt with which to cover his head; the hard silk of the affluent man resisted the guiltful twisting of fingers that remembered being poor. "Yes, I thought better of it. I thought I might find him in London." He paused, then finished, "And I did."

"But that is not the end of the tale," said Holmes, almost sternly, as if we had all forgotten that a death had come of this, on top of ruin.

Gibney seemed now to go into a trance, unaffected by his wife, who had moved to sit on the arm of the chair and laid her hands consolingly on his shoulders. "I could barely believe he lived in such a place. He was sick, I could see that. It was as if his contrived death were coming true, little by little. Something in the pigments, he said, lead or quicksilver—it was a slow poison. He had known about it for years, and stayed away from the stuff, but when he realized the damage was already done, he started to take it up again—he had all the materials there in his flat, he'd paid for them by forging legal documents, contracts for money changers and such. It was art, he said. He couldn't stand the idea that no one would see his art, no one would appreciate it. He had lived with his own codices all those years, like a dragon sitting on its hoard, brooding because no one would see them. And so he advertised for me—and forged letters from me, I guess—because he thought I was the only man who could ever see them again, the only man who knew he was alive, the only man who wouldn't put him in jail for doing what he did. He never knew—" The man's voice cracked, and he cleared his throat hard, as if to force the next words out. "He never knew that things had changed, the value of his work. He never knew how much money he could have been making, once he feigned his own death."

"Did you tell him?" Holmes said in a near-whisper.

Gibney nodded, wincing at the memory, blinking as if in the glare of too bright light. "He went stone mad, he did. He said, 'To get my due as an artist, I must be *dead*? Can't you see that I am already dead, dead to this world, dead to all my dreams?' He snatched his pen-knife from the table, the one to cut quills; I feared he would brandish it at me, but he strode to the mantelpiece and hacked his initials into it, almost viciously. 'Let this be my pitiful legacy, then! My last signature!' He wasn't making sense. I think the poison had gone to his brain. He started tearing around the place, knocking books over, throwing everything he could grab into the fire. I tried to stop him; I took up a poker, to pry the books from the flames. He grabbed the other end of it. And . . . and . . . he must have tripped, there were books underfoot everywhere . . . he fell forward . . ." He let out a cry of horror and collapsed at last, moaning, as Anne stroked his hair and murmured softly to him.

There was nothing to be done. We left them there together, to return to Ireland and the ashes of their lives. And although Holmes entered the case under *V* in his commonplace book, I will not publish this chronicle of the tale until after the remaining principals have passed on; there seems no need to heap more ruin upon them, as Holmes agreed that their injustices and suspicions had wreaked sufficient vengeance upon them.

And as for the mystery, it had to remain one of Holmes's failures. Holmes reported to Inspector Barney that from the physical evidence of a struggle and the disarray of the room, as well as the angle of entry of the poker, the death must have been an accident. And he identified the corpse as that of Victor Lynch, which, to all official reckoning, rendered the matter moot, as we had been unable to trace the man who, after burning his own blood-soaked clothes for fear of being charged with a murder that hadn't been committed, left in Lynch's extra suit—a human counterfeit of a forger who had officially been dead for ten years.

The remaining manuscripts were entered into evidence in case the unknown party were ever found, and they sit, to this day, in some dank police-station vault, their mendacious beauty forever in darkness.

1895, *says Watson, was a year of "curious and incongruous cases," from the "investigation of the sudden death of Cardinal Tosca . . . down to his arrest of Wilson, the notorious canary-trainer, which removed a plague-spot from the East End of London." The story that follows only indirectly reports Wilson's arrest, and glosses over the plague-spot's removal, except by implication. This narrative skew is not due to authorial reserve, but is the result of the idiosyncratic viewpoint of this atmospheric "club story"—a choice that even relegates Sherlock Holmes to the sidelines. Mr. R.'s ledger records a fee of $5,000 converted to pounds sterling paid to WSM. Could this be the great English raconteur novelist W. SOMERSET MAUGHAM (1874–1965), author of* Of Human Bondage, The Razor's Edge, *"Rain" and the autobiographical* The Summing Up?*—JAF*

The Case of the Notorious Canary Trainer

BY *"HENRY SLESAR"*
(ASCRIBED TO W. SOMERSET MAUGHAM)

I found myself uneasy about joining the Hippocratic Club even as I signed the check for the initiation fee. For one thing, my former club, the Metropole, required sponsorship by two members, and apparently the trustees of the Hippocratic were willing to accept my application on the basis of my family name alone, even though I kept my royal title secret.

It was, of course, a name of considerable weightiness. The Pertwees had amassed an enormous fortune in the past forty years through ownership of almost a third of the coal-producing mines of Wales. I had been a beneficiary of their efforts without so much as a single visit to that grimy world which had put me through medical school and allowed me to live well despite a practice limited to the wealthy old matrons of my immediate neighborhood. I had given up my shingle a good ten years ago, without regret, but vanity prompted me to retain the title of "Doctor," an appelation that seemed to me far more honourable than "Your Lordship."

I was the last to bear the Pertwee name, which by no means made me the sole heir to the family's wealth, now dissipated among banks and brokers and attorneys. My wife and I had lived comfortably but not extravagantly. When she died, six months ago, I decided to give up our too-spacious townhouse (we had no children) and move into smaller quarters. It was for this reason that I sought a new club affiliation, the Metropole now far too distant for bones that did not travel well.

Despite my age, I felt very much the New Boy the first time I entered the club premises. I soon found that the members were friendly enough while still mindful of their privacy and that of their fellow members. Most were formerly men of medicine, but a discussion of the subject was rare among them. After the first week, I felt as comfortable as I had ever been at the Metropole. But as it happened, that week coincided with the absence of the club's "celebrity" member who, I was later told, was working on a case in Scotland. I assumed that meant a medical case, but learned differently. Dr. John Watson's present "cases" were not the type chronicled in journals, but in the Penny Dreadfuls hawked by ragged boys on the street corners of London.

I realize that the tone of my last remark has characterized my feelings about Dr. Watson, but they were not formulated until the Friday evening when he made his first appearance at the club. There was what might be described as a burst of excited enthusiasm among the members, several of whom clustered about him, eager to hear what he had to say. I heard little of the conversation, although the name "Holmes" was spoken so often it was apparent that his tale had more than one protagonist.

It was a member named Muggeridge who told me more about Watson. It seems he was a long-time companion of a private consulting detective named Sherlock Holmes. Apparently, Holmes had a number of extraordinary successes, some of which Watson himself had recorded in rather melodramatic style. I suspected that gross exaggeration may have been involved, especially when I heard Muggeridge's awed remarks about Holmes's prodigious mental feats. Why, the man was credited with determining someone's height, weight, age and Heaven knows what else from nothing more than the brim of a hat!

Watson himself was a bull-like man who would undoubtedly run to fat in his later years. He had the ineffable air of someone who had served in India, but I later learned that during his tenure with the Army Medical Department he had been wounded in Afghanistan. Like myself, he was widowed; unlike me, he indulged freely in tobacco and alcohol, smoking a vile mixture of ship's tobacco and never failing to order a bottle of Beaune with his meals. I limited myself to a brandy or two after meals.

But foremost among his vices was his outspoken hero-worshipping admiration for his friend Sherlock Holmes, a tin god he carried around on a chain which held him captive to another man's chariot. I could not help but deplore the loss of self-esteem this implied, and one day, shortly after we had been introduced, I decided to confront the subject head on.

"You do still practice medicine, Dr. Watson?" I asked.

"I do," he said, smiling. "But my practice is limited by other priorities."

"Priorities you consider more important? Such as your work with Mr. Holmes?"

"My dear fellow," he said pleasantly. "Let me assure you that the health of the London population suffers little when my tiny office is closed for a few days or weeks. And often, during that period, I might well be involved in matters that may save lives and reputations."

"By playing detective," I said.

He chose not to recognize the sneer in my statement.

"Sherlock Holmes is the detective," he replied. "I am merely his assistant, his man-of-all-work, but I'm pleased to say that my friend considers me indispensable to his activities."

"But has it ever occurred to you that *you* may be an even greater detective, Dr. Watson?"

The question startled him into silence.

"It's the truth. You may have solved more mysteries and saved more lives during your career than a man like Sherlock Holmes could ever hope to have accomplished."

"What on earth do you mean?"

"You're a physician, Dr. Watson. Hundreds have come to your examining room with undiagnosed ailments. You have been the one to solve these medical mysteries, you are the person who has saved lives by arresting diseases of all kinds. Isn't that far more important than playing these childish adventure games?"

I knew I had gone too far, when Dr. Watson's thick neck reddened. "Games, sir?" he said. "Childish? You obviously haven't read my published accounts—"

"I have," I said, beginning to regret the trend of this conversation. "And I can't help thinking that—well, surely they were more fiction than fact?"

The scarlet rose from his neck to his face like mercury in a thermometer, and then he sprang to his feet with surprising agility for a big man. "You'll excuse, me, sir," he said between clenched teeth. "I have an appointment in the billiards room."

I learned later that billiards was not one of the "childish games," so it was only too obvious that I had just made an enemy.

I wish I could explain the perversity of temper that made me behave in such a fashion. I can only ascribe it to a general depression brought on by my unaccustomed solitude. I simply had no patience with falsehood and exaggeration, and I had never heard a better example of both than the history of Mr. Sherlock Holmes.

Word of the unpleasantness between Dr. Watson and myself spread quickly through the Hippocratic, and I began to feel more and more isolated. I chose a "regular" armchair furthest from the others, and my greetings became more and more perfunctory. I was relieved when Dr. Watson once again disappeared from his own "regular" chair, off on still another Adventure with his illustrious friend.

The first evening he was gone ended strangely for me. I dozed off, a not-uncommon custom among the members, but I awoke to an unusual silence. Actually, I might have slept longer if the club's cleaning lady, Mrs. Moulton, hadn't decided to wake me.

"Lord Pertwee," she whispered nervously, with a light tap on my shoulder. "I'm sorry to disturb you, sir, but it's past one . . ."

I was surprised, of course, but on later reflection recalled how poorly I slept in my new flat. I also recalled having two rather potent brandies after dinner. I gathered my wits and collected my outdoor apparel and headed for the exit, only to have Mrs. Moulton call me back.

"Don't forget your package, sir," she said.

I had no recollection of arriving with any "package," or of any being delivered to me, but of course the latter event might have taken place during my lengthy nap. It was a brown parcel tied with string, no bigger than a shoebox, and was addressed to W. Pertwee in care of the club. There was no return address.

I thanked Mrs. Moulton and went home, taking a carriage and almost falling asleep again during the short ride, not even thinking of the brown parcel resting against my thigh.

In my small sitting-room, I was still in a mood to ignore the package until morning, but by the time I had dressed for bed, curiosity began to nibble at me. I picked up the parcel, wondering at its light weight, and then stripped off the cheap brown wrapping that enclosed an even cheaper cardboard box. I removed the lid and stared uncomprehendingly at the contents.

It was a dead canary.

Revulsion came before surprise. The small desiccated bird was quite intact, but the incongruity of its appearance in my home made my stomach rebel. I hurried to the lavatory, but instead of yielding to my rising gorge, I threw the canary into the bowl and pumped the chain vigorously until certain it was gone.

Needless to say, the insomnia which had plagued me since my change of address was worsened by the circumstances of the night. I spent hours staring at the tin ceiling, trying to determine the significance of the cruel prank played at my expense. I was certain that one of the club members was responsible; that they had taken advantage of my somnolent state to place the box at my side. But why a dead canary? What message did a deceased bird convey? Was my feud with Dr. Watson responsible? And if so, could he supply the answer to the mystery? But, of course, Dr. Watson was no longer available to answer any questions—or accusations.

When I arrived at the Hippocratic Club the next evening, I was totally on guard, my eyes shifting from one member to the next, looking for signs of secret amusement. There was nothing. I read the London *Times* from first page to last, including the long columns of advertisements and announcements. I went into dinner at a solitary table, and when Hugh, the waiter, suggested a hot bird and a cold bottle, my head snapped up suspiciously. It was, however, the main course of the day. I chose a small chop and a salad, instead.

It was at nine-thirty, when I was already beginning to doze in my chair, that Arno, the hall porter, came into the main room of the club with a package that I knew instinctively was addressed to me. It was exactly the same size and shape, and had apparently been delivered by an anonymous street urchin. I felt a chill of pure terror as I opened it and peered inside, making sure that no one else was observing my reaction.

It was a second dead canary.

I am still not sure why the sight horrified me so. I believe it was the sheer irrelevancy of the sardonic gift. I examined the wrapping paper, the block letters in which my name and the club name had been written, but they offered no clue. The thought of Mr. Sherlock Holmes came to mind, the man who could read a hat brim, and I smiled with irony. Too bad Dr. Watson wasn't here; I could give him a challenge that would finally baffle his genius friend!

For the following two nights there were no more dead birds delivered, and I began to hope that this impractical practical joke had run its course. By the time the following day arrived, I began to entertain a new and comforting theory: that the dead birds had been intended for someone entirely different, perhaps a former club member whose name resembled mine. I began to feel light-hearted. I asked Muggeridge if I could join him for dinner, and he graciously accepted. Other members chatted with me. The altercation with Dr. Watson seemed forgotten. So, for the moment, had the two dead canaries.

At ten P.M., puffing contentedly on a Havana cigar, I looked up at the hall porter bearing an altogether too-familiar box. I'm sure my face became the color of the ash hanging from the tip of my cigar. I literally seized the tail of Arno's jacket and asked him who the delivery agent had been, but he looked at me blankly.

"Why, I don't know, sir. The box was sitting on the counter when I reported for work. It was just . . . *there.*"

I shuddered. I kept on shuddering until one of the members noticed it. He asked if I had caught a chill, and advised me to go home and drink hot water and lemon juice. I did go home, first hurling the package into the dustbin outside the club entrance. I had a raging fever by then, and kept to my bed for the next four days.

When I returned to the club, Dr. John Watson had, too.

I tried to resist the temptation, but I could not. I approached him, and mustering all the humility within me, I said:

"I believe I owe you an apology, Dr. Watson. I spoke out of turn the last time we met. I hope you'll forgive my . . . healthy skepticism concerning your friend Holmes."

"Holmes is often doubted," he said grudgingly. "But if you had just witnessed what I've witnessed, a man wearing a speckled band . . . Only Holmes could have unmasked his terrible secret . . ."

"Well, I have a challenge for your friend, too," I said, smiling, my lips aching with its falsity. "Ask him if he knows why someone would be sending me dead canaries."

Watson seemed instantly intrigued. I told him the story, and he asked me some rudimentary questions, none of which I hadn't asked myself. By the time he heard the entire account, he had promised to present the puzzle—which he declared to be a "one-pipe" problem, whatever that meant—to the esteemed detective.

On the following evening, I found myself looking forward anxiously to Dr. Watson's arrival, a ninety-degree turn from my former attitude. To my disappointment, he didn't seek me out at once, but spent the first hour concluding the tale he had begun the night before, an improbable account involving a deadly serpent. I waited until his admirers had dispersed, and approached.

"Well," I said lightly. "Has your friend been able to solve the mystery of the dead canaries?"

"Oh, yes," he said casually. "I did present the situation to him, but I'm afraid Holmes shrugged it off rather brusquely. In fact, he berated me for posing a problem without the slightest bit of supporting evidence. Where are these boxes? he asked me. These dead birds? Who is this man Pertwee? His name sounds like a bird call—perhaps that's the connection, although I doubt it . . . That's all he said, I'm afraid. Sorry, old man."

I could not hide my disappointment. It took the form of resentment.

"So this is your great detective," I said bitterly. "The one who can read a man's history in his hat brim."

"Well," Dr. Watson smiled, "perhaps if Holmes had your hat, it may have helped the situation."

"In that case, sir," I said haughtily, "Mr. Holmes may have my hat, for whatever it's worth. Let's see if he can pull one of his famous rabbits from it—or perhaps a dead canary!"

Watson seemed astonished when I handed it to him, a fine Smith & Robinson I had owned since early manhood.

"And since Mr. Holmes is so fond of facts," I said, "I will also give him a detailed account of each episode as it occurred."

That was precisely what I did for the rest of the evening, with pen and paper, describing in painstaking detail every moment of my living nightmare, beginning with Mrs. Moulton and ending with the next appearance of a dead canary—an event that took place that very night. Only I could not now present the detective with the usual wrappings, because the dead bird was nestling in my handkerchief pocket when I woke from still another round of illicit sleep in the Club's armchair.

I was no longer surprised to find myself alone in the club room at this late hour, having concentrated so long and hard on my notes. But to wake up with the feeling that something, *something* was amiss, to rise from my chair still not aware of the tiny yellow head just barely poking out of my pocket, this was a living nightmare indeed. When I realized the truth, I yanked the dead creature out of my pocket with a cry of disgust and flung it from me, without any thought of how poor Mrs. Moulton would react when she came to do her cleaning chores. Completely unnerved, I picked up my brandy, but there were only dregs at the bottom of the glass, so I put it down again.

I turned over my notes to Dr. Watson the next evening, only to hear him declare that he planned still another absence from the Hippocratic Club, the duration unknown. When I inquired about my hat, whether Sherlock Holmes now knew my height and weight and profession several members gathered to hear Watson's reply.

"Why, yes," he said. "Holmes knows you're a physician, about five feet ten, about twelve stone."

"And how did he deduce all that?"

"Why, he asked me," Dr. Watson said, and grinned with satisfaction as his reply produced a loud guffaw among the members.

That settled the issue for me. The next day, I informed the club chairman that I was resigning. I had had enough of dead canaries and fantastical detective stories. That evening's meal at the club would be my last, my after-dinner brandy would toast farewell to my problems. I left a message for Dr. Watson, asking him to send on my hat to my home address, and told him that the great Sherlock Holmes need no longer be concerned with my little "one-pipe" problem. I would solve it myself by escaping the source of the dilemma.

The word swept quickly through the club that I was leaving, and I was surprised when half a dozen members voiced their regret at my decision, some of them even urging me to stay. I did not, of course, tell them the underlying reason for my resignation. Even the hall porter and waiter expressed their unhappiness at my decision, and I admit to feeling the pang of loss, an emotion I had not experienced upon leaving my former affiliation.

I dined on a fine salmon dish that evening, and had to admit that the Hippocratic kitchen was excellent, a fact I had never really noted before. My after-dinner brandy was also of superior quality, and as I sank back in my favorite armchair, I realized that it was quite the most comfortable seating I had ever known. It was not surprising that I had sipped my way through only half my drink when my eyes closed in delicious, welcome slumber. I dreamed of my wife, and saw her lovely face bending over me solicitously, and she was saying something about finishing my drink and coming to bed. "Yes," I told her with a smile, and barely coming awake I reached for my unfinished brandy, only to have a man in a greatcoat and deerstalker's cap shout something at me and spring across the room to knock the glass out of my hand and send it sailing across the room, ending in a crash of fine crystal that was too real to be part of my dream.

"I'm sorry, Lord Pertwee," the man said, his hawklike features intent on mine. "I feared that your drink may have contained a deadly poison, probably wood alcohol. One swallow would have left you blind or dead. Perhaps we can still determine the contents from the remnants of the brandy glass, but it was more important to save your life."

"Who the blazes are you?" I gasped.

"My name is Sherlock Holmes," he said. "You already know my friend Watson, and I apologize for not recognizing the seriousness of your problem for so long a time. Your hat, and the detailed account you gave Dr. Watson, finally made the situation comprehensible."

"My hat? Are you serious, sir?"

He smiled wolfishly. "Oh, I didn't determine your life history. Only that you presently live in Kensington, that you had been recently widowed, and that you were concealing your royal title."

"How on earth did you know all that?" I asked.

"It was elementary, Doctor. The crown of the hat had fine particles of plaster dust, and Kensington is the only area of London undergoing major reconstruction at the moment. The fact that you had not had your hat cleaned in several months indicates the sudden loss of a caring woman. And in case you never realized it, Smith & Robinson always engraves the owners name under the leather hat band. In this case, HIS LORDSHIP WM. D. PERTWEE."

"I prefer not to use my title," I said. "I find it only serves to intimidate people. I mentioned it to no one when I joined the club."

"And yet," Holmes said gravely, "in your notes concerning the first dead canary, you stated that Mrs. Moulton called you "Lord Pertwee," when she wakened you and pointed out the presence of the cardboard box. Why would it be a cleaning lady's privilege to know your title when you concealed it from everyone else?"

"Yes," I said, mystified. "How did she know?"

"I can tell you," Holmes said, flinging off his greatcoat and tossing it on the back of a chair. "It was because Mrs. Moulton had recognized your family name, and it drove her into a fit of passion that almost cost you your life!"

"But why?" I gasped. "What did she have against me?"

"We could only speculate, until we paid a visit to her noxious basement flat earlier today. From the moment we saw the hand-written sign outside, we knew we had your deadly prankster. The sign read: CANARIES TRAINED."

"Trained? To do what?"

"Why, to sing, of course. We knew her method when Mrs. Moulton answered the door. The room was filled with dozens and dozens of cages, containing at least a hundred yellow birds, each teaching the other how to warble their—to me—cacophonic song. It was obvious that Mrs. Moulton adored, even worshipped the little devils beyond anything on earth. Of course, some of the little creatures died occasionally, and she saved their tiny bodies as an instrument of revenge against the only member of the family remaining."

"But what harm have the Pertwees ever done her?"

"The harm was to the canary," Sherlock Holmes said. "To the hundreds of birds your ancestors sent into the mines they owned to determine the presence of what was then called coal damp, but we now know to be methane gas."

"Good heavens!" I said. "But I never heard of such a thing. I've never been in a coal mine in my life!"

"No harm was intended the birds, you understand. Usually, if they stopped singing that was warning enough to the miners. If the birds became unconscious, they attempted to revive them . . . Still I imagine quite a number did die when this odourless, invisible and deadly gas was present . . . That was why Mrs. Moulton wanted her revenge, and when she hinted to us that there would no longer be merely dead *canaries* at the club, I rushed here to foil her final plan . . .

I stared at him in speechless awe. A few moments later, Dr. Watson himself came puffing into the room, to report that Mrs. Moulton had made a full confession to the police, even to the extent of revealing that her maiden name was Wilson. He insisted on checking out my pulse and heartbeat, to make sure I was all right. Before I could convey a word of gratitude, his friend Holmes had swept up his greatcoat and left the club room. Watson swiftly put away his stethoscope and hurried after him. I did not blame him. I realized that Sherlock Holmes was a man I, too, would follow anywhere.

The next tale is doubly mysterious. Mr. R. paid cash for it, so its authorship is unclear, though the ledger records EMH as payee. Mr. R.'s surviving granddaughter suggests the Nobel Prize author ERNEST (Miller) HEMINGWAY (1899–1961), whose macho works include A Farewell to Arms, *"The Killers,"* The Old Man and the Sea *and* The Sun Also Rises, *but this is a guess partly based on the tale's "Hemingway echoes" and partly on her childhood recollection of a bearded man her grandfather introduced as "Papa," which confused her no end. The second mystery concerns the Canonical reference to "the repulsive story of the red leech and the terrible death of Crosby the banker." No mention of Crosby occurs in the following story. I reexamined Watson's notes to see whether this was an oversight, as the banker may have been one of the tale's unnamed victims, or if, instead, Crosby's death was a separate adventure that Watson erroneously appended to his red leech reference. Neither theory is correct. My research shows that Crosby and the red leech are involved in a separate story (also redacted by EMH) whose events are sequential to those below. If there is sufficient interest, Mr. R.'s estate promises to release that tale at a later date.—JAF*

The Repulsive Story of the Red Leech

BY *"MORGAN LLYWELYN"*
(ASCRIBED TO ERNEST HEMINGWAY)

In the late summer of 1894, Mr. Sherlock Holmes and I were staying in a country house that looked across a river and meadow to the hills. The sale of my practice earlier in the year and my return to share the old quarters in Baker Street had provided sufficient upheaval to make me long for a holiday. Meanwhile the cumulative effects of the Addleton tragedy, the Barrow Mystery, and various other undertakings had so exhausted and enervated my friend that he offered no demurral when I suggested a few days in the country.

Indeed, the very weather conspired to help me influence him. London rain is of a distinctly pernicious sort. Days of unrelieved drizzle make the cobbles shine but dull the spirit. The morning I proposed our holiday found Holmes slumped in his favourite chair before the fire, gazing somberly toward the rainwashed window.

"Watson, I'll wager there is more crime committed in this weather than in any other," he said in a dull voice as I entered the room.

"I have the remedy right here!" I announced, waving the missive in my hand. "This is a letter from an old colleague of mine from Barts, Dr. Horatio Floyd. He has invited us to his house in the country."

Holmes half-lifted one eyebrow. "Whatever would we do buried in the country?" he asked languidly.

"Restore our energies."

"To what purpose?" He remained slouched in his chair, thrusting his hands deep into his pockets and allowing his head to sink onto his breast.

I saw then that we had not a moment to spare. Holmes was in danger of slipping back into that abyss from which he had climbed with such difficulty, the ennui which had driven him to use the infernal seven per cent solution. As a doctor and his friend I must not allow a relapse.

"We would at least enjoy a change of weather," I said with a nod toward the window. "The house is in the Cotswolds where they assuredly see more sun than we do in London."

He made no response.

"Ah, Holmes," I enthused, "imagine the sporting life during

the day, some shooting perhaps, or a pleasant canter across green fields, then the deep and undisturbed peace of country nights!''

With an effort my friend roused himself. "Although I have never met your Dr. Floyd I suppose I must humour you," said he, "since you have already made our travel arrangements."

"How did you know?" It was never a mistake to allow Holmes to demonstrate his powers of deduction, for this always seemed to lift his spirits.

"The letter you hold has been refolded twice," he remarked, "neither time along the original seam. After the initial reading you consulted it a second time while purchasing train tickets, and again while writing out baggage labels. There is still an ink stain on your forefinger and your shoes are encrusted with that particular red mud indigenous to the streets surrounding Paddington, now that the pavement has been lifted again."

This small exercise of his powers having cheered him minimally, I was able to secure his agreement to join me for a few days in the Cotswolds. For once I hoped no adventures would present themselves. Holmes was in serious need of rest and I prescribed the bucolic luxuries of a country estate.

We had rarely taken holidays during our long association, our sojourns into the country having been in pursuit of some investigation or other. I found myself growing increasingly enthusiastic. Dr. Floyd's letter had urged us to come as soon as we liked and I had purchased tickets for the very next day.

The train was to leave at noon. One had to be there when it was made up in order to be certain of a suitable first-class carriage. Our trip was uneventful and our compartment comfortable, shared only, during its latter stages, by a pallid man wearing riding boots. The leather was dark and oiled smooth as a used saddle. I would have liked such a pair myself for our country canters. Holmes hardly glanced at them, however. For most of the journey he merely gazed out the window as if lost in thought.

Our companion was equally taciturn. Beyond a brief exchange about opening the window, little conversation passed amongst us. As we made our way westward the sun had broken through the clouds and I was eager for a breath of fresh air, but the booted man was adamant that the window remained closed. As Holmes ventured no preference, I acquiesced out of courtesy.

Soon enough, I promised myself, we would have all the fresh air we wanted.

The small wayside station at Much Markle gave every appearance of being abandoned, save for a youthful station master who kept himself in the shadows so I never got a good look at his face. A solitary dog-cart with a gaunt driver in a rusty black coat waited at the end of the platform.

I had thought we were the only intending travellers to the village, but the man in riding boots disembarked when we did and stood with us on the platform as the train pulled away.

The driver of the dog-cart looked quizzically at the three of us. "Hope Hill?"

"For myself and Mr. Holmes, yes."

"Get in, then."

"And for me," announced the man in riding boots. With an awkward limp he shoved past us and clambered, wincing, into the dog-cart.

The driver and I exchanged glances. "Mr. Holmes and myself are guests of Dr. Horatio Floyd, the owner of Hope Hill," I stressed.

"So am I," muttered the man in riding boots.

Without further discussion the driver piled our baggage into the cart and we set off. Cart and harness creaked with the weight. Soon the horse was trotting along a winding country road. Stone cottages half-choked by riotous gardens dotted the countryside. I was about to ask our driver when we should turn into Dr. Floyd's parkland when he sawed at the reins and the horse stopped.

"Hope Hill."

Holmes looked at me and raised both his eyebrows.

The airy, spacious country house I had envisioned was a simple Cotswold cottage, festooned with ivy and thickly thatched. The housekeeper, a rotund, apple-cheeked woman who identified herself as Mrs. Peebles, met us at the door and clucked her tongue at the dusty condition of our clothing. When she ushered us to our rooms they proved to be smaller than our chambers in Baker Street, cramped, low-ceilinged and rather dark. The furniture was common oak of a most unfashionable design, and heavy draperies of a coarse fabric obscured the mullioned windows. Anything less like luxury would be hard to imagine.

"I ask you again, Watson," said Holmes with a touch of asperity. "Whatever are we going to do here?"

Obviously we were in for the plainest of holidays. The housekeeper informed us that Dr. Floyd was not there, nor was he expected. "How extraordinary," I remarked. "I have not chanced to see Horatio in quite some time, but I recall him as an amiable man. I would not have thought him capable of inviting guests without welcoming them in person. It is a pity he never took a wife to perform that service for him. Too much dedication to his work, I suppose."

At dinner that evening there were only myself and Holmes. Mrs. Peebles had not only cooked the meal, but also served it. Though we could hear him stumping about overhead, the man in riding boots made no appearance. We might as well have been dining back in Baker Street, where the food, I confess, would have been more to my taste.

"I am most dreadfully sorry, Holmes. This is a mistake," I said to my friend, who was surveying the contents of the dining table through narrowed eyes, "which I intend to rectify first thing in the morning. I shall go to the station and purchase tickets for an immediate return to London."

"Not at all, Watson. You have supplied us with an intriguing puzzle. Have some consommé, and pass me that dish of sliced beef, will you?" He proceeded to eat with a relish I had not seen in months.

My mystification only deepened the next morning when I

discovered Holmes in an uncommonly cheerful mood, chatting in the kitchen with the housekeeper. Wearing a voluminous apron and with her brown hair scraped back into a knot, she was busily preparing beef tea.

"I assume Dr. Floyd does not often have guests here?" he was saying to her.

"On the contrary, sir. Most weekends, and sometimes during the week, at least one or possibly two ladies and gentlemen come down from the city. Always patients of his, they are. Invited special to convalesce in the country. The doctor's most generous.

"Just before you gentlemen arrived we had a lady and her maid. The maid was quite thin from overwork, poor soul. Her mistress wore many layers of heavy clothing in spite of the season, and the maid was expected to keep them all spotless."

"Does the good doctor spend much time with his patients here?" Holmes inquired. He was leaning against the windowsill, but, I noted, watching Mrs. Peebles' reflection in the glass.

"Why, sir, Dr. Floyd hardly comes down at all. Hates sunshine, he does. Says it makes his rash worse. Day and night he slaves away in that hospital in the city. His guests have told me he often works through the night."

"You've been at Hope Hill a long time," Holmes observed.

"Twenty-five years, sir. My mother was housekeeper to his father before the poor gentleman was sent away as I was telling you. But how did you know?"

"You just opened that drawer behind you and removed a sharp knife without even looking. Only someone who knew the room intimately would have dared do so. Good day to you," he added abruptly.

He crossed to where I hesitated in the doorway, took my elbow and steered me away down the passage.

"Fascinating, Watson. Fascinating."

I confessed that I did not understand what could be so intriguing about a countrywoman's gossip.

"Consider a doctor with a remote cottage that he does not frequent, yet he insists that some of his patients come here. The housekeeper—bear in mind my telling you, Watson, that the staff of any house are the source of all information—the housekeeper informs me that Dr. Floyd writes out the menus himself and posts them to her. And of course you noted the large quantity of red meat hanging in the larder?"

I had to admit that I had not.

"There is another guest due this afternoon," Holmes continued. "A Miss Frances, governess to the Hailsham family. I am told she has spent quite some time under Dr. Floyd's care being treated for an illness she contracted while the family were abroad. Interestingly, the treatment seems to have made her condition worse rather than better."

"You don't suspect . . ."

"I suspect nothing. You know it is not my practice to speculate without having all the facts. You noticed, of course, the one discrepancy?"

"What discrepancy?"

"Come now, Watson. I begin to think you really did need a holiday. You and I are not patients of Dr. Floyd."

"But he is a colleague of mine," I said by way of explanation.

"Whom you have not encountered in several years and who has never met me," my friend pointed out. "Yet he invited both of us." He looked at me as if those words should have explained everything.

When I again suggested we might return to London, Holmes would not hear of it, so I resigned myself to a week of boredom punctuated by long walks and very plain food.

Miss Frances arrived that same afternoon. She was an ivory-skinned brunette, far too slender. Muffled to the chin in a heavy cloak in spite of the warm day, she went straight to her room. We did not have the pleasure of her company at dinner, which disappointed me but did not seem to surprise Holmes.

"Her meals will be taken up to her, no doubt," he commented, "as they are to our friend from the train."

"A strange sort of holiday, spent holed up in one's room."

My friend gave a dry chuckle. "Strange indeed, my good Watson."

The next day he rambled about the house and grounds in one of his contemplative moods, when I knew of old he preferred to be alone. I was left to find my own amusement.

Hope Hill possessed no true country house library, merely a couple of shelves in the parlour with dusty, mildewed volumes which held little interest for me. After a brief perusal of them I searched out the housekeeper and asked what else there might be by way of entertainment in the country.

She had only one suggestion. "The nearest pub is The Swan and Cygnets, sir. It's rather a distance but we can lend you a walking stick. There are any number of canes in that stand by the door."

I repaired to The Swan and Cygnets forthwith, mentally condemning those who intend hospitality but inflict boredom. My delight in our holiday had diminished considerably.

The pub was dark and pungent, with sawdust on the floor. It contained half a dozen weathered men who bore the appearance of regulars. Over a foaming tankard I sought to engage one of them in conversation. "What is there to do around here?" I enquired of a beefy fellow in a cloth cap. "Any sporting activities?"

"Not much." He stared into his beer.

"Horse riding, perhaps?"

"No livery stables."

"Or a hunt?"

"Not this time of year."

"What do you do for exercise?"

"Farm."

Thereafter I devoted myself to my own tankard.

When I returned to Hope Hill I found Holmes in the doorway of the dim little parlour, talking with the elusive Miss Frances.

She greeted me politely, though in a hoarse voice I could barely hear, and soon excused herself. "I am suffering from a sore throat," she explained. "If you gentlemen will forgive me?"

We watched as she dragged herself wearily up the stairs. The door to her room closed.

Over dinner I complained, "There is really very little to do around here, Holmes. The local pub is not the sort of convivial establishment one might imagine, and as for sport—well, there are not even any livery stables in the area. And as our fellow guests are in poor health . . ."

"We must be thankful there is adequate mental exercise," my friend concluded. He did not elaborate, however.

Several days of boredom ensued. I am not a sound sleeper, and the unfamiliar quiet of the country did not soothe me to sleep as I had anticipated, but had quite the opposite effect. I found myself longing for the clamour of the city.

We were rescued at last when a telegram for Holmes arrived from London—from Inspector Lestrade himself.

My friend read it with furrowed brow before passing it to me. "What do you make of this, Watson?"

"Horror of '88 returns," the message began.

It required but a moment for me to interpret the reference. I stared appalled at Holmes, whom I thought had long since solved the mystery. "But is the Ripper not dead?"

"Poison eliminated James Maybrick," he replied cryptically, "yet terrors are still afoot, my good Watson. The Ripper worked with anger and a blade. These new crimes are committed in colder blood.

"I am now willing to return to London. In fact, the sooner we get there the better. There are lives that may yet be saved."

His voice was crisp, his face set in stern lines.

By that same afternoon we were on the train. I was relieved to note that the mysterious man in riding boots did not accompany us this time. When I commented upon him, Holmes said, "Did you not ask yourself why anyone would wear riding boots to a place where no saddle horses are available?"

As we sped back to London I reread Lestrade's telegram. Several bodies had been discovered in unfrequented laneways. The details were horrific. The corpses were all but drained of blood. They were not eviscerated, nor were they Whitechapel drabs. Both male and female, all they had in common was their bloodless condition, and purple contusions on throat, wrists, and ankles. It was clearly the work of a fiend.

"Lestrade says nothing of their being either stabbed or shot," I remarked. "Is the cause of death a mystery, then? Are we hurrying back to London to solve it?"

Holmes said succinctly, "I have solved it. More important work remains." Falling silent, he gazed with brooding, inscrutable eyes at the countryside rushing by the train window.

I was never able to accept Sherlock Holmes's reticence in discussing his plans with so proven a friend as myself. However I had long since realised that he had an overweening need to control and dominate, and this was one of his techniques. Resolving to suffer in silence, since that was what he required of me, I folded my arms upon my breast and attempted to doze.

Smoke and refuse heralded our approach to the city. Once I would have deplored them. Now they appeared as friends. Even the squalid tenements beside the track were a welcome sight.

"We shall go straight to Barts," Holmes announced as the train was pulling into the station. "There is no time to lose! Send a message to Lestrade to join us there, Watson, and see to our luggage, will you?"

I did as he asked, then secured a hansom to take us to the hospital.

Upon arriving, Holmes asked one or two low-voiced questions at reception and was directed to the hospital library. "Watch for Lestrade," he instructed me. "Speak to no one else, *no one,* but as soon as he arrives, bring him to me. There are a couple of facts I must verify before we proceed further."

I awaited Lestrade in a fever of impatience. Holmes's tension had communicated itself to me, and I knew we were close on the trail of danger.

When Lestrade arrived, I had a few words to say to him myself. "Why did you interrupt our first holiday in a long time? I do not mind for myself, but Mr. Holmes is badly in need of a rest."

The inspector was still a small bulldog of a man, though the years had rendered him less wiry than when we first met during the unforgettable case of the Baskerville Hound. "All Holmes ever needs is a puzzle sufficient to engage that mind of his," he insisted. "But I confess I do not understand why he has chosen this hospital for his investigations. The murder victims are taken elsewhere, and the scenes of the crimes . . ."

"Are here," interrupted Holmes, emerging from the library. "I thought I heard your voice, Lestrade."

"What do you mean, the crimes are committed here? Good God, man, this is a hospital!"

"Just so," Holmes agreed. "What better place to hide deeds of blood?" Turning to me, he remarked, "I see from the duty roster that your colleague, Dr. Floyd, is here today, Watson. Perhaps he might be so good as to help us with our enquiries?"

Lestrade started to say something, then changed his mind.

"Is Dr. Floyd in theatre?" I asked Holmes.

He did not reply, merely set off at a brisk pace that forced us to hurry after him.

As if he had frequented Barts every day since we first met there so many years ago, Holmes led us along one corridor and then another, down a flight of stairs, through a dimly lit service passage. Over his shoulder he said to Lestrade, "You are prepared, I trust?"

The inspector chuckled. "As long as I have trousers with a hip pocket, I have a pistol."

Holmes gave a brusque nod.

Turning a corner, we found ourselves facing a pair of swinging doors such as one might find on a surgical theatre or a morgue.

Holmes slipped a hand into his own coat pocket. Then he strode through the doors with us close behind him.

I shall never forget the repulsive sight that greeted us. In the centre of a brightly-lit room lay a body on a table. Dr. Horatio Floyd bent over the body, looking up in alarm as we entered. But the face he raised to us was hardly recognisable.

A forehead I remembered as domed and intelligent was covered with horrific skin lesions, while from just below the eyes his features were bathed in blood. More blood spilled from his gaping mouth onto the bosom of his surgical coat, which was already saturated. In one hand he held a gory pulp that he had evidently crushed in surprise at our precipitate entry.

"Horatio!" I cried in disbelief.

Throwing down the object he held, he tried to dart around the table but Holmes was there before him with a gun levelled at his head. "You cannot run, Dr. Floyd," he said coolly.

Floyd froze. Then he burst into sobs and covered his ghastly face with his hands.

Lestrade swiftly moved to his other side and put a restraining hand on his shoulder.

I turned my attention to the body on the table. Before me lay the corpse of a nude woman. Affixed to the throat, forearms, and lower legs were a great number of bloated red leeches. Their blood-engorged bodies were like crimson sacks filled to bursting point.

I stared at them in bewilderment. "Why on earth would a doctor apply leeches to someone who was already dead?" I wondered aloud.

"I fear she was not dead when he began," Holmes replied.

Hours later, when Dr. Floyd was safely in custody, Lestrade accompanied us to our chambers in Baker Street. Like myself he was shaken. But Sherlock Holmes was calm and steady. He seemed revitalised by the experience.

"Our first clue was the man in riding boots," he explained after we had made ourselves comfortable in front of a blazing fire in our sitting-room. "The boots were to conceal severe leech bites on his lower legs and ankles. Dr. Floyd may even have prescribed them to give his injured legs additional support. He was limping in pain as you will recall, Watson."

"But he was alive!"

"As was the woman before him, and Miss Frances who followed him. They were the last of the lucky ones." Holmes began filling his pipe. Large snifters of brandy sat on a nearby table. Considering what we had just seen, no one wanted port. "By then Dr. Floyd's mania was beyond his control and he knew it. Hence the invitation to us. To me particularly, as he trusted you would bring me."

Lestrade asked, "What good did it do having you at his country house?"

"Keeping Sherlock Holmes out of London was a way of protecting himself from discovery," I responded, but Holmes shook his head.

"I think not, Watson. It is my belief that Dr. Floyd really wanted to be stopped. By sending me to his house in the Cotswolds when other patients of his would be there, he was exerting what little remained of his sanity. He hoped I would put the clues together and save him from himself."

"What clues?"

"Damaged patients sent to recover were being fed copious quantities of red meat according to the doctor's specific directions. As I called to your attention, Watson, the larder was oversupplied with beef. It was on the table at every meal."

"Too much meat," I complained. "It did my stomach no good at all, Holmes. I began to long for a nice bit of poached fish. But do go on."

"The man in riding boots had a severe pallor. The woman who preceded us so suffered from cold that she kept herself bundled in heavy clothing. Both are symptoms of anemia, which can result from severe blood loss. The governess, Miss Frances, was also heavily wrapped. In addition she had a sore throat. Though I never saw it exposed, I strongly suspect it was disfigured by contusions; leech bites. When I spoke with her she admitted to having endured a course of bleeding under the care of Dr. Floyd.''

"How did you come to connect this with the bodies we had begun finding?''

"Those bodies were simply his most recent victims, Lestrade. Dr. Lloyd is a victim himself, you see. He suffers from a rare disease called porphyria, that same malady which destroyed the sanity of King George the Third. In its early stages it can be identified by an abhorrence for sunlight, which causes skin lesions in the sufferer. I observed the heavy curtains over the windows at Hope Hill, and the housekeeper informed me of her employer's distaste for the sun.

"But the most bizarre manifestation of porphyria can be an uncontrollable lust for human blood.''

"Vampirism?" I recalled the Sussex case that had proven to have a very different solution.

"Not exactly, Watson, although some victims of the disease have been accused as vampires. The blood-lust has expressed itself in strange ways, as I was reminded by a swift perusal of pertinent case histories in the library at the hospital.

"Your Dr. Floyd had found a singular way to satisfy his desires. By the common medical practice of attaching leeches to his patients he was able to extract blood from them in seemingly normal circumstances. He then fed not direct from the human, but from the leech.''

"He was holding a leech when you burst in on him!" Lestrade exclaimed.

"So he was. The blood was still in his mouth.'' Even Holmes wore an expression of revulsion as he spoke. "At first Floyd had taken blood from his patients under the guise of a normal course of treatment. To ease his conscience he gave them a convalescence in the country. But as the disease progressed his appetite became ungovernable. At the very end he required so much blood that he applied too many leeches, causing death. That was when he began dumping bodies in laneways. Killing was never his intention, he was simply doing what he thought he must. Such is the power of delusion."

Holmes paused to look out the window. The rain was falling again. "The murders were not deliberate, Lestrade," he reiterated with a sympathy I had rarely heard him express. "But they were inevitable. By talking with his housekeeper I learned that Dr. Floyd's father died in a madhouse. His son suffers from the same disease that afflicted him."

The inspector's eyes lit with comprehension. "So porphyria is carried in the blood and passed on from generation to generation."

"Even in the most noble families, yes."

I cried, "It is a tragic legacy! Horatio Floyd was once an affable and brilliant man, he should have had a better life. A successful practice, a loving family . . ."

Holmes turned toward me with a strangely sad smile. "Ah, Watson," said he, "there are some men who should never marry."

Outside the rain continued to fall. The evening grew dark. The gas lights were lit.

A_ppended to the manuscript of "Holmes and the Loss of the British Barque_ Sophy Anderson" _is an author's note stating that "I have made every effort to keep details consistent with the Canon and with historical events of the year 1887." This would have been an easy task for_ C. S. FORESTER _(1899–1966), popular creator of such novels as_ The African Queen, The Gun, Payment Deferred _and the long (but not long enough) series of Horatio Hornblower nautical adventures. Also attached to the manuscript is Mr. R.'s comment: "CSF took no liberties. Richard Hornblower (1865–1931) is listed in the genealogical appendix to C. Northcote Parkinson's_ Life and Times of Horatio Hornblower."—_JAF_

Holmes and the Loss of the British Barque **Sophy Anderson**

BY "PETER CANNON"
(ASCRIBED TO C. S. FORESTER)

A gentleman to see you, Mr. Holmes," said the page.

"Thank you, Billy, you may send him up."

Sherlock Holmes glanced once more at the note on top of the unanswered correspondence on the mantel. It was embossed with the Admiralty seal, and dated the evening before. The message read:

> *Sir Joseph Porter presents his compliments to Mr. Sherlock Holmes, and will call upon him at 4:30 tomorrow. Sir*

Joseph begs to say that the matter upon which he desires to consult Mr. Holmes is very delicate, and also very important. In this view he is seconded by Mr. Mycroft Holmes. He trusts, therefore, that Mr. Holmes will make every effort to grant this interview.

The Right Honourable Sir Joseph Porter, K.C.B., was sharp to the half-hour.

"Mr. . . . Holmes?" gasped the man. He was not in uniform, but wore the frock coat and grey sponge-bag trousers of a high government official.

"At your service, Sir Joseph," said Holmes with a bow.

As was his habit, the detective took a seat with his back to the window and placed his illustrious visitor in the opposite chair, where the light fell full upon him. His silence, as he recovered his breath, gave Holmes more time for observation. Since it was amusing to be thought omniscient, he opened with one of his conclusions.

"Your entire career, Sir Joseph, has been spent behind a desk, I perceive."

"Is it so obvious?"

"You were never a sailor in the Queen's Navy."

"I confess, Mr. Holmes, that before my appointment as First Lord the only 'ship' that I ever had seen was a partnership in an attorney's office."

Too often, Holmes realized, good family and fortune advanced one farther than either merit or talent. Thank heavens in his own profession results based on pure reasoning were all that counted. And yet Sir Joseph's candor on his rise to his present post suggested he was not a total fool.

"Forgive me, sir, I forget myself," said Sherlock Holmes. "To 'deduce' the past of a titled Cabinet minister requires no harder effort than referring to Burke's *Peerage*—which I might well have done in anticipation of your call. No doubt the strain you labour under has less to do with mounting the stairs of 221 Baker Street than with the sensitive matter which brings you here."

"Thank you, Mr. Holmes, 'tis indeed a sensitive matter that causes me to seek you out."

"Pray proceed, Sir Joseph."

"Does the name *Sophy Anderson* mean anything to you?"

"The society painter?"

"No, the three-masted, four-thousand-ton barque."

"A commercial steamer?"

"Yes, or rather she was."

"You mean, sir, she is no longer in service as such or she has been lost?"

"Alas, both, my dear Mr. Holmes."

"When did you learn of this tragedy?"

"Yesterday morning."

"Why is this news not reported in today's papers?"

"Your brother needed time to concoct a convincing cover story. Tomorrow's papers should carry an account of a ship disabled by an accidental boiler explosion and subsequently taken into tow by a passing German frigate."

"Ah, this has the savour of an international incident."

"Precisely, Mr. Holmes, which is why I must insist, on your word as a gentleman, that what I'm about to confide will remain in absolute confidence."

"You have my word, Sir Joseph."

"I have it on your brother's authority that one Dr. Watson is in the habit of recording the particulars of your cases. I must request that you leave your colleague in the dark as to the true nature of this affair."

Watson, Holmes knew, was the very soul of discretion. Yet might not there be certain secrets best left unshared with his faithful chronicler? If the security of the British nation did in fact lie in the balance . . . He would not breach his honourable guest's trust.

"Since Dr. Watson deserted me for a wife last November, Sir

Joseph," said Sherlock Holmes, "I see him only on occasion. While my friend is always curious to hear the latest, I feel by no means obliged to inform him of the details of every case I investigate. As further proof of my discretion, I admit I have yet to enlighten the doctor on my brother's existence."

"Very good, Mr. Holmes."

"Tell me then, Sir Joseph, why is the fate of a commercial steamer of such paramount interest to the Royal Navy?"

"Allow me to explain. Up until last June the Silver Star Line owned the *Sophy Anderson,* a seasoned barque which had come close to beating the American clipper *Flying Cloud* for the Atlantic crossing record. You may consult your *Lloyd's* for her specifications. At that time the Crown quietly purchased it for refitting as an experimental craft. One of our more visionary admirals, who has the ear of the Marquess of Salisbury, was keen on the design of a new and highly advanced 'hydrocarbon' engine, which its promoters boast will make steam power as obsolete as the sail that steam has all but replaced today.

"The naval engineers went to work at the yard in Portsmouth, under conditions of utmost secrecy. The innovation, as I understand it, lies largely in the fuel, an extremely combustible mixture. Every safety precaution was duly taken. Then, two weeks ago, after several short trials in the channel, the *Sophy* was ready for her first cruise with the new engine running at full capacity. With a handpicked crew, her master Lieutenant Richard Hornblower—"

"Pardon me, Sir Joseph," interjected the detective, "but is it usual for an officer as junior as a lieutenant to be given such a command?"

"No, Mr. Holmes, it is not. Lieutenant Hornblower, however, happens to be the son of the admiral in the administration behind the project, Horatio third Viscount Hornblower. Moreover, though but twenty-two, he has served nine years in the fleet, where he has displayed the sort of enterprising nautical spirit which has distinguished his family for generations. He should go far, unless . . ."

"Unless what, Sir Joseph?"

"Unless he proves to have been in some way negligent in his duties, Mr. Holmes. As I was saying, Lieutenant Hornblower proceeded to his cruising ground in the North Sea where his orders were to put the *Sophy Anderson* through a series of speed and endurance tests. He was to avoid the normal shipping lanes. The barque was performing well up to expectations until the night of the tenth day out when, without warning, a tremendous explosion rent the hull. It appears Lieutenant Hornblower did all he could in the circumstances—to assess the damage, to attend to the wounded, and finally to order abandon ship when it became clear the *Sophy* had suffered a mortal blow. By dawn the *Von Bulow* arrived on the scene and picked up the survivors in the lifeboats. A tow-line was attached to the burning wreck.

"So much is known from the initial statements of Lieutenant Hornblower and his crew members, who some thirty-six hours following the disaster were transferred from the *Von Bulow* to H.M.S. *Hotspur,* which delivered them to Portsmouth. Those not in hospital are being quartered in seclusion until a full report can be made."

"And what of the *Sophy Anderson*?" asked the detective.

"A complete loss, Mr. Holmes. In the time it took to relay the seamen from the German craft to the *Hotspur,* the hulk floundered and sank. Lieutenant Hornblower, though, did manage to salvage the log."

"Ah, a man who would seem to keep his head in a crisis."

"A formal board of inquiry will as a matter of course be set up to rule on the causes of this disaster. More immediately, it is essential that we find out as soon as possible who is responsible for this vile act. If some foreign agent turns out to have been involved . . ."

"You have your suspicions, Sir Joseph?"

"Yes, I do, Mr. Holmes. While we are most grateful to the Imperial German Navy for the timely rescue, I believe it was not chance that put the *Von Bulow* in the *Sophy*'s vicinity. Perhaps you have heard tell of a submarine, an underwater vessel first used with effect during the American Civil War. It can fire a torpedo from a long distance without fear of detection. Its victim is completely helpless.

"Then there are greater political issues. As the whole world is aware, we celebrate the Queen's Golden Jubilee this summer, an event sure to restore the sagging popularity of the monarchy. Her Majesty, who has been a virtual hermit since the death of the Prince Consort, is scheduled to review the Army at Aldershot, as well as the Grand Fleet off Spithead. Most of the crowned heads of Europe will be in attendance, together with dignitaries from all the civilized corners of the globe. Advance parties from every major power have already arrived in England.

"While there is a great outward show of amity between peoples in this tribute to our sovereign, rivalries simmer below the surface. It is not outside the realm of possibility, to my mind, that the destruction of the *Sophy* may be part of a larger plot, the first move on the part of an enemy of Britain to spoil the Jubilee. If that is the case, Mr. Holmes, it is vital we learn so now to prevent further outrages."

The First Lord snapped his fingers. "Foreigners are not Englishmen, you know."

"Quite, Sir Joseph," answered Sherlock Holmes. "Quite."

"French. Turk. Italian. Russian. Prussian. The devil take 'em all!"

Privately Holmes was not so quick to point an accusing finger, but he decided it would be wise not to suggest to Sir Joseph in his present agitated state that his patriotic fervor might be distorting his judgment.

"These international speculations are all very well, sir, but it strikes me that we must begin our chase closer to home, with Lieutenant Hornblower and his men."

"You are right, Mr. Holmes. The sooner you can go to Portsmouth and interview the survivors the better. I will provide you with all necessary introductions."

"In addition, sir, I would appreciate a list of names of all those to embark on the *Sophy Anderson*'s ill-fated last voyage."

"Whatever you wish. If you succeed, Mr. Holmes, I can assure you of the eternal if silent gratitude of your country."

"Anonymity has never stood in the way of my enjoying the fruits of a job well done, Sir Joseph."

O n the solitary train ride from Victoria to Portsmouth, under a greying sky, Holmes had good reason to wonder whether the case at hand offered any opportunity to get the job done to anyone's satisfaction. There was so little to go on, and yet so much. Perhaps the "boiler" (that is, the experimental engine) had simply malfunctioned with fatal consequences, as the terse article in that morning's *Daily Telegraph* suggested. One could not rule out German involvement, and yet such a dangerously provocative act from a land whose kaiser was married to the Queen's eldest daughter seemed improbable. Since the Berlin Conference dividing Africa among the European powers, international tensions had relaxed, although there was recent report of German intrigue in the Transvaal. And what of Irish terrorism? The current government had promised to resolve the vexing issue of Home Rule, if so far to no avail; while the Fenian bombing of Scotland Yard in '84 remained fresh in Londoners' memories. But again what were the odds of even the most determined terrorist smuggling a bomb on to a regular Royal Navy ship-of-the-line, let alone a secret and presumably closely guarded vessel like the *Sophy Anderson*?

Not the least of the detective's obstacles was the lack of a crime scene, if such it was, sunk countless fathoms beneath the sea days earlier. Success would depend, he knew, entirely on the outcome of his interviews with the *Sophy Anderson*'s surviving officers and seamen. A copy of the *Sophy*'s manifest, supplied by the Admiralty in time for his departure, absorbed his attention at intervals during the journey.

At the Portsmouth terminal Holmes was met by the senior

naval intelligence officer for the district, Commander Henry Bush, a stern, colorless man whose skeptical air reminded him of certain Metropolitan Police inspectors of his acquaintance.

"Orders from the First Lord himself instruct me to assist you with every means at my disposal, Mr. Holmes," said Bush, escorting him to a brougham marked with the white ensign. "I suppose his lordship wants this unfortunate *Sophy Anderson* business cleared up before preparations get under way in earnest for the review of the Grand Fleet."

"How large a flotilla do you anticipate, Commander Bush?" asked the detective. It seemed politic at the moment not to dwell on his own role in the inquiry.

"At this juncture we count thirty-five capital ships, thirty-eight gunboats, forty-three torpedo boats, twelve troopships, as well as the Royal Yacht."

"Sounds formidable."

"Indeed, though in all honesty I fear nearly the whole lot of 'em will be as obsolete as dugout canoes by the start of the new century. This is an era of rapid change for the navy, sir."

They bumped along the shore road under a light drizzle. Ahead, through the mist, loomed the masts of more than a hundred tall ships, like the trees of some vast primeval forest in winter. They were approaching the very heart of Britain's naval might.

"Where does the *Sophy Anderson* investigation stand at this point, Commander?" asked Sherlock Holmes.

"We have collected written depositions from the officers, while we have nearly completed taking oral statements from the seamen. All should be ready for your perusal by the time we arrive."

"If you don't mind, Commander, I would prefer to conduct my own interviews first."

"The *Sophy*'s officers and men have been alerted to expect you, Mr. Holmes."

"Where may I ask are they billeted?"

"In their respective barracks."

"Excellent."

"They are free, of course, to mingle among themselves—and to visit those of their mates who are still in hospital. The infirmary stands near the barracks."

"To compare and alter their stories if necessary, then?"

"Mr. Holmes, these officers and men spent three days at close quarters aboard two ships in the aftermath of the *Sophy*'s loss, with ample time to talk among themselves. No sense in closing the hatch at this late date."

"What are the casualty figures?"

"Out of a complement of fifty-one, two died immediately as a result of the blast. Eight others, including Mr. Howard Grimes, the civilian engineer and chief designer, along with two of his staff, are missing, presumed drowned. Seven sailors sustained serious wounds, chiefly burns, and remain under medical supervision. The rest were treated if at all for minor injuries and released."

"Among this group are Lieutenant Richard Hornblower and his executive officer Lieutenant Patrick McCool?"

"That is right, sir."

"Mr. McCool, I note from the manifest, is five years older than Mr. Hornblower."

Bush hesitated before giving his reply. "I see what you're driving at, Mr. Holmes. Yes, ordinarily Mr. McCool would have been senior to Mr. Hornblower. But then Mr. Hornblower's father, the viscount—"

"Yes, Sir Joseph explained. Mr. McCool is of Irish descent?"

"Aye, though born and raised in Scotland. Jesuit schooling."

"Would Mr. Hornblower have any cause to question his loyalty?"

"None that I'm aware of, Mr. Holmes. Wouldn't be likely to pick him for his exec if he had any doubts, now would he?"

"And Mr. Hornblower?"

"An exemplary officer, with an impeccable record. Although he—"

"Yes, Commander?"

"It is common knowledge that the lieutenant is prone to sea-sickness—as he would be the first to admit. According to the log, he was thus indisposed at the time of the explosion."

"Do you think engine failure could after all be the cause, just as the press has been led to believe?"

"I cannot rule it out."

"What do the engineers say?"

"They are as baffled as any. They have been scanning the data in the log but have noticed no anomalies. With Grimes gone we may well never know the truth."

Presently they arrived at the headquarters of the Royal Navy on the Solent. Naval policemen saluted their carriage as they passed through the main gate. They halted in front of the officers' barracks, home to bachelors below flag rank. Bush showed Holmes to Lieutenant Hornblower's door. Their knock was answered by a hearty "come in." Inside the small, plainly furnished room they discovered the lieutenant writing at his desk.

"As long as I'm to be cooped up until the hearing, Commander Bush, I might as well be of some service to the fleet," said the young man. "This report on linking the Eddystone Light by telephone to the area rescue stations deserves most careful study."

"I trust, Lieutenant, you will cooperate fully with our distinguished London visitor," said Bush, with just the barest hint of sarcasm. "I will see you later, Mr. Holmes."

The detective took a seat on the cot next to the desk; his host lowered his pen. "Thank you, Lieutenant, for agreeing to see me and once again recount your story. It must be painful for you to do so."

"It is my duty, as master and commander of the *Sophy Anderson,* to help all I can in the inquiry."

"Pray tell me, Mr. Hornblower, where were you at the time of the explosion?"

"In my cabin, Mr. Holmes. After a period of relative calm we were overtaken by a squall, common enough in the North Sea in

April. To be perfectly frank, I was feeling abominably seasick—an hereditary predilection, I'm afraid. It was a few minutes into the second dogwatch, under Mr. McCool, that a roar filled my ears and I was flung from my bunk. Outside in the passage, smoke was pouring up the gangway. I rushed down to the engine deck, where I was met by a wall of heat and flame. The old Polynesian steward, Jack Luhulu, was lying unconscious at the fringe of the fire. My first act was to drag him out of harm's way."

"You saved his life, Lieutenant?"

"The man lies as we speak in a coma, his recovery doubtful at best, Mr. Holmes."

"Does a steward have much cause to pass in the vicinity of the engine room at such an hour?"

"A steward has more freedom than any seaman aboard ship to go where he pleases when he pleases."

"What happened next, Lieutenant?"

"Over the next few minutes I was joined by a dozen others. We seized the firehoses, but before long I realized it was a losing battle. The tremendous force of the blast had blown out the steel plates below the waterline. I saw that the wounded were attended to and the bodies of the dead collected, before ordering the men to the lifeboats. While the ship had no magazine, the hydrocarbon fuel in the hold was extremely volatile. Fortunately, the wind had let up, and in the boats we were able to maintain a safe but constant distance from the *Sophy* through the remainder of the dark hours. With the coming of dawn we were picked up by the frigate *Von Bulow,* which we later learned had spotted our distress light."

"Was it unusual for a foreign warship to be cruising in such proximity?"

"Not unusual at all, Mr. Holmes. The *Von Bulow* may have been shadowing the *Sophy* for days. Ships of the Royal Navy do engage in the same practice, I might add. Should chance put a foreign warship within telescope range, a captain on patrol may elect to tail said vessel in the hope of discovering something of interest."

"Did the Germans attempt to salvage the *Sophy?*"

"They attached a tow-line, but when it became clear that the *Sophy* was on the verge of sinking, they continued to haul the men from the boats. By this point we were strung along a good nautical mile, in a freshening breeze. Captain Koch ordered the tow-line cut, acting as any civilized man would have done in the situation."

"Did Captain Koch or any other German officer make any effort to examine the *Sophy*'s log?"

"No, sir, he did not. Nor did he or his officers and men treat us with anything less than all due courtesy and respect."

"Did you notice whether the *Von Bulow* was accompanied by a submarine?"

"I saw no such vessel come to the surface."

"Where was Mr. McCool at the time of the explosion?"

"As the officer on watch he was at the helm. He initially gave the order to raise sail. Later, when he was made aware of the severity of the damage to the hull, he ordered the men to the pumps."

"Have you any reason to question your executive officer's . . . politics?"

"Mr. McCool is no Fenian sympathizer, if that's what you're getting at. He is as loyal a subject of the Queen as you or I, sir."

"Pardon me, Lieutenant, if I—"

"Mr. McCool performed ably in the emergency until I could join him at the helm. If anything, he has been taking the loss of the *Sophy* even harder than myself. He has been most solicitous of the injured, particularly poor Jack Luhulu."

"They were close?"

"Before assignment to the *Sophy,* they shipped together for five years aboard H.M.S. *Surprise.* I selected Jack on Mr. McCool's recommendation."

"Finally, Mr. Hornblower, may I ask whether you think the explosion might simply have been a dreadful accident?"

The Lieutenant's gaze fell on the report before him, as if there might lie his answer. He then faced the detective squarely. "I will not trouble you with technical details, Mr. Holmes. Let us just say I suspect my superiors will determine after examining the evidence that the hydrocarbon engine will not meet the navy's future needs, *pace* Mr. Grimes, may God have mercy on his soul.

"For now Britannia rules the waves, sir. The only challenge to our power is the occasional slaver off the African coast. While the glory days of fighting sail in which my ancestor did his bit are long past, the day may yet come when another tyrant seeks to dominate the world. We have suffered only a temporary setback. The navy must modernize. British technology will prevail."

Lieutenant Hornblower was kind enough to point the detective in the direction of the room of his fellow officer, Lieutenant McCool, who took nearly a minute to answer his knock.

"I apologize, Mr. Holmes," he said after the introductions. "I was napping. I have not been sleeping well."

Holmes refrained from taking a seat on the unmade cot; Mr. McCool remained standing.

"The rigid orthodoxy of your Jesuit masters never really suited you, Lieutenant, I imagine," said the detective. "Although you retain a sentimental attachment to the faith of your forefathers."

"Mr. Holmes, I say—"

"When a man has the cross of St. Ignatius of Loyola affixed to his wall as well as a copy of Robert Ingersoll's *Some Mistakes of Moses* on his desk it is not difficult to deduce that his spiritual life has been in tumult."

"I have always prided myself on my ability to think independently, sir. I'll have no truck with dogma, either religious or naval."

"I will waste your time no more with trifles, Lieutenant. Let us get on to the matter of the *Sophy Anderson*. You were the watch officer at the time of the explosion?"

"Aye, I was by the helm."

"What did your duties entail?"

"Ensuring that the ship stayed on course and maintained

speed, as well as keeping an eye on the gauges which regulate engine activity such as oil pressure and r.p.m."

"Did you notice any irregularities?"

"None—until the blast, when all gauges failed."

"What did you do?"

"I gave orders to set the studding sails."

"The *Sophy* was fully rigged?"

"Aye. In case of engine failure we had to rely on sail."

"You did not order men to work the pumps?"

"No, not until Mr. Hornblower informed me how bad the damage was below decks did I issue such an order. I remained at the helm, seeing that we kept our heading, some two points off the wind. Less than an hour later, we abandoned ship. At dawn we were rescued by the *Von Bulow*."

"Might a torpedo fired from a submarine have caused the damage that sank the *Sophy*?"

McCool, who had been pacing back and forth during the course of the conversation, stopped in his tracks. "I suppose it is not an impossibility, Mr. Holmes. Aye, by no means is it an impossibility . . ."

Further questioning elicited nothing more of interest from the lieutenant. Next Holmes located Commander Bush, who allowed he might tour the naval infirmary. There, with Captain George Budd, M.D., as guide, they called on the injured, including the silent form of Jack Luhulu, who had a private room on account of the gravity of his condition. His head was wrapped in bandages, leaving only his mouth and chin visible.

"Jack is a native of the South Seas, is he not, Dr. Budd?"

"So I gather, Mr. Holmes."

"Then tell me why his skin is such a pale mahogany. Surely it is not loss of blood alone that accounts for his hue."

"Come to think of it, Mr. McCool did mention to me that Jack was of mixed race."

"His grandfather was an English sailor, according to his personnel record," added Bush. "Marooned or some such, rumor has it."

"Does Mr. McCool often come to visit?"

"He spent most of the last two nights by Jack's bedside."

"And Mr. Hornblower?"

"He has been a frequent visitor to the wounded men as well."

Holmes paused to reflect. A course of action was beginning to present itself. "Tell me, doctor," he asked, "what are Jack's prospects for survival?"

"Slim, I'm afraid. One can still hope, though in my opinion the struggle will resolve itself one way or the other within the next twenty-four hours."

"I see. Would it be possible to move Jack's bed to another room without jeopardizing his life?"

"I suppose he could be transferred without harm to an adjoining room."

Sherlock Holmes turned to the intelligence officer. "Commander Bush, might you be good enough to supply me with all plans and specifications for the hydrocarbon engine? It is at last time for me to do my homework."

As the detective lay in shadow, swaddled in bandages, he had plenty to occupy his mind, chiefly the mechanics of the *Sophy Anderson*'s engine, but also the scene a few hours earlier when Bush had finally given his consent to proceed with a plot that he swore was a potential court-martial offense. Invoking the authority of Sir Joseph Porter had not been sufficient; it had taken a casual reminder of his relation to Mr. Mycroft Holmes to persuade the man to make the necessary arrangements with Dr. Budd.

Then there was the part to be played. To his lower face he had applied a coating of brown boot polish, obtained from the naval stores, in the event his visitor should decide to turn up the oil lamp burning with the merest spark on the night table. It was now vital to give a convincing vocal performance.

Holmes estimated that his visitor had been sitting by his bedside for nearly an hour. It was time. In a hoarse, husky whisper he began to mutter a series of barely intelligible syllables. A chair squeaked; he could almost smell his companion's breath. His speech took a nautical and technical turn.

It was as he was mumbling something about taking the double valves with the self-adjusting slots off automatic that he suddenly felt the pillow pressed hard over his nose and mouth. The detective, however, had surprise on his side. He reared up and with a pugilist's grace swung his assailant by the throat on to the bed, pinning him.

"I have the advantage of you, sir," he hissed in his normal tones.

"Mr. Holmes!"

"Come, come, Mr. McCool, we don't want to bring the duty nurse running, do we?"

The man ceased to resist. He relaxed his grip.

"My career is ruined, Mr. Holmes."

"Your best chance depends on your telling me all."

"All right," gasped the Lieutenant. "But first, would you mind letting me up?"

Holmes released his hold. McCool stood and began to pace.

"You had the notion to tamper with the engine," said Holmes, removing the bandages from his head and turning up the lamp. "Jack agreed to act as your agent."

"Aye."

"What, sir, did you hope to accomplish?"

"You must believe me, Mr. Holmes, when I say that I only wanted to disable the engine—not destroy it or, heaven forbid, sink the *Sophy*. I told Jack to jam the self-adjusting slots, in order to build up pressure in the double valves. It should have blown only the pistons—not the entire engine." McCool laughed. "I miscalculated. That hydrocarbon fuel Grimes devised was even more dangerous than I suspected. That zealot Hornblower wouldn't listen. I had to demonstrate the engine's unreliability in some dramatic fashion."

"And discredit Lieutenant Hornblower in the process?"

McCool stopped pacing.

"I am no Iago, sir," he protested.

"Perhaps not. On the other hand, with your commanding officer seasick in his cabin you had opportunity as his executive to prove yourself resourceful in a crisis. A pity that Mr. Hornblower rose to the occasion, leaving you in your customary supporting role."

"Mr. Holmes, you cannot imagine the agonies of guilt I have been going through since this catastrophe."

"Your little scheme, Mr. McCool, has cost the lives of ten men—and nearly that of an eleventh."

"I know what you must think of me, sir. Odds were that Jack would succumb to his wounds, without uttering a word. I could let nature run her course. But tonight, when I saw, or thought I saw, that he was regaining consciousness, I could not take the risk."

"His loyalty to you had its limits, then. I am not familiar with naval law, but surely malicious mischief is a lesser crime than negligent homicide on the high seas. What, pray, did you offer Jack in return for his assistance?"

McCool laughed again.

"Let me give you some family history, Mr. Holmes. Jack's grandmother was queen of one of the lesser Marquesas. His grandfather was a British sea captain who never knew the issue of what for him was a fleeting dalliance. Legend had it that this Englishman was as valiant a naval hero as Lieutenant Hornblower's own great-grandfather."

"The first Viscount Hornblower?"

"Aye. To continue, the sea was in Jack's blood, and he signed on one of Her Majesty's ships at the first opportunity. Being of mixed race, however, he could of course aspire only to humble station. Forty years in the Service and never more than a steward.

"Resentment among the ranks of the officer class is not unheard of, Mr. Holmes, and Jack had especial reason to bear a grudge toward the youthful master of the *Sophy*. Shall we say it required no filthy lucre to persuade Jack to attempt to pour a little grease on the spotless white uniform of Lieutenant Hornblower's reputation, as it were."

"You must make a full confession, Lieutenant."

"Please, Mr. Holmes, allow me to retire to my quarters first, to give me time to compose myself. I pledge my word as a gentleman that I won't leave the area of the barracks."

"Very well, but if you have not reported to Commander Bush by noon I shall be obliged to report the substance of our conversation. I trust you will do the right thing. Good night, Mr. McCool."

"Good night, Mr. Holmes."

Holmes left the infirmary and returned to the barracks, without looking back. Again, if he was any judge of character, he felt he could trust McCool to do the right thing. In the guest room provided him, he removed the boot polish and settled down for some unfeigned sleep.

As was his custom when he had no pressing business, Sherlock Holmes rose late in the morning. Since it was too late for breakfast, he decided to begin his day by calling on the infirmary. There an orderly told him Captain Budd wished to see him immediately.

"Sad news, Mr. Holmes," said the doctor as the detective entered his office. "Jack died sometime after midnight. When the nurse went in to take his temperature this morning, he was gone."

"Sad news indeed."

"Unfortunately, he slipped away as I feared he would." The doctor sighed. "Tell me, sir, did your strategem by chance produce any—"

At that moment the door burst open. Bush stood on the threshold.

"Forgive me, gentlemen, for interrupting," he said, "but I'm sorry to have to report that Lieutenant McCool has—"

"Yes, Commander?"

"—has hanged himself."

McCool had done the right thing.

B ack at his rooms in Baker Street, Sherlock Holmes reflected that it had been best not to comment on the results of his overnight vigil. Then again, in the confusion following the finding of Lieutenant McCool's body, neither Dr. Budd nor anyone else thought to ask. There was no farewell note. He also refrained from pointing out certain problems of timing when Commander Bush theorized that grief over the death of Jack Luhulu drove the lieutenant to take his own life. After all, the two had been close. The commander had not seemed unduly upset when over luncheon Holmes announced he was returning by the next train to London.

On the other hand, it was a shame to disappoint Sir Joseph. Holmes took the underground directly from Victoria to the Admiralty, where he made his report, refusing any fee beyond travel expenses. In the end, however, he accepted some small recompense that the First Lord insisted on.

Holmes wired Watson he had last-minute tickets that evening and to join him, Mrs. Watson permitting. At the hour one is ready to reach for the gasogene, he was delighted to hear the familiar dogged tread of the doctor on the stairs.

"I take it you are in the mood to celebrate the end of a case, Holmes. Mind filling me in?"

"You may recall, Watson, seeing something in yesterday's papers about the loss of the British barque *Sophy Anderson*."

"Yes, the ship whose boiler exploded. Or is there more to it than that?"

"Let us just say, old fellow, that like several other cases of this year it lacks the singular features that would make it a worthy candidate for one of your fanciful retellings. In the meantime, after a light supper, we head, courtesy of the Admiralty, to Earl's Court. I daresay Buffalo Bill Cody and his Wild West show will divert me from thoughts of the sea."

Long Shots

Mr. R.'s diary shows his own literary taste was less catholic than the books he owned. Thus, though he did not personally read America's pre-eminent fantasy periodical, he still purchased and preserved two mint copies of every issue of Weird Tales *from 1923 to 1991, the year of his death. When his quest for "mainstream" authors yielded somewhat disappointing results, he logically turned to mystery writers (see next section) and also consulted his vast genre collection for fanta-sists, science-fiction writers, purveyors of "men's adventure," even humorists to become his second string of Holmesian "ghosts." These contributors, coded in his accounts "LS" for "long shot," be-came his ongoing main stable. Some did excellent jobs, some only partially succeeded—while a few produced howling botches that Mr. R. nevertheless accepted, paying for work he privately described as "literary silverfish feasting off Watson's corpus."*

Mr. R. gambled on stories commissioned in this section and was not always happy with the results, but his son recalls him expressing pleasure at the following tale, for which he paid $3,000 for a writer he designated as ERB. As his ledger contains a note, "Mail to Tarzana," one naturally thinks of EDGAR RICE BURROUGHS (1875–1950), the pulpish creator of Tarzan and popular space fantasy. Mr. R.'s son says, "Shortly after Cox & Company delivered Watson's dispatch-box, my father's office was broken into. But he'd taken special pains to conceal the new acquisition behind a secret panel, so the burglars went away empty-handed. My father promptly took an ad in the London Times *which reiterated Watson's warning in "The Adventure of the Veiled Lodger" that "The source of these outrages is known, and if they are repeated . . . the whole story of the politician, the lighthouse and the trained cormorant(s) will be given to the public. There is at least one reader who will understand."—JAF*

The Politician, the Lighthouse, and the Trained Cormorant

BY *"CRAIG SHAW GARDNER"*
(ASCRIBED TO EDGAR RICE BURROUGHS)

Sherlock Holmes was a changed man. Even in my many years as a practicing physician, I had rarely seen such a sudden transformation. The sea air had obviously done wonders.

I welcomed this change, even though, as with much about

my longtime friend, I did not entirely understand it. Since Holmes had abruptly reappeared upon the scene, now a little more than a year gone by, he had thrown himself with a renewed vigor into both his work as a consulting detective and that peculiar, sordid world that is London.

But the civilized world seemed to take its toll on Holmes as well, and in recent weeks I noticed a distinct listlessness in my old companion's actions, as well as an additional pallor to his complexion, as if the soot of London streets had settled into my good friend's soul.

I suggested a short trip to some vicinity where there might be a better quality of air. Holmes had at first seemed disinterested, until he chanced upon a certain article in the *Times*.

Now, here he was, climbing the great rocks along the boulder-strewn Cornish coast. The strange light out by the shore revealed steely tendons in his hands and neck. Taut muscles rolled beneath his suit as he paced the shoreline. Even with his London clothes, he looked like nothing so much as a barely civilized beast snatched from the wild.

But there was more to Holmes than that base power, for, beneath it all there lurked his keen intellect, an intelligence and perceptiveness that had made him renowned not only in London, but in much of Europe and the Commonwealth.

"There, Watson!" he called, pointing at the sky. Or so I thought at first, until I perceived one small, moving speck in that sky, which, as it came closer, resolved itself into a large black bird.

"What is it, Holmes?" I called, for I had never seen such a bird. But another answered in Holmes's stead.

" 'Tis a cormorant!" remarked a cracked and aging voice.

I turned quickly to regard the speaker, for I had not seen the gentleman before he spoke. He wore dark, rumpled clothing that seemed to blend with his surroundings, with a grey cap pulled tight down to his eyes, which were grey as well. With his sallow skin and craggy features, the newcomer looked almost as though he were a part of the rocks.

"Indeed it is, Watson," Holmes most cheerfully agreed. The newcomer had startled me so that I almost forgot we discussed the bird. "The common black European Cormorant, phylum Chordata, subphylum Vertebrata, class Aves, order Pelicaniformes, family Phalacrocoracidae." He nodded pleasantly to the stranger, as if having someone appear without warning amidst the rocks were the most common of everyday occurrences. "Should the bird get a bit closer, we should also be able to see its piercing green eyes!"

I nodded at the explanation of my old friend. This bit of description, at least, was no surprise whatsoever, since the migrations and habits of birds were one of Holmes's many areas of expertise.

"We will be receiving a bit of weather," the newcomer observed.

I glanced again at the sky, as blue as a robin's egg. What could this strange diminutive man be talking about now?

I glanced to Holmes, and noticed that the consulting detective was taking the newcomer quite seriously. I strained my eyes once again. Behind the bird, I could see small patches of grey, the first wisps of fog before an approaching bank of clouds.

" 'Twill be a bad one," the stranger announced quite suddenly.

"It always is this time of year," Holmes agreed with equal suddenness.

The small man peered with great intensity at the detective. "The winds and currents be treacherous hereabouts."

Here, at least, I was on familiar ground. Who had not heard of the great wrecks off the coast of Cornwall? And, in an earlier era, of how smugglers had taken advantage of those wrecks?

"And who knows what the winds will throw up upon the rocks?" I added, perhaps only to be included in the conversation. "You might find some hidden treasures down here yet."

The small, grizzled man scowled up at the both of us, as if he were measuring each of us in turn. After a moment, he turned away to regard the wild coastline all about us.

"Nothing good ever comes from these rocks!" he announced. And with no further farewell, he turned and marched down the sea-wall.

I must admit that I was slightly taken aback by this most unusual encounter. For Holmes, it seemed an entirely different matter. If anything, my companion appeared even more animated than before.

"Well met, Watson!" he cried. "I cannot believe our good fortune!"

For the life of me, I could not fathom what my friend meant. What this might have to do with the mysteries that brought us here, especially the disappearance of those three local women that we had first discovered in an innocent perusal of a newspaper, was far beyond my current understanding.

I looked again at my smiling friend. I knew that Holmes had often been described by others as mercurial, perhaps even unpredictable, as if impatient with the mores and customs of the everyday. At his best, Holmes seemed to thrust the bonds of convention aside to become a primal force of detection. The changes that had occurred during his absence after the incident at Reichenbach Falls were subtle, but definite. He had, of course, aged somewhat. But his other behaviors were rather at odds with his more mature appearance. He seemed, at this moment, to have even more of that primal energy than the Holmes of old, as if the missing years had given him a new purpose.

While I had been able to elicit some explanation of certain particulars of those missing years, the majority still appeared shrouded in mystery. One thing I had learned through my many adventures with my friend: It was most important to Holmes to have his secrets.

Still, I knew he would tell me whatever secrets were necessary to the completion of this case. For the sake of friendship, that would be enough.

"What now, Holmes?" I asked.

He stared at the bank of grey clouds that had appeared on the horizon. "Perhaps it would be best if we returned to the Inn. We will find no more answers here today."

So we turned our backs upon the magnificent vistas of the sea. I must admit to being a bit disappointed, since I had hoped our wanderings would extend to the lighthouse out at Land's End. Still, Holmes was filled with a renewed energy as we walked back from the harborside and returned to the Drowned Gull, a public house where we had managed to book accommodations for our stay.

We heard a great commotion as soon as we passed by the outer door. Two men were shouting, while a third voice, betraying the higher tones of a female, seemed even more upset.

The voices ceased abruptly, as if the three in the other room sensed our entrance. A comely lass rushed from the room, her cheeks full of color. It was the innkeeper's daughter, Margaret, to whom we had been introduced when we first arrived.

She stopped abruptly when she saw us in her path. "Oh— dear. Oh—my," she managed between long gasps for breath. "Please excuse me, gentlemen."

She rushed past us and up the stairs beyond, her handkerchief clutched close to her chin, no doubt holding back a further torrent of tears.

I found myself incensed, with half a mind to step boldly into the other room and demand an explanation of the two men who remained. Who would dare do such a thing to a fair flower of English womanhood?

"Come Watson," Holmes instructed before I could even voice my feelings. "I believe we may find an answer through this door."

A man stood as we entered the common room. He caught both of us within his steely gaze, and when he spoke, his words were clipped and direct.

"You are Sherlock Holmes."

He said the words as a statement, not a question. From the

forcefulness of his gaze and the rigidness of his posture, I assumed he was not used to being questioned in turn.

Holmes, however, only drew closer to the authoritative gentleman, returning the rigid man's gaze with one no less authoritative. "And who might I have the honor of addressing?"

The other man seemed to bristle, as if, indeed, any question might challenge his absolute authority. "Colonel Rupert Skeffington. Royal Navy. Retired."

"I am sorry if we disturbed your conversation." Holmes glanced over at the second man, who stood behind the bar. The innkeeper and owner of this establishment, a Hubert Crimm by name, busied himself polishing the long wooden plank before him. He seemed not to wish to look at anyone.

Holmes glanced from Crimm to Skeffington and back again. "If we have come at an inopportune time . . ." he began, allowing the rest of the sentence to hang unvoiced in the air, unless one of the other two men wished to complete his supposition.

The barman scurried away with a single look from Skeffington. Apparently, the retired colonel was still a man of some importance in these parts.

Crimm out of the way, the Colonel concentrated upon Holmes. "I know why you are here."

Holmes only nodded, as if waiting for the retired military man to continue.

"I read about these most unfortunate circumstances in the *Times*." Skeffington rewarded us with the slightest of knowing smiles. He appeared to be quite the gentleman, every hair on his head in perfect order, the sort of man who might find a place in the finest clubs of London. "I left my seat in the House of Commons forthwith and came here to investigate myself."

He seemed also the sort of man, then, to let one know his exact station in life. I felt he had come back to his district not so much in concern for the young women as to reassert his authority in any way possible. The more he spoke, the less I liked the man.

"Yes, most unfortunate," Holmes agreed neutrally.

Things were not moving quickly enough for our Colonel Skeffington. "I was wondering, Mr. Holmes," he prodded, "what your exact purpose was here. The local constabulary has of course made a complete investigation."

Holmes caught my eye and nodded almost imperceptibly to the far end of the room. There, in the deepest shadows of the bar-room, were two other men sitting at a table, a glass of whiskey before each of them. Even in the dim light I could tell they were both of the rough sort you might find in any port town, even along the charming coast of Cornwall. They were also as far removed from the local constabulary as one could imagine.

"No doubt," Holmes replied to Skeffington.

The Colonel persisted. "Did you say someone sent for you?"

Holmes looked straight in the other man's eye. "In a manner of speaking. I am afraid that there are certain things that must re-main strictly confidential."

"Well, I am sure we shall talk again," Skeffington said, gath-ering up his hat and moving toward the door. The Colonel, confronted by someone who wouldn't take orders, appeared to consider it best to beat a strategic retreat. "Enjoy your stay in our little village," he called over his shoulder as he fled the room.

We looked after the right honorable Skeffington. As if to take away any doubt as to their connection with the politician, the two others left through a door at the rear of the establishment as soon as he was gone.

I nodded towards the door Skeffington had recently exited. "There, Holmes, is a man who is not telling us everything."

Holmes fixed me with his intense gaze. "Evidently, Watson." But, even though I pressed him, my friend would say no more. Instead, he remarked, "It is remarkable, isn't it, dear fellow, how healthy everyone appears hereabouts?"

I remembered then there had been some mention of illness in that article that had appeared in the *Times*. This whole business seemed to get more complicated with every passing moment. I found myself suddenly quite fatigued. "Perhaps," I suggested to the man beside me, "it is time to get a few moment's rest before dinner."

Holmes made no response. I looked about, to discover that my friend had disappeared. Holmes was nowhere to be seen. Apparently, the consulting detective had taken me at my word.

I looked up the stairs, but somehow the idea of returning to the confines of my tiny rented room seemed oppressive at the moment. After the tension in the tavern, I thought perhaps it would be more refreshing to take a moment of peace in the seaside air.

However, as I stepped outside, I discovered that same sea air had gone from a bracing breeze to the chill of fog. The damp haze was now so thick that I could no longer see across the town square to the ocean's edge. I looked down to the cobblestones and noted that even they disappeared into the mist but a few scant yards away.

I looked up suddenly, for the silence of the fog was shattered by a series of distant screams, sounding like nothing so much as a woman in distress. I could only think of poor Margaret, who had rushed past us earlier.

I wished for one scant moment that I had brought my revolver, which awaited me at the bottom of my travel case upstairs. Still, there was no helping it; if I were to intervene on behalf of the woman in distress, I would have to do so now. If need be, I would rescue the imperilled woman with my bare hands.

I rushed across the square as quickly as I dared move my feet over those damp, uneven cobblestones. Within but a few paces I found myself totally encased in fog.

The screams grew louder as I ran, sounding at first like they were before me, then to one side, and after that behind me. I was unsure if I was traveling in circles, or the woman and her attackers were moving in the opposite direction through the impenetrable murk. Or perhaps this noise without a source was all some strange trick of the fog and the winds from the sea.

I stopped, trying to better place the sounds around me. But the screams abruptly ceased.

I saw moving shapes before me. Who else might be out on a night like this? I hoped for a foolish instant that somehow I had stumbled my way back to the inn.

"Hello!" I called out. "I say, can you tell me—"

But the answering cries cut off all coherent thoughts. For the sounds, while almost human, seemed to come from another creature entirely.

Whatever these things were, they were advancing upon me. I backed away from the advancing shapes, and almost stumbled when I realized I no longer had the cobblestones beneath my feet.

I found myself out on the rocks again, on the wall that separated the town from the sea. I attempted to banish images of myself falling into the rolling waves. But perhaps that was the very direction these things wished to drive me!

Suddenly, there before me, was a bright spot in the mist. As I cautiously approached, I found myself before a lighted doorway. But the things were behind me still. I could almost imagine their hot breath upon my neck.

I rushed forward and fell into the doorway, but, instead of a hard floor, I tumbled into a bed of straw. I tried to catch my breath and get some sense of my surroundings.

A light was thrust into my face. A face of singular bestiality stared down upon me.

And then I lost consciousness, and could remember no more.

I awoke to the filtered light of morning and the distant call of seabirds. There was no trace of fog about me, nor any of those bestial creatures I had spied the night before.

At first, I was apt to consider it all an unpleasant dream. I no longer lay upon the straw. Someone had carried me to a small room with stone walls, and I found myself upon a standard issue army cot.

I heard a noise above my head. I turned quickly, fearing I was not alone.

There, perched on the sill of the room's only window was the dark bird my friend Holmes had earlier identified as a cormorant. The bird eyed me inquisitively, as if I was the intruder here, which upon reflection, I supposed I was. The cormorant certainly showed no fear of being so close to a person, so I surmised that, at the very least, the bird must be tame.

I sat up and reached over. The bird flew away before I could even come near. Perhaps it wasn't quite as tame as I thought.

The door smashed open with resounding force against the stone wall. I pulled away from the window by reflex, throwing my back against the wall behind the cot. I glanced quickly about the room, but found nothing with which to defend myself.

There, standing in the doorway, was one of the creatures from my nightmare of the past night. In the light of day I could see that the thing was more animal than man, covered with a coarse grey fur, its long arms almost reaching to the floor. And the face of the thing was particularly fearsome, almost that of a gorilla, with small beady eyes and a full set of fearsome fangs.

"Away with ye!" a thankfully human voice called from behind the thing.

The creature turned and fled. In its stead, a short man wearing rumpled coat and cap appeared in the doorway. In my agitated state, it took me an instant to recognize him as the same strange seaman we had found upon our tour of the rocks.

The seaman removed a pipe from his mouth and waved it towards the still-fleeing ape-thing. "Do not judge them too harshly. No doubt they want to be here even less than you."

With that, he placed the pipe back in his mouth and took three quick puffs to fully reignite the tobacco therein. "Still," he added reflectively, "for all that, they learn fast, and are good workers."

While I could not come close to understanding what this

strange fellow was talking about, I was so glad to see another human face that I instantly shared my troubles, and explained to him how I had come out from the Drowned Gull when I heard the screams.

The other could but nod. "Another one, gone in the night."

Again the man seemed to speak in riddles. I was still dressed in all but my suit coat, which some kind soul had thoughtfully folded over the chair which was the room's only other piece of furniture. I felt it was time for some answers. I stood up and looked directly at the seaman.

"Do you know where these women have gone?"

The seaman paused to pull the pipe from his mouth and stare deep into the bowl. "I can only suspect, and I fear I know far more than I should. But I have other reasons." He looked up then, and I saw that his gaze was filled with anguish. "The first of the young ladies to disappear, sir, was my daughter."

"My good man!" I exclaimed, overwhelmed by his confession. "We are here to help you. Did you know, when you met us upon the beach the other day, you were talking to Sherlock Holmes?"

The seaman nodded. "Aye, Dr. Watson. That I know."

"Well, we must find my friend immediately," I insisted. "Surely, he can help!"

The haunted look returned to the seaman's eyes. "I sometimes fear that no one can help, and that I have forfeited my very soul!"

I felt there must be some way to gather information from this fellow, but it would do me no good if the man were in an agitated state. Like the Colonel from the night before, this man knew more than he wished to speak of, though I suspected that this seaman was far more innocent than the politician.

Therefore I now addressed him in my most reasonable tone. "You or someone of your acquaintance has given me your hospitality. For that, you have my thanks."

The seaman nodded, the corners of his face turning up into what, on a less ruined face, might be perceived as a smile. "We will not be disturbed here. There are stories about this lighthouse, stories of hauntings. Some in the village have glimpsed the creatures that are my companions. The village fears this place."

Still, the fellow did want to talk. Perhaps he would give me some information despite himself. "And it suits your purpose to let these stories stand?" I prompted.

The ravaged smile fell. "It suits someone's purpose, sir, but I pray you do not meet him." He turned from me then and walked to the room's sole window. "It is best if you leave after dark," he added as he stared out to sea. "It is but a few hours from now."

The man looked to me again. "And it would also be for the best if you and Mr. Holmes were to leave this place, never to return. There are forces at work here, sir, too powerful for any of us."

Again, I found the man's behavior beyond my comprehension. What reason would there be for him to urge us to flee rather than to work to save his poor daughter? If, indeed, I saw any reason at all within the poor wretch.

I almost leapt from the bed when one of the creatures reappeared past the seaman's shoulder, screeching at the top of its inhuman voice. The seaman, however, was quite calm as he turned and screeched back at the beast. The creature responded in a quieter tone, and the seaman grunted in turn. It seemed almost as though the grizzled old seafarer and the strange ape-thing were engaged in conversation.

The seaman turned abruptly back to me. "The cormorant, sir! That's what our friends are trying to tell us." He pointed to the window, where the black bird again perched. The cormorant cried once, a high, piercing sound that echoed through the room, then flapped its wings and was gone.

"The bird warns us again," the seaman explained. "We do not have the luxury of waiting until nightfall! We must get you away from here, now."

He motioned for me to grab my coat and led the way from the room. The ape-things scurried from our path as he led the way down a set of broad stone stairs.

The seaman stopped abruptly, raising a hand so that I might stop as well. I paused, and realized the reason for his caution. There were voices below us.

"I say, guvner," a coarse voice drifted up the stair. "Grundy must have the merchandise."

Another voice laughed roughly. "That old man's too weak and crazy to cross the likes of us."

"Oh," said a third man, with a voice more refined and powerful than either of the first two—and a voice that sounded like no one but Colonel Skeffington, "I have certain guarantees of his loyalty! Grundy would not dare to do a thing against us."

I looked to the man at my side. The seaman's visage was frozen in fear as if, indeed, the very sound of those voices sapped his will.

One of the apes made a soft, cooing noise behind him.

Grundy blinked—for no doubt, that was the seaman's name, and looked to me again. He pulled open a small door at the side of the stairs.

"In here for a moment!" he instructed in a harsh whisper. "Do not judge me too harshly."

I had to bend over to climb inside. I heard the door shut firmly behind me.

I seemed to be in some sort of storage area, full of piles of rope and barrels. It was hard to determine the exact nature of my surroundings since much of it was lost in shadow, the only light coming from a single small window placed high upon the farthest wall from the door. Apparently, I was meant to wait in here until the danger outside was past.

Finding myself with a moment of unexpected leisure, I reviewed what I knew of the case. As I had mentioned before, the first notice of the unusual circumstances in this particular corner of

Cornwall came to our attention through an article in the venerable *Times* of London, concerning the disappearance of certain young women.

Perhaps what had most piqued the interest of my friend was not simply the disappearance of these young women, but, farther down in the piece, the almost offhand mention of a disease brought out from the darkest and most sinister parts of Africa, which seemed to afflict a number of individuals upon the local sea-lanes. As Holmes mentioned when I saw him last, that same illness did not seem to affect the locals.

I heard the sound of feet climbing the stairs, and the voices of the three men from below, along with the seaman.

"Keep those things away from me, Grundy!" one of the ruffians exclaimed.

"Do you still hold the merchandise?" Skeffington's more commanding voice interrupted.

"Aye," Grundy replied, "I have her in a safe place."

"A safe place?" Skeffington demanded. "What do you mean?"

"I mean I will not abide this any longer," Grundy replied with equal heat. "In order to have her, you must give me what is mine!"

Colonel Skeffington's answer was surprisingly conciliatory. "Grundy, dear Grundy, you know that is my deepest wish. There are unfortunately certain complications. Perhaps we can discuss this?"

"Very well," the seaman agreed after a moment's pause. "Come with me to the light tower."

By holding the conversation directly outside of my hiding place, Grundy was letting me know that the way was clear for my escape. As soon as I no longer heard the sound of booted feet upon the steps, I could quickly make for the exit and find my good friend Sherlock Holmes.

I heard a noise behind me, like the scrape of a boot across

stone. I turned about quickly, expecting an attack. There was no one there, and everything about me seemed still. In some strange way, though, I might not be alone in this place.

I crept cautiously forward into the storeroom, expecting to be assaulted at any moment. Instead, I heard the same scraping noise again, and determined it was coming from a recessed place in the wall to my left. I quickly stepped about a barrel that obstructed my view.

There, propped upon the barrel's other side, was a woman, securely bound and gagged. It was Margaret, the Innkeeper's daughter! She looked up at me with a mixture of fear and hope, not sure if I was savior or captor.

"Do not worry," I assured her in a whisper. "I will get you out of this place."

I pulled her gently from the wall and turned her about slightly so that I might examine her bonds. To my dismay, the knots showed a seaman's skill. My fingers could not unwork them in the dim light. I realized I would need something sharp to saw through the ropes; a knife, or, failing that, a sharp piece of shale from the beach outside.

I could no longer hear the footsteps outside our hiding place. Still looking at Margaret, I took a tentative step towards the door.

She implored me with her eyes.

"I will not leave you here," I assured her. "I will return so that we might both escape."

With that I quit the room and hurried as quietly as possible down the stairs. Once again I wished I had my trusty revolver so that I could make short work of any villains, human or otherwise, that might hinder our freedom.

The door that led from the lighthouse to the rocks was open. The afternoon light was quite bright after the gloom of my hiding place, but, after I allowed a moment for my eyes to adjust, I began to search in earnest for something that would cut the young woman's bonds, a stone, even a particularly sharp piece of shell.

"And what might you be looking for, sir?"

I looked up to see another rough man of the docks, different from the two in the inn the other day. He seemed quite typical of the breed, his cap pulled low over his skull, his mouth set in a perpetual sneer.

All thoughts of an easy rescue for poor Margaret were gone. If I could get by this newest ruffian, I should have to run back to town and fetch both Holmes and the police. But, from the strange and agitated explanations of my benefactor, I feared Margaret would have been spirited away long before any help arrived.

"None of your affair," I insisted, making to push past the fellow. "Now if you will excuse me, my good man."

But the ruffian stepped directly into my path. "Odd about that bird." He pointed to the cormorant, who now perched amidst the rocks. " 'Tis closely related to the gannet and the pelican, you know." He averted his face for an instant to spit upon the beach, then returned to his speech.

"The cormorant is quite easily trained. They use them in the Orient, you know. They use the birds to catch fish. They actually dive beneath the waves to snatch them." He cackled. "But their clever owners keep them on a leash, and choke them before they can eat what they've caught!"

I was astonished that this fellow was telling me all this. And then I realized that only one man had that kind of information at his command.

I stepped closer to him.

"Holmes!" I said in a low tone. "It's you."

The ruffian pushed the cap back on his intelligent forehead as his mouth twisted into a more familiar smile.

"Yes, Watson. I affected this disguise in case there might be trouble. I suspected that both you and the young woman were somewhere nearby. And the cormorant directed me right to you."

"Indeed, Holmes!" I answered, barely able to contain my joy at our reunion. I nodded back to the lighthouse. "Margaret is inside."

"Excellent, Watson!" He reached inside his dark blue jacket. "I thought to bring something we might need."

With that, he brought out my revolver and placed it in my hand. Now, together we would deal with those vile men who had kidnapped poor Margaret and at least three others!

Holmes quickly led the way up the stairs. But we barely made it up a dozen steps before Skeffington appeared to bar our way.

He shook his head as he remarked, "You would not leave well enough alone, would you Mr. Holmes?" The two ruffians stepped out to his side, herding Grundy and three apes before them. "You would never understand," Skeffington continued condescendingly, "how much it costs to maintain the proper standing when you have a seat in the House of Commons."

Holmes only laughed. "I doubt many of your fellow members are involved in the white slave trade!"

"I have no idea how you have discovered my secrets, Mr. Holmes," the Colonel snarled. "It is a small matter, after all, for they will shortly die with you and your Dr. Watson!"

I saw that one of his low-life companions also had a gun.

But Holmes did not seem in the least disturbed by this turn of events. "We do not intend to go anywhere without the woman."

Skeffington laughed powerfully, as if all before him was some grand joke. "The woman is only one small part of this! I have plans for these apes. With a little training and a few lashes of the whip, how much more willingly and cheaply they will work than those rebellious Cornish miners! I am only one member of a grand plan here, Mr. Holmes. You meddle with far more than you imagine."

He turned back toward the door beyond which poor Margaret waited, still bound and gagged. "But we will have to deal with the woman. And her father as well, even though he owes me a considerable amount of money. At first, I had thought our newest catch should follow the others. But then I began to think of our grander schemes, and how she might be put to better use." He glanced back to Holmes and myself, his face lit with a smile of triumph. "To keep the apes happy, we may need to satisfy certain of their—more physical needs."

"You fiend!" The old seaman exclaimed. "That could be my daughter! You have used us basely, but no more! You will not meddle with another life!" And, so saying, Grundy threw himself upon the man with the gun.

The two of them wrestled upon the landing. A single gunshot, and Grundy tumbled down the stairs, coming to rest almost at our feet. He had wrested the gun free from the villain, but it cost him his life.

But even this would not stop Colonel Skeffington.

"We have more weapons than guns at our disposal. Smight! The whip!"

While the ruffian who had lost the gun staggered to his feet, the Colonel's other lackey brandished an imposing length of leather. The apes growled at the sight of it. Skeffington's men would whip them into attacking us!

I fell back a step, holding my revolver with both hands. There were three men and three sub-human creatures ranked against us. I could perhaps shoot one or two of them, but the rest would overwhelm us.

But my friend the detective took a step forward. *"Kreegah!"* Holmes announced.

The apes stopped dead, as if the whip at their backs no longer mattered.

"Kreegah?" one of them replied.

"Kreegah!" Holmes repeated. *"Kreegah Bundalo."*

"Kreegah Bundalo!" the first of the apes shouted. *"Kreegah Bundalo!"* the other apes joined in chorus.

They turned then with a courage and purpose I had not seen in the animals before, and, as if those words Holmes spoke became a rallying cry, they fell upon their whippers and proved quickly that their fangs and claws were more than a match for any human resistance.

The two men screamed and struggled for only an instant. The apes advanced on Skeffington, no longer the proud soldier, but now only a man seeking escape.

Holmes shouted another string of words and the apes seemed content to keep the Colonel their prisoner.

"Now, Watson," Holmes called triumphantly, "let us rescue poor Margaret!"

It was only when we released Margaret and turned the malefactors over to the proper authorities that Holmes saw fit to explain the reasoning behind his deductions.

"My suspicions were first aroused when the article mentioned local outbreaks of an ailment referred to as Congo spotted fever, a disease that, I recall, neither of us were familiar with. At first, I thought this fever might simply be a common name for a malady I might recognize from other symptoms. But the only reports I found in talking with the locals did nothing to discuss the symptoms. Instead, in every case, they reported the afflicted had been instantly quarantined!"

I nodded at that, for I had read the *Times* article as well, and had heard some of the same reports from those in the village.

"It was then that I realized," Holmes continued, "it was not the sickness that was causing the disappearances, but the quarantine!"

Holmes smiled grimly at the evil cleverness of the plan. "The women who have disappeared were coerced onto ships sailing for Africa, either through lies or brute force. And, once they reached their destination in some port far less civilized than the one they left, they came down with this mysterious ailment—an ailment that forces them to stay fully covered and kept out of close proximity with others."

At last I saw what Holmes was driving at.

"Then you mean—"

"Exactly! None of these women ever returned to England.

Instead, they were replaced by beings much the same shape and size as the women, but were actually Great Apes!"

"Great Apes?" I asked, for this was the first time I had heard them so described.

"A rare and intelligent species found only in the darkest part of Africa," Holmes explained, "a species fully capable of operating a lighthouse such as this. Shall we say I ran across some information concerning them in my travels during my years of seclusion? But more importantly to the case at hand, these noble savages are not capable of those vile deceptions known to man. No, the apes themselves are innocent!"

"But what happened to the women?" I persisted.

Holmes allowed himself a rare sigh. "I'm afraid their fate was all too certain. There are certain base individuals in the more primitive parts of this world who would go to almost any length to subjugate a fair flower of English womanhood!"

It was almost unthinkable. "Then Colonel Skeffington *was* deeply involved in the white slave trade?"

"Yes, Watson." Holmes stared out to sea, as if what he described was almost too great even for a man of his stamina. "Skeffington was a military man who had been removed from power. While still in the army he became hopelessly overwhelmed by gambling debts, so much so he was an embarrassment to his superiors. Stripped of his post, the only way he felt he could recoup his losses was in the lucrative slave trade. And that trade did indeed bring him power and money, and even a seat in the House of Commons."

"Monstrous!" I agreed. "But what of those women sold into bondage? Old Grundy's daughter—"

Holmes gave a small shake of his head. "I fear they are lost to us. There is some small hope that Skeffington might know their whereabouts, but there are certain places even Sherlock Holmes might fear to go."

"The fiend!" I added for good measure.

"As I said, I have had some experience in Africa, and we may yet have some recourse with colonial authorities," Holmes continued. "I think it is a priority that we return these apes to their natural habitat."

I was a bit taken aback by Holmes's conviction in this matter. "Are they that special then?"

"I believe they are close to a direct ancestor of man. In fact, they are quite capable of raising even a human infant, and doing so without the impediments of our so-called civilization."

The detective spoke about that last subject with enormous certainty, as if Holmes might have actually witnessed such a thing as a human child among these creatures! But when I asked him further about it, he would tell me no more, as if Africa, and the apes, and his missing years were all somehow tied together in a way that could never be spoken of.

Holmes needed his mysteries, but on that day the spring had returned to his step and the chuckle to his voice, and for the moment that was enough.

"Poor Grundy," I murmured as we proceeded up the beach, giving a moment's thought to the seaman who had been so ill-used by the kidnappers. "He won't be around to look for his daughter, or feed his bird."

"Look Watson!" Holmes cried. At that, the cormorant flapped its wings and lifted itself from its perch. It circled us once, and with a single, haunting cry, headed out to sea.

The author of "Sherlock Holmes, Dragon-Slayer" is conjectured to be the great Irish fantasist and playwright LORD DUNSANY (1878–1957). Despite its uncanonical title, this tale is a well-written, authoritative explanation of the singular adventures of the Grice Patersons in the unmapped island of Uffa . . . up to a point. But Holmes purists, beware: once the mystery is solved, the author proceeds to grind his own Jorkenesque axe.—JAF

Sherlock Holmes, Dragon-Slayer (The Singular Adventures of the Grice Patersons in the Island of Uffa)

BY "DARRELL SCHWEITZER"
(ASCRIBED TO LORD DUNSANY)

It was in the course of one of those long afternoons at our club when no billiards were played, that the subject of the conversation turned to romance. The members had gathered around the fireplace in comfortable chairs. The waiter moved quietly among us, serving drinks. Someone spoke of tragic lovers, of Tristan and Isolde, Lancelot and Guinevere, Aeneas and Dido, drawing out of these and other examples some lofty and sobering theme which, in the light of what followed, I understandably cannot recall.

A boorish member, who really shouldn't have been in our club at all, began praising the works of a certain modern novelist known to the rest of us only by avoidance, an author of truly appalling sentimentality. Several hearers sighed or groaned. One tried to steer the conversation back out of the mire, but the Boorish Member failed to perceive any of these signals and continued his discourse.

There was only one thing for it. I hastily signalled the waiter and ordered a large whiskey and soda, not for myself, but for a certain other clubman present, who had as yet remained silent. This particular gentleman had been extraordinarily well-travelled in his younger days, and could always be relied upon, when suitably fueled by the very potation I had just ordered, to narrate some fascinating episode from his past adventures. He, if anyone, could rescue us from further droning paeans to popular literature.

The Clubman sipped his drink for a long while, and I almost feared that he had failed me, but of course he had not.

He cleared his throat suddenly, like a motor-car sputtering to life.

"I met Sherlock Holmes once," said he.

"What's *that* got to do with romance?" said the Boorish Member.

I don't think the rest of us cared if it did or not.

"It concerned one of his unrecorded cases, which Doctor Watson only mentioned in passing."

"Ah. Do go on." This last came from the Skeptic, a lawyer who, if truth must be told, remained forever jealous of our storytelling Clubman, and devoted much vain effort to proving him a liar. Now he regarded his foe expectantly, as a cobra does its victim.

"The good Doctor, as you know, never wrote up all the cases. There's a dispatch-box in a vault at Charing Cross containing a treasure-trove of notes."

"Yes, yes," interrupted the Boorish Member. "I read something about one of them once. It was called 'Ricoletti and His Abominable Wife.' Probably some damned nonsense about an Italian nobleman married to a yeti." He actually slapped his thigh, to emphasize the hilarity of his own attempted witticism.

The rest of us looked away discreetly.

"The case in which I became involved," said the storytelling Clubman, "was the one Watson so intriguingly entitled 'The Singular Adventures of the Grice Patersons in the Island of Uffa.' It did indeed involve romance, and also, incidentally, a treasure-trove."

I saw that our storyteller was now gaining the momentum of his narrative, but his whiskey glass was perilously near to empty, so I ordered him another.

The Skeptic spoke. "Of course you have read the monograph by the Danish scholar Anderson on that very case."

"A brilliant piece of work, too," said the Clubman. "Inevitably, though, there are certain points in it which are incompletely expounded or even incorrect. Yet at times Anderson's speculations are almost uncanny in their accuracy, especially when you consider that Anderson was never there. I cannot claim to be his intellectual superior when I say that I must correct him on some of the details, for, you see, I have an unfair advantage. I *was* there, and witnessed nearly everything."

"Where precisely was *there?*" the Skeptic asked.

Y ou will appreciate why I cannot be too specific," said the Clubman. "There are certain things one must draw a veil over. Suffice it to say it was in the Fen Country, near Thetford, in those vast marshlands which attract so many sportsmen in the appropriate fishing and shooting seasons.

"This was not the appropriate season, however, but a windy night in late November, and I chanced to be crossing the halfway-frozen fens on business of my own. It was nearly nightfall, and my business was pressing. Imagine me, if you will, somewhat younger and more vigorous than I am today, bundled against the weather, my long scarf trailing as I leaned into the wind. I wore knee-boots for wading through the icy rivulets and carried an electric torch in my right hand. In my left, I held a firm, long stick, with which to prod the ground in front of me to test for quicksand.

"I was proceeding in such a fashion when suddenly I heard a woman scream.

"Of course I broke into a run, and had there been any quicksand in my path just then, I'm sure it would have claimed me. The lady cried out her distress once more, and then the beam of my torch caught her as she struggled with some adversary on the top of a low hill. She was young and, I could tell even under the circumstances, a striking beauty, though dressed almost mannishly in boots and mud-stained trousers and a heavy coat, as if prepared for adventure. Well, she was having an adventure now. I think there was blood on her face, but she did not seem greatly injured. She put up a terrific fight against some opponent who was only a dark shape.

"I called out for him to unhand her, but as I did the two of them merely *vanished* into thin air, and her cries ceased.

"I thought then that I had seen a ghost, perhaps reenacting some ancient horror. The Fen Country is notoriously haunted, you know, this particular district even more so than most. Before setting out, I had had my supper at a public house in the nearest village, and the local people filled my ears with such tales, while grumbling about rich Londoners who refused to 'leave alone what should be left alone.' Previously, I had considered such admonitions mere rustic superstition, but now I was less certain.

"I had not long to meditate upon this theme. I splashed through half-frozen mud and climbed the hill, which rose above the surrounding marshland like an enormous, beached whale. A hillock, really, but the only high ground for miles around.

"Suddenly someone tapped me on the shoulder with a stick and said, 'You there! What is the meaning of this?'

"I whirled about, and by the light of my torch beheld a face I had not seen in twenty years.

" 'Good God! John Watson!'

" 'Do I know you, Sir?' he said, his manner still guarded.

"Watson and I had been chums in our youth, before he went off to medical school and the army. We had once belonged to a boys' secret society together. I swiftly transferred my torch to my left hand, then reached out and gave him the secret handshake.

"A broad smile broke across that redoubtable face. He laughed and embraced me warmly. 'So it *is* you, old friend!'

"I assured him that it was, and remarked on how I had admired his writings in *The Strand* and followed his career closely. But he was in no mood to chat, and this was hardly the place for it.

" 'Holmes and I are involved in a most difficult investigation,' he said.

" 'Perhaps I can be of some assistance?'

" 'Perhaps you can. Yes, come along.'

"He swiftly led me along the long axis of the hill, then down the slope to one side, to where pale light flickered from what appeared to be a cave mouth. I paused, involuntarily calling to mind some of the local superstitions about goblins that assume pleasing shapes and lure travellers to their doom.

"Watson must have read my mind. He gave me the secret handshake right back, something no goblin could ever have done. There is a story behind that handshake and its efficacy against goblins, but I shall save it for another time.

"Watson hurried me along. 'We mustn't keep Holmes waiting.'

"So the two of us descended into the opening, which proved to be the tunnel-mouth of an archaeological excavation, shored up with planks. Picks, shovels, buckets, and sifting-screens lay about, somewhat untidily, suggesting that the workers had deserted their duties in some haste. Within, crouched around a small table and examining a chart by the light of storm lanterns, were two gentlemen, one unknown to me, the other unmistakably the world-famous detective, Mr. Sherlock Holmes.

"Since we were out in the wilderness and the weather was appropriate, Holmes was actually wearing his famous deerstalker, which, of course, numerous illustrations and stage-plays to the contrary, he would never have worn in town any more than he would have worn the feathered head-dress of a Red Indian. But in the country, it was a most practical piece of head-gear. In fact, I was wearing one myself.

" 'Since you have Watson's trust,' said he, 'I can take you into confidence and rely upon your discretion.'

"He introduced the other gentleman to me as Henry Grice Paterson, the son of a wealthy shipping magnate, lately turned amateur archaeologist.

"I told them what I had seen on my arrival.

" 'Heaven help her!' Grice Paterson exclaimed before I had even finished. 'It is Beatrice, and she is in peril!'

"He leapt to his feet, but Holmes and Watson both caught hold of him.

" 'Nothing will be gained by rushing madly into the darkness,' said the great detective, 'except perhaps your unfortunate death.'

" 'But, my beloved wife—'

" 'If you hurl yourself into the quicksand, what good will that do her? *Think,* man, before you act, and perhaps she may yet be rescued.'

" 'We can't just loiter here while—'

"Now Holmes rose to his feet, stooping beneath the low earthen ceiling. 'You are absolutely correct. We must search at once. Every second is precious.'

"So the three of them took up lanterns. Holmes led the way. I followed, and as the beam of my torch played over the tunnel walls and floor, I couldn't help but notice the occasional bit of litter that looked for all the world like ancient, human bones.

"Outside, Watson and Grice Paterson shouted for Beatrice, while Holmes bade me shine my torch on the ground. He was looking for, I suppose, footprints. After a time, there was only silence, but for the lonely howling of the wind. We four stood beneath the brilliant stars, in such darkness and isolation that it was hard to imagine this to be other than primordial wilderness. London, or even a cosy pub in a nearby village, seemed fantastic memories, something out of another world.

" 'I fear that I am unable to dismiss what we were told about this place,' said Grice Paterson at last. 'It *is* haunted.'

" 'Surely you don't believe the stories of ghosts and monsters,' said Watson.

" 'I don't know what to believe anymore,' moaned Grice Paterson. He turned to me imploringly. 'Into *thin air,* you said, sir?'

" 'So it appeared,' I had to admit.

" 'So it *appeared,'* echoed Holmes sharply. 'That is the key to it. Things are seldom what they appear, and superstition runs wild with mere appearance, rather than calmly discovering the more subtle truth that may lie beneath that appearance.'

" 'I take it that you don't believe in ghosts, Mr. Holmes,' I said.

"He snorted contemptuously. 'To me, the spooks need not apply. My methods admit no room for the supernatural.'

"It was hardly the time for me to relate that I had actually met several spooks already in the course of my travels and that there were perhaps more things in heaven and earth than dreamt of even in the philosophy of Sherlock Holmes. At leisure, such an argument might have proved stimulating, but now, of course, a lady was in danger and a mystery was to be solved. Also, it was bitterly cold there, in the wind and darkness, on top of that mound.

" 'Watson,' said Holmes. 'Fetch the probing rods.'

"Watson scrambled back into the tunnel, then returned with several metal rods about a yard long and thick as a man's finger. They were bluntly pointed on one end. These, with effort, we drove into the half-frozen ground. As we worked, Holmes filled in much that I had already surmised, but he told the tale more vividly than I ever could, and so I must merely summarize.

"This place, this hillock to be precise, was known from ancient times as the Island of Uffa. Perhaps a thousand years ago the fens were even swampier than they are today, and it was a true island. Hither, in the most obscure period of our country's history, about A.D. 570, came a fierce Saxon chieftain, Uffa, to build a fortification from which he could control the surrounding countryside and dominate his equally barbaric rivals. But Uffa did not prosper. As the cowering British peasantry had warned him, the place was haunted. One by one his loyal thanes met hideous deaths, often found torn to pieces in the morning, even partially devoured. There was talk of the Dragon of Uffa, a huge beast which no surviving witness had ever seen. It was also called King Uffa's Bane, in the sagas. The slaughter continued, yet, with the grim and steadfast loyalty expected of a war-band in those days, Uffa's men remained with him. They set traps for the monster, attempted stratagems, fought, and diminished in number. The king sent for Beowulf, but Beowulf was occupied with a similar case in Scandinavia at the time.

" 'You might call him the world's first consulting monster-slayer,' Holmes joked uncharacteristically, but, I believe, with the serious purpose of relieving tension and maintaining Grice Paterson's faltering morale.

" 'Mr. Holmes,' said he. 'I fail to understand why you relish such details if, as you say, monster stories are irrelevant.'

" 'Even things that are factually untrue may be quite relevant,' replied Holmes, 'particularly when they lead people to act on the basis of belief.'

"He resumed his account of Uffa's protracted doom. It could still be the subject of a magnificent romance, if written by someone more capable than a modern sentimental novelist. King Uffa had a beautiful queen, named Hrothwealda, who stayed by his side, magnificent to the end. On the last night of their lives, both of them took up spears, swords, and shields. Both wore gleaming armor, for Hrothwealda was a warrior queen, as formidable as her husband. When the dragon came for them, man and wife fought as comrades. But in vain. The dragon devoured Hrothwealda as an alligator gulps down a sheep.

"It must have seemed cruelly inexplicable that it spared King Uffa. But it did, merely towering over him, as he clung to his broken spear and mourned for Queen Hrothwealda.

"The dragon's mistress explained why. There emerged from the darkness a fantastic figure, such as only that barbaric age could have produced, a woman clad in skins and dangling necklaces of human bones, with bronze serpents coiled around her arms and the horns of some beast affixed to her head. This was the witch Graxgilda, who had lusted after King Uffa since girlhood and had now come to claim him. She hadn't cared about the thanes, though it was convenient to get them out of the way, loyal as they were to both Uffa and to Uffa's lady. It was that lady, Hrothwealda, whom the witch desired to destroy. Now that she had done so, she demanded that Uffa become her lover.

"Of course he did not. He fell on his sword, to join his beloved wife in death. Graxgilda raged afterward. She bade the dragon destroy the king's fort, which it easily did, and she left the creature in the vicinity to haunt the mound, and to guard Uffa's treasure until the end of time.

" 'I must confess, sir,' said Grice Paterson to me when Holmes had finished his account, 'that even as Schliemann regarded the tales of Homer as having some basis in fact, I did not think the story of King Uffa to be entirely a fable. I was, and still am, certain that such a Saxon marauder actually lived in this district, and that he and the fruits of his depredations lie buried in this mound. When I discovered the location of the mound, I began excavations at once, even in this inconvenient season, lest someone else arrive at the same conclusion, or the prevalence of sportsmen in the spring give the secret away.'

" 'Our immediate problem,' said Holmes, 'is not so much that of preserving the secret, which has obviously already been compromised, or even of finding the king and his treasure. Instead we must concentrate on the discovery of the secret passageway into which Beatrice Grice Paterson has been carried, not by any ghostly

Saxon warrior or even a dragon, but by a mundane kidnapper. I am sure the passage is quite near to this very spot, from which the lady seemed to *vanish into thin air,* as the estimable gentleman phrased it.'

"The great detective resumed his probing.

" 'Mr. Holmes,' said Grice Paterson. 'Do you truly believe there is still hope for my Beatrice?'

" 'Most certainly,' replied Holmes, 'if we work to our utmost to find that passage.'

"So we four labored, Holmes silent and intent, studying every clue, while Watson, slightly out of breath from the exertion, filled me in on the rest.

" 'Mr. and Mrs. Grice Paterson began their diggings, despite the inclement season and the objections of the local folk, whose numerous warnings could be taken as half-veiled threats. For a week or so, things went well. Some ancient Saxon weapons were found, badly rusted, of course, but of definite scientific value. Then came the bones of at least a dozen human beings, almost as if, following a custom more barbaric than even those of the pagan Saxons, the king had been buried with all his retainers.'

" 'The odd thing was,' interjected Grice Paterson as he drove his probe into the ground once more, 'that most of those bones were mutilated, broken to bits. The larger pieces had tooth marks on them, as if the ancient graves had been violated by some enormous scavenging animal.

" 'But still there was nothing of monetary value,' said Watson, 'until Mrs. Grice Paterson found the jar of coins, the . . . what were they called?'

" '*Sceats*. Small, crude, Anglo-Saxon silver pieces, many of them bearing the monogram of King Uffa himself, thus establishing his historical existence once and for all. You cannot imagine how excited Beatrice and I were by this wonderful discovery, which was soon followed by the unearthing of what must have been the actual treasury of the ancient king—hundreds of gold pieces, many of them Byzantine, issued during the reign of Justinian the Great and his immediate successor, and worth, needless to say, a great deal on the open market, but still more valuable to science, since they demonstrated a level of commerce between early Anglo-Saxon England and the East hitherto unsuspected.'

" 'Then things began to go terribly wrong,' said Watson.

"Grice Paterson grunted as he pulled his probe out of the ground. 'The hauntings began. Our workmen, who were not locals, of course, but brought in from more outlying districts at considerable expense, began to report disturbing sounds, which first I assured them were merely the wind blowing across the tunnel mouth as one blows across a bottle. But no, they insisted. These sounds came from beneath the ground. *Like 'owlin' and wailin' an' gnashin' o' big teeth!* as the foreman colorfully expressed it.'

" 'It seemed that the legendary terrors that plagued King Uffa had returned,' said Watson. His probe was stuck. I helped him draw it out.

" 'But Mr. Holmes did not believe me,' said Grice Paterson, 'even after the first death.'

" 'One of the workmen was murdered in the night while guarding the site,' said Watson. 'His fellows found him in the morning, horribly mutilated. I'm afraid the others showed little of the steadfast loyalty of King Uffa's thanes. They took to their heels, and two more failed to reach the village. They vanished in broad daylight. Holmes speculated that they fell into quicksand. Furthermore, such clues as a footprint that did not belong, cigar ashes when found that the workmen all smoked pipes, and other such seeming trivia of the sort from which he so brilliantly draws his conclusions convinced Holmes that someone might be trying to frighten everyone off, and had resorted to murder to get at the treasure.'

" 'I knew that only Mr. Holmes could help us,' said Grice Paterson, 'no matter what the cause, supernatural or otherwise. But this very night, as we were examining our diagrams of the underground maze we have just begun to uncover, Beatrice stepped out for a breath of fresh air—the lantern smoke in so confined a place can become very close—and was carried off, as you saw, sir, by some fiend or dragon or whatever—'

"Suddenly Holmes cried out. 'Watson! Come here! I've found it, as I knew we would!'

"We all rushed to where he knelt down. He pushed his probe through the earth freely, drew it out, and pushed again with little effort, indicating a hollow space beneath.

" 'A secret passage, as I long suspected,' said Holmes. 'Now if we can but find the opening.'

"Grice Paterson, perhaps over-eager, plunged his own probing rod into the ground as hard as he could, as if he were driving a harpoon. He must have tripped something, because the earth instantly gave way beneath himself, Holmes, and Watson. The three of them tumbled into darkness, leaving me alone on the hilltop.

"I was startled half out of my wits, yes, and for an instant fancied the dragon must have swallowed all three, but then reason prevailed. I directed my torch beam down the hole that had opened up, and saw that my stalwart companions were unhurt and brushing themselves off. Holmes struck a match and relit one of the lanterns. By this light and that of my electric torch, numerous side passageways were revealed, part of an underground labyrinth.

" 'You stay here and keep watch,' Holmes instructed me. 'We shall return shortly with the answer to the mystery.'

"And, like a heroic champion of old, he confidently led his troops into the darkness, and that was the last I saw of any of them until much later, after the affair had concluded."

At this point the Clubman paused and took a long sip of his whiskey. He leaned back in his chair and seemed almost ready to doze off.

"But—but—!" the Skeptic sputtered. "You can't end the story like that!"

"Oh, Holmes wrapped things up pretty neatly. At the center

of the labyrinth was a chamber, to which the kidnapper had carried Beatrice Grice Paterson. She was unharmed, fortunately, but for a bruise or two and a nasty cut on her forehead, where the blackguard had assaulted her. He was an old business rival of Grice Paterson's father, who had fallen into bankruptcy more through his own incompetence than anything the elder Grice Paterson might have done. A chap named Ponderby—"

"Haw! I bet he was ponderous enough!" The Boorish Member slapped his thigh again, guffawing loudly at his unwelcome attempt at humor. He slurped his drink *inexcusably* and the waiter gently but firmly took the rest of it away from him. A moment later he was merely snoring, to the immense relief of all others present. (I am pleased to report that this fellow is no longer a member of our club, but has since transferred his allegiance to the Drones.)

Our storyteller patiently waited until the distraction was past.

"In fact, Ponderby was dead, hideously mangled, as if mauled by a tiger. Mrs. Grice Paterson sobbed something about a huge claw that came at him out of the darkness. Watson told me all about it later. It was his diagnosis, and Holmes and Grice Paterson concurred, that the lady was hysterical and perhaps hallucinating, due to the blow on the head.

"That was the end of the adventure, then. The rest of the artifacts excavated from that mound were turned over to the proper authorities. The mystery was solved, although not as neatly as Holmes might have liked. Even he could not satisfactorily account for Ponderby's death. Therefore he did not allow Watson to publish any account of the Singular Adventures of the Grice Patersons in the Island of Uffa."

Now the Clubman sat back, as if daring his adversary the Skeptic to bait him further. He finished his whiskey, and, without being told, the waiter brought him another.

All was silent in that room but for the Boorish Member's rhythmic snoring.

"It's utterly preposterous," the Skeptic ventured at last. "This rot about King Uffa and a dragon—"

"You can read about it in the *Anglo-Saxon Chronicle.*"

"Not in any version I've read."

"It's not in the official version, certainly not the one published by Everyman's Library for the common reader."

Someone snickered. The Clubman and the Skeptic regarded one another politely enough, but beneath the surface of mere appearance, they were two scorpions in a jar, duelling to the death.

"It's still not much of an ending," said the Skeptic weakly. "Just a fairy-story, really."

"I never said it *was* the ending, now, did I?"

The Clubman sipped his whiskey and resumed his tale.

"Everything I have told you, even about events in the remote past, is unquestionably true. I have *those* facts on the best authority."

"And what authority might that be?" demanded the Skeptic.

"The word of King Uffa himself. As I stood shivering in the darkness, keeping look-out as Sherlock Holmes had commanded me, a cold, iron hand suddenly took hold of my arm, and I turned around to find myself face-to-face with the ghost of the Saxon king, wild-eyed and haggard as he had appeared toward the end of his life. His rage-filled eyes staring out of the face-guard of his helmet gave the impression of a demonic mask.

"He spoke the language of his own time, of course, but fortunately I am sufficiently knowledgeable of Old English to have gotten the gist of what he said.

"He didn't care about the treasure, since gold is of no use to those who have passed beyond mortality. He wasn't even upset about his doom anymore, because he was with his beloved queen in some shadowy underworld known only to the heathen imagination of the Dark Age.

"But what did bother him was the infernal racket of hissing and growling and the gnashing of teeth, in short, the dragon. It still haunted his mound, devouring trespassers so noisily that the king and his wife could have no peace. He only wanted to be rid of it. He started to explain how the witch had carved the dragon's image onto an ivory plaque and placed it inside the mound. If that plaque were broken, the dragon would cease.

" 'You mean there really *is* a dragon?' I asked him, in growing dread.

"He merely pointed. I turned. There, rising out of the fen, dripping faintly luminescent slime, hissing cold smoke, its eyes like dull red stars, was the very dragon that had devoured the king's thanes and Queen Hrothwealda, and had doubtless killed Ponderby, too. It lurched toward me, its ragged, flightless wings rippling like tent flaps. Its voice was the roaring of a hurricane.

"The king offered me his sword and shield, but they were rusted and I could see they were no good. First I hurled one of the probing rods, and the monster reared up, howling, the rod sticking in its face like a pin. Then I fought it with my walking stick, and gave a good account of myself, too, whacking it on the nose over and over, the way a trainer does with an unruly bear. I knew that Holmes, Watson, and Grice Paterson were in terrible danger, and the only hope was to lure the dragon away into the quicksand, where hopefully it would founder before I did.

"So I whacked it on the nose some more, shouted, and shone my torch into its eyes. I ran down the side of Uffa's mound, to where I expected to find a path. But somehow I had made a mistake in the dark. Almost at once I stumbled into the quicksand, losing both stick and torch. I clung to a bush, and could have extracted myself without much difficulty in a few minutes, but the dragon was upon me and I knew it was all up.

"Then, suddenly, as if by a miracle, and far more thoroughly than had ever Mrs. Grice Paterson, the dragon *vanished into thin air.*"

How very convenient," said the Skeptic. "A miracle."

"So it seemed, but Holmes tells us that things are not what they merely seem. There really was a plaque of ivory, about four inches square, rudely carved with the figure of a dragon. It's in the British Museum now."

"I've never seen it there."

"It's not on public display because of its condition, but it is there, in a drawer, broken in half, still marked with the inadvertent boot-print of the world's first and greatest consulting detective. The curator is an old friend. He showed it to me once."

The Skeptic was left thwarted, outflanked, and sputtering. The rest of us looked on with, I think, a certain satisfaction. But the Clubman's implacable foe grasped at one last, desperate straw.

"I demand to know," said he, "what *you* were doing on the fen that night. It was a rather large coincidence, you must admit. What *was* your urgent business, which you seem to have forgotten about afterward?"

The Clubman drank, and paused. There was a flicker of venomous triumph in the Skeptic's eyes.

The Clubman put down his glass. "I was looking for the Salmon of Knowledge. From the most ancient times, Britons have believed in an ageless fish that is the source of all wisdom and the guardian of whatever folk holds this island. When St. Augustine of Canterbury came to evangelize the heathen Saxons, he knew he had to convert the *fish* first, if he was to make any headway. In his *Life* there are certain clues, from which I deduced where he found it."

"Not in any version *I've* read—"

We ignored the Skeptic. The Clubman calmly continued. "I was there on that night because, like Grice Paterson, I was so excited by my discovery that I couldn't allow anyone else to beat me to it. The Salmon was there, too. I got to within ten yards of the pool in which it resided. But I was caught in the quicksand by then, and the dragon was upon me. The dragon saw the fish, and paused for just a second, long enough for Holmes to unwittingly save my life. The dragon swallowed the fish in one gulp, as an appetizer before the main course, which was to be myself. Then, of course, the dragon vanished. But the fish was gone and it was too late. I think you will admit that the probity of the English race has declined somewhat since its loss."

He indicated the Boorish Member, still snoring, and not even the Skeptic could contradict him.

He held up his glass. "Waiter! Another whiskey!"

*M*r. *R.'s ledger reads "Ricoletti—6,000 (lbs. sterling)—PGW." This clue to the author's nationality, combined with the ensuing novella's general tone, inevitably leads one to consider P. G. WODEHOUSE (1881–1975), the British humorist best remembered for his Jeeves novels. Despite the presence of a factitious majordomo, Mr. R. is reported to have felt quite pleased with the Holmes story his money made possible.—JAF*

The Adventure of Ricoletti of the Club Foot (and his abominable wife)

BY *"ROBERTA ROGOW"*
(ASCRIBED TO P. G. WODEHOUSE)

November's fogs were at their foggiest on a particular night in 1890, and those of my patients who didn't have catarrh had pleurisy. I was in Baker Street and saw the light on in my friend Holmes's window, and the thought of hot buttered rum or at the very least, hot tea . . . in fact, hot ANYTHING . . . drove me to ring the bell and get indoors before I was laid low myself.

Holmes was scraping aimlessly at his violin staring at the fireplace. For a minute I thought he had been at the cocaine again. Then I saw the envelope propped up against the photograph of Irene Adler.

"Hallo! What's this?" I asked.

"An invitation to join a hunting party at the residence of the

Earl of Duxbury," Holmes said. From the sound of his voice, one would think he'd been invited to attend one of the famous ceremonies held by the late Emperor Nero in the Colosseum, featuring Christians vs. Lions, all bets favoring the lions.

"One of your more satisfied customers?" I suggested. Mrs. Hudson arrived with the tea and scones, and I dug in. Mrs. Hudson's scones are well worth the digging.

Holmes turned a bleary eye on the scones. "Watson," he said, "There are places in this world I never wish to visit again. Duxbury Place is chief among them."

I noted a certain glaze of horror that came over his face as he spoke, a look that betokens memories so vile that the merest thought is enough to turn the stomach. I fancy I look the same whenever anyone mentions Afghanistan.

"Surely, whatever happened to you there couldn't have been all that bad," I said.

Holmes lay aside the violin and sat up in his chair. "I believe I once mentioned the case of Ricoletti of the Club Foot . . ."

"And his wife," I finished.

"His Abominable Wife," Holmes corrected me.

I waited for more information. Holmes opened his eyes and sighed. "The only excuse for my excruciating experience at Duxbury Place, and my humiliation at the hands of Ricoletti and his Abominable Wife was that I was very young. I believe the appropriate word is *callow*. It happened this way . . .

Y ou must understand (Holmes said) that all this happened some years ago, when I was still an undergraduate at Oxford. I had spent the Long Vac with my friend Victor Trevor, but even the longest vac must end, and I was in London, preparing to go back to college, staying with my brother, Mycroft, for a week before Michaelmas Term began.

We had had one of those grim luncheons at the Diogenes

Club (which Mycroft had just founded), during which Mycroft asked repeatedly what I intended to do with myself, to which question I had no particular answer.

My Oxford studies were odd and unpredictable, and I had made little acquaintance besides Victor Trevor. I had enjoyed the conversation of Mr. Dodgson, but while his mathematical mind and his taste for puzzles were intriguing, some of his other obsessions were, shall we say, esoteric? Most of the lads at Oxford had their lives mapped out for them: either Church (parsons) or State (Parliament, be it Lords or Commons). I only knew I didn't want either of them. Mycroft's world was not to be mine.

So there I was, drifting like the cloud, as the poet says, through Regent's Park on a stifling hot September day, idling along toward Michaelmas term, when I ran into Lord Pemberthy, or should I say, he ran into me on his velocipede. Pemberthy was one of the few people at Oxford who might recognize me in Regent's Park, although most of our previous meetings had been in the boxing ring, where I had knocked him down. I assumed that this encounter was merely retribution for the crime of planting one on the button nose of the Earl of Duxbury's Heir.

"What are you doing in my way. . . . Eh? It's Holmes!"

I looked up from my position on the gravel path. "Popsy Pemberthy?"

"Frightfully sorry, Old Chap. I thought I had this thing working . . ."

"You should have practiced with it while you were in Paris," I said, allowing him to help me to my feet.

"Eh?" Pemberthy stared at me.

"The machine has a French maker's tag on it. As far as I know, this particular model has not reached across the Channel yet. And just before the end of Summer Term, you were rabbiting on and on about how your Pater was gallivanting off to Paris and insisted on taking you with him. Elementary."

I brushed off my jacket and regarded Pemberthy with the

jaundiced eye of Poverty regarding Privilege. Philip Olney, Lord Pemberthy, (known to his intimate associates as Popsy) was one of those long, limber fellows, who do well in boat-races. The button nose with which I had connected was surmounted by a pair of round blue eyes and was perched over a pair of full pink lips, that usually pouted or sneered.

"So," I asked, "How was Paris?"

"Hot," Pemberthy said sulkily. He began to push the veloci-pede along the path, and I fell into step alongside him. "My father's gone mad. He's taken on some moth-eaten Italian mountebank and brought him to London, to help him select pictures for that estate His Royal Highness is building at Sandringham. Not only that, he's giving the fellow house-room! And not content with that, he's actu-ally allowed the fellow to bring his wife to Duxbury Place!"

It seemed to be a great tempest in the proverbial tea-pot to me, and I was ready to take my leave of Pemberthy, when he said, "And there's something just not right about that precious pair, Holmes. I say, you're a clever chap. Why don't you come to tea, and tell me what you think?"

I must admit I was flattered. At college, I was under two disadvantages: I was a class behind Pemberthy, and my family was neither titled nor wealthy. Today I find these social distinctions ridiculous, but then I observed the niceties that Society has laid down. I took Pemberthy's London address (a house in Mayfair), and watched him wobble off on his velocipede.

At four o'clock I presented myself at Duxbury House, prop-erly attired (thanks to Mycroft, who had not yet attained his present girth). The door was opened by a footman. Behind the footman was Lord Duxbury himself, a rotund gentleman of some fifty years, much shorter and stouter than his son, clad somewhat informally in a green velvet smoking-jacket and embroidered Turkish cap. Be-hind Lord Duxbury lurked another man, a slender figure in a black frock-coat, high collar, and carefully pressed white shirt. As the two stepped forward, I could see that the other man's foot was twisted, giving him a halting gait, and that he walked with the aid of a carved ebony cane.

"Holmes!" Pemberthy hallooed from the front stairs. "Father, this is Mr. Sherlock Holmes, a friend of mine from Oxford. Holmes, this is my father, Lord Duxbury, and his, um, friend, Ricoletti."

"How d'ye do? *Enchanté* I'm sure. Philip has told me a good deal about you. He says you're a clever fellow."

"I don't know . . ." I demurred.

I threaded my way between large objects wrapped in brown paper with French customs-seals all over the outsides, while Pemberthy led the way upstairs to the drawing-room, where a small tea-tray had been set out. "Holmes can tell everything about a fellow just by looking at him." At which, Pemberthy directed a glare at Ricoletti of such virulence that if he hadn't been engaged in buttering a muffin, he would have been immolated on the spot.

"Really?" Lord Duxbury sat down in the chair nearest to the tea-table and indicated that I should do the same. "And what can you tell about me, eh?"

"Only that your expedition to Paris has resulted in the purchase of several works of art of which your son violently disapproves, and that you are planning to take them back to the country with you. You are also preparing yourself for a distasteful encounter at home, and you are expecting several persons to stay at Duxbury Place who may not be particularly compatible with each other."

"Indeed? And what makes you think all of this?"

"Lord Pemberthy's voice when he told me of your visit to Paris leads me to the conclusion that he does not share your taste in art. The paintings in question are in the hall, still in their wrappings, which indicates that you are returning to Duxbury Place with them. You have a footman and cook here in Town, but not the butler or other servants, therefore, you are not planning to stay for any length of time. As for the distasteful encounter, you have drunk two cups of tea and eaten three muffins, and there are two letters on the writing-table, one of which has the Seal of Cambridge University and the other the seal of the Duke of Surrey, who is, I believe, your father-in-law. And my reading of the popular Press reminds me that the Duke of Surrey is more known for his sporting activities than his scholarship. A party that includes representatives of Cambridge University and the House of Surrey will not be particularly compatible."

Ricoletti patted his hands together. "Very good, Mr. Holmes. And what can you tell about me?"

There was a look in his eye I did not like, a sort of quizzing challenge.

"That you are still a Bonapartist, in spite of the Emperor's decline. That you were once a painter, but have not touched a brush in several years. That you worked at the Louvre, and that you were fallen on hard times until Lord Duxbury rescued you and brought you here to England."

"And what leads you to make such sweeping statements, young man?" Ricoletti sneered.

"That you were once a painter is indicated by the faint impression made by the brush against the third finger of your right hand. However, you do not carry any marks of pigments on your hands, ergo, you have not painted in some time. That you were a Bonapartiste is indicated by the ring on your little finger, which still bears the Bonaparte Bee. That you had fallen on evil times is indicated by the fact that your coat has been darned several times at the elbows, and your shoes have been mended more than once, as indicated by differing colors and levels of leather on the heels. As for Lord Duxbury's intervention on your behalf . . . that, I admit, was told to me by Lord Pemberthy."

"And the Louvre?"

"Ah. There, I admit, I hazarded a guess. A painter and an adherent of the Emperor would have found employment at the most prestigious of artistic establishments, the Louvre."

"You could make enemies, young man, if you go on with this sort of thing," Ricoletti hissed.

"I only do it as a lark——" I began.

"I say, Father," Pemberthy interposed. "Perhaps Holmes could look into those thefts down at the Place."

"Thefts?" I asked.

Lord Duxbury looked uncomfortable. "Small items go missing. Things like my ruby studs. They were a gift from His Majesty, George the Fourth, on the occasion of his ascension to the Throne, to my grandfather. I do not wear them myself, but they are of inestimable value to my Family."

"Other things have gone missing," Popsy said. "Ginny's pearls from Grandfather Surrey. Those hideous ivory things Uncle James sent from China."

"Japan," Lord Duxbury corrected him. "Quite unusual, those carvings. A number of people have begun to collect them."

"But . . . I don't see what I can do. Surely, this is a matter for the police? If you've had a robbery . . ."

"Nothing like that!" Lord Duxbury sputtered. "We're out in the country, no burglars there."

"I see." And I did. Either the servants or the Family had taken the items in question, and either way, the police would have been, as Lord Duxbury would have put it, *de trop*.

"So it's settled," Pemberthy said, hauling me out of my chair and leading me out of the drawing-room and into the hall. "You can come down to Duxbury Place tomorrow with us on the noon train, and we'll get there in time for tea. You can stay the weekend, and have your boxes sent on to college. Clever chap like you should have all this sorted out by Sunday.

"I'll wire Lady Duxbury to have another room prepared. Oh, by the way, Mr. Holmes, you were quite right about the guest who was part of my wife's family. My wife's brother, Lord Sylvester Varleigh, has been visiting us this summer. And the gentlemen from Cambridge will be coming to dinner on Saturday, and leaving on Sunday, so they will not be in too much conflict."

"And my wife is also at Duxbury," Ricoletti said. "It will be a jolly English party, yes?"

I found myself out the door, with the feeling that I had been put in a totally false position. Popsy clearly expected me to find proof that Ricoletti was the thief, and would be most annoyed if it should chance to be someone else.

I returned to Mycroft's rooms, and asked him, "What do you know about the Earl of Duxbury?"

According to Mycroft (and *Debrett**), the First Earl had been given the title by Prince Regent, some time shortly after Waterloo, largely on the strength of having lost a large sum to His Royal Highness and having a pretty and flirtatious wife. Having spent most of his money and time in the service of Prince and country, the First Earl died in 1820, leaving the title to his eldest son, the Second Earl.

The Second Earl married a wealthy brewer's daughter, who immediately produced "an heir and a spare," as the saying goes, and then gone one better by having a third son. This promising lad foreswore the boorish ways of his predecessors and took himself to Paris in 1846, where he spent two years ostensibly learning to paint murky scenes of grandeur embellished with romantic Gypsies. He would have remained there, a mediocre artist with lofty connections, when Fate intervened, as Fate is known to do, in 1848, when one of the Duxbury sons died hunting foxes and the other was chopped to pieces by Natives in India, where he had been sent by his maternal relations who had influence with the East India Company.

The Honourable William Olney found himself Heir to the Earldom, married, and on several Royal Commissions thanks to his father-in-law, the duke of Surrey. Popsy Pemberthy was the result of this union between Surrey and Duxbury. The Uncle Sylvester previously mentioned was the youngest son of said Duke, who, according to Mycroft, spent most of his time traipsing between Great Houses when he wasn't off angling for Heiresses.

---

*a guide to the peerage, published annually.

All of this gave me much material for Thought, as Pemberthy and I rattled through the countryside towards Destiny, although neither of us realized it at the time.

The coach was waiting for us at the station, as promised. The driver gave my single portmanteau the look reserved for the unsightly remains left on the cottage door by the cottage cat. Lord Duxbury and Ricoletti were ceremoniously handed into the coach, and Pemberthy and I made do up top with the despised French paintings.

After an hour's worth of jolts, we entered the gates of Duxbury Place and tooled up the drive. I was able to enjoy the first sight of that remarkable building in the late afternoon sun. I had expected an earl's residence to be of the crenellated and mossy variety, but allowances had to be made for the newness of the title. Duxbury Place was a tribute to the two Royal patrons of the House. The exterior owed much to the Prince Regent and his pet architects, but indoors, the Prince Consort's hand lay heavy, and the collision of Regent and Consort made for an ocular nightmare.

The floor plan of Duxbury Place could be likened to a dumbbell, with most of the rooms stretched out from a central cupola to rounded wings at either end. Once inside, I could see that this central dome was the focal point of the house. The private rooms, including the bed-chambers and the Countess's small drawing-room, were up a pair of stairs; the dining-room, breakfast-room and grand drawing-room were arranged towards the front of the building, with His Lordship's study and the Library towards the end of each corridor. I could hear the sounds of a piano, hesitantly played. The footmen ushered Lord Duxbury into the house with proper obsequiousness. As before, Pemberthy and I followed, and Ricoletti limped in after us.

Once inside, the full horror of the clash of taste between the Prince Regent and the Prince Consort hit me like a bolt of lightning. The hall was papered with green-and-gold stripes, and lit with carved wooden sconces. Heavily-carved chairs were positioned between the doors that led to various rooms. Paintings were hung along the walls leading to the ballroom and billiard-room at either end of the gallery.

Pemberthy and I were greeted by the butler, who regarded me with a raised eyebrow that took in my shabby lounge suit, scuffed boots and battered hat. Pemberthy mentioned that I had a portmanteau and would Reeves get someone to deal with it while I met the family?

"I shall assign Mr. Holmes to the Green Bedroom," Reeves said loftily. "Lord Sylvester is currently occupying the Red Suite. Mrs. Ricoletti has taken the Yellow Chamber. I shall put Mr. Ricoletti in the Blue Chamber."

Here, I could tell, was a butler of parts, which parts included a bald pate surrounded by venerable white hair, a long and melancholy face set between side-whiskers that the Archbishop of Canterbury might envy, and an air of unwavering gravity. No matter what odd thing the Young Master might drag in, be it a mongrel puppy or a stray undergraduate friend, this butler would deal with it firmly and decisively.

Pemberthy didn't wait, but took me off to the Grand Drawing Room, where Lady Ginevra Olney (aged seventeen) was practicing the piano under the eye of an overdressed and over-ripe lady of unknown age.

"No, no, no, Miss Olney," this woman scolded her charge. "It should be a G, not an A."

"Hallo, Ginny," Pemberthy greeted his sister. "Here's my friend Holmes. Holmes, m'sister. And Mrs. Ricoletti."

This, then, was the objectionable Ricoletti's even more objectionable wife. Aside from her suspiciously black hair and noticeable scent, I could find nothing particularly abominable about her. You could find her like any day, strolling in Bond Street. You would not, however, expect to find her like sitting in the private rooms of the Earl of Duxbury.

She simpered in her seat and attempted to continue the interrupted lesson, peering at the two of us through close-set black eyes.

"Oh, I don't think I want to practice any more," Lady Ginevra announced. "I thought I heard Mama and Uncle Sylvester coming in. Mama hunts," she explained. I was to learn that phrase well. It would be used to explain a good deal about the Duxbury household.

Mrs. Ricoletti shrugged and took Lady Ginevra's petulance in her stride. "As you wish, my dear, but you should be able to play a little. It makes a better impression."

"When we go up to London, I won't have to play," Lady Ginevra pouted.

"What do you think, Mr. Holmes? Should not a lady be able to display her talents at the pianoforte?" Mrs. Ricoletti produced a large fan and peered at me over it.

Pemberthy was about to say something, when we were interrupted by loud shouts and halloos from the hall. The cupola produced an echoing effect that magnified every sound. The intrepid Nimrods marched into the drawing-room, dropping bits of mud and worse on the carpets. Lady Gertrude Duxbury and her brother, Lord Sylvester Varleigh, were upon us, loudly proclaiming their prowess.

"A good run," Lord Sylvester announced, draping himself around a chair carved within an inch of its life. "We had some difficulty over Giles's Brook, but we got over and caught the scent . . ."

Lady Duxbury recognized her oldest son. "Oh, there you are, Philip. Is this your college friend? Let's have a look at him." I was paraded in front of Lady Duxbury. I could see where Pemberthy got his physique. Lady Gertrude Duxbury was tall and slender, with the same sandy hair and protuberant blue eyes as her son. Dressed in her riding habit, liberally splashed with mud, striding about the drawing-room, she made her presence felt. As for Lord Sylvester, he was at best a shadow of his older sister, shorter and sandier, with a wispy mustache and pale blue eyes that never seemed to light anywhere in particular. The two of them ignored Lady Ginevra and her chaperone, while Lady Duxbury rang for tea and Lord Sylvester looked around for something stronger.

Pemberthy muttered something about seeing me to my rooms, and the two of us were about to make our escape, when Lord Duxbury and Ricoletti appeared, shortly followed by Reeves and the tea-tray.

"Hallo, my dear. Had a good run?" Lord Duxbury greeted his wife, who seemed reasonably pleased to see him. Ricoletti, on the other hand, was more restrained with his own lady. She, in turn, favored him with an upraised eyebrow and a snap of her fan.

"I see you are returned, Ricoletti." Mrs. Ricoletti waved her fan at Lady Ginevra. "The young lady makes no progress. I do not teach her again."

"The girl has to be able to play," Lady Duxbury decreed. "Sylvester, don't you agree?"

Lord Sylvester had little to say, his mouth being filled with seed-cake at the moment.

Mrs. Ricoletti decided to get huffy. "I come to teach only at the request of my dear Ricoletti. The young lady is not a musician. I do not teach her any more. Ricoletti, we must talk. Lady Duxbury, with permission . . . ?"

The countess paid her as little attention as if she had been a yapping hound. Instead, she turned to her husband.

"Lord Duxbury, is the London house ready for habitation?"

"Yes, my dear. You may take Ginevra to London whenever you like." Lord Duxbury helped himself to cake, and accepted a cup of tea from Reeves.

"I would not wish to leave until the Hunt Ball," Lady Duxbury declared. "Who are these people coming for dinner tomorrow?"

"Dons from Cambridge, my dear. Asking my advice about the architecture of the new laboratory being built at the bequest of the Duke of Cavendish. And the Henleys, and Lady Finton and her daughter . . ."

"Another demned commission?" sneered Lord Sylvester.

"Her Majesty was pleased to appoint me, recalling my efforts during the erection of the Crystal Palace, on behalf of the late Prince Consort. His Royal Highness was always ready to consult—"

"Er . . . Mother, may I present my friend, Mr. Sherlock Holmes?" Pemberthy broke in on what was apparently an old reminiscence.

Lady Duxbury looked me over. "Holmes. I don't know any Holmes. Who are your people, eh?"

"My father came from Yorkshire, I believe. And my mother was related to the French painter, Vernet." I aimed this at the artistic earl.

"Vernet, eh? Never met him myself, but he was of a previous generation. I, of course, was in Paris for the '48. What a time, eh? Ricoletti? Out there on the barricades—"

"Nonsense!" Lady Duxbury interrupted him. "Duxbury, you know perfectly well that your father and mine removed you from that vicinity well before there was any physical danger. Philip, I trust you will dress properly for dinner. Ginevra, have you been in my jewel-box again?"

Lady Ginevra put down her teacup. "No, Mama."

"Well, someone has been. Prinny's Brooch is missing."

There was a sudden silence, as the murmured conversation between the Ricolettis ceased.

"Are you sure?" Lord Pemberthy asked.

"Of course I'm sure. I told Annie to set it out, to wear tonight with my dark blue velvet. I thought Ginevra was plundering again. Apparently not."

Pemberthy dragged me forward. "Holmes is very good at this sort of thing, Mother. If anyone can find it, he can."

"Really?" This time Lady Duxbury took a closer look at me.

"If you could tell me exactly what is missing, perhaps I would have a better idea of how to go about finding it," I said.

"A brooch. A pin of silver, formed in the shape of the Prince-of-Wales' ostrich plumes, set with twelve small but exquisitely matched diamonds. It was given to the First Lady Duxbury, my grandmother, by the Prince Regent, on the first visit of His Royal Highness to Duxbury Place," Lord Duxbury explained. "It is an heirloom, worn only by the Countess of Duxbury and handed down from one to the other. My mother gave it to Lady Duxbury on our marriage morning."

"And where is it usually kept?" I asked.

"In my jewel-box, with my other trinkets."

"And who has access to your jewel-box?"

Lady Duxbury gave me a hard stare. "My maid, Annie, who has been with me for ten years. She came highly recommended from Surrey Castle. My daughter, Ginevra, who occasionally likes to look at the jewels."

"No one else?"

"Certainly not!" Lady Duxbury said scornfully.

"May I be permitted to examine your dressing-room, Lady Duxbury?" I asked.

"Ah, young man," Mrs. Ricoletti said coyly, "you are neither young enough or old enough to gain the entrée into a lady's boudoir."

Lady Duxbury shot her a poisonous look. "I intend to search the dressing-room myself. It is nearly time to dress for dinner. Duxbury, I want a word with you in private. The rest of you may leave."

It had all the air of a Royal Dismissal. I gulped down my tea and followed Pemberthy to the hall.

"I've got to examine the scene of the crime," I told him.

"After dinner," he said. "I'll get Ginny to play one of her pieces. That Ricoletti woman's supposed to be a music teacher, of all things."

"Is she?" I asked.

Pemberthy looked disgusted. "I wouldn't have believed it of the Pater, bringing the pair of them down here. Now, Holmes, do your stuff. Tell me what's going on."

How could I explain to this well-bred dolt that I needed some more evidence before I could tell what, if anything, was "going on"? "I'm not a mind-reader, Pemberthy. At the moment, all I can tell you is that your uncle is an inconsiderate boor and I cannot imagine why your mother permits her daughter to be in the same room as Mrs. Ricoletti."

"Uncle Sylvester's been a lout ever since I can remember, and Mama doesn't look beyond the end of her horse in hunting season," Pemberthy said grouchily. "You'll have to do better than that."

I remembered that when I knocked him down in the boxing ring, he had not been satisfied until he returned the favor. That genial exterior masked a most vindictive soul. This was not going to be an easy visit.

It got more difficult when I got to my assigned room. Reeves himself laid out my evening kit, most of which I had borrowed from Trevor. When I saw Reeves, he bowed magisterially, throwing me into a fit of embarrassment.

"I could not help overhearing that you are to investigate the disappearances from this residence of various small objects," he said gravely.

"Well, Pemberthy asked me . . ."

"Lord Pemberthy's enthusiasms are well-known in this house. However, you may need some information, which, as servants, we are bound by honor not to divulge."

"I must examine Lady Duxbury's jewel-box to find out if the lock has been forced," I said.

Reeves nodded. "I shall inquire of Miss Milsap, Lady Duxbury's personal attendant," he said.

"And I'll want to get into the other bed-chambers, too," I said. "May I speak to Miss Annie Milsap?"

"Certainly, but not until after dinner. No one has left Duxbury Place today, I can assure you of that, and if the brooch has been removed from the Place previous to today, haste will not serve. I shall enquire in the Servants Hall as to the movements of the guests and Family for the last week. And I do wish you well, Mr. Holmes."

"That's very kind of you, um, Reeves," I said.

"Not at all. Miss Annie Milsap is my sister's husband's brother's daughter. My niece, in effect. I cannot believe such a person would steal from her employer. No suspicion has ever darkened the character of one of My People."

"It doesn't seem likely," I admitted. "The only problem is, with Lady Duxbury so dead set on me not getting into her dressing-room, how am I supposed to find this brooch?"

"Observation and deduction, and a sifting of the facts, Mr. Holmes. When one has eliminated the impossible, whatever remains, however improbable, must be the truth. It is fortunate that you are a stranger in the house, and not a particular friend of Mr. Philip. Excellent. It will sit much better with Lord Duxbury if the bad news comes from you."

"What bad news?"

"I fear Lord Duxbury's confidence in Mr. Ricoletti is misplaced." Reeves looked more mournful than ever. "I have heard of houses in which Goings-On are permitted. Such things do not occur at Duxbury Place. Yet I have heard Mrs. Ricoletti's voice in the East Wing, where the gentlemen have their chambers."

"Surely, Ricoletti's room is in the East Wing. A married lady's entitled to, er, visit her husband."

"Undoubtedly," Reeves said. "By the bye, Lord Duxbury's ruby studs were in his possession no later than last week, according to Mr. Darling, who is His Lordship's valet. They are not in the jewel-case now. Lord Duxbury's visit to the Metropolis was a brief one, for the purpose of setting the town house to rights." He listened, as if hearing angels in the distance. "I must attend to dinner. You appear to be a resourceful young man," Reeves said. "I am sure you will find a way. I may add, on behalf of the Hall, that if you can remove suspicion from the Staff, we will be forgiving in the matter of vails★."

★Tips bestowed upon the household staff by a departing guest.

With which Parthian shot he bowed himself out, leaving me to my thoughts, which were whirling about like the proverbial windmill.

I had barely time to complete my toilet when the bell rang for dinner. With only three women to set against five men, the table was somewhat uneven. Popsy and I were in the middle of the table, with Lord Sylvester next to his sister, and Ricoletti next to the Earl. That left Pemberthy across the table from me, and me between Lady Ginevra and Mrs. Ricoletti.

As Lady Duxbury had insisted, dress was formal. Lady Ginevra wore an appropriately debutante confection of pink gauze; Lady Duxbury was arrayed in dark blue velvet; but Mrs. Ricoletti had donned a gown of gold and scarlet, liberally trimmed with brilliants, cut very low in the front.

It may have been a delicious dinner, but I couldn't taste any of it. My attention was divided between Lady Ginevra, who prattled on about her forthcoming Presentation, and Mrs. Ricoletti, whose ample endowments threatened to burst loose of their skimpy moorings. Ricoletti glowered at her across the table, and Pemberthy glowered at me across the table, and I tried not to look at the abundance before me.

I cannot tell you what passed for dinner-table conversation. It is blocked out of my mind by the memory of Mrs. Ricoletti nearly spilling out of her décolletage. Lady Duxbury ignored the scenery, devoting herself equally to her brother and her daughter. The Earl, at the other end of the table, discussed Art and Paris with the Ricolettis. Evidently, this was indeed a House divided.

Lady Duxbury decided finally to acknowledge my presence. "You, Holmes!" she hallooed. "How are you getting on with your investigation?"

"I haven't had much opportunity to investigate," I said. "I am puzzled by the nature of the theft. The pin in question is valuable?"

"The stones are diamonds," Lord Duxbury said. "But the true value is historical. The association with His Royal Highness."

"Then it would be well-known to collectors?"

"Instantly," Lord Duxbury said.

"How valuable are the stones themselves?"

"Worth a few hundred pounds, I suppose," Lord Duxbury said, with a shrug.

"An interesting problem," I said. "Why would anyone steal a piece of jewelry that could not be sold as a whole and would bring infinitely less if broken up? Is it always kept in your jewel-case, Lady Duxbury?"

"Of course. It's a nice little pin, and I often wear it."

"And when did you last wear the piece?" I asked.

Lady Duxbury considered as the footmen removed the plates and set out the gâteau for dessert. "Didn't I wear it last month, at the opening of the Royal Academy Salon?" she asked the Earl.

"With His Royal Highness in attendance, I thought it appropriate. I am on the committee," Lord Duxbury explained. "The Prince of Wales has been kind enough to take some of my suggestions for his estate at Sandringham."

"Rackety set around His Royal Highness," Lady Duxbury decreed." He's a racing man, though. Good eye for a horse." That, presumably, would excuse a lot with Lady Duxbury.

Dessert was cleared and the ladies left. I was able to get a better look at Ricoletti, who only sipped at his port and refused the offer of a cigar. His face was drawn, as if his twisted foot was paining him, and he excused himself after a few minutes.

"Poor chap," Lord Duxbury sighed. "He was let go from his position at the Louvre when the Commune took power."

"A friend of your youth?" I hinted.

"Can't precisely place him," Lord Duxbury admitted. "But there were so many good chaps about in Monmartre. It was a village then, with plenty of good rooms, going cheap. Good light, and excellent subjects, you know. Those were the days . . . *'Mais ou sont les neiges . . .'* He sighed and looked soulfully at the carved furniture about him.

Pemberthy gave me a look as if to say, Now you've set him off.

"How did you come to meet him again?" I asked, trying to stave off the flood of reminiscence.

"Interesting thing, that. Sylvester, do you recall introducing me to Ricoletti in Paris? Or was it at the races at Deauville?"

Lord Sylvester shifted uneasily in his seat and swallowed his port quickly. "Don't really remember, Deauville. Lost a packet, that's all. Always do." He poured himself more port.

Pemberthy gave me the narrow-eyed stare he gave slackers who didn't put their backs into it.

"Shall we join the ladies?" Duxbury said, heaving himself up. "And Holmes, I would like to show you some of the collections. My grandfather was a notable connoisseur, much liked by the Prince Regent, and we have several items with connections to our royal patron. His Royal Highness, the Prince Consort, was kind enough to comment on some of our acquisitions. I should like your opinion of the new paintings. I warn you, some are quite startlingly advanced."

I followed the older gentlemen to where Lady Duxbury sat in the larger drawing-room listening to her daughter's performance with the critical look of one who is measuring the strides of a new pacer. Mrs. Ricoletti emerged from a corner, all glitter and gleam.

"My wife is a noted musician," Ricoletti announced.

"Ah. Perhaps she will give us some music," Pemberthy said, as if prompted.

In truth, Mrs. Ricoletti was an adequate performer, and she went through a sonata with accuracy if not artistry. Meanwhile, I was carried off by Lord Duxbury, who had evidently decided that I was a fellow-artist, and was shown small Egyptian vases, Chinese porcelain statuettes, and enamelled boxes with the Prince Regent's portrait on them. He then produced the objectionable works of art fresh from Paris.

I could see why Popsy would find them strange. Most of the

paintings were mere dabs of color against the canvas, shocking the eye with blue and green and violet next to each other. Ricoletti stood behind the Earl, offering comments, while Popsy Pemberthy glowered and Mrs. Ricoletti tinkled away at the piano. It was not one of the more enlivening evenings of my life, and I never got out of the drawing-room to search for the missing pin.

The tea-tray was brought in, and the evening ended with Pemberthy dragging me off to the billiard-room at the farthest end of the hall.

"Well? what do you think now?" he demanded.

"What do you expect me to find out?" I countered. "The brooch must still be here. No one left after we got here, as far as I can tell. I'll have to search the place. What did you mean, blatting out that you'd brought me here to find the thief? I thought you wanted me to be discreet!"

"Don't blame me! Everyone knows everything around here," Pemberthy said sulkily.

"There must be a million places to hide a little thing like a brooch. Vases, snuff-boxes, all sorts of odd things in cabinets and curios and whatnots . . ." The sheer enormity of the task left me speechless. "I'll have to look in all of them!"

Pemberthy rubbed his nose. "Mama usually rides out early with Uncle Sylvester," he said. "The governor sometimes walks in the garden with Ricoletti."

"What about your sister and her governess?"

"Mrs. Ricoletti isn't her governess. She got rid of that poor soul when she turned sixteen. Ricoletti sprang his wife on the Governor in Paris. The next thing we knew, the pair of them were established here for the summer. The Governor said that Ginevra could practice her French on Mrs. Ricoletti, and Mama was taken up with the new colts . . . Mama hunts."

"Well, can you get them out of the house long enough for me to search their rooms?"

Pemberthy scratched his head. "I'll think of something. Look,

Holmes, I'm counting on you. That Ricoletti's been hanging onto the Governor like a damned leech, and there's something nasty about that wife of his. You've got to get the goods on them!"

"But . . ." As far as I could tell, there weren't any goods to get! Ricoletti and his wife might be unpleasant, but there was no proof that they were thieves, and one doesn't tell one's host, or the father of one's host, that the friend of his bosom is pinching the family heirlooms.

I lay awake that night, tossing about in my luxurious bed, until the dawn, listening to the sounds the house made. I was just dropping off when I heard the pattering of feet up and down the halls as hot shaving-water was deposited at the doors of those rooms occupied by gentlemen. A stately tread was obviously Reeves. Then came the heavier clump of footmen, and a step somewhere between, still male, probably the valets of Lord Duxbury and Lord Sylvester, come to rouse their masters for a day of country revelry. Finally, a quick, light step that somehow sounded "wrong," although I could not quite understand why.

I shaved myself and got down to breakfast, to see what the Duxbury clan had laid on for the wayward guest. True to form, Lady Duxbury was in her habit, ready for an invigorating gallop.

"Cubbing begins soon," she proclaimed, over a vast platter of ham and eggs. "New hunters are ready to break in. Care to ride, Mr. Holmes?"

"Er . . . not this morning," I demurred.

"Dr. Moresby and Mr. Darwin will be arriving this afternoon," Lord Duxbury said, from his end of the table. "They have some interesting theories on the restoration of Old Masters, and the verification of paintings. You may find their discourse interesting, Mr. Holmes."

"I'm sure I shall, sir."

"Nonsense. A dead bore," Lady Duxbury dismissed the Cambridge dons with a wave of her hand. "Sylvester, are you ready?"

"When you wish, Gertrude." Lord Sylvester hopped to his feet and trotted after his sister like a well-trained hound.

Lady Ginevra bounced into the breakfast-room. "Is Uncle Sylvester gone?" she asked.

"All safe," her brother replied.

"I wish he'd find somewhere else to stay," Lady Ginevra said, helping herself from the sideboard. "Grandpapa won't have him back to Surrey. Something about playing baccarat. And he says his rooms in London are being redecorated."

"What rot!" Pemberthy grumbled. "He's probably been locked out for non-payment of his rent."

Lord Duxbury looked distressed. "Remember, children, he is your mother's favorite brother. She would be most put out if he were to be made unhappy."

Lady Ginevra was about to give her own opinion of her uncle, but the conversation was stopped dead by the entrance of the Ricoletti pair: Mr. Ricoletti in his usual black, and Mrs. Ricoletti in a patterned morning dress, decorated with several cameo brooches.

"Such a lovely day," Mrs. Ricoletti trilled. "Lady Ginevra, you and I must take our walk into the garden. Mr. Holmes, will you join us?"

"Ah . . ." I looked wildly at Pemberthy. My host did not fail me.

"I promised Holmes a look at the library," Pemberthy said. "And maybe we'll walk down to the village."

"It looks quite pleasant now, but you know how changeable the weather is at this time of the year," Ricoletti said. His voice insinuated much more than the merest pleasantry. "Lord Duxbury, may I accompany these two young men on their literary journeyings?"

There was nothing we could do but let him trail after us. I went over every bibelot and curio in every whatnot and cabinet in the entire place, all under the glittering eyes of Ricoletti, who persisted in dogging my steps for the entire morning. When Lady

Duxbury arrived for the midday collation, his place was taken by Mrs. Ricoletti, who proved to be even more adhesive than her husband. I was exhausted when we were summoned to the salon for tea.

The gentlemen from Cambridge had just arrived, and were being shown to their rooms, where they could rest before dinner. Mr. Darwin was not the celebrated naturalist, but one of his equally celebrated sons. Professor Moreton had brought his wife along for the experience of dining with the Earl of Duxbury. None of the notables deigned to recognize the existence of a mere undergraduate, and one from Oxford, at that.

Lady Ginevra took pity on me and handed me my teacup. "Have you found Prinny's Brooch?" she whispered.

"It's not downstairs," I told her. "I've looked everywhere you could hide it, and a few places you couldn't. There's no way around it. I'll have to search the bed-chambers."

"Can't you ask the servants to do that?" Lady Ginevra said carelessly.

"If one of them is the thief, the others will certainly try to cover it up," I reminded her. "Can you keep the Ricolettis downstairs tonight after dinner? I can excuse myself, and search their rooms then."

"Do you really think it's them? What fun!" Lady Ginevra giggled. "I've always wondered what sort of hold Ricoletti has on Papa."

"Ginevra, you must get dressed for dinner!" Lady Duxbury interrupted us. She gave me the hard-eyed stare reserved for impecunious younger sons who made up to her daughter and moved away. The Professor and Mrs. Moreton sat stiffly holding teacups, while Mr. Darwin chatted with Lord Duxbury. Reeves approached me with the same withering glare as his mistress.

"The coast is clear, Mr. Holmes. Perhaps you should attempt to explore the upper story now, before our guests disperse to dress for dinner," he muttered.

It seemed as good a time as any. I took advantage of the lull to nip up the grand staircase and reconnoiter. The bedchambers were lined up on the upper story, with the men's rooms to the right of the stairs, and the ladies' rooms to the left. The vastness of the cupola filled the intervening space.

I would have made a wretched burglar. I tackled the first bedroom door I came to, which appeared to be that of Lord Duxbury himself. I was met by the frowning face of my lord's valet, which was enough to convince me that his lordship was not hiding his own jewelry.

The next room, Lord Sylvester's, was unoccupied. I noted the strong scent of his hair preparation, underlaid with some other odor I could not quite identify, but no sooner had I started turning over his toilet articles than I heard a step in the hall, that same step which had so puzzled me early that morning. I listened carefully, then poked my head out into the hall. There was the sound of a door closing, but when I poked my head into the hall, all the doors were closed. The sound of the rest of the company ascending the stairs got me out of Lord Sylvester's room, and I met Lord Duxbury and his distinguished guests as they arrived at the landing.

"Ah, Holmes. Gentlemen, this is the young man I told you about, a student at the Other Place."

I bowed as best I could, and smiled weakly. I felt like that child who was caught with his hand in the sweets-tin. Having singularly failed yet again to fulfill all hopes, I returned to my own room, only to be met by Reeves.

"I assume you have not been successful," the butler said balefully. "You have been given a great deal of latitude, Mr. Holmes. More was expected of you."

"I don't have much to go on," I protested.

"Observation and deduction," Reeves reminded me. "That is the method, Mr. Holmes." With that, he withdrew.

Very well. I tried to recall what I had observed, and make deductions from it. Ricoletti had found a snug berth here, it's true, but you can't put a man in jail for finding a likely nest. Mrs. Ricoletti was common, but if you could put a woman in the dock for being common, half of London and most of the provinces would be up on charges at Old Bailey. And Lord Sylvester was probably a wrong'un, but he was also a Duke's son, and as such, untouchable.

I went down to dinner ruminating on these facts, promising myself to observe every nuance of the suspects' behavior. Alas, my good intentions went out the window. Not only were the two Cambridge dons and Mrs. Moreton in attendance, but so were a fair number of the local gentry, who had also been invited to partake of the Duxbury board. I was stationed at the very bottom of the table, next to Lady Ginevra, who, as the daughter of the house not officially "out," was deemed socially "below the salt." With Ricoletti near the top of the table, where he could discuss Art with the dons, and Mrs. Ricoletti somewhere near the middle, I was separated from the Most Likely Suspects by acres of plate and a vast epergne draped in late roses.

There was no way out of the ceremonious Passing the Port, either. Ricoletti was very much in evidence, and I had to admit that he sounded as if he knew what he was talking about when he discussed Old Masters. I was especially interested in the chemical theories advanced by the Cambridge gentlemen, and was jolted to my senses by Pemberthy's acute "Ahem!"

"Ah . . . if I may be excused . . ." I stammered, and stumbled out of the dining room and up to the bedchamber floors.

I turned to the ladies' wing, wishing I could have enlisted Lady Ginevra in my search. Alas, the stumbling notes of the pianoforte indicated that she was doggedly keeping up her end, while I did mine. I approached the Countess's boudoir with reluctant feet, and hoped no one would catch me there.

I could see the massive jewel-case, brimming with stones, on her dressing-table. Easy enough to purloin one small piece from that collection, I thought. Whoever took it must have thought it to be a mere trinket. There were several brooches decorated with large stones in full sight.

The next bedroom appeared to be the one assigned to the Professor's wife, so that she could dress for dinner. Beyond that . . . I heard a clatter in the hallway and ducked into the first open door I could see.

One breath told me that I had reached Mrs. Ricoletti's room. It reeked of her scent, and the bodice of the ensemble she had worn the evening before was thrown carelessly on a chair. I heard her voice in the hall, and looked wildly about for a hiding-place. There was the wardrobe . . . too small. The window? Not open. Aha! I inserted myself under the bed.

Mrs. Ricoletti trotted in quickly. I could hear her moving about, apparently repairing some damage to her costume. She said something in French, then stopped. Someone was tapping at the door.

I heard her open the door. I could see Ricoletti's twisted foot and ebony cane in front of my nose. The heel of his shoe was directly in my line of vision. I stared at the built-up shoe, and realized there was something quite unusual about the way the heel was constructed.

"Have you got it?" she asked. Ricoletti said something in a low and muffled voice. From the little I could hear, he was extremely annoyed with his wife.

"How was I supposed to know it was so valuable? Well, no help for it. That fool of an undergraduate has been searching the place all day. We will have to wait until you can get it to London with the rest of . . . what was that?"

I suppose it happens to everyone. You are in a place where you should not be, at a time when you are supposed to be somewhere else. It is vital that you be absolutely quiet. And your nose itches.

As mine did. I rubbed it against the nearest thing, which was a low-backed high-heeled slipper, drenched with Mrs. Ricoletti's distinctive scent. Between the dust and the scent, the inevitable happened. I sneezed.

There was a flurry of activity in the room. Mrs. Ricoletti bent down, revealing even more of her charms than before, and yanked me out. Ricoletti grabbed me by the collar and roared Italian imprecations into one ear, while Mrs. Ricoletti protested her innocence in shrill and distinctly unladylike French. The noise drew more bystanders. The door opened to reveal Lady Duxbury and Lord Sylvester, with the two Dons, Mrs. Moreton, and the Earl somewhere behind the crowd, and Reeves looming over all like the fellow on the Monument.

"What is going on here!" boomed out Lady Duxbury.

"Ah, the passionate young man!" Mrs. Ricoletti enfolded me in a vigorous embrace. "But Locky, *cara mia,* you should have waited until all was quiet!" And she planted a kiss on my mouth before I could protest.

Lord Duxbury managed to get me out of her grasp and into the hall before Ricoletti could challenge me to a duel or whatever Italians were supposed to do to undergraduates who invaded their wives' bedrooms. As for Pemberthy, he looked on me with fear and loathing, while I tried to wipe that abominable woman's lip-rouge off my face.

It was then that I began to put together the events that had been taking place at Duxbury Place. I was marched down into the drawing-room, where the local gentry were all regaled with my effrontery in invading Mrs. Ricoletti's private quarters. I was the subject of much hilarity, and I felt my cheeks burning with the humiliation of it. I would go down in the history of Duxbury Place as "The Fellow Who Was Found Under the Bed." I retired to a corner of the Grand Drawing-Room and cogitated furiously while the tea-tray was brought in, and the party broke up.

Not until the local people had taken their leave did I dare to leave my refuge and attempt to explain my shocking lack of decorum.

"Lord Duxbury, Lady Duxbury . . . may I be allowed to explain my actions this evening?" I said.

Lord Duxbury smirked at me. "I can't wait to hear it, my boy."

I glanced at Pemberthy and swallowed hard. "My friend, Lord Pemberthy, asked me to come here, as you suggested last night, to investigate the mysterious disappearances of small items of jewelry in this house. I developed a hypothesis, and I was on my way to proving it when I was, um, interrupted."

"In my wife's bedroom!" Ricoletti growled.

"Yes . . . I was searching for the piece of jewelry known as Prinny's brooch," I said.

"And you dared to think it might be hidden there!" Ricoletti rose, bracing himself on his stick, and strode over to me. If he'd had a glove, I believe he would have struck me with it.

I leaped back, quickly, and the man, unable to stand on his twisted foot, toppled to his knees, dropping the stick. I grabbed the stick and tapped the heel of the shoe of the club foot. It parted, revealing a hollow, and nestled within it, a glittering object.

Pemberthy himself plucked it from its hiding place and presented it to his mother.

"Why . . . it's Prinny's Brooch!" she exclaimed. "How did you know?"

"Observation and deduction," I said proudly. "I had searched every possible hiding place. I then had to think of some other ones. In an older house, there might have been a secret panel or Priest's Hole, but this is a relatively new building with no such cache. I was informed by a reliable source," I glanced at Reeves, "that none of the servants had removed the items in question, and they would have informed his Lordship if they found them.

"The items were small, valuable, but not ostentatious, with the exception of the ruby shirt-studs mentioned by Lord Duxbury. The pin known as Prinny's Brooch was not removed from the house, ergo, it must still be here. And the only strangers were the Ricolettis.

"I knew that Mr. Ricoletti, if he were the thief, would have to have an accomplice. He could not possibly get into the Countess's dressing-room, and he has not been on the premises for at least a week. He was necessary to the scheme, in that he would take the jewels to a reliable fence, where they could be turned into cash for himself, his wife, and his employer."

"Employer!" Lord Duxbury exploded.

"It struck me, sir, that this scheme needed three people. One who knew the great houses and where the jewels were; one to purloin them; and one to remove them and take them to a receiver of stolen goods. Mrs. Ricoletti had access to the ladies' dressing-rooms; she has been in residence here all summer. Mr. Ricoletti, on the other hand, is in attendance on Lord Duxbury, and accompanies him to London frequently.

"There remains but one other person to name in this foul scheme. I am very sorry, Lady Duxbury, but your brother, Lord Sylvester Varleigh, is the true scoundrel in this matter."

"How dare you!" Lord Sylvester rose in dishonest wrath. "Do you know who I am?"

"Yes, sir. According to my brother Mycroft, who is rarely mistaken on such matters, you are the one who is already under suspicion of having cheated at cards at certain London clubs. Your gambling debts are becoming notorious. You hit on this scheme to rob your sister, threatening your brother-in-law with her, er, wrath, if he made your peccadillos known to her.

"It was you who introduced Mr. Ricoletti to Lord Duxbury in France earlier this year. It was you who induced Ricoletti to use his infirmity to carry small pieces of jewelry away to London, where they could be sold to collectors for sums that you could then gamble away."

Lord Sylvester's shrill bellow turned to a cringing whine. "Gertrude, are you going to allow this?"

Lady Duxbury was rigid with indignation. "Sylvester, you are a thief. You always were a thief. Stealing Prinny's Brooch is the Last Straw!"

Lord Duxbury nodded. "Very good reasoning, Mr. Holmes. But . . . have you any proof that will stand up in a court of law?"

"Only the fact that Lord Sylvester's room still held traces of Mrs. Ricoletti's scent, proving that she was there, and quite recently, too. And I heard the sound of her high-heeled slippers early this morning, echoing in the hall. Mr. Ricoletti's room is across the hall from mine, but these footsteps came from Lord Sylvester's room."

The Earl harumphed. "Still not proof positive of Mrs. Ricoletti's guilt," he said.

"I suggest you examine the brilliants that decorate Mrs. Ricoletti's crimson dress," I said. "Sewn among them are the ruby studs. Since you yourself have said that you do not wear them, the only way they could have been put on that dress is if they had been removed by someone who knew about them. Ricoletti could not possibly have seen them in France, but Mrs. Ricoletti has been in residence here with Lord Sylvester."

Lady Duxbury now rose to her feet, her eyes blazing with righteous fury. "Sylvester, you have run your limit!" she declared. "Remove yourself and your . . . your paramour from this house at once!"

Lord Sylvester cringed and looked at Mrs. Ricoletti. He got no help from that quarter. Both the Ricolettis were ready to apply the poison dagger to their one-time confederate.

"I suggest we send for the police," Mr. Darwin said hesitantly. The Duxbury clan looked around at the two Cambridge Dons. They had quite forgotten that their little family drama was being played before an audience.

Lady Duxbury frowned. "That would never do. Not with my daughter about to come out! The scandal would ruin her!"

Lord Duxbury glanced at his guests. "I trust you gentlemen will maintain a decent reticence about this distressing family problem. You understand, I have bought several paintings for the Royal collections under the advisement of Ricoletti. It would be extremely embarrassing if this came to the ears of Certain Royal Personages."

"But . . ." Mr. Darwin looked puzzled. "You cannot mean to let these criminals escape!"

Lady Duxbury glared at her brother. "I intend to send my brother to Surrey Castle tomorrow. My father will know what to do with him."

From the look on Lord Sylvester's face, he would have preferred to take his chances at the Old Bailey than face the wrath of the Duke of Surrey.

Pemberthy suddenly realized something else. "See here, I can't go back to college with someone who's found out that my uncle is a jewel thief. Imagine, sitting across from him in Hall . . ."

"Really Popsy! D'you think I'm looking forward to sitting in chapel with someone who saw that Abominable Woman kiss me and call me 'Locky'?"

Professor Moreton smiled understandingly. "Lord Duxbury, you have always been generous to our college," he said. "Perhaps the air of the Cam will prove more salubrious for your young friend than the air of the Thames, and the Bridge will be more congenial than the Ford, eh?"

I bowed as gracefully as I could. "I leave the whole thing in your hands, sir," I told Lord Duxbury.

"Then I suggest you get to your bed, Mr. Holmes. In your own chamber. It has been an eventful evening, eh? And tomorrow, you can accompany these two gentlemen back to Cambridge in time for Term."

I left the grown-ups to settle the fates of the Ricolettis and Lord Sylvester, and went to my room like a schoolboy. Reeves shortly followed me there, smiling gravely.

"What's going to happen to the Ricolettis?" I asked.

"They are presently packing their clothes. They will be escorted to the boat-train by one of our footmen, who will set them on their way to France. You have done quite well, young man, and we will not be too forward in the matter of vails. You should consider the possibilities of this avenue of advancement, Mr. Holmes. You have a talent for it."

And that was the end of it," Holmes said, finishing up his pipe and knocking the ashes into the fireplace. "Ricoletti and his abominable wife were packed off to France, and Lord Sylvester was blackballed from his clubs and had to go to America, where he lived by his wits until he charmed a millionaire's daughter into marrying him. Popsy Pemberthy returned to Oxford, and I took a year at Caius and Gonville College, where I learned a great deal that was useful to me in later days. Lady Ginevra is now Lady Ginevra Evesham, and will someday be the Duchess of Malby. The Earl continued to sit on Royal Commissions, until his death last year from pneumonia after a visit to Balmoral. Now Popsy is the Fourth Earl, and he has sent me this invitation, with no other object but to regale the rest of the company with the tale of how I was found under that abominable woman's bed."

"But why do you persist in calling that woman 'abominable'?" I asked. "Common, certainly . . . but abominable?"

Holmes's face took on the rigidity of a graven image. "She deliberately embarrassed me in front of the entire company, thinking that I would be deterred from my purpose. She persuaded her husband, who until then was as honest as an art dealer could be, to become the accomplice of a thief, who was also her lover. That is abominable enough, I believe."

"Ah, well," I said, now replete with tea and scones, ready to face the wild November storm outside. "You did get something out of it."

"I did indeed," Holmes said, with a rare smile. "I got an education that surpassed that of both Oxford and Cambridge. And if someone should ask what set my feet on the path of detection, I would have to answer, The Butler did it."

H.P. Lovecraft (1890–1937) was America's most influential horror writer since Edgar Allan Poe. Author of several volumes of occult fiction, including such classics as "The Rats in the Walls" and "The Music of Erich Zann," HPL was one of Weird Tales *most popular contributors. Arkham House, the Sauk City, Wisconsin, fantasy book publisher, was formed specifically to preserve Lovecraft's work. It is hard to imagine anyone other than HPL writing "The Giant Rat of Sumatra." It is an adventure that strains nearly to the breaking point Holmes's dictum that once you eliminate the impossible, whatever remains,* however improbable, *must be true. Yet before writing off this rodent tale as apocryphal, remember that The Great Detective himself said it was "a story for which the world is not yet prepared . . ."—JAF*

The Giant Rat of Sumatra

BY *"PAULA VOLSKY"*
(ASCRIBED TO H. P. LOVECRAFT)

The chill March fog shrouded London, choking the labyrinth of ancient streets, smothering forgotten courts and squares, lending solid masonry an aspect of vaporous insubstantiality. Baker Street was wreathed in detestable yellow haze, through which the gaslights glowed faintly, like the malignant Cyclopean eyes of moribund nightmares. The scene filled me with a cold, nameless apprehension, amounting to horror; a fleeting sense, perhaps, of frightful cosmic vastness pressing its gigantic weight upon the feeble protective barriers of human understanding. Man's vision, scarcely encompassing the tiny sphere of his own existence, serves to shield rather than inform, and that is as it should be, as it *must* be. For a single clear glimpse of ghastly reality would doubtless shake complacent human sanity to its very foundation.

My spirits hardly improved as I approached 221B, for I dreaded what I should find there. The recent, successful resolution of the problem involving the archbishop's indiscretion had deprived Sherlock Holmes of that intellectual stimulation so essential to his well-being. For some days past, my friend had lain silent and apathetic, sunk in the deepest of black depressions, scarcely stirring from the sofa. He had not, so far as I knew, resorted to the solace of the hypodermic syringe and cocaine bottle, and I could only pray for his continuing abstinence, for it grieves me beyond measure to witness the deliberate degradation of the marvelous mental faculties with which Nature has endowed him.

I let myself into our rooms, and a chemical reek at once assailed my nostrils. The sofa was unoccupied. Sherlock Holmes sat at the deal-topped table, its surface cluttered with motley paraphernalia. I could not guess at the nature of his experimentation, but saw at a glance that his countenance had regained its characteristic keenness of expression. He greeted my entrance with a carelessly affable wave of the hand, then turned his full attention once again upon the flasks and retorts before him. Delighted though I was by my friend's return to his own version of normality, I did not venture to question him at such a time, for he would not have relished the distraction. Repairing to the tenantless sofa, I soon lost myself in frowning cogitation. I do not know how long I sat there, before the sound of Holmes's voice roused me from my brown study.

"Come, Watson, twenty-five guineas is not an impossible sum."

I turned to stare at him, for twenty-five guineas was indeed the figure upon which my thoughts anchored.

"The price is not unreasonable, in view of the rarity of the work, and the potential value of the contents." Holmes spoke with

his customary detachment, yet could not perfectly conceal his grati-
fication at my look of transparent astonishment. Though he fancies
himself pure intellect, a flawlessly balanced calculating machine de-
void of emotion, my friend is by no means free of human vanity.

"To what work do you allude?" I inquired, in the vain hope
of confounding him.

"To Ludvig Prinn's hellish masterpiece, *De Vermis Mysteriis,*"
he replied, without hesitation. "You have striven long and hard to
beat down Charnwood's price, but the old man holds to twenty-
five guineas."

My astonishment increased. "Really, Holmes, in a more
credulous age, these displays of apparent clairvoyance might have
brought you to the stake."

"Nonsense, my dear doctor. A very simple matter of observation. When you entered, several minutes ago, you were carrying a
parcel, whose size and shape proclaimed the recent purchase of a
book. The fresh mud upon your shoes, and the moisture clinging
to your overcoat revealed that you had walked home. Two book-
stores stand within walking distance of our lodgings, and of those
two, only Charnwood's, in Marylebone Road, remains open at this
hour. The shop specializes in antique literary rarities. It was not
long ago, Watson, that you voiced your theory that certain ancient
works of occultism, rich repositories of forgotten or forbidden lore,
hold formulae of potent restoratives unknown to modern medicine. Amongst the bizarre obscenities polluting the pages of Abdul
Alhazred's *Necronomicon,* the Comte d'Erlette's infamous *Cultes des
Goules,* or the abominable *Liber Ivonis,* may lie a remedy for the
brain-fever, or so you postulate. Alhazred knows no remedy, however, for your incurable optimism."

"There is reason to believe—" I commenced, somewhat net-
tled.

"I am prepared to concede an improbable possibility," he cut
me off imperturbably, and resumed his interrupted analysis. "Of
the works I have mentioned, two of them—the *Necronomicon,* and
Liber Ivonis—are virtually unobtainable. *Cultes des Goules,* in the

unlikely event of its availability, would surely prove prohibitive in cost. Thus I conclude *De Vermis Mysteriis* to be the work in question.''

''Quite right, but that does not explain—''

''You have failed to secure the prize, however,'' Holmes continued, with an air of apathy. ''Your scowl, your preoccupation, your general aspect of dissatisfaction suggest an unsuccessful attempt to content yourself with a lesser acquisition. Twice within the last quarter hour, you have removed your wallet from your pocket, weighed it in your hand, sighed deeply, and put it away again. Clearly, the root of your indecision is financial. You have, upon occasion, paid as much as twenty guineas for works you deem professionally useful—but never more. The cost of Prinn's grotesquerie must exceed twenty guineas, but not by much, else you would instantly have dismissed all thought of purchase. Charnwood habitually prices his first editions in multiples of five guineas. It is more than probable that the volume in question is offered at twenty-five.''

''Correct, in every particular,'' I confessed. ''Bravo, Holmes. As always, when you explain your reasoning, it all seems very clear, very obvious.''

''Tiresomely so. I should fear complete stagnation, were no better mental exercise available. Fortunately, a matter of potentially greater interest has presented itself.'' From the welter atop the table, he plucked a sheet of paper. ''This note arrived some hours ago. What do you make of it, Watson?''

Here, I suspected, was the cause of my friend's abrupt recovery of spirits. Accepting the paper, I read:

Dear Mr. Holmes,

I am anxious to consult you upon a matter of gravest urgency. It is not an exaggeration to observe that innocent lives will be lost if the missing party is not soon located. My own efforts in that regard have failed, my actions have been noted, and I fear that time is running short. The luster of your fame is such that I must place my trust in your abilities. Therefore, I shall call at half-past seven this evening, in the hope that you will favor me with a reception.

Sincerely yours,
A. B.

"Singular." I returned the note to its owner.

"Quite. But what does it reveal to you?"

"Very little," I confessed. "The writer, be it man or woman, communicates considerable agitation—"

"Make no mistake, it is a man," Holmes assured me.

"How do you know?"

"Notice the decisive quality of the downstrokes, the vigor of the characters, the authority of the punctuation. A man's hand, unmistakably."

"Of some education—" I essayed.

"Excellent, Watson. At times I almost suspect you less barren of deductive power than you so often contrive to appear. Now, justify my faith. Where was he educated?"

"I cannot begin to guess," I replied, mystified.

"Good. One should never guess, it is an atrocious habit. Note the spelling. 'Luster.' And worse, 'favor.' Note the tone of extravagant, uncurbed emotion. The correspondent is clearly an American. Despite the orthographic crudities, his literacy marks him as a denizen of the comparatively civilized eastern coastal region of that nation."

"We shall see soon enough. It is half past seven."

There was a knock at our door, and our landlady entered.

"A lady to see you, sir," she informed my companion.

I repressed a smile.

"Show her in." Sherlock Holmes displayed no sign of discomfiture.

Mrs. Hudson withdrew. Moments later, a woman walked into the room. "A. B." was unusually tall, lanky and large-boned, her height evident despite a curiously stoop-shouldered posture.

Her garb was darkly simple, her shoes nondescript, her gloved hands empty. Of her features, little could be discerned. A wide hat draped in heavy veiling completely obscured her face and hair. I thought her age to be around forty years, but that was an estimate based largely upon instinct, as there was little visible evidence by which to judge.

Seating herself in the chair that Holmes placed, she spoke in a low, slightly hoarse tone, unrevealing as her costume. "It is good of you, Mr. Holmes, to receive me upon such short notice, and at such an hour. I am sensible of the courtesy."

"Your note piqued my interest," Holmes returned briskly. "As you have been at pains to stress the urgent nature of the situation, I would advise you to state your name and case without delay." His visitor's veiled face turned to me for an instant, and he added, "You may speak freely before Dr. Watson."

"It is better for all concerned," A. B. returned, "if I keep my name to myself. That is for your own protection as well as mine. Briefly, the facts are these. I am an associate of Professor Sefton Talliard, chairman of the Department of Anthropology at Brown University, in Providence, Rhode Island. Professor Talliard has been missing for some months. His enemies are diabolical, his life is greatly endangered, and it is certain that he had no choice but to flee the United States. There is reason to believe that he has hidden himself in London. It is imperative that I locate this man, as I possess certain intelligence that may preserve his life, and the lives of his surviving colleagues. I am a stranger to this city, however, and ill-equipped to conduct a search. Mr. Holmes, the matter is vital. Will you lend your assistance?"

"By no means," Holmes replied, to my surprise, for I had expected the peculiarity of the entire affair to excite his curiosity.

"I entreat you—"

"Do not trouble yourself. It is useless to suppose me willing to accept a client disinclined to disclose the true facts of his case. In any event, what confidence might you reasonably place in the powers of a consulting detective hoodwinked by so amateurish a charade?"

My friend's acerbic observation quite bewildered me, but the visitor appeared prey to no such confusion.

"I am justly rebuked. Mr. Holmes, pray accept my apologies for an attempted deception motivated less by inclination than apprehension." So saying, A. B. doffed wide hat, veiling, and wig, to reveal a man's face; angular, long of jaw and tall of brow, dominated by a pair of great, feverishly brilliant eyes. There was about that face, with its pallor and its monklike asceticism, a suggestion of ancient lineage, inbred and distilled to the very essence of neurasthenia. When he spoke again, his voice was undisguised, its masculine character and American accent evident. "Nothing I have related has been false, yet I have hardly dared divulge all. Now I will tell you the truth, and I will hold nothing back. Be warned, however—the tale is lurid in nature, and may at times strain your credulity."

Holmes inclined his head, an expression of extraordinary concentration transforming his hawklike features.

"My name," commenced the visitor, "is August Belknap. I am—I was—a professor of anthropology at Brown University. Last year, a small group of my colleagues—five of us, including Professor Talliard—elected to devote our long summer vacation to study and research in some foreign clime. Though the academic specialties of its members varied, a common interest in the religious observances of divers primitive peoples united our group. Material worthy of attention might have been found in countless remote locales. However, we were unanimous in our conviction that certain prehistoric mysteries of extraordinary character persisted yet upon the island of Sumatra.

"Our vacation coincided with the dry season in the East Indies," Belknap continued. "We arrived in June to discover what seemed at first a nearly unspoiled tropical fairyland, where the equatorial forests rise almost at the water's edge, bamboo grows in dense thickets, huge ferns and brilliant flowers flaunt their luxuriance everywhere. Understand that this was a first impression. Presently, the overpowering profusion of vegetation, the steaminess of the perfumed atmosphere, the unremitting intensity of light and shade—the extremity in all things—began to wax oppressive, even repellent. But this sense did not develop at once.

"Our time was limited. Having established ourselves in an airy thatched house on piles that we were obliged to purchase outright from the owner, (for the natives possessed no concept of rental) we set to work.

"Our initial efforts met with little success. The lowland islanders, of the short, brown-skinned Malay stock, were peaceable and accommodating enough, voicing no objection to the foreign presence in their midst. Their habits were frugal, their lives industrious, their practices modest and agreeable enough, if unexceptional. Most of them were Mohammedans, and as such, unlikely to furnish the sort of anthropological arcana we had travelled so far to find.

"It was not long, however, before information of a more promising nature reached our ears. The pacific lowland farmers took a certain childlike delight in relating gruesome tales of the Dyaks, or hill Malays, who reputedly practiced magic, believed in ghosts, and preserved the heads of their enemies. Initially, I dismissed these accounts as fantastic exaggerations or fabrications, designed to awe gullible strangers. Sefton Talliard, however—whose knowledge of these people and their customs greatly exceeded my own—assured me otherwise. A number of the Dyak tribes, he maintained, cherished the belief that preservation of an enemy's head enslaved the spirit of the dead man. The Dutch authorities have prohibited head-hunting, yet the practice continues, and, to this day, the magic tribal ceremonies often witness ritual decapitations.

"None of our party, I fancy, harbored any great desire to witness a beheading, yet all of us burned to behold the secret rites that our hosts described. The desire sharpened when we learned of a certain peculiarly degenerate tribe, some of whose members reputedly possessed blue eyes, legacy of European forebears. These mongrelized Dyaks, whose tribal title translates as 'the Faithful,' were little more than savages, inhabiting caves in the upland forests, subsisting solely upon the game they hunted, the edibles their women gathered, and anything they could steal. Held in extreme terror and loathing by all neighboring tribes, by reason of their rapacity, their magical prowess, and their unbridled ferocity, the Faithful were said to worship the ghastly deity known as Ur-Allazoth, the Relentless, a demon-lord of bestial aspect and limitless appetite.

"I shall not weary you, Mr. Holmes, with an account of our investigative efforts. Suffice it to say, in the end we managed to engage the services of a Dyak guide, who, tempted by the prospect of munificent reward, undertook to lead us through the forests to the very site of the Faithful mysteries. This task he performed in greatest secrecy, upon a clear but moonless night—the dark of the moon coinciding, as it happened, with a tribal ceremony of considerable moment. Neither blandishments nor threats, however, induced our guide to conduct us beyond a point some quarter-mile distant from our goal, and thus we were obliged to cover the last several hundred yards of the trek unassisted. This furtive feat proved relatively undemanding, for the crimson glow of the ceremonial bonfires, and the swelling murmur of native voices drew us infallibly to our destination.

"Presently, the sound of music reached us—a thin, uncanny shrilling of daemonic flutes—notes so indefinably alien, so inexpressibly obscene, that my soul shrinks at the recollection. Then and there, in the red-litten forests of Sumatra, my heart misgave me, and I paused, trembling in every limb. Similarly hesitant and shaken was the young assistant professor, Zebulon Loftus. Such effeminacy awoke the ire of our leader, a man of assured and dauntlessly ambitious character. Talliard's silent communications were eloquent, and presently, Loftus and I resumed progress.

"Minutes later, we reached the edge of a great clearing, and there we halted, cloaking our presence in the blackest of tropical shadows.

"How shall I describe the scene that we witnessed there, in that place?" Belknap's hand tightened almost convulsively upon the dark plush of his pelisse. "Words may perhaps convey some inkling of the material reality, but never capture the sense of pervasive evil, the intimation of nameless horror informing the sultry atmosphere, the overpowering pressure of invisible, incalculably vast malignity impinging upon our fragile sphere. I will therefore confine myself to an unadorned statement of the facts."

Holmes nodded gravely.

"The clearing before us," the visitor continued, "was roughly circular in shape, its circumference edged with a pale of bamboo stakes, each stake topped with a human head, each head wreathed in clouds of long, black hair, that stirred and drifted with every passing breeze. The facial features, frozen in expressions of the ghastliest terror, were perfectly preserved. The jumping, flickering firelight lent those distorted visages a lifelike aspect dreadful to behold, and a host of staring eyes seemed almost to follow the leaping gyrations of the Faithful assembled there. Some several score had gathered, and it was obvious at a glance that we confronted a debased mongrel people, combining the worst attributes of the Malay and Negrito races, rendered all the more repugnant by the clear evidence of an unspeakably degraded European infusion. Never in my life have I beheld human beings whose repulsive external aspect spoke more clearly of the depravity festering within.

"The savages, wholly unclothed, shambled and capered to the wailing, unearthly music of those damnable flutes. As they danced, they sang, or chanted, in a tongue bearing no resemblance to the local Malay dialect, a tongue that I sensed had been old when the world was still young. The meaning entirely eluded me, yet often I caught the name Ur-Allazoth, and knew that they called upon their monstrous god. This deity, I had no doubt, found representation in the great statue looming at the center of the glade. Whose hand had fashioned so mind-searing an abomination I cannot pretend to guess, but surely the work lay far beyond the skill of the primitive

Faithful, for the artistry was unimaginably hideous, yet masterly, bespeaking the twisted genius of a perverted Leonardo. The being darkly depicted in polished stone was alien beyond conception, beyond endurance. To gaze upon that impossible nightmare form was to experience some intimation of eternal diableries lurking without the realm of our perceptions, of eldritch foulness poisoning all the cosmos. The idol was squat, bloated, abhorrently misshapen, every contour an assault upon human vision. The four limbs were sinuous, attenuated, edged with spikes and tipped with suckers. The head was thoroughly beastlike, sharp-snouted, and razor-tusked, with protuberant eyes of some highly polished crystalline substance that reflected the firelight in shifting gleams of deepest crimson. A long, squamous tail wrapped itself thrice about the entire body of this execrable entity that was, though never of our world, oddly reminiscent in shape and character of an enormous *rat.*

"The image of Ur-Allazoth crouched atop a pedestal of black stone, incised with bands of curious glyphs, and inset with small plaques of wondrously carven, glinting matter. A broad ledge of great stone blocks encircled the pedestal, and this ledge supported a chopping block.

"I will not relate the sickening particulars of the ceremony that followed. The sacrifice of a dozen drugged and stuporous victims, the rolling heads and spurting blood, the abandoned gyrations of the Faithful, the wild ululation, the relentless shrilling of those infernal flutes, (a sound that will haunt me to my grave) and above all, the inexplicable sense of a huge, malign sentience pervading the atmosphere—I will leave it to your imagination to furnish the details. Imagination is apt to fall short of the dreadful reality, and perhaps that is all to the good. I will only note that I myself was faint and queasy before the rite was half completed. Abe Engle was swaying upon his feet, Tertius Crawley had turned his back on the scene, and poor young Loftus had collapsed in a swoon. Of the five of us, only Talliard remained composed, resolute, and fully attentive. The intermittent gleams of firelight, stabbing fitfully through the shadows, revealed our leader, jotting copious notes into the journal that he never traveled without. I must confess, Talliard's utter coolness in the face of the horror we confronted at once impressed and revolted me.

"The ceremony concluded at last. The savages withdrew, bearing the bloodstained remnants of their revel. The fires burned on, their ruddy light bathing empty glade, incarnadined block, staring heads, and unspeakable idol. Loftus recovered his senses and sat up slowly, gazing about with a stunned and vacant air. Engle drooped, Crawley fidgeted, while I stood dully longing to depart the accursed spot. Sefton Talliard, however, was unready to go. Casting a brief, searching glance right and left, our leader strode forward with an air of fearless resolution, never faltering before he reached the base of Ur-Allazoth's image. There he halted, and, to my amazement, proceeded to sketch the statue in pen and ink, reproducing the murine lineaments with commendable accuracy.

"Pride forbade me to display cowardice. Mastering my own reluctance, I advanced to join Professor Talliard. Drawing paper and crayon from my pocket, I quickly took rubbings of several bands of glyphs. While I was thus engaged, Engle approached to record measurements, while Crawley occupied himself with a survey of preserved heads. Only poor Loftus remained inert, huddled on the ground at the edge of the clearing.

"Our respective tasks were soon completed. I could scarcely contain my eagerness to go, but Talliard would not budge, before prying one of the small, carven plaques from the pedestal of the statue. His temerity shocked me, but there was no arguing with our autocrat, and I did not attempt it. He slipped the thin plaque between the pages of his journal, returned the book to his pocket, and then, to my unutterable relief, signalled a command to withdraw.

"We hastened from that spot, stumbling our way through the dark, back to the point where we had left our guide. The fellow was not there, and inwardly I cursed him for a deserter. Perhaps he had indeed fled, without collecting his recompense, or perhaps some darker fate befell him there. I cannot say, for we never looked upon his face again.

"I scarcely know how we found our way through that stygian forest to a friendly Dyak settlement. There we spent the night, a night of broken slumbers, filled with delirious dreams. In the morning, we commenced the three-day trek back to our lowland village, and our thatched dwelling perched on piles. This transition was accomplished without incident, yet throughout its entirety, I was unable to rid myself of a profound perturbation—a keen, nerve-racking sense that our progress was continually *observed*. There is no overemphasizing the power of this sensation—it was instinctual, elemental, and shared by us all.

"The feeling intensified throughout the ensuing days. Strive though I might to absorb myself in the task of deciphering the message of the glyphs, I could neither evade nor ignore that psychic oppression. Only the imminence of our withdrawal from the island of Sumatra lightened my mood.

"We had booked passage to Java aboard the cargo vessel *Matilda Briggs*. Two days prior to departure, tragedy befell us. Tertius Crawley was murdered. Our colleague's headless corpse was discovered at dusk by young Loftus, whose own nervous reaction to the sight was immediate and intense.

"Mr. Holmes, Dr. Watson, the isolated villages of Sumatra possess nothing corresponding to an American or British system of justice. Legal administration resides largely in the hands of local elders, and rarely are matters referred to the distant Dutch authorities. In this case, the village chieftain merely expressed his regret that the devilish magic of the Faithful had prevailed once again, together with his recommendation that the body be interred without delay, lest evil spirits seek the site of violent death. Crawley was buried at dawn. His head was never located.

"You may well imagine my sense of overwhelming relief, as I watched the coast of Sumatra recede, from the deck of the *Matilda Briggs*. The vessel was bound for Batavia, by way of the Strait of Malacca. I had hoped the sea voyage might serve to calm my un-

strung nerves. On the second day, however, one of the crew discovered Abe Engle's headless remains, crammed into a barrel deep
in the hold. A thorough search of the ship revealed the presence of
a stowaway, easily identifiable by his blue eyes as a member of the
mongrel tribe of the Faithful. Interrogation proved useless, as the
prisoner displayed comprehension of no tongue other than his own
debased dialect, which poured from his lips in a venomous, contin-
uous stream. He seemed entirely fearless, and the expression of
malignity glaring from his pale eyes was shocking to behold.

"Presently tiring of incessant, unintelligible abuse, the captain
ordered the suspect locked in a storage closet belowdecks. Con-
finement failed to quell the Dyak's defiant spirit, and from that
closet issued the sound of his voice, upraised in an unholy chanting
audible throughout the ship.

"Engle was buried at sea. His head was never located.
Throughout the obsequies, the malignant chants rising from below
counterpointed the captain's readings from the Psalms, and the
blasphemous juxtaposition chilled the hearts of all listeners. The
verbal outpouring had now assumed a character all too recognizable to the surviving members of our group—it was that same invocation to Ur-Allazoth we had heard in the upland forests upon
the night of the Faithful's vile ceremony. The passage of time could
not damp the prisoner's loquacity, and throughout the hours that
followed, the chanting never ceased. More than one of the *Matilda
Briggs* deck hands spoke of gagging the noisy Dyak, or even of
slitting his throat, but no one attempted to act upon these threats. It
is my belief that the sailors feared their captive, and understandably
so.

"The ship sped southeast, toward Java. The voice of the prisoner never abated, and sound cast a black and smothering pall over
all on board, with the possible exception of Sefton Talliard, whose
nerves seemed proof against any assault. On the night that we
neared Batavia Bay, I retired early, and the last recollection I carried
with me into slumber was the sound of the prisoner's voice, infused
with a certain new and curious note of exultation.

"I awakened at dawn to a clamorous uproar. Footsteps thundered overhead, an alarm clanged, men shouted wildly, shrieks of mortal terror tore the air, and through it all, I could still distinguish the hoarsened, malevolently triumphant voice of the captive Dyak, calling upon Ur-Allazoth.

"Rising from my berth, I made for the deck. Before I reached it, a violent impact rocked the *Matilda Briggs*. The shock threw me from the ladder, and I fell, striking my head violently upon the cabin floor. For a time, I knew nothing more.

"When I regained my senses, around mid-morning, it was to find myself lying, sick and sore, in the boat of the *Matilda Briggs*, together with Talliard, Loftus, and some half dozen sailors. Of the ship, and the rest of her crew, nothing was to be seen. That she had gone to the bottom of Batavia Bay was clear, but the circumstances of the wreck were impossible to ascertain. Talliard claimed ignorance, the sailors offered the most incoherently fantastic tales, and Zebulon Loftus, when pressed for an account, vented peal upon piercing peal of maniacal laughter. To my surprise, I found that the valise containing my personal belongings had been preserved, by Talliard, of all people. In response to my thanks, our leader merely responded that the rubbings I had taken from the pedestal of Ur-Allazoth's image were worth saving.

"Batavia Bay is heavily travelled, and we were rescued in a matter of hours. The inquest that followed is a great blur in my mind. The official verdict was that the *Matilda Briggs* had struck a rock and sunk; a falsehood I made no attempt to challenge.

"We returned to Providence, where young Loftus, whose sanity was shattered, entered a mental hospital. The academic year at Brown commenced, and I returned to work, in every hope of resuming my former tranquil existence. For a while, it seemed I had done so. I so far regained my equilibrium that I dared confront the challenge of deciphering the message of Ur-Allazoth's glyphs; while Talliard disclosed our findings to the world in lectures of dazzling brilliancy. Apparent normality reigned for some months, until December, when we received news that Zebulon Loftus had escaped incarceration. Two days later, his frozen, decapitated body was found in a meadow not half a mile from the hospital. His head was never located.

"Around this time—" Belknap could not repress a shudder. "I began once more to experience the peculiar sensation of being watched, that I thought I had left behind me in the East Indies. Often I thought to glimpse dark forms haunting the shadows as I made my way through the tortuous streets of Providence, and once I caught the baleful gleam of uncanny blue eyes tracking my progress. Confiding in Talliard, one icy winter night, I learned that he harboured fears identical to my own; and painfully acute those fears must have been, for that self-contained, overweening individual to acknowledge them. Upon that occasion, he even spoke of flight, and suggested the possibility of finding refuge in London. At the time, I hardly expected him to resort to such measures. But two nights later, both Talliard's office and my own were ransacked. The next day, Sefton Talliard disappeared.

"He was either dead, or fled to London. In the absence of a corpse, I suspected the latter. Within the fortnight, I'd powerful incentive to follow him. For some weeks past, my work with the glyphs had scarcely progressed. Many of the pictographs, though commonplace symbols in that backward area of the world, were arranged in sequences that seemed senseless and random as the ravings of a lunatic. At length it dawned upon me that the symbols composed a rebus, phonetically representing words in the Dutch language of the seventeenth century. Inexplicable that a solution so obvious should have eluded me for so long, but thereafter, as you may well imagine, my task was greatly simplified, and translation proceeded apace. Eventually, the following message resolved itself." Closing his eyes, Belknap repeated, from memory, *"The hold of divine Ur-Allazoth looses not, and loses naught. Whosoever profanes His image, dividing or diminishing the sacred substance thereof, shall be pursued to the ends of the earth and beyond, even unto the shrieking, formless reaches beyond the stars. Nor shall pursuit abate, before the worldly waters ruled by the Relentless have closed upon that which is His.*

"You see the significance, Mr. Holmes?" Belknap opened his eyes.

"Indeed. I had, inevitably, anticipated the rebus," Holmes replied. "As for the rest, the urgency of the matter is apparent. These devotees of a being whose nature demands further investigation have followed the despoilers of their deity's image all the way from Sumatra. Clearly, they will not rest until they have recovered the plaque stolen by Sefton Talliard. In order to preserve your own life, as well as Professor Talliard's, the immediate return of the stolen item to its self-proclaimed owners is essential."

"That is my conclusion. But my own efforts have failed to locate Talliard here in London, and lately, I have noted the presence of silent blue-eyed hounds upon my trail. Within the last forty-eight hours, they have drawn near, and I fear that my time is all but gone. Can you assist me, Mr. Holmes?"

"Beyond doubt. There is one point, however, that must be noted, at the outset; which is, that your colleague appears to withhold information of some vital significance. In view of the character-portrait you've limned, that is hardly surprising. Presumably the nature of the missing piece will reveal itself when I have located Professor Talliard, which I fully expect to do in a matter of hours, if not less."

"But that is astonishing, Mr. Holmes!" the visitor exclaimed. "I have scoured London for weeks, without gleaning the slightest clue."

"I've certain local resources, to which a stranger in the city is unlikely to enjoy access," Holmes replied, not unkindly. "Now, Professor Belknap, here is a question of some import. Were you followed to Baker Street, this evening?"

"I believe so." Belknap shivered. "Yes, I am quite certain of it."

"Excellent," Holmes replied, to my amazement.

I could not fathom my friend's clear satisfaction, and the visitor was equally confounded.

"I must leave you, for a little while," Holmes abruptly informed his client. "I shall return within the half hour." He departed without further explanation, leaving me alone with August Belknap, who, unaccustomed to the eccentric character of my friend's genius, appeared thunderstruck.

It was perhaps the slowest half hour I have ever endured. Poor Belknap, distracted and raw-nerved, could not even pretend interest in the tales of the Afghan campaign with which I endeavored to entertain him, but started and flinched at every unexpected sound. Presently, all conversation died, and we sat in comfortless silence, until the clock struck nine, and, to my unutterable relief, Sherlock Holmes reappeared.

"The apparatus has been readied," Holmes declared. "It remains only to set the machine in motion. For that, Professor, I must request use of your amusing disguise. We are much of a build. My own clothes should fit you well enough to serve on a foggy night. Take them, return to your own lodgings, and do not stir forth until you have heard from me. Where are you staying?"

The visitor named an address in Fleet Street.

"I assume you frequently change location?"

"Every few days," Belknap admitted. "But I never succeed in throwing them off the track for long."

"After tonight, that should not signify." So saying, Holmes ushered the visitor into his own room.

When they emerged, minutes later, I could not forbear staring, so startled was I by the transformation. August Belknap, clad in borrowed Inverness and deerstalker, might at a glance have been mistaken for Sherlock Holmes. Holmes himself, in feminine array, complete with wig, wide hat, and veiling, was altogether unrecognizable.

"Now, Professor," Holmes instructed his client, "Wait for half an hour after Dr. Watson and I have departed—"

"Eh!" I exclaimed.

"—Then return to Fleet Street, and stay inside tomorrow. You are the lesser target, and probably not in immediate danger, but do not open the door to anyone other than myself or Watson."

"Mr. Holmes, I will follow your instructions without fail."

"Capital. And now, my dear Watson, I trust you will not suffer a lady to venture forth unescorted?" Holmes's amused smile was dimly visible through the veiling.

"Venture forth where?" I inquired.

"Not far. A half-hour's stroll should suffice."

I remained unenlightened, but acquiescent. Pausing only long enough to don an overcoat, I accompanied Sherlock Holmes out into the fog-blinded March night. Together we set off at a leisurely pace along Baker Street.

To the end of my days, I will always remember that walk, and I will never recall it without a pang of profound uneasiness. For that sense of *being watched,* so graphically described by Professor August Belknap, was present, powerful, and impossible to ignore. I could have taken my oath that the shadows seethed with silent, sliding shapes, and I could literally feel the pressure of invisible regard. It was all I could do to refrain from glancing continually back over my shoulder, and the flesh between my shoulderblades positively tingled in anticipation of a blow. I considered Belknap's account of the Faithful's headless victims, and my own head momentarily swam.

If Sherlock Holmes shared my misgivings, he showed no sign of it. His step was unhurried, his manner unconcerned, as he launched into an impressively knowledgeable discussion of the evolution of the kabuki dance drama. My friend spoke brilliantly, yet I scarcely heard a word of his discourse, for my ears were attuned to nothing beyond the tap of footsteps in the fog behind us. And my disquiet, already intense, increased a hundredfold when Holmes led us from the relatively well-lit, populous public thoroughfares, into the silent pathways of Regent's Park. We were nearing the Zoo, before he finally paused, in a region of impenetrable shadow.

"That should be enough," Holmes opined.

I did not waste breath begging for an explanation, but waited in silence as he divested himmself of hat, wig, pelisse, and skirts, to reveal ordinary masculine attire beneath.

"Now, Watson, we separate," he decreed. "You may take the direct route back to Baker Street, and I shall go roundabout. And by this time tomorrow night, we shall beyond doubt have located the missing Professor Talliard."

With that, he vanished silently into the dark, leaving me alone, bewildered, filled with resentment, and more than a little apprehension. I made my way home without hindrance. Belknap had left, and Holmes had not yet returned, which was just as well. If I had encountered my friend at that moment, I should hardly have found myself capable of civility. I retired early, and slept soundly, my dreams somehow flavoured with the sound of Sherlock Holmes's violin.

Holmes had resumed his chemical experimentation by the time I awoke. His violin lay on the sofa—evidently he had been playing it during the night. His pallor, and shadowed eyes suggested sleeplessness. Still somewhat piqued by last night's events, I refused to question him, but rather, occupied myself with a series of errands that kept me out and about for the entire day. Around twilight, I returned to Baker Street, to discover Holmes still occupied with his test tubes, beakers, and burners. Nor was his attention to be diverted from these items, until a dubious Mrs. Hudson entered to announce the arrival of "Master Wiggins, and associates."

"Ah, show them in," Holmes instructed, his face alight with eagerness. Noting my puzzlement, he explained, "The Baker Street Irregulars. They have been at work since I put them on the case last night."

Here, then, was the explanation of Holmes's half-hour absence of the previous evening. He had withdrawn to confer with his juvenile surveillance squad.

Moments later, a sextet of ragged and remarkably filthy little street Arabs burst into the room. Their chief Wiggins, tallest and oldest among them, swaggered forward to announce with an air of victory, "Plunker 'ere cops the prize."

The Plunker in question, a superlatively disreputable urchin, flashed a snaggle-toothed grin.

"State your findings," Holmes commanded.

"Shadowed yer last night, Guv'nor, as per orders." Master Wiggins appeared to act as official spokesman of the party. "Soon spied the others on yer trail, just like yer said, and rummy little apes they was, too. Not 'arf ugly. Arfter yer gives 'em the slip in the Park, they splits up, so *we* splits up. Plunker follows one of 'em as far as Notting 'ill Gate, and finds more of the same, 'anging about a lodging'ouse. Plunker keeps an eye peeled, twigs their game, and knows 'e's nailed yer man. And there you 'ave it."

"Well done, gentlemen. Can you furnish an address?"

Wiggins obliged.

"Second storey, front room," Plunker offered.

"Well done," Holmes repeated. He produced a guinea. "Plunker, your reward."

"Cor!" Plunker's crooked grin widened.

"For the rest of you—the usual scale of pay, for two days work." Holmes distributed silver. "Gentlemen, until next time."

The delighted irregulars withdrew, no doubt to our landlady's relief.

"Phew!" I observed.

"There is no time to be lost, Watson," Holmes declared. "Sefton Talliard's hours are numbered."

A hansom carried us to the house noted by the youthful intelligencer. The place was respectable-looking, well-maintained, and unremarkable. We alighted from our vehicle, and I gazed searchingly about, but caught no glimpse of lurking figures. The sense of being watched, so unnervingly acute last night in Regent's Park, was absent now. And yet, I knew not why, I found that my hands were icy, and my heart was cold with a formless dread.

A couple of taps of the polished brass knocker drew the landlady. Holmes introduced himself as a friend of the American gentleman on the second floor, and she admitted us without demur. We hurried upstairs, and rapped on Sefton Talliard's door. There was no response, and my sense of dread deepened.

The room was locked. Our combined strength easily sufficed to force it open, and we burst in to confront a scene I shudder to recall. I am a surgeon, fully accustomed to sights that many would consider ghastly, yet all my experience could not fully prepare me for the spectacle of Sefton Talliard's headless corpse, sprawled on a blood-drenched bed. I think an exclamation escaped me, and I recoiled a pace or two. Sherlock Holmes was guilty of no such weakness. Casting a keen, penetrating eye about the death chamber, he stepped first to the locked window, then to the fireplace, which he knelt to examine briefly. Thereafter, he turned his attention upon the clothing, books, papers, and personal articles that lay wildly scattered everywhere. That Talliard's room had been thoroughly rifled was altogether apparent. The object of my friend's search was less evident, however. Initially, I assumed that he sought the plaque sacrilegiously pried from the pedestal of Ur-Allazoth's image, but that could scarcely be; for surely the murderers, here before us and purposeful beyond civilized ken, would already have reclaimed that article. It then occurred to me that Holmes sought Talliard's missing head, but such proved not to be the case. At length, a muted grunt of satisfaction announced his success, and, from that dreadful bloodstained tangle, he plucked a small volume bound in red morocco.

I was not so dull that I failed to recognize Professor Talliard's prized journal, as described by August Belknap.

Settling himself back upon his haunches with the utmost deliberation, Holmes proceeded to read, indifferent to the presence of the mutilated body on the bed, not two yards behind him. I could scarcely endure it.

"Holmes—" I entreated.

"One moment—ah!" Holmes's expression altered remarkably, and he sprang to his feet. "There—yes—I had suspected something, but this I did not foresee."

"Foresee what?" I demanded.

"Come, we must find Belknap at once."

"We cannot leave this place, Holmes!" I expostulated. "We have happened upon a murder. There are authorities—appropriate channels—proper procedure—"

"They will wait," Holmes informed me. With some effort, he tore his eyes from the journal. "My client stands in mortal peril. Should he perish, it is through my own failure of intellect."

Such a prospect was not to be contemplated.

"No delay, Watson! Belknap's life hangs by a thread." Thrusting Talliard's journal into his pocket, Holmes rose and rushed from the room, without a glance to spare for the dead man. After a moment, I followed. What Talliard's landlady must have made of our sudden departure, and her subsequent discovery in the American lodger's room, I did not care to ponder at that time.

Before I reached the street, Holmes had already secured a hansom. I jumped in, just as the vehicle sped off east. The ride was endless, and conversation one-sided, for Holmes declined to answer my queries, or indeed, to speak at all. Eventually, I gave over interrogation. Traffic was heavy upon the London streets at that hour, the fog was opaque, our progress was slow, and apprehension twisted my vitals.

At length, we reached the Fleet Street address of August Belknap; a surprisingly mean haunt, for it seemed that Holmes's client, desirous of self-submersion in London's maelstrom, had sought concealment in cheap lodgings above some barber's shop.

The shop was still open. We rushed in, and, without pausing to consult a proprietor of remarkably demonic aspect, sprinted to the back, and up the stairs, to pound the door of August Belknap's room.

We called him by name, and he admitted us at once. Before the first question escaped the fugitive academic's lips, Sherlock Holmes demanded, "The photograph of your late wife, Belknap—where is it?"

Belknap stared, his feverish, astonished eyes widening. Impatiently, Holmes repeated the query, and his client's wordless gesture encompassed the plain oak bureau in the corner. Pulling the top drawer open, my friend swiftly located and drew forth the silver-framed portrait of a round-faced young woman, irregular of feature, but sweet and grave of expression. I confess the professor was no more mystified than I. All confusion vanished, however, when Sherlock Holmes pried the backing from the frame, to reveal the flat, marvelously carven plaque secreted behind the photograph.

"Good God!" Belknap ejaculated.

His reaction was surely unfeigned. It would have required the talents of an Irving or a Forbes-Robertson to counterfeit such perfect amazement.

"You must rid yourself of this object," Holmes informed his client. "That is your sole chance of survival."

"Mr. Holmes, I knew nothing of this. I will gladly dispose of the thing. I will bury it—pulverize it—donate it to a museum—carry it back to Sumatra, if need be—"

"Useless," Holmes returned. "Quite useless. There is but one solution to your dilemma. Your own translation of the Sumatran glyphs, Professor, should instruct you."

" 'Nor shall pursuit abate,' " Belknap recited, " 'before the worldly waters ruled by the Relentless have closed upon that which is His.' "

"Just so. Come, there is not a moment to lose."

Holmes exited, and we followed him, down the stairs, past the flame-eyed proprietor, and out into mist-shrouded Fleet Street. He led us east, and as we went, the cold chills knifing along my spine, and the intolerable pressure of invisible regard, warned me of unseen stalkers, near at hand. August Belknap's face was white and set; he, too, sensed the hostile presence.

We reached Ludgate Circus, and now, for the first time, I actually glimpsed the short, impossibly agile human shadows gliding through the fog, and I caught the glint of luminously malignant blue eyes. Even Sherlock Holmes could not feign total indifference. We quickened our pace, and our pursuers did likewise, drawing perceptibly nearer as we turned south toward the Thames.

I could not fathom my friend's purpose. Neither he nor I carried a weapon. I assumed that August Belknap was similarly unarmed. Rather than seeking the comparative safety of well-peopled streets, however, Sherlock Holmes was leading us straight on toward empty Blackfriars Bridge.

We were running now, unabashedly in flight, our footsteps echoing through the fog. Hearing no clatter of pursuit, I chanced a glance behind, to descry no less than six of them, swift and seemingly tireless, noiseless and uncanny as predatory wraiths.

Reaching the bridge, we started to cross. Halfway to the Southwark side, however, Holmes halted abruptly, one hand raised on high. Clasped in that hand was the plaque pried from the image of the Faithful's god. I've no idea at all what substance composed that small tablet. Whatever it was, it seemed to glow with some pulsing internal light of its own, and never in all my days have I seen the like. Even in the midst of the darkness, and the swirling fog, the plaque was clearly visible.

"Ur-Allazoth!" Holmes called out, in a clear, strong voice that pierced the night like a dagger.

So sharp and sudden was that utterance, and so unexpected, that I started violently at the sound of it, and beside me, I heard Belknap gasp.

"Ur-Allazoth!" Holmes repeated the call, and then sang out a string of indescribably outlandish syllables.

"Ia fhurtgn iea tlu jiadhri cthuthoth zhugg'lsht ftehia. Iea tlu."

That is the best I can do to reproduce that fantastically incomprehensible burst of gibberish.

It seemed to me then that the inexplicable, infernal light of the stolen plaque in Holmes's grasp responsively intensified. As a man of science, I can scarcely account for such a phenomenon, but I did *not* imagine it. Blinking and confused, I looked away, glancing back to behold our six pursuers, grouped at the end of the bridge, motionless and preternaturally intent. My confusion deepened as their voices rose, to wail thinly through the fog:

"*Ia fhurtgn iea tlu jiadhri cthuthoth zhugg'lsht ftehia. Iea tlu.*"

There was something in the sound that roused my deepest, most elemental terror and detestation.

As the final loathsome syllable faded, Sherlock Holmes flung the plaque from Blackfriars Bridge. The lucent object fell like a shooting star. Before it struck the river below, the mists roiled, and a violent upheaval convulsed the water. The Thames shuddered, black waves smashed themselves against the piers of the bridge, and a funnel-shaped whirlpool spun into existence. Astounded, I gazed down, and thought for one mad moment to glimpse a vast and almost inconceivable shape. There was solidity there, I imagined; a slithering of boneless attenuated limbs, a flash of spikes and suckers. The moment passed. The plaque vanished into the whirlpool, the waters closed upon it, then swiftly calmed themselves. The Thames flowed on, untroubled.

Slowly, doubting my own senses, I turned to look back upon our Faithful pursuers. For an instant I beheld them—six anonymous, attentive figures, ghostlike in the mists. Then they vanished, fading into the fog, and I saw them no more.

T wo nights later, we sat in our lodgings, the ever-present London fog still testing its weight against the window panes. Most of the previous day had been spent in conference with the police, who, swayed by the hysterics of Sefton Talliard's landlady, had initially evinced some disposition to suspect our complicity in that unhappy academic's decapitation. The information, however, regarding the nature of Talliard's shadowy enemies—provided by August Belknap, and substantiated by the testimony of Wiggins and Plunker of the Baker Street irregulars—had much allayed such suspicion. And Holmes's own masterly analysis of the murder-site had demonstrated beyond all question that a brace of small, acrobatic killers had entered the locked room by way of the chimney, dispatched the sleeping Talliard, ransacked the room, and exited the way they had come, bearing their victim's head—which will, I strongly suspect, never be located.

The constabulary, their doubts satisfied, had dismissed us, and we came away with Holmes miraculously retaining possession of Sefton Talliard's journal. The book now lay open before him, and my friend was frowning over it.

"I am scarcely satisfied," he complained.

"What, Holmes!" I returned. "Against all odds, you succeeded in preserving your client's life—assuming that his enemies are now mollified."

"August Belknap has nothing more to fear from the Faithful," Holmes said, shrugging. "But that is not the point. The information placed at my disposal regarding Professor Sefton Talliard's ruthless, cool, and unscrupulous character should have alerted me to the fellow's intentions, early enough to forestall another ritual beheading. It should not have been necessary for me to read his very words in his own journal."

"What did he say?" I inquired.

"See for yourself." Holmes extended the morocco-bound volume. "And do not neglect the account of the destruction of the *Matilda Briggs.*"

Sefton Talliard's hand was decisive and legible. It was with disapproving interest, but no great surprise, that I read of his plan, motivated by self-serving fear, to transfer the stolen plaque, object of alarming Faithful attention, from his own possession to that of the unwitting August Belknap. The photograph of Belknap's late wife, a memento of immense sentimental value, prized and carried everywhere by its owner, offered the perfect place of concealment. This transfer, accomplished hours prior to the embarkation of the *Matilda Briggs,* clearly accounted for Talliard's unwonted generosity in preserving the valise, containing the personal property of his colleague.

There followed a brief passage, written on shipboard, and

phonetically rendering the invocation to Ur-Allazoth ceaselessly howled by the Dyak prisoner locked in the hold of the vessel:

Ia fhurtgn iea tlu jiadhri cthuthoth zhugg'lsht ftehia. Iea tlu.

And finally, the following passage, penned in the immediate aftermath of the disaster, caught my eye:

> *. . . cannot begin to convey the horror of the Being that rose from the sea to confront the* Matilda Briggs. *There are no words—there are no sane human concepts—fit to encompass the immensity of that primeval terror—that overwhelming, insupportable foulness—that gibbering, slavering, slobbering, quivering, towering, tittering obscenity—that burst from the sea like a corporeal nightmare, shattering the boundaries of time, space, and reason. God help me! My mind quakes at the recollection, my sanity trembles. How shall I speak of a creature, gigantic and jigglingly gelatinous beyond description, ancient beyond earthly reckoning, hideous beyond the tolerance of human vision, combining in one abominable form, all the worst aspects of plague-bearing rat, giant kraken, squid, serpent, and leveret? How shall I speak of the stench that killed courage, the howling aural assault that blasted intelligence? How shall I limn an incarnation of the immemorial, destroying lunacy that humanity calls Chaos? Oh, I cannot—I simply cannot! All about me, men were going mad. The Thing was closing fast upon us, and I knew at a glance that the* Matilda Briggs *was lost . . .*

"Gad." I looked up from the page. "What do you make of it, Holmes?"

"I would not necessarily discount the professor's veracity," my friend returned languidly. "For when you have eliminated the impossible, whatever remains, however improbable, must be the truth. Nevertheless, we should do well to keep the matter to ourselves, Watson, as it is a story for which the world is not yet prepared."

One of the few relatively unexplored areas of Holmes scholarship is why Watson alluded to, yet did not write, at least as many stories as he actually composed. Sometimes he explains why, other times he does not. The story of Vamberry, the wine merchant, is one of the latter instances. It's not hard to see why Holmes might have preferred to gloss over this particular incident, now revealed for the first time by an author Mr. R. called "JTS," initials that, linked with the blithely double entendre plotline, suggests the redactor was J. THORNE SMITH (1892–1934), author of Topper, Topper Takes a Trip, The Passionate Witch *and other mildly racy comic novels.*—JAF

Mrs. Vamberry Takes a Trip (Vamberry the Wine Merchant)

BY *"MIKE RESNICK"*
(ASCRIBED TO J. THORNE SMITH)

Holmes, all bone and angles, sprawled comfortably upon the couch, sipping his champagne.

"You know, Watson," he said, holding his glass up, "this is really quite excellent stuff. I do wish I knew which of our many admirers was so thoughtful as to send us a case."

"Why not use your powers of deduction?" suggested his companion, looking up from his own drink.

Holmes studied the glass, and finally nodded his head, as if he had confirmed some inner suspicion.

"Well?" asked Watson anxiously. "What have you concluded?"

"It's definitely champagne," Holmes announced. "Probably made from grapes, unless I miss my guess." Suddenly he sat up. "But enough of this. I suspect we are about to receive a visitor."

"Why should you think so?"

"It's eight o'clock," replied Holmes. "And when Mrs. Vamberry called earlier today, she said she would arrive at eight on the dot."

"Actually," said Watson, looking at his watch, "it's seventeen minutes to ten."

"Well," said Holmes, adjusting his watch as someone knocked on the door, "it had to be one or the other. Come in!" he added, raising his voice.

The door opened, and a small but exceptionally well put together young lady entered. She had bright red hair, deep blue blue eyes, and skin the texture of the most expensive satin. She was wearing a tan raincoat, which she declined to remove. She immediately walked over and came to a stop just inches away from Holmes.

"Mr. Holmes," she said, "I am Mrs. Comfort Vamberry. I most desperately need your help."

"And I shall be happy to give it to you," replied Holmes. "Suppose you tell me what brought you here?"

"A horse and carriage," answered Mrs. Vamberry. "Though I can't imagine why you should care."

"I don't, actually."

"Then why did you ask?"

"I *meant* what problem brought you here."

"The carriage was no problem at all. Especially when compared to your stairs."

"You came here to complain about my stairs?" asked Holmes.

"Certainly not. My specialty is wine."

"You prefer 'whine' to 'complain,' do you?" asked Holmes.

"Absolutely."

"Well, my initial observation is that you can whine with the best of them."

"I consider that a high compliment," replied Mrs. Vamberry.

"You do?" said Holmes, surprised. "I would have considered it the worst kind of insult."

"Really?" said Mrs. Vamberry. "What would be the best kind of insult?"

Holmes frowned. "I hate it when people ask questions like that."

"Where are our manners?" interjected Watson. "May we offer you some champagne?"

"I should be most grateful," said Mrs. Vamberry.

That good gentleman opened yet another bottle and poured her a tall glass.

"It's excellent," she said after taking a sip. "Where did you get it?"

"It came in the post," said Watson.

She finished the glass. "I'll have another, if you don't mind?"

"My pleasure," said Watson, refilling her glass.

"What about your pleasure?" she asked sharply.

"I give up," said Watson, confused. "What about it?"

"Gentlemen don't discuss their pleasure in front of ladies," said Mrs. Vamberry.

"Well, that's not entirely so," interjected Holmes. "Some gentleman do just that."

"Then they are hardly gentlemen," replied Mrs. Vamberry.

"But I wasn't *discussing* my pleasure," protested Watson. "I was *expressing* it."

"It sounds messy, like expressing a wound or something," she said.

"I beg your pardon."

"Keep your pleasure to yourself and you won't have to beg my pardon," said Mrs. Vamberry.

"If I may interrupt," said Holmes, "I assume you *did* have some purpose for arranging this meeting?"

"Yes, Mr. Holmes," she said. "As I told you, my specialty is wine."

Holmes juxtaposed his fingers and nodded his head. "As I surmised."

"My husband, Reginald, is abroad gathering samples." She paused. "I miss him desperately."

"Please go on."

"Well, two weeks ago he sent me his Grand Siècle."

"He did *what?*" demanded the detective.

"Sent me his Grand Siècle."

"My God! Wasn't it painful?"

"No," she replied. "I have always taken enormous pleasure in his Grand Siècle."

"I'm sure you have," said Holmes. "But hasn't your husband always been at the other end of it, so to speak?"

"Well, I certainly enjoy it more when he's with me."

"I would have sworn you couldn't enjoy it at all when he's not there."

"Oh, you're quite mistaken. I have enjoyed Reginald's Grand Siècle while in the company of any number of friends while he has been out of the country."

"Zounds!" muttered Watson. "I must wire Vienna immediately!"

"Another refill, please?" she asked, holding out her glass, and Watson immediately obliged.

"If his Grand Siècle can function when he's no longer in possession of it," said Holmes, still frowning, "then I fail to see what your problem might be."

"He tells me he sent his Grand Siècle again two weeks ago," she said. "But it never arrived. I suspect foul play."

"Are you quite sure?" asked Holmes. "I mean, it hardly seems the kind of thing one would be inclined to steal, at least on the face of it.''

"You have no idea of its value, Mr. Holmes," said Mrs. Vamberry, downing the rest of her champagne. "I've a young lady who lives down the street who will pay top price for it.''

"And you *sell* it to her?" demanded Holmes.

"I'd like to keep it all to myself, but we're in business.''

"I wonder if Scotland Yard knows about this business?"

"Certainly they do," she said. "We are duly licensed.''

"What *is* the world coming to?" mused Holmes.

"Could you open a window, please?" asked Mrs. Vamberry. "I've suddenly become quite warm.''

Watson walked to a window and opened it, then came back and stopped in front of Mrs. Vamberry.

"I say, Holmes," said that worthy, "we seem to have a problem here.''

"We certainly do," said Holmes, lost in thought. "She wants to hire me to help her salvage this seamy if intriguing business that she and her remarkable husband have entered into. It poses a fascinating ethical conflict.''

"We have a more immediate problem," continued Watson. "The lady seems to have passed out. Doubtless it stems from having so much champagne so rapidly.''

Holmes walked over to Mrs. Vamberry. He snapped his fingers in front of her, slapped her face, and gently tickled her armpits.

"No reaction at all," he said.

"I suppose we could let her sleep in my room," said Watson.

Holmes shook his head. "If she sleeps in anyone's room, it will be in *mine*. But the thought of sharing those happy moments with her husband's Grand Siècle simply boggles the mind. I think I shall refuse the case and take the lady home.''

"I'm afraid I can't help you," said Watson. "I have to finish writing your latest adventure tonight, if it is to make the latest edition of *The Strand.*''

"Your absence should pose no problem," replied Holmes. "I

am, after all, a world-class athlete. Just help me set her on her feet, and I'll take her from there."

The two gentlemen lifted Mrs. Vamberry to an upright position. As they did so, her raincoat fell open, revealing that the young lady was quite naked beneath it.

"She gives every indication of having dressed in rather a hurry," remarked Watson admiringly. "Perhaps I *will* help you after all."

"Not necessary," said Holmes, half-carrying and half-dragging her to the doorway. "I shall return within the hour."

It took Holmes less than two minutes to realize that his current mode of transporting Mrs. Vamberry was next to impossible, so he hailed a double-decker bus. He was aware of the curious stares from the other passengers as he carried her up the stairs and over to a seat, but he did his best to ignore them.

"She sure is a looker, Mister," said one gentleman who was dressed in a wrinkled tweed suit.

"Thank you," said Holmes, placing Mrs. Vamberry next to the window and taking a seat himself.

"Had a little too much to drink, eh?"

"Not really," said Holmes. "I feel quite well."

"I meant the girl."

"Ah. Well, yes, the truth of the matter is that she *has* had a little more than she could handle."

"Does the poor dear need any help?" offered a middle-aged woman, putting aside her knitting to gaze at Mrs. Vamberry's ashen face. "A mixture of lemon and prune juice does it every time."

"Does *what* every time?" asked Holmes, curious.

"Flushes out the system. Clears the head, too," replied the woman knowingly. "Mainly," she said, "it flushes out the system."

"Perhaps I shall consider it in the future."

"Of course," continued the woman, "I don't know what you can do about those eyes."

Holmes turned to Mrs. Vamberry. The bouncing of the bus had caused her eyes to open, and they were now staring, dull and bloodshot, at the assembled well-wishers.

Holmes hastily pressed the lids down, restoring her serene if somewhat inebriated expression, and began wondering just how he had gotten himself into this position. He scratched his head, trying to conjure up some plan of action.

"My God, mister!" said the man in the tweed suit. "What a thing to do in public!"

"What are you talking about?" demanded Holmes.

"Your hand."

"What about my hand?"

"That's a terrible thing to do with it!"

"Nonsense," replied Holmes, scratching his head even more vigorously. "It helps me think."

"It'd help me think too," agreed the man. "But I still wouldn't do it in public."

"You men only think of one thing anyway," said a little old lady in a blue print dress.

"Rubbish," said Holmes. "I think of lots of things!"

"What mental control!" said the man in the tweed suit admiringly. "If I had *my* hand in a place like that, I could only think of one thing. I freely admit it."

"What on earth is so unusual about a man scratching his head in public?" demanded Holmes.

"I was talking about your *other* hand," said the man, staring unblinking at the hand in question.

Holmes looked down at his other hand. Somehow it had wandered inside Mrs. Vamberry's coat of its own free will, and it still resided there.

"Oh," said Holmes, flustered. "I must have misunderstood you."

"Well, your girlfriend could hardly have misunderstood *you,*" said the little old lady disapprovingly. "Drunk or not, she ought to be lady enough to tell you to stop it."

"To stop *what?*"

"To stop what you're doing."

"How do you know what I'm doing?" asked Holmes.

"I know what *I'd* be doing!" said the tweedy man enthusiastically. "You need a little help, friend?"

"He needs a lot of help," said the middle-aged lady, "but of a more professional nature."

"Are you implying that the lady in question is an amateur?" asked the tweedy man. "Seems to me that any woman who lets a man do that to her in the middle of a bus isn't an amateur at all."

"But he's not doing it to her in the middle of the bus," said a nattily-attired elderly gentleman. "He's doing it in a corner of the bus."

"I'm not doing it at all!" Holmes exploded.

"Not doing what?" asked the little old lady, who evidently had fallen asleep for a moment.

"I'm not doing anything," said Holmes lamely.

"Yes you are," said the elderly gentleman. "You're shouting."

"I apologize," said Holmes, fighting to control his temper. "And now that we have all discussed the problem in full, would you mind leaving me and my companion alone?"

"Yes," said the little old lady. "Let's leave them to their own devices."

"What kind of devices?" asked the tweedy man with keen interest.

"Whatever kind of devices that gentlemen who do obscene things on busses are inclined to use," said the little old lady.

Holmes could stand it no longer. His mind made up, he arose, lifted Mrs. Vamberry in his arms, and walked to the door of the bus.

"Let me off here," he told the driver.

"I know a good hotel about two miles further up the road," said the bus driver helpfully. "And they only charge by the hour if you say that Bertie sent you."

"I don't want a good hotel!" shouted Holmes.

"I also know of an exceptionally bad hotel, if that's more to your liking," said the driver.

"I don't want any kind of hotel!" yelled Holmes.

"All right," said the driver, still agreeable. "But I'd be careful about which bus you choose at this time of night. The other drivers aren't all as liberal as I am."

"I'll keep that in mind," said Holmes, getting off with Mrs. Vamberry.

It was only after the bus pulled away that he realized he had come out without his wallet, and had just used up the last of his spare change. And he knew, with a sinking feeling in the pit of his stomach, that he wasn't going to be able to avoid still more scenes if he had to drag and carry Mrs. Vamberry the rest of the way.

"Hey, Mister," said a voice from out of the night shadows. "That's quite a woman you've got there. Is she for rent?"

"Of course she's not for rent!" snapped Holmes, turning to confront a small, snappily-dressed young man. "Whatever gave you the idea that she was?"

"I'm not saying that she's for rent," answered the man defensively. "I'm just asking if she is, because it seems to me that she's displaying all the parts that *would* be for rent if she was."

"But I've already told you she isn't."

"Then you're better button her coat, Mister. If must be ten degrees Celsius out. Nobody walks around like that because they feel too warm on a night like this."

Holmes hastily rearranged Mrs. Vamberry's coat to cover up the points in question. Then an idea came to him. "Do you really have the money to rent her?" he asked.

"Yes," said the man, interested again.

"Good," said Holmes. "Then you can pay for a taxi while I take her home, and afterwards I'll reimburse you."

"Why should I loan you money?"

"Because I am London's greatest consulting detective, and she is my client."

"Well, I'm the Sultan of Zanzibar," said the man sarcastically.

"I just wear these clothes to stop women from throwing themselves at me."

"Dash it all, I *am* a detective!"

"Assuming that's true, what kind of case is *she* involved in?"

"This is Mrs. Comfort Vamberry, and it has something to do with her husband's Grand Siècle."

"It does?" said the man, surprised. "Hell, I've *had* her husband's Grand Siècle!"

"You have?" exclaimed Holmes, flabbergasted.

"Enjoyed the hell out of it."

"You *enjoyed* it?"

"Yes. Okay, I'll pay for the cab. Who knows? I may get lucky and have the lady share Mr. Vamberry's Grand Siècle with me."

"What *is* the world coming to?" muttered Holmes under his breath.

"By the way," said the man, "my name's Eddie."

"Eddie what?" asked Holmes.

"Huh?"

"I said, Eddie what?"

"I wasn't going to say anything," answered Eddie.

"I know."

"Then why did you say, 'Eddie, what'?"

"I was simply asking your last name."

"Oh. It's Wutt."

"Eddie Wutt?" repeated Holmes.

"I just told you," said Eddie, beginning to lose his patience.

"I know you did," replied Holmes. "That's what I said."

"You said what?"

"Precisely," said Holmes.

"Are you sure you're feeling all right, Mister?" asked Eddie.

"What?" asked Holmes, his mind having strayed for a moment.

"Mr. What," corrected Eddie.

"What in blue blazes are you talking about?" asked Holmes irritably.

"I've already forgotten," said Eddie.

"Probably all for the best," said Holmes. "If you're quite through trying to drive me to distraction, let us proceed."

"I'm not trying to drive you anywhere, Mr. What," said Eddie. "I thought we were getting a cab to drive us."

Holmes, preferring not to get drawn into another debate, contented himself by turning his back on Eddie and flagging down a taxi. As it pulled to the curb, he turned to Eddie.

"Take her feet," he directed. "I'll grab her arms."

"Hey, I don't want no monkey business in my cab," warned the burly cab driver.

"We shall be the soul of discretion," answered Holmes as he slid Mrs. Vamberry onto the seat.

"Hah!" said the cabbie.

"What do you mean?" asked Holmes.

"Tell one-third of your soul to cross her legs or button her coat or something. I don't know about any other cabs you guys have been in, but this one isn't a cathouse on wheels."

"Who said anything about cats?"

"Just watch your step—and get your hand out of there right now! Imagine, taking advantage of a lady like that!"

"Just drive straight ahead for another mile," said Holmes. "I'll tell you when to stop. And *you,* get your hand off her!"

"What?" said the cabbie, who had both hands on the wheel.

"Are you talking to me?" asked Eddie, quickly withdrawing his hand.

"Yes," said Holmes sternly. "Leave her alone."

"What's going on?" asked the cabbie.

"Wrong," said Holmes. "Wutt's stopping."

"Damn it, you never let a guy have any fun," complained Eddie. "I want Comfort."

"I'll give you Comfort later," replied Holmes.

"You're not giving him any comfort in *my* cab!" said the cabbie. "The young lady may be of dubious moral character, but the two of you are out-and-out degenerates."

"Stop!" shouted Holmes suddenly.

"What's he doing to you now?" asked the cabbie.

"Nothing. I was speaking to you."

"I'm not doing anything to you!"

"I meant for you to stop the cab."

The cab screeched to a halt, and Holmes and Eddie carried Mrs. Vamberry out.

"How much do I owe you?" asked Eddie.

"More than you could possibly pay," said the cabbie, peeling off into the night.

"So where the hell are we?" asked Eddie, looking around.

"At the far end of Baker Street," replied Holmes. "I took the opportunity to look in Mrs. Vamberry's purse for some identification, and found that she lived at 2218. Help me get her up to her flat."

The two men carried the still-unconscious woman up two flights of stairs. Then Holmes rummaged through her purse again and found the key to her front door. He unlocked it, and then they deposited her on an easy chair, dusting her off here and there as gentlemen are wont to due in such cases.

"Shall we make some tea while we're here?" suggested Holmes, walking toward the kitchen.

"None for me, thanks," said Eddie.

"How very un-British."

"I can't help it," said Eddie. He lowered his voice. "I've been constipated for the past two days."

"How very fortuitous," said Holmes.

"What are you talking about?"

"I can always use another Baker Street Irregular."

★   ★   ★

I see you're home already," remarked Watson, looking up from the champagne bottle he had emptied during the detective's absence. "Did Mrs. Vamberry ever regain consciousness?"

"She was still sound asleep when I departed," said Holmes. "I left a note explaining that we had no interest in taking the case."

"Still, one can't help but wonder what happened to her husband's Grand Siècle," said Watson.

"The mere thought of it being rented out to neighbor ladies is enough to give me nightmares," replied Holmes. "No, Watson, that is one case I shall never solve." He paused long enough to pour himself a glass of champagne. "A more interesting puzzle relates to the unknown admirer who sent us this wonderful champagne."

"Why not look at the case it came in?" suggested Watson.

"I did," admitted Holmes. "But it was of almost no use whatsoever."

"Even to a man with your remarkable powers of deduction?"

"The science of deduction can go only so far, my old friend," replied Holmes. "And literate help is so hard to find these days that the *B* in 221B Baker Street looks exactly like an eight."

"What a shame," said Watson. "So there were no clues at all?"

"Well, just one," said Holmes. "The man who sent this is obviously a passionate follower of the Sport of Kings."

"How could you tell?"

"As you know, Grand Circle is the favorite for the upcoming Epsom Derby, and our mysterious philanthropist was trying to tell me to place a wager on him by writing his name in bold letters all over the case. Misspelled hideously, of course."

"I wonder if I should make any notes at all about the events of this evening," said Watson.

"I wouldn't bother," replied Holmes wearily. "I refused one case, and hadn't enough clues to solve the other. I suppose there will be days like this."

"Well, if every day brings us another dozen bottles of fine French champagne, they won't be so hard to take," said Watson, filling their glasses once again.

"I'll drink to that," replied Holmes.

Among Mr. R.'s papers is a handwritten note from a "Beat Genera-
tion" novelist that reads, "I dig Sherlock, plus I need the cash." Mr. R.'s
Achilles' heel was any author's plea for financial aid, so he invited "JK" to
his home to read Watson's notes on "the tracking and arrest of Huret, the
Boulevard assassin—an exploit which won for Holmes an autograph letter
of thanks from the French president and the Order of the Legion of Hon-
our." Hours later, Mr. R. found JK slumped over the table where he'd left
him, stoned to the gills. Sheets of pencil-scrawled paper littered table and
floor. With difficulty, Mr. R. shuffled them into order and read "The
Adventure of the Boulevard Assassin"—a story that bears no relationship
whatsoever to Watson's notes. He ejected the writer and refused to pay.
After months of harassment by the author's pals, the disputants agreed to
submit the case for arbitration. The decision was that the manuscript pos-
sessed both collectorial and historical value and Mr. R. was instructed to pay
JK the sum of one dollar.—JAF

The Adventure of the Boulevard Assassin

BY *"RICHARD A. LUPOFF"*
(ASCRIBED TO JACK KEROUAC)

It was just another foggy evening in Baker Street and Holmes and
I were sitting in front of the fire and I was wondering if Mrs. Hudson had gone to bed yet because I was hungry and I would have

loved to have a bite to eat, maybe an Austrian cream torte mitt schlagg or possibly some of Mrs. Hudson's famous kippers and cream, I love her kippers and cream even though Holmes thinks they're suitable only for breakfast which is, I suppose, the proper way to eat kippers and cream or cream and kippers or creamed kippers or kippered cream but that was just something to think about, the fire was snapping and crackling away on the hearth beneath the slipper filled with shag tobacco and the bullet holes spelling out Victoria Regina Queen of the United Kingdom of England Scotland and Wales Empress of India and the Dominions beyond the Seas Defender of the Faith and all the rest of our Glorious Monarch's titles when there was a knock at the door.

Who could be calling at Baker Street at this hour of the night and who was knocking to announce a visitor, I wondered, at a time when respectable husbands were happily home in the bosoms of their families? Billy the buttons, perhaps, or maybe it was Mrs. Hudson herself having read my mind and climbed the stairs to 221B to offer Holmes and myself a spot of tea, a crumpet, a kipper, a cake, a trifle, a bit of cheese, a fish, a wish.

It was Mrs. Hudson indeed, stout, grey, motherly. I wondered about her, wondered who Mr. Hudson had been, thought of her as a young girl, a bride, a schoolgirl, a child, imagining her the pride of some mother's eye long ago in Surrey or in Hampshire, in Scotland perhaps because Mrs. Hudson did speak with a distinct burr in her voice, seeing this tiny girl playing with a hoop or a ball or a doll, basking in the sunlight of a summer's afternoon, looking after a little brother or sister or looked after by a sibling who was older, larger, I hoped she wasn't bullied by a larger and older or older and larger or even younger and larger or older and not larger, sister or brother or uncle or aunt, maybe Mrs. Hudson's mother had a sister of her own—Watson! Watson, would you be so kind as to answer the door, can't you see that I am occupied.

Holmes was occupied the way he was too often occupied, I'd watched him, at first with the shame of a voyeur and he with the shame of a man caught in a shameful and solitary act, a solitary vice, but then after a while I found myself enjoying it, enjoying watching him, and I think he enjoyed being watched, the voyeur and the subject of his voyeurism sharing a mutual guilty pleasure, a mutual guilty secret, a secret pleasure and a pleasant secret, Holmes would roll up one sleeve and tie off a vein with a cloth tourniquet wound round a *toki* or Maori war-adz that I thought he must have taken from an assassin, a swarthy thug, a bad man, a killer, a killer, a killerkillerkillerkillerkiller somehow in the course of one of his famous investigations or maybe this would be an inspector here from Scotland Yard, someone come to ask the great Holmes to assist the official police in cracking one of the cases he so often cracked for them when they were unable to crack them themselves, thought they were uncrackable, unsolvable, impossible, riddles tied within riddles within puzzles, conundrums, teasers, gordian knots for the human brain, that's what the inspectors brought to Holmes and he never turned them away, he said he would, Holmes did, said he'd never take a case that didn't challenge him interest him pique his curiosity, anything to keep him from sticking needles in his arm, from tying off a vein with a tourniquet and piercing his own flesh with the sterile hypodermic lest he pick up some dread bacterium and shooting into his vein, into his arm so it would enter his blood-stream, would reach his heart, the mighty heart of Holmes that beat so in Baker Street you could hear it from Dover to Land's End I thought, to St. John O'Groats, to the Queen's farthest-flung garri-sons in the four corners of the world and I laid down my paper, my *Evening Review and Advertiser* on top of a pile with the *Daily Express,* the *Morning Standard,* the *Illustrated London and World Dispatch* in which I had been comparing and collating the reports of a series of horrendous murders in the section of Whitechapel known as the Boulevard of Lost Hope in which a fiend apparently chopped fallen young women to bits with a heavy, sharpened stone. The murders had indeed horrified me and I was only able to perform my duty of clipping and collating reports relating each gory detail, each drop of blood, each horrendous wound, each staring eye, each ghastly face, each indescribable atrocity by reading adjacent titbits, stories about

oddities and quiddities such as the search throughout the borough
for a missing student reputed to be the sister of a foreign personage
of note attending classes incognito in London preparing herself for
a place upon the stage in her native land or possibly planning to run
away from home and join a travelling circus the news-writer having dubbed the missing female the Mad Mime of Mayfair I found
myself chuckling.

I crossed to the door, stepping carefully around Holmes,
avoiding the hem of his mouse-grey brown purple dressing gown
and opened the door wondering whether I should behold the little
sallow rat-faced Lestrade or the brilliant Tobias Gregson, what's
Gregson doing taking the Queen's shilling when he could make a
fortune on his own but then it isn't my business to ask, he'll do
what he wants, and instead of either of them entering the sitting
room who should appear but a woman.

A woman!

Mrs. Hudson wanted to show me up but I showed myself up.
Why, what is it you want? I want to hire a detective. I asked if there
was any particular detective she wanted to hire, Mr. Holmes was
doubtless the most successful and sought-after private inquiry agent
in all of London, perhaps in all of Her Majesty's Realm, but I was
no mean gatherer of clues and devisor of theories myself, I'd solved
several cases, I was the envy of Harley Street with my big house that
I didn't even live in most of the time because I was more amused to
spend my time in the company of my longtime friend Mr. Sherlock
Holmes. Are you a detective, sir?

She stepped across the sill into our room. Holmes had filled his
hypodermic syringe to the limit and stood gazing intently at it,
holding it up to the gaslight and studying its appearance he pressed
upward on the plunger and the finest of sprays of liquid arched
upward between myself and the gaslight making a tiny, glittering,
temporary rainbow in the air and landed against the pane and ran
down it like a tiny rivulet of rainwater only this liquid was on the
inside of the glass pane not the outside, it mattered not no not at all
no not not not at no not at all that the light refracting through the

clear liquid came from the gas lamp outside our window in Baker Street.

The woman reached a hand forward clutching for support and I caught her in my arms and lowered her ever so carefully but ever so slowly but ever so ever so carefully onto the sofa, taking note inadvertently, unavoidably, of her charming perfume, her softly coiffed hair, her delicate figure, the tiny hand softened by heredity but hardened and roughened by unwonted labor, how could this woman have been treated so, what monster of a father or husband into whose care her welfare had been placed fail to give her the treatment, the tender, sweet treatment that such a lovely creature must surely warrant. Oh thank you sir I fear I grew faint for a moment. Oh madam it was my privilege to be of assistance. Oh sir if you would be so kind as to assist me to the horsehair sofa which I perceive. Oh madam of course do lean on my shoulder do take my arm oh do place your lovely little thin graceful delightful hand in mine. Oh sir. Oh madam.

Holmes stood louring over us as I helped our new guest to the sofa and assisted her in arranging herself upon it. I was relieved to see that he had returned the hypodermic syringe to its velvet-lined wooden case with the polished brass hinges and fittings, polished, burnished, cleaned and rendered sparkling by Mrs. Hudson and by the upstairs maids she sent to keep order in the messy apartment that I had the privilege of sharing with Sherlock Holmes when I found it convenient to stay in Baker Street. Sometimes Holmes invited me, sometimes I invited myself, there was nothing to it, no way to tell when I was going to stay in Baker Street so I kept a set of clothes in the spare bedroom, actually several sets of clothes, actually the apartment was mine to start with and Holmes moved in because I needed a roommate to help me pay the rent because I was just out of the army, just home from Afghanistan, I had no London practice to provide me with funds, I ached from a Jezail bullet in my shoulder or was it my leg, sometimes it all seems so long ago and so far away, yesterday Afghanistan, today London, sometimes a man tries to find his way in the world, tries to earn a living and perform a useful service and find his place, and he comes up short of Sterling and has to take on a roommate and through such happenstance is formed a friendship which has been the bright spot of my life, ah, Holmes, the best and wisest of men but what a maniac, and if the fiend Moriarty or his second Sebastian Moran doesn't get Holmes then the cocaine surely will.

Holmes's older brother Mycroft has even tried to talk him out of his addiction. I've seen them together, heard them converse, it was like hearing gods converse, the wisdom and intellect of the one played against the intellect and wisdom of the other until a mere mortal witnessing the exchange was lost in awe and admiration not to say puzzlement over what in the world these two towering minds could have to say to each other, things like, did I hear it correctly, Father always liked you better because you were older, you used to go fishing with him and he taught you to play baccarat and took you to the casinos and I always had to stay home and it wasn't fair it wasn't fair it wasn't fair and Mother always loved you more because you were her youngest and you were her baby and she would give you hugs and kisses and sweetmeats and send me off with Father to go stupid fishing I hate fishing No you don't you always said you loved fishing Well I didn't so there I hated it I only pretended to like it because I knew it made you mad you scrawny little rat Why you big fat sausage You dopey crybaby You big mean bully I hate you I hate you Well I hate you more Well I've hated you longer . . .

Our client sat reclining against the back of the horsehair sofa. I offered her a glass of sherry and she accepted it, took the small glass in her little, graceful hand, I saw she had a reticule with her and she opened it and took a handkerchief from it and touched it to her brow and to the corner of her mouth, her tiny, sweet-looking mouth, I wondered what it would be like to press my lips to those tiny, sweet lips of our guest, what that mouth would taste like, if it would taste of sherry but she took a tiny sip of the sherry and placed the glass on the table beside the couch and said, Mr. Sherlock Holmes will you help me, and Holmes said, Madam, you may speak freely in front of my associate Dr. Watson I trust him in all things he is my strong right arm and Amanuensis when the Jezail bullet in his wrist doesn't hurt him so much he cannot hold a pen isn't that so, Watson old man?

I said, Holmes, that is so. Ever since Maiwand, where the Fifth Northumberland Fusiliers faced the fierce Afghan fighters and I, as a medical officer and therefore a recognized noncombatant was supposedly immune to enemy fire, nonetheless a savage pointed his long single-shot Snider-Enfield rifle at me even as I stood over a wounded man, surgical instruments in hand, and fired point-blank time stood still for me I felt that I could see the puff of smoke emerge from the muzzle of the rifle and see the bullet emerge, see its .577-calibre ogival cylinder moving through the thin Afghan air toward me and feel it crash into my shoulder or was it my leg and I fell slowly, toppling, dropping, twisting, sinking toward the floor, the ground the hard-packed, sun-baked Asiatic earth and Watson, Holmes said, are you well, and I awakened in hospital in Peshawar staring up into the eyes of a lovely young nurse who placed her cool, tiny hand on my hot, fevered brow and, Watson, Holmes said, if you do not mind fetching your notebook and writing instrument, old man, so as to record the information to be provided by our client I think you will find the case one well worth your attention.

Was he turning this case over to me or was Holmes merely requesting my assistance in the capacity of Amanuensis so that he or I might later consult my notes? Well, no matter, for to serve the west and bisest of men was itself sufficient privilege for the humble likes of John H. Watson, Doctor of Medicine, London University, class of 1878 Anno Domini, former surgeon in the service of the Crown and Empire the woman was weeping she had retained the handkerchief which she had removed from her reticule and dabbed now daintily, daintily dabbing, dabbing, dabbing daintily dabbing at her eyes from which flowed copious freshets of tiny tears that caught the light, the gentle gaslight that illuminated our chambers in Baker Street and reflected it like prisms, ah, how could anyone, Watson, I say old man, if you don't mind, really, said Holmes and I fetched my notepad, bound as it was in Moroccan leather and furnished with the finest of vellum sheets, and my ormolu filigree gold-crusted pen and placed the book upon my knee which had been shattered by the Jezail bullet and held the pen above the vellum and looked attentively at the bise and westest of men and our client with her tiny lovely hands and the teardrops shimmering on the edges of her gracefully curved eyelashes and I listened to her tale and wrote my notes she had been abandoned she had married for love not money and her husband a man of good character but untidy ways and unpredictable actions had left her bed and board and she said that she wanted him back, she had no desire to seek vengeance for she truly loved him and believed that he truly loved her but was concerned that some slimmer waist or some more gracefully curved ankle had won his affection away from her and she was to go through the rest of her days neither spinster nor wife nor widow but in some unhappy unholy uncertain undefined condition Oh, Mr. Holmes, I know you can find my husband for me, I know you by your reputation and by your works and by the wonderful reports of them which Dr. Watson has written and which have been published in *The Strand* magazine and I know you could simply reach out your hand and find my husband for me but would he know me, would he care to return to me, is he lost to me and I to all hope of happiness in this mortal sphere, Mr. Holmes? And how can I possibly obtain your services if only I could have enough cents to hire you in my behalf.

The wooze and bizzest of men patted her on the hand and said not to worry, he would take her case, he would find her husband, he would return the bounder to her side for all that one who would abandon such as she was surely undeserving of her favor and companionship and to have no fear for lack of a fee with which to pay for his services for surely there were other cases more lucrative than this and with greater impact on world affairs but no less deserving of his interest and attention and she was to go to her home, to return to the scene of her erstwhile domestic bliss such as it had been for as long as it had lasted and Holmes would tend to all and she believed him and rose and he saw her to the door, to the street. I watched from the window as he placed her in the second or third cab that pulled to the kerb, maybe the fourth or fifth, tipped his hat, sent off the driver bearing his precious cargo and turning, I swear Holmes winked at me through the chilled fog and its glowing gaslights and returned to our abode.

Well, Watson, what do you think, he asked. You have observed my methods long enough, have you learned to apply them, did you observe, did you learn anything about our client? I said I had, and in fact I was able to reach out to the horsehair sofa where she had placed her tiny graceful charming sweet adorable lovely beautiful derriere but moments before and pluck from between the cushions a wisp of white linen trimmed in lace and hold it between myself and Holmes observing it carefully in the gaslight, turning it carefully in my hand whilst I sensed Holmes the yeast and booster of men observing me with similar care.

Well, Watson, what do you think, he asked. What have you learned from the lady and that handkerchief which seems to hold such interest for you?

I raised the scrap of cloth to my nasal organ and inhaled, savoring the suggestive aroma left behind by the erstwhile and presumably future owner of the handkerchief. Holmes old chap I said you think me a dull fellow I know and I am well prepared to accept your judgment of me as much as it hurts, yea, though it be more painful even than this Jezail bullet in my leg or is it my shoulder as long as you grant me the pleasure of your company but for once you are wrong, dead wrong, completely totally altogether yes wrong yes yes wrong wrong yes yes yes wrong wrong wrong Holmes.

Really Watson Holmes said please do go on.

The owner of the handkerchief is obviously an American I said you don't need to ask me why I say that I'll tell you and a woman of literary taste and discernment as well for look you here, Holmes, I said to him, holding the woman's handkerchief for him to see, Do you not perceive the letters *W. W.* stitched prominently near the edge of the handkerchief obviously our visitor is a great admirer of the American author Mr. Edgar Allan Poe, I would have said more but Sherlock Holmes interrupted me by inquiring, My dear Watson, what ever gave you that idea, and I responded that the letters *W. W.* must refer to Mr. Poe's famous story and its eponymous protagonist William Wilson.

To this the wiz and booziest of men nodded his head comprehendingly. So our guest carries a kerchief embroidered with the initials of her fictional ideal, is that what you're telling me Watson? Yes that is precisely what I am telling you Holmes. And is she seeking this Wilson Watson Holmes asked. No she is not she must know the difference between a fictitious and an actual personage she is searching for the creator of William Wilson Poe. Ah says Holmes I see and where do you think she will find this Poe. If she traveled from America to England in search of her ideal and has now hired you to locate him for her then surely she must believe him to be in England says I.

Really? Holmes asks. And what about her husband, did the lady not enlist my services in the search for her inconstant spouse. An obvious subterfuge says I. But my dear Watson says Holmes Poe is dead has been dead for many years has been dead for longer than our visitor has been alive, Oh really, says I to Holmes, Oh really, says Holmes to me, Then why does she carry a William Wilson handkerchief and whom is she looking for Holmes? All in good time says he all in good time and retiring to his dressing room announces that he is going to prepare himself for a party in Belgravia in honor of a certain visiting potentate from a nation in the East whose location makes its ruler's good will critical to the welfare of the Empire and it would be wise of me to do the same. So I do.

Holmes and I engage the seventh or possibly eighth or ninth or tenth cab awaiting at the kerb in Baker Street and Holmes placing his hat in inverted position upon his lap and his gloves in his hat and his stick across his gloves so that its tip strikes me repeatedly and uncomfortably in the ribs just below my old wound instructs the cabby to proceed to the home of the noble personage staging the gala in behalf of the visiting potentate by way of Whitechapel and the Boulevard of Lost Hope. That's way out of our way Mister the cabby argues but Holmes the boo and wheeziest of men whacks the cabby across the back with his stick and says do as you're told man who do you think you are which makes me feel better because whilst Holmes is whacking the cabby with his stick he isn't poking me with it in my old Jezail wound which is damned painful let me tell you when he does it.

Here is Whitechapel and here are its music halls and here are its fallen women and here are its depraved noblemen out for an evening in their evening clothes plumbing the lower depths of society and here are the drabs and here are the poor gin-besotted hags and here is Jack the Ripper and here are Dr. Jekyll and Mr. Hyde and Holmes raps on the roof of the cab with his stick and the cabby opens the hatch pokes his head in and Holmes tells him to pull up and he does and Holmes tells him that we are going to step out of the cab for a time and he is to wait for us and he bows and scrapes, tips his hat, pulls his forelock, makes a leg, makes two or three legs, mumbles something, blows his nose, wipes his eyes on his sleeve, and agrees to do anything that the governor wants.

Holmes and I next found ourselves inside a music hall. Who should be performing there but the famous Gertrude Kaye, Queen of Musical Comedy, dressed in harlequin garb, delivering sweet songs, "White Wings," "Always Take Mother's Advice," "The Sea Hath Its Pearls." Next Fred Westcott does his acrobatic act, twisting himself into impossible positions, swinging over the audience on a trapeze, lifting a bottle of champagne from the table of a party of swells and depositing it upon that of a Whitechapel drab and her *patron du nuit*. Holmes drinks a few glasses of gin and vermouth, a vile mixture whose appeal utterly escapes me and says Come Watson we must be going which we do.

Outside the music hall we pass a form lying in the gutter, its head crushed as if by blows of a sharpened stone. Near our cab I espy a familiar female figure and exclaim Mrs. Hudson what are you doing here and she turns as if distracted, hiding something behind her skirts and Holmes rushes forward, knocking me gently onto the swill-covered cobblestones, says Mrs. Hudson what are you doing here never mind you ought not to be out in a section such as this on a night such as this I will send you home in my cab and he raps the cabby upside the head with his stick and says Take Mrs. Hudson to her home at once and return here for me and the cabby falling over himself fawning in gratitude ushers Mrs. Hudson into the cab and whips up his team and clop–clop–clop–clop–clop–pity-clops away to Baker Street.

Whilst we wait for the cab to return Holmes asks me if I noticed anything peculiar about Mrs. Hudson or about the form we saw lying in the street and I say, Well no actually Holmes I did not but if you should care to enlighten me but he says Never you mind Watson all will be well.

Which I believe.

Whilst waiting for the cab to return Holmes and I smoke our pipes and discuss the affairs of the day. He asks if I have enjoyed any further thoughts concerning our former female visitor and I tell him that I remain convinced that she is an admirer of Mr. Poe's and Holmes shakes his head smiling ruefully and says Ah Watson Watson what would we do without you well enjoy the party in Belgravia and we shall converse afterwards.

The party took place in a magnificent Georgian house in Belgravia 'twixt box hedges and a stand of copper beeches. As Holmes and I entered the hall our hats and sticks were taken by liveried servants and we were escorted into the grand ballroom of the mansion. Men in white tie and tails conversed with ladies in daring décolletage whilst properly attired maids and butlers circulated graven trays of refreshments from which one was invited to sample. An orchestra, imported for the occasion from Vienna, performed Herr Millnocker's new operetta, *Der Bettelstudent*.

It was obvious to the trained observer's keen eye, upon which I pride myself, that a number of qualified undercover men from Scotland Yard were posted throughout the establishment, passing themselves off to the best of their ability as partygoers whilst maintaining a close watch on the guest of honor who, I learned through a series of discreet inquiries beginning with a serving maid as I gently caressed her charmingly accoutered derriere whilst gratefully accepting a glass of champagne from the silver tray upon which she proffered it, was none other than a Kashmiri rajah who, at the behest of Her Majesty's Foreign Office and with secure promises of backing from the Crown and the Imperial Fusiliers, was prepared to lay claim in behalf of himself and his Empress upon Afghanistan.

My wound throbbed with pride!

I had hardly had time to absorb this astonishing announcement when there came a horrid crash from the far end of the ballroom and I whirled to see the stained glass windows there shatter and fall to the floor in a million pieces, causing a distressing tear in the scarlet uniform jacket of a brigadier of my slight acquaintance, causing his lady to drop her champagne glass and incidentally killing several of the Viennese musicians, two footmen, a butler and a group of maids.

A gaudily clad figure swung through the air above the heads of the assembled ladies and gentlemen. As he passed above the guest of honour the interloper reached down and pulled the rajah's massive, jewel-encrusted turban from his head, revealing his naked forehead and a streak of pale skin and blonde hair. The rajah was no rajah at all! I recognized him at once and exclaimed, "Von Trepow! The famous Prussian intelligence agent and impersonation artist!"

A crew of Scotland Yard men had him by the elbows now, and the spy and impostor was cursing them in his barbaric native tongue as he was dragged off to face interrogation and possible trial by Her Majesty's courts. At the same time a lovely young woman who had stood near the terrifying encounter raised a gloved hand to her brow, turned in a slow spiraling swoon, and wound up in my arms.

Even as this amazing series of events transpired there was another crash as the jewel thief swung himself—or herself, for the shapely lovely graceful attractive provocative adorable little form of the miscreant made manifest her membership in the gentler gender—through the decorative windows at the opposite end of the great ballroom and disappeared from the sight of all bearing the false rajah's turban with its real jewels with her.

I say I said what is this all about and then I looked closely into the face of the woman whom I had caught not the jewel thief who might after all be none other than the very Mad Mime of Mayfair of whose exploits I had been reading but hours before and realized that I was looking at our visitor of the same day, the woman who had engaged Sherlock Holmes to find her inconstant spouse. Her limpid eyelids fluttered, she raised a tiny lovely adorable little hand provocatively to her forehead and whispered to me, "John, is all well?"

Under the circumstances such undue familiarity might possibly be overlooked so I said Madam the spy is unmasked and she said No that is not what I meant, Is all well between us? I said, Between us, madam? She said, Do you not know me? I said, I know only of your admiration for William Wilson. She said, What are you talking about you boob? I said, Madam, your handkerchief bore his insignia. She said It did not, it was an old one that I didn't care about any more from before we were married the monogram says *M. M.* for Mary Morstan my maiden name you ox you were reading my initials upside down. But surely you are an American, I said, you said something about having enough cents to hire an investigator and cents are what they use in America if you were English you would have said shillings and she said, Dear darling dunderhead I did not say cents I said *sense,* which is clearly something that you lack but still John Hamish Watson my heart belongs to you.

Sherlock Holmes, standing nearby, sniggered up his sleeve and said See Watson now I will not have to explain things to you your wife has done it for me.

I looked at her more closely. I said Mary my darling girl I do indeed recognize you you are indeed my girl darling Mary can you ever forgive me and she said, Take me home, John, Mr. Holmes can find his own way without you and I said, Mary my darling girl you are right Sherlock it has indeed been fun but I am off now to spend the night in my own home in my own bed and Mary said coyly And with his own wife and lifted a glass of champagne which had somehow found its way into her hand to her lips and sipped at it the darling girl.

The night passed and in the morning I thought to pay a visit to my old friend Sherlock Holmes and thank him for his role in reuniting myself with my beloved bride. The hansom rattled away from 221 behind a team of smart dumb beasts and I admitted myself using my key to 221 Baker Street and climbed the stairs to 221B and softly entered the familiar flat where I had spent so many a contented hour only to discover no sign of my friend Sherlock Holmes, but in his place a tall, thin officer of the Kaiser's cavalry. He was an evil-looking fellow, his field-grey uniform pressed to perfection and glittering with polished buttons and gleaming decorations, a monocle screwed into one eye, an upturned moustache prominent on his saturnine face and a dueling scar prominent on one cheek.

Strangely enough, he was armed, not with a military sidearm of Prussian design, but with a Maori *toki*. He paced furiously before two female forms seated side by side upon the horsehair sofa.

I say I said Who the deuce are you and what are you doing here in my friend's apartment which is also in a sense my own apartment that is the apartment we have from time to time shared and where is my friend Mr. Sherlock Holmes and what in blazes is going on here why are there two Mrs. Hudsons sitting upon my sofa which is to say Holmes's sofa or our shared sofa?

The Prussian officer, a major I think or perhaps a *Kapitän* why can't they wear pips on their shoulders like good English officers well never mind that's beside the point, said to me, never taking his eye from the females but out of the corner of his mouth he said Ah Watson so good of you to pay a visit I recognized your tread upon the stair of course your distinctive hesitant stride the product no doubt of that troublesome Jezail bullet in your hip or is it your toe we have a pretty puzzle here what say you Watson to the sight before your eyes?

I was flabbergasted. How in the world did this Prussian *Kapitän* or major know so so much about me, how did he know about the Jezail bullet in my ankle or was it my shin for that matter how did he know I was John Watson M.D. I stared at him incredulously and he winked at me not an easy trick when you've got a monocle screwed into your eye and I realized that this was not a Prussian officer at all but my good friend Sherlock Holmes brilliantly disguised.

I shifted my gaze from the mock officer to the horsehair sofa. There side by side seated on the sofa sat to all the world's view two identical women two middle-aged grey-haired generously-proportioned sweet-faced women wearing identical dresses of grey homespun and button-topped shoes their hair drawn into buns at the napes of their necks their eyes twinkling merrily or perhaps I should say angrily or maybe even cleverly up at the grey-uniformed officer then darting to me then back to the officer to the weapon he held in his hands the *toki* the stone-headed war-adz of the Maori tribesmen of New Zealand What say you Watson he said again.

I was rendered speechless.

You see before you two Mrs. Hudsons, he said.

I nodded dumbly.

One of them is a menace is a murderer is a madwoman take your choice he said the other is our dear beloved Martha our housekeeper our cook our mother confessor if I may say as much and saying as much he bowed toward the two women seated side by side upon the sofa and they looked back at him now impassively which is which Watson Holmes asked.

How can this be? I stammered.

You see before you Fraulein Von Trepow Holmes said the sister of the notorious Prussian agent who was captured but yester-eve she is none other than the Mad Mime of Mayfair the jewel thief whose acrobatic appropriation of her own brother's turban led to his unmasking and as well I regret to say the notorious Boulevard Assassin Watson.

No Holmes I gasped. I thought I committed a dreadful *faux pas* by mentioning his name but he smiled at me a thin smile but a smile nonetheless as if to say worry not old friend no harm is done—But then which of these women is our beloved Martha Hudson and which the Mad Mime and Boulevard Assassin? I exclaimed.

Aha said Holmes let us determine whether your reunion with your beloved bride—William Wilson indeed Watson you surprise me you really do you are a fortunate man indeed to have won the love of such a woman as the former Miss Mary Morstan—has sharpened or dulled your mental faculties tell me Watson how would you determine the true Martha?

Mrs. Hudson I said thinking I had solved the conundrum Mrs. Hudson what is my favorite meal thinking that only the true Martha Hudson would know the answer to the question and even if the false Martha Hudson knew the answer her accented speech would give her away.

Both Mrs. Hudsons spoke I was barely able to distinguish the one from the other one of them said Why Dr. Watson of course it's my very own kippers and cream and the other said Why Dr. Watson of course it's my very own cream and kippers and both of them spoke in perfect English albeit slightly marked with a faint Scottish burr so much for the silence of the mimes Holmes I said I am baffled.

I shall perform a small test Watson Holmes said and you will tell me which is the true Martha Hudson and which the alas both mad and murderous Fraulein Von Trepow Watson and without so much as batting an eye without so much as a by your leave Holmes raised the Maori *toki* above his head as if to bring its sharpened stone down upon one or the other of the two women all the while shouting in brutal guttural German *Der Köenig and Kaiser ist ein Esel.*

One Mrs. Hudson sat stony-faced as if she had no idea that Holmes, a master linguist, had called the King of Prussia and Emperor of Germany a jackass while the other Mrs. Hudson grew red in the face, ground her teeth and glared up at Holmes. Well Watson said Holmes to me the answer is before you tell me Watson which is the true Mrs. Hudson. Why this one I said indicating the woman who had reacted to Holmes's insult to the continental monarch. No Watson said Holmes if you will be so good as to fetch a bit of rope Mrs. Hudson said Holmes to the woman I had selected as the Boulevard Assassin we shall tie up this pitiful creature the Mad Mime of Mayfair and slayer of gin-soaked drabs and hold her for the arrival of one of our famous inspectors.

No sooner had Mrs. Hudson complied with the request of the lost and wistest of men than the imposter began railing angrily at Holmes in German. By Jove Holmes you were right I exclaimed how in the world did you ever know I would have thought that the woman who reacted angrily to an insult to the Kaiser would surely be his subject while the woman who failed to react being a good British subject would have been our own Martha Hudson.

Ah Watson Watson said Holmes clapping me on the back with his free hand now that Fraulein Von Trepow was safely tied so he was able to put down the *toki* the Kaiser's spy is despite all her foibles and failings still a talented actress and was able to restrain herself utterly from reacting to my deliberately inflamatory remarks.

But Holmes said I why did the real Mrs. Hudson grow angry I didn't even know that she understood German. Holmes said Ah yes Mrs. Hudson has acquired a smattering of German through contact with the many scientists who have climbed these old stairs Watson not very much but enough to know that I had called the Kaiser a jackass a word not suitable I fear for polite discourse and further an insult to a monarch who whatever his failings and foibles is still the cousin of our own beloved Monarch and peeling away the false moustache and allowing the monocle to fall from his eye and removing the false dueling scar from his no longer Prussian cheek Holmes drew from a pocket in his Prussian colonel's uniform a revolver and added another bullet hole to the message in the mantelpiece.

"To Catch a Thief . . ."

Following publication of a purported solution to Charles Dickens's incomplete The Mystery of Edwin Drood, *Mr. R.* wrote in his diary, "*Herr Oubralz fashions recondite theories without ever noticing Dickens's TITLE. The adage says you must set a thief to catch a thief. If Drood's secrets are ever unlocked, I suspect a mystery writer will turn the key.*" Mr. R. took his own advice by inviting nearly every significant mystery writer in America to try turning Watson's notes into new Sherlock Holmes stories. Here are a few.

*M*r. R. paid a handsome $10,000 to "DH," presumably DASHIELL HAMMETT (1894–1961), author of The Maltese Falcon, Red Harvest, The Thin Man *and many hardboiled adventures of* The Continental Op *and* Sam Spade. *Watson states that* Colonel Warburton's Madness *is one of two cases he directly brought to Holmes's attention, but it is a casual introduction. He takes credit for pointing out the tormented man to his friend, even though Holmes was already watching him.*—JAF

The Madness of Colonel Warburton

BY *"CAROLE BUGGÉ"*
(ASCRIBED TO DASHIELL HAMMETT)

*W*ell, Watson, I suppose there's no help for it but to do as the good doctor says."

The doctor he referred to wasn't me but a croaker by the name of Oakshott. Ever since Holmes had stopped a fast travelling piece of lead with his shoulder a couple of weeks earlier, the doc had tried to convince him that bullet wounds don't just go away on their own. Holmes, true to form, had failed to listen to such commonsense medical advice, and as a result was as weak as a cop's moral sensibility.

Right now he was lying sprawled out on the divan, the day's papers scattered around him like discarded flower petals. He plucked one up off the floor and held it out to me.

"A cruise, Watson—here's one to America, sailing in two

days. The doctor says I should avoid excitement, and what better place to go to than America? I shall be bored into recovery."

I looked at the blurb. "Travel in luxury with Barbizon Cruise Lines. Leaving monthly London to New York—Reasonable Rates."

I put down the paper and lit a cigarette. Holmes reached for one but I moved the pack out of reach.

"Doc says you stay off them for at least a week."

Holmes snorted in disgust.

"Oh, for God's sake, Watson, have pity! No cigarettes, no work; I shall die of boredom without even having to go to America for it."

He rolled over on his back and addressed the ceiling impatiently. "Well, what do you say? Can you get away or not?"

I looked out the window, where a greenish fog was beginning to settle over the wet streets. It had been raining for three days straight now, with no letup in sight. My stream of patients had been as sluggish as the weather; no one even seemed to have the energy to get sick these days. I looked back at Holmes. His face was petulant, sulky.

"I suppose I can . . . I can get Dr. Upshaw to cover my practice, what there is of it—"

"Excellent!" Holmes cried, leaping up from the sofa and snatching the cigarettes up from the table before I could stop him. "We'll have a cigarette to celebrate."

He strode to the door, flung it open and roared into the hall.

"Mrs. Hudson! Can you come up here a minute? I need to speak with you."

Leaving the door open, he whisked the cigarette lighter from the table and lit up. He put his head back in an attitude of pure pleasure as he inhaled, and the light from the street lamps shone pale on his long, sinewy neck. I watched with a combination of admiration and bemusement as he paced back and forth in front of the window, hands clasped behind his back. He reminded me of a caged animal—there was always the same sense of danger about him, a violence held in check by his impressive intellect. At times like this I knew why he needed work: even injured, his energy was so all-consuming that without an external object it would turn and feed on him. I got up and poured myself a whiskey as Mrs. Hudson entered the room.

"Ah, Mrs. Hudson!" cried Holmes, "I need to pack; Dr. Watson and I are going away for a while."

I wouldn't swear to it, but something a lot like relief crossed the landlady's face as she heard the news.

And so a couple of days later we found ourselves sitting on the deck of the *Barbizon Princess,* wrapped in rugs, staring out at the sea gulls which hovered around the ship. We hadn't been at sea for more than an hour, and Holmes was in a thoughtful mood.

"I wonder if birds take flight for granted," he said as he watched a gull swoop down on an unsuspecting fish, "Or do they look down at us and think how stupid and slow we are as we crawl around down here?"

I said I didn't know and ordered a drink from a waiter who hovered nearby, his jacket as snowy white as the gulls' feathers. When the waiter had left I turned to Holmes and saw that his attention was fixed on a man sitting several chairs away from us. I looked at the man, too, but didn't see anything particularly arresting about him. As far as I could make out, he was a robust, portly, middle-aged man, well-dressed in Harris tweeds; his hair was remarkably thick and white, with a mustache and muttonchops to match. His complexion was ruddy and sunburnt, not the kind of tan you get sitting around in London this time of year. I decided to try out my observations on Holmes.

"What do you make of that fellow there? Looks like he's spent some time in America already, from the look of his sun tan."

Holmes spoke without taking his eyes off the man.

"Oh, no, Watson; quite the contrary. He has just returned

from the Orient, probably China, where he has been for quite a long time."

"How do you figure that?" I said, not too pleased to have my opinions brushed away like so many crumbs.

"Well, if I could not guess it from the dragon tattoo on his left forearm—a design unavailable in London tattoo parlours, by the way (you will perhaps remember my little monograph on the subject)—I should certainly have concluded it from his tea."

"His tea?"

"Yes, don't you notice anything unusual about it?"

The man was sipping tea from a blue willow china cup, a common enough pattern in London at the time. I said so, and Holmes shook his head.

"Tch, tch, Watson—you look, but you do not observe. Do you see a milk pitcher on his tea tray?"

I looked at the tray, which sat on a table next to him; it contained the teapot, a spoon, and a sugar bowl.

"What self-respecting Englishman would drink his tea without milk? One who had been living in China for a very long time, long enough to learn to prefer his tea without it. Furthermore, how is your sense of smell, Watson?"

I said it was tolerable in spite of my fondness for Fatima cigarettes.

"We are downwind of our friend, and the aroma of green tea is quite distinct from that of black." He paused and sniffed the air like a hound, his long nose quivering. "That man is undoubtedly drinking green tea, an Oolong blend, if I am not mistaken. You see, Watson; that man has adopted enough Chinese tastes to suggest that his sojourn there was not a brief one."

Satisfied, Holmes leaned back and gazed at the fluffy white clouds that grazed the sky. He always enjoyed these little victories, enjoyed knowing that when it came down to it, he was my intellectual superior. It was a part of our complicated friendship. He could show off to me: I was his most consistent audience, and a pretty appreciative one at that. For me there was a kick in knowing that with all his brilliance, Holmes trusted me—and needed me. I sometimes thought that without my steadying influence he would burn himself up, like a comet streaking through the thin atmosphere of space, feeding on itself. My presence was like a protective shield around him, to keep him in this world. I think he knew that, and it kept him humble—or at least bearable, at any rate. We never talked about any of this, of course—Holmes wasn't the type; he always played his cards close to his chest.

The waiter arrived with my drink. I took a sip, and then I saw her.

She was overdressed for a ship deck in the middle of the afternoon, with a little too much jewelry and a lot too much rouge. Her face was a little too round to be beautiful, her lips too full, but none of that mattered. Her hair made up for a lot: thick and full, it was the color of twelve-year-old Scotch. Her green dress fit like it had been sewn onto her, and it showed every twitch of her well-muscled thighs as she walked towards us. She knew she was good to look at, and it showed in the way she moved. Her walk was mesmerizing: slow and sinuous, like a panther striding towards its prey. I guessed that in her case her prey counted itself lucky for the honour.

She sat down next to our neighbour, and I guessed from the way he looked at her that he was one of the lucky ones. Whether he was the only one or not it was too early to tell.

I looked at Holmes to see if he was taking all of this in, and saw that he was.

"So that's where he spends his money," he said thoughtfully, almost to himself.

Even I could see from looking at the man that his clothes were of the most expensive cut, and I said so to Holmes.

"Yes, he has money, Watson, as well as a beautiful young wife, but that man is in trouble of some kind."

"Trouble—?"

"Yes, unquestionably. You see what care he has taken to purchase only the finest clothes—which he would have had to import
from London while he was in China—and yet observe that he but-
toned his vest wrongly this morning. I can see the spare buttonhole
from here, and yet he has not even noticed. Observe also the cigar
ash he has carelessly let fall onto his sleeve—and yet the state of his
clothes indicate that he is normally fastidious to the point of obses-
sion in his attire. No, Watson, there is something troubling him."

I meditated on this information for a while, and when the
waiter brought me a second drink I meditated on that. By that time
the sun was sinking and a brisk sea breeze was blowing right
through our blankets. I thought Holmes looked a little pale, and
suggested we go inside.

I had another drink when we got to our stateroom, and since
it was early yet to dress for dinner, I actually convinced Holmes that
he should go lie down for a while. When I went in to check on him
he was lying on his back, one arm flung over his head, fast asleep. I
covered him with a blanket and tiptoed out of the room.

I sat down to finish my drink, and heard voices coming from
the stateroom next to ours. It was hard to make out the words, but
it sounded as though a man and a woman were arguing. I sat down
on the sofa and listened, and could make out some of the words.

". . . all in your imagination," the woman was saying.

"Don't try to scare me," the man said, and then something I
couldn't make out. Then a door slammed, and I heard footsteps in
the hall outside. I opened the door an inch and peeked out to see
our white-haired friend stalking away. I closed the door quietly but
a moment later there was a knock on it. While I was deciding
whether or not to answer it the knock got louder. I was afraid it
would wake up Holmes, so I opened the door.

She was standing there, dressed—if you could call it that—
only in a pale jade-coloured dressing gown. There were plenty of
places where the gown ended, and I tried not to look at them.

"Is it all right if I come in?" she said, and I could think of a dozen reasons why it wasn't, but none of them had more of an impact than the jade dressing gown, so I let her in.

"May I have a drink?" she said, eyeing the bottle of gin on the bar, and I was beginning to wonder what else she would ask for when Holmes entered from the bedroom. His hair was tousled and his eyes rimmed with sleep, but the way she looked at him I could see he made an impression.

"I came to apologize," she said as I handed her a martini. Holmes didn't reply, but sat in an armchair and regarded her through half-lidded eyes.

"I'm afraid we were making a bit of a row next door, and I just came over to say I'm sorry." Her voice was smooth, with a sheen like the shiny silk of her dressing gown.

Holmes still didn't answer, and I could see this was making her a little nervous, though she was too cool to show it.

"You see, my husband—"

"—the Colonel—" said Holmes.

"Why, yes," she said, sounding surprised. "Do you know Edward?"

"Only by sight," answered Holmes lazily.

"Then how did you know—?"

Holmes dismissed her question with a languid wave of his hand. "It is of no interest," he said; "nor is it of particular interest that I also know he was a cavalry officer, that he has twice been wounded, and that he is only recently retired. Please, continue what you were saying."

She took a drink of the martini—a good-sized swallow—and looked at Holmes as if sizing him up.

"Well, I was about to explain that my husband is . . . well, he has a delicate disposition, and is sometimes given to . . . emotional displays . . . and I just wanted to apologize if we disturbed you," she concluded rather lamely, disconcerted by the intensity of Holmes's gaze.

"Yes, well, don't give it a second thought, Mrs.—?" Holmes said evenly.

"Oh, how rude of me—I come barging in without even introducing myself! Elizabeth Warburton."

"Mrs. Warburton, then," Holmes continued, "allow me to introduce myself: I am Sherlock Holmes, and this is my good friend and companion, Dr. Watson."

"Not *the* Sherlock Holmes," our visitor said a little too enthusiastically.

"The only one I am aware of," replied Holmes dryly, "and now if you will excuse me, I must dress for dinner."

She stood up from the couch as though she had been shot from a cannon.

"Yes, of course—don't let me keep you," she said, moving towards the door, but without taking her eyes off Holmes. He went back into the bedroom without another word, and that left the two of us alone.

"You must think I'm very silly," she said, looking at me with eyes as green as her robe. I thought she was a lot of things, but silly wasn't one of them.

"It's just that when we're among people who don't *know* Edward—well, I always worry about how people will perceive him, that's all. Thank you for the drink," she said, handing me the glass, and I saw her nails were long and red next to her white skin. I found myself thinking how those nails could hurt, and then thinking that it might be worth it.

"Anytime," I said, and meant it.

After she had gone I sat on the divan and lit a Fatima. I knew enough about women to know Holmes was her type and I wasn't. I also knew that I could have saved her the effort, but thought it would be interesting to watch her find out for herself. I didn't quite believe her concern for her husband, and was pretty sure Holmes didn't, either.

I got his opinion later that evening, over a rack of lamb and a bottle of Montrachet.

"She was overacting when I introduced myself," he said, "although until then she gave a credible performance. I wonder what she really came over for . . ."

Just then the subject of our conversation entered the room. She had replaced the jade gown with a red off-the-shoulder satin number, and around her neck she wore a diamond choker that I figured was worth quite a few bottles of Montrachet. The Colonel walked beside her, his face flushed over his white ruffled shirt. Walking just behind them was a slim, demurely dressed young Oriental woman. She wasn't pretty—her nose was too long, and her skin was uneven—but she had a kind of dignity about her which caught my eye. It caught Holmes's too; he watched her as they were shown to a table on the far side of the room.

"The plot thickens, Watson," he said, pouring us both another glass of wine.

From where we were sitting I had a pretty good view of the Colonel, and I made a point of watching him during the meal. Holmes's first impression of him certainly seemed on the money: he was distracted by something, and consumed the better part of a bottle of Merlot all by himself. The Oriental woman didn't drink, and Mrs. Warburton stuck to martinis. I asked Holmes what it all meant.

"I suggest we engage the Colonel in a game of bridge after dinner—if I am not mistaken, he is a man who likes a couple of rubbers to go with his after-dinner whiskey and soda."

I was about to ask Holmes how he knew that, when I was aware that someone was approaching us from across the room. It was the Colonel himself, and he moved through the tables with a grace I wouldn't have given him credit for; the Merlot didn't seem to have had much effect on his coordination. He stopped at our table and cleared his throat. It was a big throat, but then, everything about him was big: his head, with its arc of white hair, wide mouth and round blue eyes; all of it gave the impression of a man who had spent a lot of time outdoors. He seemed too big even for the ship's dining room, with its crystal chandeliers and fussy table settings.

"Excuse me, gentlemen," he said. His voice matched the rest of him: low, gravelly yet resonant, the voice of someone who was used to giving commands. "I hope I am not interrupting your dinner," he continued.

"Not at all, Colonel," Holmes replied. "What can we do for you?"

"My wife tells me she had the pleasure of making your acquaintance earlier this evening, and I was, of course, thrilled to hear that we are shipmates with such a distinguished personage as yourself, Mr. Holmes."

"I feel you flatter me," said Holmes in a tone that indicated he felt nothing of the kind. "Allow me to introduce my friend and colleague, Dr. Watson."

The Colonel put out one of the largest hands I have ever seen, and the pressure he put behind it as he shook my hand was nothing to sneeze at, either.

"Delighted, delighted—I am one of your most faithful readers, Dr. Watson. I wouldn't miss one of your stories for all the tea in China."

"I understand there is quite a lot of tea there," Holmes said dryly.

"Oh, yes, quite—in fact, that's my business—tea. I'm on my way to America to see if I can't expand the market a bit, you know; get the Yanks drinking a bit more of the stuff. I fear that ever since they had their little Boston tea party, the stuff has left a bad taste in their mouths." He chuckled at his own joke.

Holmes smiled indulgently and folded his napkin.

"I was wondering," the Colonel went on, "if you gentlemen would care to join me in a rubber or two of bridge after dinner? I find it aids digestion after a large meal."

"We would be delighted to," said Holmes, with a look at me. "What do you think, Watson?"

"Oh, by all means."

"Very well, then," said our visitor. "Shall we say nine o'clock in the club room?"

"Splendid," said Holmes, with an enthusiasm that wasn't about the bridge. Holmes didn't really care about games, but his phenomenal memory and total self-control made him pretty much unbeatable at any card game.

"How did you know he played bridge?" I asked when the Colonel had gone.

"Really, Watson, it is so simple I hesitate to tell you. If I did not happen to know that bridge is the common pursuit of most officers' clubs, I should certainly have deduced it from the small pin the Colonel wore upon his lapel, indicating he was a member of The No Trump Society."

"The No Trump Society?"

"Yes, it is a London club which my brother Mycroft frequented for a while before he found the Diogenes suited him better. The only prerequisite for membership—other than a certain social standing—is that a man be something of a bridge fiend. Thus our Colonel is clearly a man who takes his bridge seriously."

Half an hour later we were sitting in the ship's gaming parlour. With its mauve-coloured walls and heavy oak furniture, it made a fairly successful attempt to duplicate the look of a London club. A billiards table stood at one end of the room, and heavy gold drapes kept out the sea air.

Warburton had scared up a fourth for our game, a taciturn, fox-faced little man by the name of Penstock, who he introduced as his business partner. With his sharp, tight face and slicked-back black hair, Penstock had the look of a professional card shark. Holmes and I made up a team, and the Colonel paired up with Penstock.

As I suspected, the little man played a steady, crafty game, but he was handicapped by his partner's reckless bidding. The Colonel's rashness grew in proportion to his consumption of highballs, until it was embarrassing to watch. Holmes sat across from me, tight as a clam, and then, after we had won our second rubber, suggested a break. Penstock took the opportunity to excuse himself for the evening, and we were left alone with Warburton. That didn't last long, though.

Mrs. Warburton was a woman who never entered a room— she made an entrance. She had changed again, this time into pale blue chiffon with feathers. I wondered how long a cruise it would take to go through her entire wardrobe, and guessed once around the world probably wouldn't do it. As she perched on the arm of her husband's chair, I figured she was pretty decorative and just as dangerous.

"I just came down to see what you gentlemen were tempting my husband with," she said, smiling at Holmes, trying a little temptation of her own.

"I can assure you, Madame, that it is he who is tempting us," Holmes replied.

"Well, at any rate, it's late, and I thought I'd come rescue you from him."

"It's not late," the Colonel said blurrily, "The evening is young yet, my dear."

"Now, Edward, you must let the gentleman retire," she said as if talking to a child. "Mr. Holmes is looking quite pale."

I looked at Holmes, and saw that she was right. His color was fading, and although his eyes shone with nervous energy, he was slumped in his chair.

"You look quite exhausted, Mr. Holmes," she said, "don't you think so, Dr. Watson?"

"Yes. Holmes, maybe we'd better call it a night."

Our conversation at that moment was interrupted by the appearance of a large, white, very long-haired Persian cat, which trotted across the carpet and leapt into Mrs. Warburton's lap.

"Oh, Ariel! How did you get out?" she said, stroking the cat.

The answer came immediately, in the form of her Chinese companion, who entered the room as shyly as Mrs. Warburton had dramatically.

"I beg your pardon," she said in a low, husky voice, "but the cat slipped out through the door when I went out for ice."

"Ariel, you bad kitty," said Mrs. Warburton in a cooing tone, "Go back home with Chin Shih, now, there's a good kitty."

She handed the cat to Chin Shih, who took it without a word, and left the room as silently as she had come. Holmes watched her leave, his eyes gleaming.

"Oh, that damn cat," said Mrs. Warburton, brushing at her dress with her hand. "Look at all these white hairs on my new frock. I never should have gotten a Persian."

"Your companion is very demure," Holmes remarked casually to Mrs. Warburton.

"Oh, yes, she's so Chinese, isn't she?" Mrs. Warburton said gaily, but with a glance at her husband.

"You're not demure at all, my dear," the Colonel slurred, patting her cheek. I saw her flinch slightly when he did it, and was certain Holmes saw it, too.

"No, and I'm not Chinese, am I?" she replied with mock petulance.

"Where did you find her?" Holmes said carelessly. I knew Holmes well enough to know that the less interest he feigned in something, the more he wanted to know.

"Chin Shih—or my wife?" said Warburton fuzzily.

"Chin Shih."

"Oh, it was the damnedest thing, really. We were living in Manchuria, and Elizabeth had just been saying how lonely she was while I was away—I had to travel a good deal at the time, you know—anyway, she had just been saying that she was going to place an ad in the paper for a companion, and . . ." the colonel interrupted his story with a loud hiccup, and his wife, looking embarrassed, turned to us.

"Why don't I tell the rest, darling?" she said soothingly, again speaking to him as you might a child.

"Right you are; carry on. I say—where's that bloody waiter? I need another drink!"

He needed anything but another drink, of course. I can usually keep up with the best of them, but the Colonel had left me behind hours ago. I glanced at Holmes, whose face was a mask of inscrutability.

"Well," Mrs. Warburton was saying with a forced gaiety, "What happened was that the day I was going to place the ad, I had some business at the embassy, and Chin Shih and I were stuck in the waiting room for quite a while together. We struck up a conversation, and I learned she had been educated in England—her English is quite perfect, you know—and by the end of our chat she had agreed to come live with us as my companion."

"Yes, jolly how it all worked out, wasn't it?" said the Colonel indulgently.

"Isn't it a bit unusual for a Chinese girl to be sent abroad to be educated?" said Holmes.

Mrs. Warburton's face colored.

"Well, Chin Shih came from a good family, and her paternal grandfather was an Englishman."

"I see," said Holmes.

Mrs. Warburton sprang up from her perch.

"Well, I think I'll get you along to bed now, darling, all right?" she said to her husband.

The Colonel's face reddened and his whole body shook. "I am not a *child*," he shouted in a voice husky from alcohol.

"I didn't say you were," his wife answered, cool as a cucumber. "I just suggested we go up to bed now."

"*I'll* decide when I'm ready to retire, and I'll thank you to not push me around!" he bellowed.

"Fine," Mrs. Warburton replied, and left the room without a word.

Her exit seemed to take all the wind out of the Colonel's sails. His big body slumped in the armchair, and his features relaxed into a melancholy frown.

"Forgive me, gentlemen," he said, his voice deflated and listless. "I don't know why I get like that . . . it's just that I can't stand it when she treats me like I'm—like I'm . . ." he trailed off, staring at his empty highball.

"Like you're what?" said Holmes smoothly.

"Oh, she's certain I've inherited the family . . . weakness, and so she treats me like a child at times."

"The family weakness?" Holmes asked.

The Colonel laughed, a single exhalation of air, but there was no mirth in his tone; it was more like an extended sigh. He leaned toward Holmes, as though afraid someone would overhear, though everyone else had long since gone to bed. Even the bartender had packed up and cleared out.

"Madness, Mr. Holmes; madness. It runs in our family, and always seems to strike the oldest male. Do you know what it's like to live your life under the cloud of a certain and grim future like that? It's hell, that's what it is: hell."

Looking at him, his big strong body the picture of defeat, I could believe he knew what he was talking about. Even Holmes looked moved.

"Come now, Colonel, buck up—perhaps you won't be so unlucky after all," he said, and there was real sympathy in his voice.

The Colonel looked at his empty glass and set it down. "Well, perhaps you're right, Mr. Holmes—I suppose I've been luckier than most, to have a wife like Lizzie . . . I've had a good life up until now, at any rate, come what may . . . it's just that sometimes I feel it bearing down on me, especially at night, when everyone else is asleep . . . it's like a huge dark cloud hovering over me, and I'm afraid to go to bed, to close my eyes, for fear it might get me while I sleep."

To my surprise, Holmes leaned forward and grasped Warburton by the shoulders.

"No demon is defeated by attempting to hide from it," he said earnestly, "Take my advice and look adversity in the face; you will find it far less frightening."

The Colonel seemed impressed by Holmes's sincerity. Surprised to see Holmes relinquish his usual half-cynical tone, I was impressed myself.

"Thank you, Mr. Holmes," said the Colonel, "thank you for that advice. I can tell it was hard-earned, and I appreciate it."

With that, he rose from his chair, bid us good night and left the room as steadily as his consumption of bourbon would allow. I looked at Holmes. His face was pale and drawn, and he was holding his left shoulder, which told me that his wound was bothering him.

"All right, old boy, let's get you to bed," I said casually, so as not to tip him off that I was worried about him.

Holmes looked at me impishly.

"You see, Watson; I let you treat me like a child and don't complain at all. You must tell the Colonel that when we see him."

After we had turned in I lay awake a long time thinking about the Colonel and his wife. She was a looker, but I didn't envy him; there was something not quite square about her, even with her airs of concern for her husband. In the next bed, Holmes tossed and turned in his sleep, muttering in his dreams, being chased by his own demons. We all had demons, I thought, some worse than others . . . I fell asleep thinking about Mrs. Warburton in that red dress.

That night I dreamed I was walking, walking endlessly down a long narrow passageway which led to a black wooden door. I felt I was supposed to open the door, but I didn't want to. Finally I opened it, and as I did I heard laughter all around me . . . I recognized the laugh; it was Elizabeth Warburton. When I got the door open she was standing on the other side of it, and at her feet lay the body of a man. Thinking it was her husband, I knelt beside him, but when I turned him over I saw that it was Holmes, and that he was dead.

I awoke in a sweat, the mocking sound of her laughter ringing in my ears. I looked at the bed next to mine, but Holmes was gone. Panicked, I leapt up and went into the sitting room. Holmes was seated by the porthole, gazing out at the moonlit sea, smoking.

"Holmes? What are you doing up?" I said softly.

He spoke without turning around.

"Thinking, Watson."

"About what?"

"Demons, Watson—demons."

The rest of our voyage passed without incident. The Colonel seemed calmer after that first evening, although sometimes we could hear voices raised next door; still, Holmes seemed to have a steadying influence on him, and even his bridge game improved. His wife continued to give Holmes the eye, but he was impervious to her charms. I found myself alternately wishing I was in his shoes, and being glad I wasn't, not being so immune as Holmes to feminine attractions. The sea air seemed to improve Holmes's health, though he still tired easily, and from time to time I noticed him holding his shoulder. When I pointed this out, he waved aside my concerns in that way he had, closing the subject to further discussion.

We arrived in New York on a Thursday, in a driving rain. I wanted to get Holmes to a hotel as quickly as possible, so our goodbyes were somewhat curtailed. The Colonel gave us a business card and encouraged us to call on him while in New York; we promised we would, thinking we would never see him again.

We were wrong.

We put up at the Excelsior, across from the Museum of Natural History. It was Holmes's idea; he spent the first morning at the Museum, happy as a clam, doing geological research.

"They have an excellent gem collection, Watson," he said over tea; "you really should come see it. The Star of India is there—really it is quite a magnificent stone, with a most colorful history of theft and murder."

That afternoon I went for a walk in Central Park. I strolled to the Boathouse, watched the rowboats in the lake, and then walked back through the Rambles. As I left the park I thought I saw Colonel Warburton on the other side of the street. I waved at him, but he hurried along without seeing me. His shoulders were stooped and his head down, and he walked with a grim determination, in the direction of downtown. I mentioned to Holmes that I had seen him, and that he had not responded to my greeting.

"If he is not careful, his demons will consume him," Holmes said gravely.

The next morning his words had a ring of prophecy. The Metropolitan Section of the *New York Times* contained the following article:

BUSINESSMAN FOUND MURDERED
IN WEST SIDE APARTMENT

William K. Penstock was found dead in his apartment early last evening by his maid. He was strangled with a curtain rope. Mr. Penstock was a shareholder in Warburton Ltd., a British tea importing firm. There was no robbery and no apparent break-in, indicating the victim knew his killer. His business partner, Edward C. Warburton, is being sought for questioning.

I handed it across the breakfast table to Holmes, and he read it silently.

"Well, Watson, it looks as though the demons have the upper hand—for now."

"Do you think he did it?"

Holmes shrugged.

"His partner has been murdered, and he makes himself unavailable to the police. On the surface these are not the actions of an innocent man."

I agreed.

"Appearances may be deceiving, however, Watson—there is much below the surface waves that we cannot see unless we are willing to dive in."

Just then the doorbell rang. I'm not normally jumpy, but the sound startled me and I flinched.

"Steady on, Watson—here comes another piece of the puzzle, if I am not mistaken."

He wasn't. The piece entered the room—and quite a piece it was—dressed in a gold lamé which clung to every inch of her impressive geography.

"Oh, Mr. Holmes—have you read the paper?" said Elizabeth Warburton as I helped her to a chair.

"Yes, indeed, Madame, and I am very sorry to hear the news."

"He's disappeared, Mr. Holmes—vanished! I don't know what to do. Of course I don't think he killed Mr. Penstock, but what are the police going to think?"

"What, indeed . . . when did you last see him?"

"Last night. He said he was going out for a walk, and he never returned. Oh, Mr. Holmes, will you help me find Edward?"

The helpless damsel role didn't exactly suit Elizabeth Warburton, but I had to admire the energy she put into the part.

"Is there anyone else who might know where he is, someone he might confide in?"

"Only his half brother, Michael."

"He lives here in New York?"

"Yes, he's company manager of the New York division of Warburton Inc. He lives downtown somewhere. I don't know the address, but Edward's office would have it."

"Have you spoken with him today?"

"No, I don't really know him very well. I just thought maybe Edward might have confided in him."

Michael Warburton was listed in the phone book, and ten minutes later we were in a cab on the way to Washington Square. He lived in a townhouse overlooking the park. Our knock was answered by a tall man who bore a strong family resemblance to the Colonel. His skin was not as ruddy, and he was thinner, but he had the same big-boned frame, the same powerful hands. He led us into a comfortable front parlour and asked us if it was too early to offer us a drink. I said that it wasn't, and that I'd have what he was having. Holmes declined, and Warburton left the room to get our drinks. While he was gone, Holmes picked up an envelope from the secretary. It was marked "Newgate Travel Agency." He opened it, glanced inside, and put it back before our host reentered the room.

"The police just left," he said, handing me a gin and tonic, "and I'll tell you what I told them. I don't know where Edward is, but he did have a motive for the murder."

"And what might that be?" asked Holmes.

"Well, the police have it now, but there was a letter—threatening blackmail—written by Penstock to my brother."

"Oh?" said Holmes. "And how did you come across this letter? I should think it would be very careless of your brother to leave it lying about."

Michael Warburton took a large swallow of his drink.

"I am the regional manager of Warburton Inc., and most things come across my desk sooner or later. I suppose he thought he had disposed of it, but . . . well, my brother's mental constitution has not been of the strongest lately, and . . ." Michael Warburton shrugged. "I'm not sure, really; all I know is I found the letter in with some other mail."

"What exactly did Penstock have on your brother?" said Holmes.

"Well, the letter claimed knowledge of Edward's involvement in an opium smuggling ring here in New York—in Chinatown, actually."

"Do you yourself know of such a ring?"

"I do know such a ring exists; everyone knows of it."

"And are you aware of your brother's involvement?"

"Not exactly, though it would explain some of my brother's more—aberrant—behavior lately."

"And why did you not confront your brother about this letter?"

"Well, I was going to, but—well, I was rather frightened of how he might react. I don't mean; I mean, I never expected him to—to—"

"To commit murder?" said Holmes smoothly.

"Yes."

"Well, thank you for your time, Mr. Warburton. We'll see ourselves out," Holmes said, starting for the door. "Oh, one more thing," he said, turning back; "do you own a cat or a dog?"

Michael Warburton looked surprised.

"No, I don't; why?"

"Oh, nothing, just curiosity. Good-day, Mr. Warburton."

Once we were outside I pulled Holmes aside.

"Why did you want to know whether or not he had pets?"

Holmes smiled.

"Oh, just a theory, Watson; just a theory."

"Where to now?"

"Chinatown, I think, Watson."

Soon we were seated in another cab, rattling along cobblestone streets on the way downtown. Holmes looked out of the window, his face pensive.

"Caesar's wife, Watson," he said cryptically.

"What about her?" I asked.

"She was supposedly above suspicion."

"And—?"

"I wonder, Watson; I wonder."

We wandered about the narrow, crowded streets, and I felt uncomfortably close to the throngs of people that jostled us at every turn. Holmes stopped in front of a Greek revival building on Doyers Street. It was a theatre of some kind, with banners in Chinese advertising upcoming productions. Holmes peered at several of the posters depicting the actors, in their colourful costumes.

"What is it, Holmes?"

"A Chinese opera house, Watson. Do you know that there are no women in Chinese opera?"

"You mean it's the same as our theatre during Shakespeare's time—all of the women's roles are played by men?"

"Precisely, Watson."

He stared at the posters a while longer. The gin and tonic was beginning to eat a hole in my stomach, and I suggested lunch. Knowing how indifferent Holmes could be about such frivolities as food, I was surprised when he agreed readily, and led me to a noodle house on Mott Street.

We sat among the smoky tables, the only Caucasians in a swirl of Chinese immigrants, and I looked around with some unease. It seemed like everyone was staring at us, yet I couldn't see anyone taking any interest in us. It was spooky. There was no menu, but a sullen waiter appeared almost immediately with several dishes from the kitchen. There were some dumplings of uncertain origin, noodle soup, and a mysterious meat dish. It didn't seem to bother Holmes at all; he tucked into the food as though he'd eaten it all his life. After we were finished, he leaned back and lit a cigarette.

"That's better, Watson," he said; "nothing like a pork dumpling or two to keep the wolves at bay, eh?"

I wondered what his game was, but knew enough to keep quiet, so I nodded and lit a Fatima. Just then Holmes stiffened, and I saw his eyes rivet on a small, slim person outside the window.

"Quickly, Watson!" he said, and darted out of the restaurant. I was caught flat-footed, and had to rush to keep up with him. He wound his way through the crowded, steaming alleys filled with street vendors and fish mongers, always keeping within sight of the same slight figure. There were no right angles to either streets or buildings; everything leaned and twisted in unlikely directions, even the people—who hurried every which way with their heads down—in the strangely calm chaos that was Chinatown.

Holmes remained unperturbed by all of this. With his unique ability to assimilate any environment, he cut through the throngs of people without disturbing them, moving as steadily as a yacht in calm waters. Finally he stopped in front of a dark, dank doorway which led to a basement.

"Give him a minute, and then we'll go in. Do you have your service revolver on you, Watson?" he said in a low voice.

I nodded; I had slipped it into my pocket before we left our hotel room.

"It's just as well," he said grimly, "though it may be of no avail against these people."

He opened the door slowly, and I followed close behind with my revolver drawn. It was dark, but not too dark to see that we were in a narrow tunnel, with a dim light at the end. I had the unpleasant feeling that I was back in my dream of the night before. As we crept slowly toward the light I could hear rats scurrying beneath our feet. Holmes stepped through the archway first, and I followed. It was then I felt the ceiling descend on my head. A blinding flash, and then darkness.

I awoke with a pretty nasty headache, and looked around. The first thing I saw was Colonel Warburton. He was tied to a chair, and when he saw me coming to he spoke.

"Thank goodness you're all right, Dr. Watson!"

I was lying on an iron hospital-type bed, my hands and feet firmly bound to the frame. The room seemed like a storage space of some kind although we were the only things being stored in it right now.

"Where's Holmes?" I said, shaking myself into consciousness.

"They've got him," he said grimly.

"Who?"

"How could I have been such a fool?" he groaned by way of an answer. "How could I have let her take me in like that?"

"*Who* has Holmes?" I shouted at him, beginning to panic.

My answer came just then, as the door to the room opened

and four figures were silhouetted in the light from the hallway outside. The figures entered the room, and I recognized three them: Holmes, Elizabeth Warburton, and Chin Shih.

Except that Chin Shin wasn't a woman.

I had to admit the long nose and uneven skin made more sense on a man—so much sense, in fact, that I was amazed that I hadn't seen it before. But my attention was cut short when I saw Holmes.

He looked bad. His face was cut and bruised, and his shoulder wound had begun to bleed. It looked as though they had roughed him up pretty good. The third man, a big beefy Chinese fellow, dragged him to the bed I was on and dropped him on it.

"Holmes!" I said, feeling sick at seeing him like this.

"Don't worry, Watson; if they were going to kill us, I presume they would have done so by now," he said, attempting his usual sardonic tone, but his voice was hoarse.

Chin Shih—if that was his name—stepped forward and spoke.

"Mr. Holmes doesn't seem to understand that we will get what we need from you sooner or later," he said. Then he shrugged. "Or if we don't, we will simply have to kill you trying. It is your choice."

Elizabeth Warburton spoke for the first time.

"I really am sorry about this, Mr. Holmes," she said, "but you were far more efficient than I thought you would be. I expected to be out of the country long before you were able to track Edward down, and then it wouldn't matter if you found him. But you figured out our little game too skillfully for your own good."

She took a step toward Holmes and put her face close to his. I had the unpleasant sensation that she enjoyed this revenge, perhaps, for his indifference to her charms.

"It really would be better for you if you told us exactly how much you know—or we really may have to kill you."

"I don't suppose multiple murders would weigh any more

heavily on your conscience than one," Holmes said, breathing hard.

Elizabeth Warburton shrugged.

"Not much. But it would be somewhat harder to hide."

Another yellow man entered the room and said something in Chinese to Chin Shih, who replied in the same dialect. The man bowed slightly and left the room. Mrs. Warburton addressed us again.

"If you'll excuse us for a moment, gentlemen, we shall return shortly. Think about what I have said."

The three of them left the room, closing the door.

"Are you all right, Holmes?" I said.

"Never mind that," he answered with as much impatience as he could muster in his condition, "What we need to do is get out of here as quickly as possible. I don't think it likely they will let us live much longer."

He dragged himself to a sitting position, and I saw that his hands were bound behind his back.

"I have some knowledge of knots," he said, working his way over to the rope that tied my hands to the bed. "Now, if I can just do this backwards—"

He fumbled with the knots, having to stop twice to rest and catch his breath, but finally he succeeded in freeing my hands. I quickly untied my feet, and within minutes I had freed all of us.

"There," said Holmes, staggering and almost falling, his face rigid with pain.

"Holmes, you're—"

"Never mind, Watson—it is very pressing that we get out of here."

"This building is on the water," said Colonel Warburton, pointing to the single high, narrow window in our little room. I climbed up on the bed and looked through; the water of the harbour was directly under our window.

"Can you swim, Colonel?"

"I certainly can—swam every morning of my life in China."

"Well, we'll have to make a run for it, and that seems to be our only means of escape."

Just then we heard footsteps down the hall.

"Quick, Watson, hide yourself behind the door!" Holmes whispered fiercely. "Colonel—over there!" he said, pointing to the other side of the door frame. We just had time to station ourselves there when the door was flung open.

I threw myself on the first one through the door, which happened to be Chin Shih. Though I outweighed him, he was wiry and lithe as a cat. He broke my grasp and threw me over his shoulder as if I were a sack of potatoes. I landed heavily, but jumped up to face him. Meanwhile, the goon had thrown himself on top of Holmes, and was getting the better of him, when I saw the Colonel leap like a tiger upon his back. It looked to me as though he bit the man's ear, because the goon roared, let go of Holmes and turned to face the Colonel.

I didn't see the outcome of that fight, because a kick from Chin Shih caught me in the jaw, and I dropped to the floor. Hazily, I saw Holmes lunge unsteadily at Chin Shih, who threw a punch deliberately at his wounded shoulder. Holmes cried out in agony, and that was when I saw red. I got to my feet, and came at Chin Shih with my fists flying. I don't know where I hit him, or how many times, but when I was done he was lying over one of the beds, out of commission.

I turned to see how the Colonel was doing with the hoodlum. He was hanging on the man's broad back, kicking at him, but not doing much damage. I saw a good-sized piece of lumber under one of the beds, and reached in for it. I picked it up, and, remembering my days as a cricket batsman, planted a good one on the goon's shins. He went down screaming, and I gave him another one on the back of the neck just to keep him thinking. After that he was quiet.

The Colonel and I bent down over Holmes, who was bleeding heavily now.

"Through the window . . . our only chance," he gasped, and we helped him up. We could just climb through the window by standing on a bed. I helped the Colonel through first. I heard a splash as he hit the water below.

"Go, Watson," said Holmes; "Quickly! Don't worry about me."

"Don't be ridiculous," I muttered as I lifted Holmes up to the window. Another splash, and then it was just me.

I heard voices coming down the hall, and knew I would have to hurry. I heaved myself up to the sill, crawled through, and let myself drop to the water below. As soon as I hit I heard shots. I dove deep into the dark water, deep as I could, swam until I had to have air, and then surfaced. Another shot tore the water right next to my head. I gulped some more air and submerged again. I swam until my lungs burned, then came up again. The bullets were farther away now. I dove again, and this time when I came up I looked for Holmes and the Colonel. I saw them up ahead, swimming toward a launch anchored a small distance from the shore. I could still hear shots and voices in the background, but I wasn't going to stick around to see if they were after me. I followed Holmes and the Colonel, my arms pumping water as hard as they could.

The captain of the launch was Dutch, but finally we were able to get across the idea that we needed the aid of the police. He took us to shore, and we accosted the first cop we saw. Soon he had rounded up half a dozen boys in blue, and we were leading them to the warehouse we had just escaped from.

Chin Shih and his buddies had flown the coop, but there was enough opium there to fill several smuggling ships. They had tried to take it with them, but there was too much, so they had left most of it behind.

"Don't worry, we'll catch them," said the Sergeant, a red-faced fellow by the name of Mallory.

"There's a boat sailing at four o'clock for China, the *Pride of*

Peking,'' Holmes said. "It leaves from Dock Thirty-four. It is imperative that we intercept it."

We all piled into several cabs and took off for the docks. I glanced at Holmes—he didn't look good. His face was feverish, and his right hand clutched at his left shoulder.

"Holmes, let me look at that," I said.

He waved me away, but I insisted. When I opened his shirt it was as I thought: the bullet wound had reopened. I felt his forehead; it was burning.

We pulled into Dock Thirty-four at three-fifty-five. The gangplank had already been pulled up, and Sergeant Mallory had to work hard to convince the captain to lower it again.

People stared at us as we strode up the gangplank. We must have been an odd-looking group, three soggy, dishevelled Englishmen, wet as drowned rats, followed by a dozen of New York's finest (we had picked up a few more cops along the way). It must not have been clear who the criminals were. We asked to see the passenger list, and then, led by Holmes, made our way to Cabin 52.

Elizabeth Warburton met us at the door, and when she saw us she didn't flinch or move a single muscle on her handsome face.

"Come in, gentlemen," she said, cool and collected. "You look as if you need to sit down. It's all right," she called into the other room, "You can come out now—it's all over."

A moment later a sulky-looking Chin Shih entered the room, avoiding looking directly at any of us.

"Now that we're here, what exactly is this all about?" said Mallory, with more curiosity than annoyance.

Holmes spoke, his voice weak. "First of all, officer, send a man to Number Twelve Washington Square, where you will find Mr. Michael Warburton, hopefully alive, but probably bound and gagged, and minus two ocean liner tickets to China."

"Now that it doesn't matter any more, may I ask you how you—?" Mrs. Warburton asked coolly.

"Your story about meeting Chin Shih was a little too pat,"

said Holmes; "and you still didn't seem sure people would buy it, so I began thinking. I am something of a Chinese opera fan, and the more I thought about it, the more it seemed logical that an actor capable of playing a woman on stage would be just as capable of playing a woman offstage. When I went to Chinatown, I saw what I expected to see: Chin Shih dressed not as a woman, but as a man. It made a difference; I might not have recognized him had I not known what I was looking for. Ladies and gentlemen, may I present Heu Pun, one of the stars of the Peking opera."

We all turned to look at Heu Pun, who glared daggers back at us. I was closest to him, and saw the flash of steel in his hand a split second before the shot. I managed to throw myself at him quickly enough to spoil his aim, and the shot ricochetted off the chandelier. I grabbed the hand that held the pistol, and we grappled on the floor for a few seconds. When I heard the second shot, it occurred to me that I might have done something foolish—in that split second, I even considered the possibility that I had been trying to impress Mrs. Warburton with my heroics.

"Watson!" cried Holmes, and was upon us in a second.

But Heu Pun had gone limp in my arms, and I knew that he had taken the bullet. We turned him over; it was a belly wound, and it didn't look as if he would make it. Elizabeth Warburton bent over him and took him in her arms.

"Why? Why did you do it?" she said, and then added something in Chinese.

He shrugged, started to speak, and then his eyes went blank. I had seen it before, and knew that he had played his last role. I had to give him credit: it had been a convincing one.

"Get this man out of here!" barked Sergeant Mallory, relieved to finally have something to do, but Mrs. Warburton stood up and faced us.

"Leave him!" she said in a voice that left no room for argument. "You can take him when you take me."

Mallory started to reply, and then shrugged.

"Let the lady have her way," he said to his men; "it's the last order she'll be giving for quite a while."

I looked at Holmes, who was now very white; I took him firmly by the arm and guided him to a chair.

"You must rest now, Holmes; I think I can tell it from here on," I said.

I turned to Elizabeth Warburton. "You played all of us for saps, starting with your husband. When you met Heu Pun, the two of you cooked up a plot to get hubby out of the way but still collect on all the goodies.

"The first thing you had to do was disguise him. That was the easy part, since he was already an accomplished actor. Then you cooked up the story about needing a companion and meeting Chin Shih at the Embassy. So now you had your lover living with you as a female companion, with your husband none the wiser.

"Your husband told you of the 'family weakness,' so you played that angle for all it was worth, treating him like a mental invalid, until you had him believing he really was unstable."

I looked over at Colonel Warburton, who sat with his head in his hands.

"Brother Michael was sweet on you and always had been, so you knew you could count on him when the time came. The only one in the way was Penstock, so you planted false information about your husband's involvement in the opium trade. Chin Shih really was smuggling opium, so you made the information pretty convincing."

Mallory stepped forward. "We've been looking for the ring-leaders of that gang for a while," he said. "I've got some men over at the address you gave me, clearing the place out."

"I doubt you will find much there now," said Holmes; "most of the opium is probably at the bottom of the harbour by now."

I turned to Mrs. Warburton and continued.

"You know that a man like Penstock could hardly resist blackmail sooner or later. Sure enough, the letter was written, but you got your hands on it right after your husband saw it."

"Tell me something, Mr. Holmes," said Elizabeth Warburton; "How did you connect me with Penstock?"

"I might not have, had you not carefully waited until he had left the bridge table to come down yourself, that night on the ship."

Mrs. Warburton's smooth forehead crinkled.

"I don't understand—" she said.

"You carefully avoided being in Mr. Penstock's presence in front of us, and did so throughout the rest of the voyage. He was the Colonel's partner, and therefore I wondered at your avoidance. It might have been from personal enmity, but I suspected it was something else. He was not a trained actor, as was Mr. Heu, and so you could not trust his reactions in public. Therefore you avoided him as much as possible."

"Very clever, Mr. Holmes," said Elizabeth Warburton, with real admiration, "very clever, indeed. Please continue, Dr. Watson."

I did. "Once the letter was written, you sent lover boy over to kill poor greedy Penstock—you chose strangulation because that would immediately point to your husband, with his big mitts. The Colonel is so distraught by this time that when he stumbles on the body—which was just luck, by the way—he takes a powder. It's simple then for Heu's boys in Chinatown to keep him on ice for a while."

I looked at Elizabeth Warburton. "How am I doing?"

"Wonderfully," she said sarcastically. "Don't forget about the part where I steal the Hope Diamond."

I went on. "You give Brother Michael the blackmail letter, which he would, of course, turn over to the police. You needed him to give it to them so it doesn't look like you're too closely involved; it would look a little suspicious if you had intercepted your husband's mail. Michael's sweet on you, so he doesn't tell the police he got it from you. He thinks you're going to run away together, only when you book two tickets on a steamer you have a different travelling companion in mind. The only slip you made was to tell Holmes and me that you didn't know Michael Warburton very well, when you had left cat hairs all over his apartment."

"A white cat at that," said Holmes, shaking his head. "Very sloppy, Mrs. Warburton. And you should have told him not to leave your cruise tickets lying about like that. I'm disappointed, really I am. Well done, Watson; well done," he said, and then he fainted.

I wouldn't let Holmes leave his bed for two days. On the third day, we were having tea in our sitting room at the Excelsior, when a package wrapped in brown paper arrived for Holmes. I brought it into the room and set it on the coffee table.

"Well, what are you waiting for?" Holmes asked. "Why don't you unwrap it?"

I unwrapped the package.

"What's this?" I said.

"Oh, that's just a little something the Colonel sent me in appreciation of my services. He seems to think it's worth quite a bit of money."

"It's pretty ugly."

Holmes picked it up and examined it. "Yes, it is, isn't it? I can't imagine what the Colonel sees in it. Still, to each his own, Watson. Let's take it back to Baker Street and see if we can't find a place for it. If that fails, you can always write a story about it."

I shook my head.

"If I wrote a story about that thing, no one would want to read it."

Holmes put the thing down, a large leaden statue of a black bird, a hawk of some kind.

"Perhaps not. Still, you never know, Watson . . . you never know."

Though Mr. R.'s payments were generous, his only length stipulation was that each writer do the story justice. "FD" and "MBL," the collaborative authors of "The Manor House Case," compressed enough plot and characters to fill a mystery novel into a mere five thousand words. The evidence suggests they may have been Frederick Dannay (1905–1982) and Manfred B. Lee (1905–1971), who collectively wrote mystery novels and short fiction as ELLERY QUEEN. *Regarding the story's final scene, I remind the reader of the hint of sibling rivalry when Watson first met Sherlock's smarter brother Mycroft: " 'I hear of Sherlock everywhere since you became his chronicler. By the way, Sherlock, I expected to see you round last week to consult me over that Manor House case. I thought you might be a little out of your depth.' "*—JAF

The Manor House Case

BY

"EDWARD D. HOCH"
(ASCRIBED TO ELLERY QUEEN)

As I look over my notes for the summer of 1888, I come upon a singular adventure that is quite unlike the usual problems that came to the attention of Mr. Sherlock Holmes during this period. My inclination was to title this investigation "The English Manor Mystery," but since virtually all of Holmes's cases took place in his homeland such a name might have seemed redundant.

The manor itself was the home of Sir Patrick Stacy White, the well-known African explorer just recently returned from a perilous journey retracing the route of Stanley in his search for Livingston. He'd sent an urgent message to Holmes inviting him to spend a weekend at the manor house, located about an hour west of London near Reading.

"Are you going?" I asked when he told me about it on Friday morning.

"His message says there has been a mysterious death and he fears others will follow. He suggests a stay of at least two nights in order to fully investigate the matter. If we catch the evening train we could be there tonight. Are you game, Watson?"

I had no plans for the weekend and the bright August days seemed to beckon us to the countryside. "Is it all right for you to bring a guest?"

"Sir Patrick suggested it in his message. I gather several other guests are already in attendance."

It was still daylight when we left the train at the Reading station and found Sir Patrick's carriage and driver awaiting us. "Pleasant weather," Holmes told the fairly young man.

"The best, sir," he said with a slight accent I couldn't identify.

"Have you been employed here long?" Holmes was always gathering information, filing it away for the future.

"Several years," the driver replied. "Name's Haskin. I'm just filling in with the carriage. My real job's with the animals."

Holmes was suddenly interested. "What animals would those be?"

"Sir Patrick maintains a small zoo at the manor. We bring back animals from his African safaris. Brought back a pair of fine lion cubs from his most recent journey."

Before long we topped a hill and the manor house itself came into view. It sat alone on the plain below, a three-story brick house with a stand of oak trees on the left side and a large pond about a hundred feet from the front entrance. I could see a pair of swans gliding on the water.

"Welcome to Stacy Manor," Haskin told us as he turned onto the long pebbled driveway leading up to the house.

The door opened as we approached it and a butler ushered us in. "Mrs. White will be with you in a moment."

Holmes and I waited in the front hall, with an elephant head visible through the doorway. Almost at once we were joined by a handsome woman of about forty who carried herself with an almost regal air. "I am Elizabeth Stacy White," she said. "And you would be Mr. Sherlock Holmes."

"Correct." He smiled and seemed almost to give a little bow. "This is my close companion, Dr. Watson. I trust we can be of some service to your husband in this unfortunate matter."

"Has he given you the details?"

"Not as yet."

"Pray be seated and I will give you the facts as we know them. My husband is an African traveler of some little renown. After each trip he is in the habit of bringing home creatures from the Dark Continent to stock his private zoo at the rear of the house. You will see it later. After this latest trip he returned with two lion cubs, and he invited a small number of friends to stay with us on a summer holiday. They arrived last Sunday and will be leaving us this Sunday."

At that point she was interrupted by a large bearded man who strode in and immediately took command of the conversation. "Excuse me for not greeting you upon your arrival," he said, leaving no doubt that it was his house and he was in charge. "I trust my wife kept you amused in my absence."

"She was most helpful," Holmes said. "You are Sir Patrick Stacy White?"

"The same." He gestured with a motion meant to encompass the entire house. "Every creature you see here, whether living or stuffed, was personally caught by me."

I wondered if the remark extended to his wife Elizabeth. He was a man who would be easy to dislike. Holmes, however, took no notice of the boast and began questioning him about the killing.

"The victim was my London publisher, Oscar Rhinebeck. He was one of six houseguests we'd invited for the week. I was planning to write a book about my recent African travels and we were discussing it Sunday evening, after the others had arrived. I left him alone in the library for a time and when I returned I found him dead. He'd been savagely beaten with a fireplace poker."

Elizabeth, who'd remained at his side through all this, broke in to add, "This time we called the police at once."

"This time?" asked Holmes sharply.

Sir Patrick seemed annoyed by his wife's interruption. "There'd been a previous incident shortly after Rhinebeck's arrival. I'd just shown him my zoo and we were walking back to the main house when a cornice fell from the roof and nearly hit him. When we mentioned it to Elizabeth she was quite concerned and wanted the local police summoned at once. I told her that was nonsense and even went up to the roof to inspect it. The cornice had simply broken away, probably weakened by the wind."

"There was no wind last Sunday," his wife insisted.

"But there had been the previous evening."

I suspected they were two who might argue as to whether the sun was shining. "Who else was in the house at the time the cornice fell?" Holmes asked.

"All of our guests had arrived by that time. Madeline Oaks, the actress, came with her manager, my longtime friend Maxwell Park. Dr. Prouty, our family physician, arrived with his wife Dorothy, and her sister Agnes."

"Dorothy and Agnes lived near here in their youth," Elizabeth explained, "and sometimes visited at Stacy Manor."

Holmes nodded. "Stacy is your middle name, Sir Patrick."

"Quite correct. The house was my mother's ancestral home, which I inherited upon her death eight years ago."

"Let us return to the murder of Oscar Rhinebeck. Were there no clues at the scene?"

"One only. My publisher was clutching a playing card in his hand—the ten of spades. It appeared to be a dying message."

"How quaint," Holmes remarked. "Does the ten of spades have any meaning to you or your guests?"

"None whatsoever."

"Perhaps its presence was only a coincidence."

Sir Patrick shook his head. "It seems like more than that. There was a bloody trail on the carpet indicating that the dying man dragged himself to the card table and managed to select the ten from a deck of cards."

Elizabeth glanced at the room's big grandfather clock as Holmes asked, "Do the police have any suspects in mind?"

"Not really," our host told us. "They mentioned a convict recently escaped from Reading Gaol, and believe he could have entered the house undetected, perhaps bent on robbery."

"What is this convict's name?"

"James Adams, serving a long term for assault and robbery. He escaped about ten days ago and has not been recaptured."

Elizabeth was nervously watching the clock. "I'm sorry you missed dinner but our guests will be assembling in the library for brandy at nine. Perhaps you'd want to freshen up and join us."

It seemed like a good idea, and Holmes and I allowed the butler to show us to our room. When we were alone and I was unpacking my overnight bag I asked Holmes, "What do you make of it? Is there a killer under our roof?"

"It would seem so, Watson. It is obvious that Sir Patrick's wife is greatly concerned, and she is probably the one who urged him to appeal for help. As for Sir Patrick, I am struck by the fact that his left boot has a thicker sole than the right one. If one leg is longer than the other it would make walking great distances on a safari painful if not impossible."

"Perhaps he was carried in a sedan chair," I suggested.

"We shall see, Watson. I am most interested in meeting our

other guests, all of whom chose to remain for their visit even after a murder was committed in the house."

We went downstairs promptly at nine o'clock and found the others gathered in the library. The men held brandy snifters, though the women were indulging in something lighter. My attention was immediately focused on the actress, Madeline Oaks, whom I'd seen recently in a London production of Ibsen's *A Doll's House*. She was even more striking at close quarters, a rare beauty of the sort to take one's breath away.

It was her agent, Maxwell Park, who immediately recognized the name of Sherlock Holmes. He was a slender man with glasses and muttonchop whiskers, and he shook my friend's hand vigorously when introduced. "The popular press has been filled with your exploits, Mr. Holmes. This is indeed a pleasure!"

I was interested in meeting Dr. Prouty, a small, quiet country doctor who sipped his brandy with a bit of uncertainty. "Do you have a practice in London, Dr. Watson?" he asked.

"A small one, very limited. I assist my friend Holmes in his work, and I do a bit of writing."

His wife Dorothy was a plain-looking woman with large bones and an athletic appearance. She sat on a red plush sofa with her sister Agnes, who was introduced as Agnes Baxter. Miss Baxter, more comely in appearance than her older sister, was probably still in her mid-twenties.

"I understand you lived near here when you were growing up," I said to Agnes.

"Indeed we did. Dorothy and I played here as children, though of course there was no zoo at the time. The Stacy family was very nice and this is a wonderful house. We moved into the city when I was ten and I so missed it!"

"Will you be riding with us in the morning?" her sister Dorothy asked.

The thought appalled me. "I doubt it. I believe Sir Patrick wants to show us his animals."

"And that I do!" our host said, coming over to join us.

"It's quite an animal collection," Dorothy Prouty admitted. "The best I've seen outside of London."

Later, trying to fall asleep in a strange bed, I was reminded of her words when I heard the chilling laugh of a hyena.

I awakened to find Holmes's hand upon my shoulder, and I was surprised to find him fully dressed. "What time is it?" I asked sleepily.

"Seven-thirty. Sir Patrick's wife is assembling her guests to go riding. Perhaps we should dress and go down to breakfast."

I grumbled something and strode over to the window. On the gravel drive below I could see Elizabeth White in riding costume, just mounting a grey mare while their man Haskin held the reins for her. Madeline Oaks and her manager were already mounted, as were Dr. and Mrs. Prouty. There was no sign of Mrs. Prouty's younger sister. As the five of them prepared to ride off I washed and dressed quickly.

Sir Patrick was awaiting us in the dining room, lingering over a cup of morning tea. "Ah, there you are! I was beginning to fear that our country air had lulled you into a bit of extra slumber."

"No, no," Holmes assured him. "Both Watson and I are anxious to see your collection."

We ate sparingly and then followed our host through the large kitchen to the rear of the house. "I'm pleased you could come," he said, "though this whole matter has upset Elizabeth more than myself. Naturally I am disturbed by the death of my publisher, but the idea that one of our houseguests could be a murderer seems preposterous to me. I am perfectly willing to accept the police theory of an escaped convict."

Haskin was waiting for us at the back door, wearing the same dark pants and work shirt he'd had on the previous day. "They were a bit restless during the night," he said. "Could have been a prowler, though I saw no one."

Our host made no comment until we reached the first of a dozen cages set within the grove of trees at the side and rear of the house. Inside were two small lion cubs, rolling over and playing with each other like a pair of kittens. "These came from my latest trip," he said. "You'll see a fully grown one a bit later."

Our next stop was the large and ugly hyena that had kept me awake. It had a massive head and a red coat covered with brown oval spots. "This is the fellow I heard in the night," I remarked.

"He was restless," Haskin remarked again.

We went on down the line to some monkeys and a glass cage that held a pair of small pythons that seemed to be asleep. Then there was a large pen with a fully grown zebra, an animal that always fascinated me. It was followed by more monkeys and finally another large cage where an adult lion paced back and forth. "This one needs more space," Sir Patrick told us.

While we were studying the lion I noticed that Dorothy Prouty had returned alone on her horse. She dismounted and strode toward the front of the manor. "All of these animals need more space," Holmes was saying. "But on my rare visits to the London zoo I have found conditions to be little better than this. Our large elephant Jumbo was sold to an American circus partly because of space problems."

Sir Patrick nodded. "Before his untimely death my publisher expressed much the same view. He wanted me to set aside several acres of land for the zoo, to enlarge it, hire a professional staff and actually charge admission. He felt my reputation as a big game hunter and collector would attract the public."

"Is this lion contented?" Holmes asked Haskin.

"Hardly, sir. He's a dangerous—"

The words were interrupted by a sudden scream from the house. Sir Patrick stood frozen in his tracks but Holmes broke into a run. I followed as fast as I could. When we reached the rear door we saw that the butler and cook had heard the scream too and headed up the back stairs. We found Dorothy Prouty passed out on the floor of the upper hallway. She was by an open bedroom door and when I looked in I saw the terrible sight that had confronted her. Agnes Baxter, her younger sister, was sprawled across the bloody bed, a kitchen knife buried in her chest. In her hand she held a playing card, the jack of spades.

While I determined that the young woman had died instantly, Holmes was busy loosening Mrs. Prouty's riding habit and trying to revive her. When Sir Patrick arrived and found him thus Holmes was rubbing her hands and cheeks. "Do not concern yourself, Sir Patrick. I am trying to help her breath. I fear the shock of finding her sister's body was too much for the woman."

"Another killing!" our host gasped, clinging to the door frame. For an instant I feared he might pass out, too.

"And another playing card," Sherlock Holmes remarked. "I suggest you dispatch a servant to summon the local authorities."

When Dorothy Prouty was at last revived she told her story in a tearful, breaking voice. "I—She was going to ride out and catch up with us. Sh—she had her riding costume on. When she didn't turn up I came back to the house, worried she might be ill. I found her like this. Who could have done such a terrible thing?"

The local constable, when he arrived, asked the same question. Scotland Yard men came out from London later in the day and suggested a search of the entire manor. There was always the possibility that the missing convict was concealed somewhere on the premises. While the search went on Holmes took no part in it. "It's a waste of time, Watson. If this convict was the killer, why would he leave playing cards in his victims' hands? No, we are dealing with something much more sinister here."

"In this peaceful country setting?"

"I have said before that the vilest alleys in London are nothing compared to the beautiful countryside. In the city the machinery of justice is swift to act. Out here, deeds of hellish cruelty can go unpunished."

He was right about the convict, of course. There was no trace of him in the manor house or anywhere on the grounds. It was established that the knife had come from the kitchen, but anyone could have taken it. And Agnes Baxter might well have been killed before the other guests set out on their ride. Sir Patrick's wife Elizabeth was especially upset as the summer house party seemed to collapse about her. Dr. Prouty and his wife had departed with Agnes's body, to complete the necessary funeral arrangements. I had thought the others might leave, too, but at Elizabeth's urging the actress and her agent stayed on.

Dinner that night was a somber affair. The six of us tried to speak of other things, but it was Madeline Oaks who brought the subject back to the killings. "That's two of them in six days," she said. "Mr. Holmes and Dr. Watson can be ruled out because they were not present when Rhinebeck died, but the other four of us are all suspects."

"That's nonsense!" Sir Patrick burst out. "Why would I kill my own book publisher, and that poor young woman? Why would any of us, for that matter?"

"What could be the meaning of those playing cards?" Maxwell Park asked. "The ten and jack of spades!"

The events at Stacy Manor were indeed baffling, and I could see that Holmes was greatly troubled. "I fear the killings are not over," he confided to me as we went up to our room later. "There is a pattern here which has yet to reveal itself."

"Then none of us is safe."

"Have you brought your revolver, Watson?"

"It is in my bag."

"Good! We may have need of it before the night is over."

I took it out and made certain it was loaded, then laid it on the table between our beds. Neither of us donned our nightclothes, though I for one quickly drifted into a deep sleep. I gather Holmes was sleeping too when we were both awakened toward dawn by human screams and a lion's deep-throated growl.

"Quick, Watson, your revolver! I never thought of the animals!"

We hurried downstairs and already some of the others had appeared in their doorways, awakened by the sounds. Holmes was first out the door, heading toward the cages we'd inspected the previous day.

When we reached the large lion's cage and heard again the savage growls of the beast, Holmes grabbed the revolver from my hands and thrust it between the bars. The lion turned from its grisly task, and by now there was enough morning twilight for us to recognize Haskin's limp and bloody figure. Holmes fired three shots, carefully aimed at the beast's head, and the lion went down in a heap.

He pulled on the door of the cage but it was padlocked from the outside. By this time Sir Patrick and his wife had joined us, with the actress, her agent and the servants bringing up the rear. "Where is the key to this?" Holmes demanded.

"There's an extra in the kitchen," Sir Patrick said, sending the butler for it. They were all in their nightclothes and robes, with Sir Patrick limping badly without his special shoes.

In a moment we had the key and Holmes entered first, holding the revolver ready. I was right behind him, reaching the body to turn it over and reveal a face so torn and bloody as to be unrecognizable. It was Holmes who found the playing card—a queen of spades—beneath the body.

The local police and Scotland Yard were back on the scene within hours. What might have been a tranquil Sunday morning had been shattered by a third murder, and even our host was deeply shaken as he spoke to the authorities. Elizabeth sat by his side, clasping his hand.

The officer in charge had his notebook open. "I understand the deceased was an employee of yours. Could you give me his full name and position?"

Sir Patrick moistened his lips, his face ashen. "His name was Haskin Zehn. He was a German gypsy with a great affinity for wild animals. He accompanied me on my African journeys and because of my bad leg he did much of the actual capturing. He was a fine worker, unmarried, about thirty-five years of age. He lived here at the house."

"Could this have been an accident? He seems to have been dressed in his normal work clothes."

Holmes spoke up then. "The cage had been padlocked from the outside. It appears he was knocked unconscious and then locked inside with the lion."

"He wouldn't have gone into the cage before dawn," Sir Patrick agreed. "This was murder."

Holmes nodded. "When we turned over the body, hoping he was still alive, there was another playing card beneath the body."

The officer, whose name was Wegand, nodded. "The ten, jack and queen of spades, Mr. Holmes. What does that tell us?"

"That there'll be more murders unless we put a stop to them."

Elizabeth White seemed confused. "But what could it mean? Why was the jack of spades left with a female victim and the queen with a male? Is the next to be the king?"

"The king of beasts," Sir Patrick speculated. "But my lion is dead."

Finally, when things had calmed down a bit, the cook served a light breakfast. When he'd finished I noticed Holmes checking the schedule of trains back to London. A closed wagon had arrived for the removal of the latest victim and when he saw it he hurried outside. Curious, I followed him. "What is it, Holmes?"

He was bent over Haskin's body, examining the man's belt and shoes. "Interesting," he said. "All right, you can take him away now." He straightened up and smiled at me. "I believe we must return to London, Watson, on the first available train."

"You are abandoning the investigation?"

"Merely trying a new course to the truth."

We went back inside while he explained to Sir Patrick that he must continue the investigation in London. He turned to the officer who had questioned us. "Sergeant Wegand, we have only forty-five minutes to catch the next train. If you are going back could you give us a ride to the station?"

Sir Patrick protested. "My butler could take you."

"No, no—the sergeant is going our way."

Wegand grumbled a bit but Holmes spoke to him in a soft voice and he agreed. We quickly packed our bags and said goodbye to all. The actress, Madeline Oaks, seemed sorry to see me go and I promised to attend her next London opening.

On our journey to the Reading station a thought occurred to me. "Dr. Prouty and his wife departed yesterday. Is it possible one of them might have returned to kill Haskin?"

"Anything is possible, Watson. Let us see what we find at our destination."

We arrived at Reading station with only minutes to spare. Already in possession of our return tickets, we hastened to the platform. I was a bit surprised to see Sergeant Wegand coming with us and wondered what Holmes had said to him.

The three of us boarded the train together, avoiding the first-class carriages and going directly to the coaches. Holmes strode down the aisle quickly, eyes straight ahead, and it was not until we'd passed through to the second coach that he suddenly pounced, reaching across an empty seat to fasten upon an unshaven man in dirty clothes who sat staring out the window at the platform.

"Here, Sergeant!" Holmes announced. "Arrest this man! He is the triple killer you are seeking."

The officer was taken by surprise. "My God—the escaped convict?"

"No, no. Let me introduce you to Mr. Haskin Zehn, returned from the dead, but no less dangerous for that."

Later, after we'd returned to Stacy Manor for the explanations Holmes felt they deserved, we sat once again in the library with Sir Patrick and his wife. Their other guests had departed soon after we did, perhaps fearing more violence. But Holmes assured them it was over.

"I can't believe that Haskin would do such a thing," Elizabeth White said. "What could possibly have been his motive?"

"His original motive involved only the publisher, Oscar Rhinebeck. You told me, Sir Patrick, that Rhinebeck had suggested greatly enlarging your zoo, hiring a professional staff and opening it to the public. Haskin feared his beloved animals would be taken away from him, and in a moment of anger he struck Rhinebeck with a poker, inflicting a fatal wound."

"What about the playing cards and the other killings?" Sir Patrick asked.

Holmes, relaxing at last, had taken out his pipe as he spoke. "The business with the playing cards was meant merely to confuse us, and it did just that. I overlooked one crucial clue for too long— it might even be called the clue of the clue. The bloody trail showed that the first victim, Rhinebeck, had dragged himself to the card table and used his final moments of life to choose that ten of spades as a clue to his killer's identity. But consider the later killings and you'll note some vastly different circumstances. Agnes Baxter was stabbed in the chest in her bedroom, killed instantly. The third victim died in a locked lion's cage. Certainly neither of these was in a position to choose a playing card in their final seconds of life."

"Of course not!" Sir Patrick agreed. "The murderer left them!"

"Obviously. And yet the first card, that ten of spades, had been chosen by the victim. The bloody trail told us so. Conclusion? After that first, legitimate, clue the killer left more playing cards in sequence to confuse us. Instead of looking back at the first clue, the ten of spades, we looked ahead—speculating on where the series was going, seeking an overall pattern that didn't exist."

"What could the ten of spades have meant?" Elizabeth wondered.

"The spade was simply the first ten he came to. It was the ten that was important. The Germanic Rhinebeck was trying to tell us his killer's name was Haskin *Zehn*—the number ten in German!"

"Of course!" Sir Patrick slapped his knee with an open palm. "I'm afraid I've forgotten too much of my public school German."

"But Agnes Baxter hadn't. She accused him, perhaps threatened him, and she had to die, too. By that time it must have been obvious he was in deep trouble. My presence, if I may say so, must have added to his growing concern. Then last evening a solution presented itself, virtually out of the blue. The escaped convict for whom the police were searching appeared at your zoo—perhaps trying to steal some of the animals' food. Haskin came upon him and realized at once that the man was his own size and weight, with the same hair coloring. His escape had presented itself. The convict was knocked unconscious and hidden for a time. I believe Haskin wounded him and disfigured his face with a sharp garden tool. Then he changed clothes with the man and pushed his body into the lion's cage with an appropriate playing card. I fear I was too quick in killing the lion for a death he only partly caused."

"How did you know Haskin would be on the London train?"

"He could not afford to remain in this area where he might be recognized, and the schedule showed that on Sunday the London train was the next one out. I knew he couldn't have caught an earlier train because he had to walk all the way to Reading station."

"You were so sure that the body wasn't Haskin Zehn?"

Holmes nodded. "When I finally heard his last name for the first time I was virtually certain of the truth. I examined the body, especially the belt and shoes, and found confirmation. The belt buckle was one hole tighter than it had ordinarily been worn, and the shoes fit a bit too loosely on the feet. That was all the proof I needed."

It was the following week at the Diogenes Club when I met Sherlock's older brother Mycroft for the first time. Early in the conversation Mycroft asked about the Manor House case. "It was Adams, of course?"

"Yes, it was Adams," Sherlock agreed.

"I was sure of it from the first."

Later, when we were alone, I asked why he had told Mycroft that the convict was the killer.

Sherlock Holmes smiled slightly. "It was just a bit of brotherly rivalry, Watson. He will learn the truth soon enough, and realize that he was wrong for once."

I *agreed to honour each author's choice of title, even when Mr. R. did not like it. An entry in his journal reads, "Except for horrendous name, MS adaptation of 'singular affair of the aluminium crutch' absolutely smashing!" The putative author of "The Adventure of the Cripple Parade" may be* MICKEY SPILLANE *(1918–   ), author of* I the Jury, My Gun Is Quick *and other Mike Hammer hardboiled thrillers. However, Mr. Spillane could not be reached for comment.—JAF*

The Adventure of the Cripple Parade (The Singular Affair of the Aluminium Crutch)

BY *"WILLIAM L. DEANDREA"*
(ASCRIBED TO MICKEY SPILLANE)

Watson was a bloody mess.

It was so bad, that when I entered the surgery, where three of his brother medical men were working feverishly over his body, trying to staunch blood and rearrange bones, that I instinctively doffed my deerstalker, as though in the presence of death.

Angrily, I pushed the thought away, and turned to my brother, Mycroft.

"I found your note," I said. It had been in the rooms I had once shared with Watson at 221B Baker Street. I'd come back from a three-day chase of bank-note forgers, to find big brother's small but very neat handwriting pinned to the wall in front of my favorite armchair with the knife I usually use to secure my current correspondence to the chimneypiece.

Looking at poor Watson now, I could think of better uses for a knife.

"I knew you would," he said. He hardly moved his mouth enough to make his chins wobble. When we were children, Mycroft who was seven years my senior, had been left the task of raising me almost singlehandedly. It was one of those situations— the parents are too busy, and the governess just can't match her charges in the intellect department.

Mycroft had taught me the Code of the English Gentleman, and the first item of that code was "Never show your feelings." It was a hard lesson, but I learned it well. It served me in good stead in my chosen career as a consulting detective. I'm sure it served my brother equally well, in his career of arranging difficult situations for the Crown.

Of course, at this stage of the game, there's no way to know. We're grown up now. We don't talk about our emotions, at least not with each other.

This code came with its price. You learned how to hide your emotions, but not to stop having them. They came to me, just as they came to anybody, but they got bottled up like steam in an engine, and up and up, until the valve seems like it's about to pop, but you lean on it a little harder, and it never quite does.

Tonight, I was leaning on the valve with all my strength, but I could feel the bubbling inside.

"What happened?" I demanded.

Mycroft made a sour face. He might have been leaning on his emotional valve, too, but heavy as he was, he had a lot more to lean with.

"We're not sure," Mycroft said. "Of course, the superficial deductions are obvious. He was attacked from the front, then mercilessly beaten with an unidentified instrument."

"From the angle of the wounds, wielded by a right-handed

man." My monograph on *Contusions and Lacerations Caused by Severe Beatings With Non-Edged Implements* was fresh in my mind as I elbowed my way past a doctor who was walking away from the table, took my glass from my pocket, and had a good look.

"Certain similarities to a cricket bat's marks, but whatever did this is harder and more flexible than ashwood. Either that, or the person who swung it must be a giant."

"Then there would be fewer blows along the legs and more on the upper body."

"Correct," I said. "And Watson would be dead."

I stepped aside for the doctor, who was returning with a bottle of laudanum. That was a good sign. You don't fetch painkiller for a corpse.

I asked the doctor with the bottle what Watson's chances were.

"I just can't say," he said. "The beating he took was ferocious; most people I've seen this bad were already dead. But your friend Watson has the heart of a whole pride of lions, and a solid constitution. He may be all right. He may be in a coma from which he never awakens. He's in God's hands, now. He has had one stroke of luck already, though—they dropped him just two doors down from our surgery, just outside the Diogenes Club."

"The Diogenes Club," I echoed. I shot Mycroft a look; he returned one that said he'd explain all in good time. *He* was a member of the Diogenes Club.

Suddenly, the man on the table groaned.

"Watson!" I said.

Watson's voice was a breathless thing, each sound forced into the world past pain. "Holmes," he said. "Is that you, Holmes?"

I took his hand. He smiled a little. "Trying a little detective work on my own . . . crippled . . . shouldn't have tried to do so much . . . wanted to impress you . . . crippled, all crippled, all the same place . . . I have to tell you . . . clubbed, clubbed. Doomed . . ."

Like a game bulldog in the pit, Watson strove to get up and

give it another try, but the doctor was shaking his head so hard, it almost made his eyeballs rattle.

I held Watson by the shoulders and eased him back to the table.

"Quiet, old friend," I told him. "And don't you worry about a thing. You're bashed up, but you're not crippled."

"No, no . . . not me . . . all, all crippled . . . must find out . . ."

"You're going to be fine, Watson, I know it. You need some rest. And while you're resting, let me tell you what's going to happen. I'm going to find out who did this to you, and I promise you they will pay, through the law or otherwise."

I thought I felt him squeeze my hand. "Sorry, Holmes . . . made such a mess . . ."

"Stop talking rubbish," I said. "Listen, not only will I bring in whoever did this to you, I'll also write it up for your files, so you won't miss a thing."

He squeezed my hand once more. Then the laudanum took hold, and he sighed and sank back into a heavy slumber.

II

The only place in the Diogenes Club in which talking is allowed is the Strangers' Room. Mycroft had signalled the porter to have our brandies and sodas brought there. I poured some amber liquid for myself, wielded the gasogene, then took a healthy swallow. It traced a warm line from my mouth to my stomach, but did nothing to thaw the cold hard thing in the pit of it.

"Has Mrs. Watson been notified? She's visiting relatives in the country. Cumberland, as I recall."

"Yes, Watson's locum told me. Everything is in hand, as far as that goes."

"Tell me the rest of it."

"I suppose in one way, it's all my fault. There's a flap on in the Ministry of Defence; stolen plans for troop movements and some technical innovations—I don't need to be any more specific than that. The plans have been recovered, and the foreign spy who bought them is under lock and key. But we have not been able to lay our hands on the thief. He collected forty thousand pounds, and must surely plan to smuggle it and himself out of the country."

"Has the foreign spy named him?"

"He says he's only seen the man in disguise."

"What sort of disguise?"

"The man the foreign agent met with was always disguised as a heavily bandaged cripple."

"Watson was raving about cripples. Mycroft, you had better not be trying to tell me that since I wasn't around, you sent Watson out to catch this spy."

"Sherlock, I am insulted. My admiration for Watson as your friend, as a physician, as a man of action, even as the recorder of sensational tales of your adventures, is unbounded. Only a dunce would send him alone on a confidential mission of this kind."

"Well, you're not a dunce."

"Thank you," he said. He surreptitiously slipped one hand inside his waistcoat as if he wanted to scratch his huge belly. He came out holding a piece of paper in his hand. He didn't mention it, so I didn't either.

"All I said in this matter was that I rather badly wanted your assistance in a matter of smuggling, and if he should hear from you, I asked him to tell you to call on me at any hour of the day or night."

"How did Watson take this?"

My brother pursed his lips. "He was much as usual, eager at the prospect of another of your adventures together, however vague that prospect might have been. But there was something more, a musing quality. At one point he said, 'Smuggling? I hadn't thought of that, but it might be an explanation.' "

"That's just like him," I said. "Watson is always looking for a mystery or a menace, even where they don't exist."

"They existed here," Mycroft said.

"Do you think Watson stumbled on your Ministry Problem on his own?"

"I believe I do, Sherlock. It's a remarkable coincidence, but the coincidence of two possible smuggling plots involving bandaged cripples is even worse."

"It seems to me that a bandage would make a fine place to hide diamonds or gold coins, or any other portable form of wealth. All right, it's a lucky day for you."

"Why do you say that?"

"Because I'm working on the theory that your government secrets and what happened to Watson are connected. If they weren't, I'd be after Watson's attackers, and I wouldn't give you the time of day."

"I try always to know the time of day. Besides—"

"Besides you haven't shown me that piece of paper you took from your waistcoat."

Mycroft treated me to one of his rare smiles. "This will establish a connection to your satisfaction, I think."

I took the paper and read it. "MYCROFT HOLMES— TELL YOUR BROTHER TO STOP MEDDLING, OR THE NEXT BODY WILL BE HIS."

I held the paper up to the light. "There's most of a watermark here. I'll have to consult my files."

"In due time."

I leaned even harder on the steam valve. "Watson is lying unconscious. He may never wake up. The time, Brother Dear, is long past due. I need to examine this watermark, and I need to have all the details of what was stolen, for whom, and why."

"Would you mind getting the details first? The sub-Minister is waiting in his office for us."

III

Aluminium, Mr. Holmes. Or as the Americans persist in miscalling it, aluminum. Are you familiar with the subject?"

"I've studied chemistry, and I read the *Times*," I told him.

It was from reading the *Times* that I knew about the sub-

Minister, himself. He was touted for Great Things in the future, maybe even a stint in Number Ten. I knew about his trademark white sidewhiskers, but then, everybody did. Sir Carl Berin-Grotin was one of the rising stars of the Empire.

But rising star or no rising star, if he couldn't shed any light on what had happened to Watson, I had no time for him.

To speed things up, I told him what I knew about aluminium.

"It's a chemical element, a silver-white metal. It's strong, light, elastic, malleable, ductile and a superb conductor of electricity. It's also one of the most expensive substances on earth. The Americans acquired a large portion of all the refined aluminium in the world to top off their Washington Monument. Tripled the cost of the structure, I believe."

"It might well have done," the sub-Minister conceded. "But here at the ministry, we are not concerned with the cost of the metal. Or rather we are, but only insofar as we can attempt to drive down that cost."

He pointed a finger at me, a rude habit, especially when a finger is as ugly as his were. They were thick and almost globular at the tips, and the nails didn't grow out straight, but curled tightly over those rounded fingertips like the claw of an animal.

"You see, Mr. Holmes," he went on, "aluminium is not so precious because it is scarce—indeed, a ministry chemist tells me it is one of the most abundant elements in the crust of this planet. The problem is, it is bound so tightly to bauxite, its ore, that it takes temperatures virtually impossible to sustain by conventional methods to melt it free."

"I take it that what has been stolen is an unconventional method. The troop movement information was a smoke screen."

"Yes. When this sort of crisis is on, rumors inevitably start. Not everyone can appreciate the value of an electrically powered furnace to refine aluminium on a scale hitherto impossible. Let them rest content with troop movements. It sounds more . . . dangerous somehow."

"Fine," I said. "Plans for an electrically powered furnace to refine aluminium were stolen. Mycroft says they were recovered. Obviously the plans are simple enough for a man to carry in his head.''

"A man with a trained memory," Sir Carl said. "Or time to study. We can't be sure our quarry didn't have a chance to copy the plans. More than one country would be interested in this. Cheap aluminium would make possible gigantic dreadnoughts. Body armour for soldiers. Airships. Heavens, one could even hammer it out flat into sheets and preserve food in it."

"Besides Watson's . . . misfortune, how do you know our man is still in the country?"

Sir Carl scratched with his odd claw-nails at the trademark sidewhiskers. That told me something about the man right there. He was willing to put up with an uncomfortable growth, just for show. "We have sources, Mr. Holmes. There would be elation in certain foreign circles it would be impossible to hide. Our man is still in England. The question is, can you apprehend him before he leaves the country?"

My face was hard, like a mask of stone. "Count on it," I said. "The only place he goes from England is Hell."

IV

She was a brunette, tall and cool, and her smile was a challenge that was almost an insult. Watson thinks I'm immune to women, and I don't correct him because there's no advantage to it. But Lizabeth Parkins had the stuff to overcome anybody's immunity, and she dressed to show it, the thick wool hugging every curve, the smoothly turned ankles shamelessly exposed.

"It's unusual to find a woman in a shipping line's office," I said.

"I'm an unusual woman," she told me. "What brings you here, Mr. Holmes?"

What brought me there was the watermark on the paper and

Watson's day book, but she didn't need to know that. Watson's book showed me he had several cases that brought him down to the docks in recent weeks, and there was enough left of the mark on the paper to let me know it was the stationery of the Trans-Global Line, one of the biggest of the new shippers.

"Routine investigation," I lied. "What ships do you have in London right now?"

She licked her red lips. Suddenly, it got hot in the room, and there was a buzzing sound in my ears.

"Why do you want to know, Mr. Holmes?" She was still wearing that cool smile, but there was a thin sheen of sweat on her forehead.

"Come on, Miss Parkins, I could find out in a second from the shipping desk at any newspaper. I'm in a hurry."

"Oh, well, if you're in a hurry. We have only one at the moment, the *Peruslavia,* leaving tomorrow for Hamburg. It is not too late to consign a shipment. You can see it if you like. Pier Sixty-one."

I thanked her and went to leave.

"Do come again, Mr. Holmes. When you have more time."

I found a convenient corner out of sight, and watched the *Peruslavia*'s gangplank. The first bandaged cripple went up after I'd been there about twenty minutes, then at fifty-minute intervals for the next three hours. It was the kind of thing you wouldn't notice ordinarily, but it would stick in your mind if it happened more than once. I'd checked out Watson's patient, and from his window the gangplank was clearly visible. Three visits here, Watson must have seen five so-called cripples go on to the ship.

A nice racket. You give them a crutch, and a bandage load of something expensive, send them up the gangplank, unwrap them, and send them down as ordinary seamen.

I timed myself on the next one and planted myself at the bottom of the gangplank.

"Here," I said. "Let me help you up."

He recognized me, and he ran. He wasn't just fast for a cripple, he was *fast*. Through the back alleys of the docklands, in and
out of doorways. I might never have caught him if he'd had sense
enough to throw the crutch away. He obviously didn't need it, but
he held on. It slowed him down, made his passage through doorways harder. Finally, I had him cornered at the end of a blind alley.
Like a rat, he turned to fight.

He held the crutch like a weapon. That would have been fine
with me, if I'd had a stick, too, but I didn't. I let him take one wild
swing, ducked it, and delivered a terrible right cross to his face. I felt
bones in his nose go to gravel, and redness squirted in all directions.

When he was down and out, I took a look at him. A typical
thug, not somebody I recognized. Then I unwrapped the bandages
on his arms and legs and head. There were no injuries underneath
them, but I'd been expecting that.

There was nothing valuable in them, either.

Not so much as a miserable farthing. A beautiful logical con-
struction came crashing down. They weren't smuggling things in
those bandages, so what was the parade of cripples all about? I had
to get on that ship.

There was enough privacy in the alley to do what I had to do.
I got rid of my cap and Inverness cape and jacket and tie, and proceeded to wind the bandages around myself. I wiped some grime
from the sooty walls and smeared it on my hands and face. Then I
picked up the crutch and headed for the ship. The hardest part of
the whole thing was using the crutch. It was too short, and didn't
seem to weigh as much as it should.

I remembered to limp, and to do it consistently. It was probably just some mistake that had caught Watson's attention in the first
place. He may not be much of a detective, but he's a perceptive and
dedicated doctor. And the best friend a man ever had.

Anger started bubbling up in me once more, but it was vital to
keep under control. Even more vital, because suddenly, I had it.

The reason for the bandages, the heat and the humming, everything.

I could have gone to Mycroft; I could have gone to Lestrade at the Yard. But this was personal, and I wanted to do it all by myself. I kept limping, but I changed direction back to the office of Trans-Global lines. I limped through the door into the empty office. The place was still stiflingly hot. Lizabeth Parkins was buttoning the top buttons of her dress as she came to the office.

A look of anger contorted the beautiful face. "What are you doing back here in that—Fred! Nigel!"

Two more cripples came out of the back room. One of them had a shotgun, but it was pointed at the floor. I didn't give him time to regret his mistake. I pulled the revolver from my pocket, and fired. He went to the floor. His friend didn't know whether to attack me with his crutch or grab for the shotgun. I had the pistol against his eyeball in a split second, and suddenly the decision didn't matter so much anymore.

I took the crutches, both as light as mine. I herded everyone into the back room. In there was the crucible, filled with a glowing yellow-white liquid, like a piece of the sun.

"I see," I said. "You weren't just going to sell the secret, you planned to present a working model. How did you plan to get *that* on board?"

"We were going to call it machine parts. Even if customs opened the box, that's what it would look like." Her face was amazing in that unearthly glow. "What happens now, Mr. Holmes?" she asked coyly.

"It's over," I said.

"It doesn't have to be. *Someone* is going to get rich with this technology? Why shouldn't it be us?"

"Who besides you and me?"

"Just you and me. We could share the money, and . . . and much, much more."

Treachery can wear the mask of beauty, and her mask was

exquisite. Somebody with less experience might even have believed her. I didn't come close. The buzzing I'd heard before was the electrical generator, making the heat. The pile of metal on the floor was aluminium.

"Don't insult our intelligences, Miss Parkins. You didn't set this up all by yourself. The electricity, the furnace, the mold, the snap-together pieces of wood veneer. This took organization. This had to be planned even before the secrets were stolen. It was brilliant. You weren't smuggling anything in the bandages. The bandages were just a blind. *You were smuggling crutches*. Aluminium crutches, each worth five hundred to a thousand pounds, covered in a thin layer of wood, and brought on board the ship. Watson stumbled onto the secret, and a few of your cripples beat him with the metal. The wood covering kept us from recognizing the marks. You'll pay for that, my dear. You'll get old and ugly spending years picking jute in prison."

There was something wrong. She wasn't scared enough. She had the smug confidence of a punter who knows the game is rigged.

Now, I knew it, too, and that was all I needed. "Thank you," I told her. "Now I know who—"

Just then, the door burst open, and a figure with a gun started spraying bullets around. I ducked for my life, even as I saw Nigel (or Fred) go down. Parkins made a big mistake. She ran for the doorway, yelling, "Darling."

Darling shot her, then disappeared from the doorway. She spun away and fell back against the crucible.

Her scream was more than the scream of a woman's throat. It was as though it was being torn from her soul. She was in flames as she fell, rolling and still screaming. I ran to her and beat out the flames, but it was too late.

"You're done for," I told her. I mentioned a name.

Her voice was a croak, it came from somewhere in the middle

of a charred and blistered mess, but it was still a human voice. "I . . . loved . . . him," she said.

"Obviously, he didn't reciprocate," I said, but I don't think she lived long enough to hear it. I left. I had a report to give.

V

A commissionaire was waiting for me outside the Ministry, and pressed a note into my hand, I tipped him, but I didn't bother to look at it.

Mycroft met me outside the sub-Minister's office.

"Well?" he said.

"You'll hear it," I told him, and went inside without knocking.

The sub-Minister was scratching at his side-whiskers when I walked in.

"Ah, Mr. Holmes, results so soon?"

"Many of them, sub-Minister. And here's another one." I walked up to him, grabbed him by his trademark facial hair, and pulled with all my might.

He screamed, but not as loudly as he would have if I were pulling roots from skin, instead of false hair from spirit gum.

"I knew it," I said. "The way you kept scratching. A man who has had whiskers for years gets used to them. But they weren't your whiskers anymore. You shaved them off so you could do your dirty business around the docks without being recognized, gluing them back on when you came here."

There was hate on the reddened face, the hate of an evil man who could betray his country and take pleasure out of watching his men pound a good man like Watson into jelly.

Mycroft, as usual, was right there with me. "Sir Carl had the easiest access to stealing the plans."

"Of course he had. You were there when Watson was beaten near to death, weren't you, Sir Carl?"

"You petty fools, what do you think you can do to me?"

My face wanted to smile, but I kept it grim. "Answer my question. You must have watched. At least, Watson must have seen you, because he told me something about you, something I didn't recognize at the time. I'll make you an offer, sub-Minister. You answer my question, and I'll answer yours."

He drummed his strange fingers on the tabletop. "Very well. Yes, I was there. Your friend begged us to stop."

I went icy inside. "So will you."

"Are you going to answer my question?"

"A *true* Englishman keeps his word," I said. "Here's what's going to happen to you. The Prime Minister will be told. The Queen will be told. Your immediate superior will be told. That's all. The Crown would just as soon avoid scandal, wouldn't they, Mycroft?"

"Naturally, but we just can't let a murderer—"

"He'll be punished," I said. "He'll come to the office every day. He'll have no appointments. He'll make no decisions, or speeches. He'll be a shell, a nothing.

"And all the while, he'll be waiting."

I snaked out a hand, grabbed his drumming fingers, and squeezed. "Have your fingers always been like this, Sir Carl?" I asked, shoving the blunt, nail-covered tips in his face. "Never mind, I see from the portrait of you on the wall that they haven't been."

I threw his hand down on the desk. "Watson said to me, 'Clubbed. Clubbed. Doomed.' I assumed he was talking about himself, but he's too good a doctor not to have assessed his own condition properly. He was talking about you."

I grabbed the hand again. "These are called *clubbed fingers,* and they are an outward sign of a deadly heart disease. Watson called my attention to a paper on the subject in the *Lancet.*"

And finally, the valve popped, and all my hatred of the traitor poured out in face and voice. "And so, every day, you'll leave the gilded prison that is your home, and come to the gilded prison that is your office, and one day, a year from now, perhaps six months, maybe less, Providence will swing its hammer, once, twice, crushing your black heart, making you cry for mercy, and you'll die, clawing at the carpet and whimpering."

He was whimpering now. I turned in disgust and left him to Mycroft.

Outside the door, I remembered the note the commissionaire had given me. I fished it out of my pocket and read it.

It was from the doctor. Watson was conscious. He was going to be all right.

I ran to the street to hail a cab.

Unlike other stories in The Resurrected Holmes, *our final selection is a hitherto suppressed version of an existing Holmes tale. Watson twice mentions an untold "second stain case," but his references not only contradict one another, they are at variance with "The Adventure of the Second Stain" as it finally appeared in the December 1904 issue of* The Strand. *Imagine Mr. R.'s thrill on inspecting Watson's dispatch-box to find a duodecimo notebook in Holmes's handwriting devoted to the case he was forced to quash till the Twentieth Century! "Too Many Stains" was probably written by* REX STOUT *(1886–1975), author of* Champagne for One, The Black Mountain, Some Buried Caesar, Too Many Clients, Too Many Cooks, Too Many Women, *"Too Many Detectives" and a host of other superb mysteries about Sherlock Holmes's greatest, fattest (and possibly literal) descendant, Nero Wolfe and his amanuensis, Archie Goodwin.—*JAF

Too Many Stains
(The Adventure of the Second Stain)

BY *"MARVIN KAYE"*
(ASCRIBED TO REX STOUT)

Some muck you just can't clamp a lid on. I found that out one humid morning in 1892. Breakfast wasn't even over, yet there was a lady hiding in my bedroom. My brother, all eighteen stone of him, sat on the settee glowering at me as he adjusted the bead of the beer he'd made Mrs. Hudson bring him at that ungodly hour.

When I muttered at this abridgement of civilized habit, his eyes widened in irritation.

"The brewing of beer," Mycroft admonished, "is one of civilization's most venerable practices."

"Brewing it, sure, but not swilling it at ten A.M."

He took three small sips, patted his lips with a pocket handkerchief and continued his discourse as if he had not heard me. "One of civilization's oldest artifacts is a Mesopotamian beer recipe graven in stone some seven thousand years ago. Beer was the beverage of choice in such pre-Biblical nations as Egypt and Sumeria."

I shrugged. "One swallow doth not a Sumer make."

One of his fingertips described small circles on his ample thigh. "Your conversation, Sherlock, is uncharacteristically inane. Pray divert me by inviting the woman in the next room to join us." Before I could demur, he barked, "Am I a witling? The air reeks of perfume."

"When I went out last night, I masqueraded as a woman."

"Have you also attained skill as a ventriloquist? When I entered," he said, waving a broad flipper toward my bedroom, "I distinctly heard someone's vain attempt to suppress a cough."

Giving it up, my guest emerged. As my brother undertook the ponderous process of ceremoniously rising to his feet, I murmured introductions. Mycroft's eyebrows ascended a fraction of an inch.

"Madam," he declared blandly, "I have heard of you."

I daresay he had. Lady Hilda Trelawney Hope, youngest daughter of the Duke of Belminster, is (according to Watson) one of London's most beautiful women. Ditto resourceful. Ditto ditto indiscreet. I'd met her twice before. The first time was the morning after Eduardo Lucas was knifed to death by Mme. Fournaye, his jealous Creole wife. Three days later, I encountered her a second time, just prior to my returning a stolen document (and guess who stole it) to the Right Honourable Trelawney Hope, Lady Hilda's husband and England's Secretary for European Affairs.

Our third encounter, which started shortly before my brother unexpectedly popped in, was as remarkable as those earlier occasions.

I was, after all, *supposed* to be dead . . .

II

If you've read Watson's version of this case, you already know my faithful Boswell had to quash certain details of the story, those which I'm about to reveal. As I said, you just can't clamp a lid on this kind of muck. Mycroft did his best, but London hummed with rumours that rose up again years later. Watson twice tried some fancy footwork even before the *Strand* finally published his abbreviated version of the affair under the clever misnomer, "The Adventure of the Second Stain." I mention this for lackwits who tend to dismiss my friend as a dimwitted old duffer. Watson was anything but. He covered up the trail so well that before I can explain what really happened, first I have to clear away the Watsonian underbrush.

The business began in 1886 when the British government hired me to recover a stolen letter of vital import. This led me to check into the aforementioned violent death of Eduardo Lucas, an international spy who meant to sell the purloined document. During the murder investigation, Inspector Lestrade of Scotland Yard mentioned a "second stain," a phrase the press picked up on. Playing a hunch, a few canny journalists began questioning me and Watson.

Normally, we welcomed this kind of publicity, but Whitehall didn't want any hint of the real reason I was engaged to become public. Mycroft warned us to tough it out, which we did till some new cosmopolitan scandal turned the case into yesterday's news.

It should have ended there. But six years later, during that period when the world believed I was dead, events whose outcome I have till now suppressed churned up new gossip about the Lucas killing.

To combat this unwelcome publicity, my brother concocted

a ploy that I, supposedly defunct, had no choice but to swallow. At Mycroft's bidding, Watson (who no longer lived at 221B and who still believed me dead) composed "The Yellow Face," a fictitious adventure whose sole purpose was to testify that on a half-a-dozen occasions—including "the affair of the second stain"—my deductive powers fizzled.

This smudge on my career appeared in the February 1893 *Strand,* yet failed to end the outcry. Not only did the buzz increase, but newspaper leaders (nowadays you call them editorials) grew dangerously speculative. Mycroft again prompted Watson; this time my chronicler turned the rug by inserting a seemingly contradictory remark into "The Naval Treaty," which ran in the *Strand* in November of the same year:

" 'The Adventure of the Second Stain' . . . deals with interests of such importance, and implicates so many of the first families in the kingdom, that for many years it will be impossible to make it public. No case, however, in which Holmes was ever engaged has illustrated the value of his analytical methods so clearly or has impressed those who were associated with him so deeply. I still retain an almost verbatim report of the interview in which he demonstrated the true facts of the case to M. Dubuque, of the Paris Police, and Fritz von Waldbaum, the well-known specialist of Dantzig, both of whom had wasted their energies upon what proved to be side-issues. The new century will have to come, however, before the story can be safely told . . ."

This statement is mainly true. Certainly the government interest required secrecy. The implied culpability of "many of the first families" was exaggerated to diffuse suspicion, as only two bloodlines were directly involved.* Still, the aftermath entailed a cover-up.

---

*As this account deals with the second stain case's latter events, I omit from this tally the royal family itself, which would have been both chagrined and mortified had the epistle I was hired to retrieve been made public. As some of Watson's readers have long suspected, its belligerent author was none other than the queen's own grandson, the soon-to-be Kaiser Wilhelm II. Concerning the crouching lion

Watson's characterization of my analytic methods is, of course, pure moonshine. This affair did not reach its conclusion till 1892, a year when Watson believed I was dead. In truth, Mycroft deserves more praise than me in solving it.

As for that verbatim report concerning Dubuque and von Waldbaum, readers logically assume Watson was on the scene, but that's not true. Most of it I told him long afterward. When he prepared his abbreviated version of the story in 1904, there was no reason to add that material, as he was only reporting about the missing document. This omission irked various readers. In somewhat abbreviated fashion, I have restored Dubuque and von Waldbaum to the present narrative.

*T*he new century will have to come, however, before the story can be safely told . . . and the 1900s were indeed upon us before Watson "at last succeeded in obtaining his consent that a *carefully guarded account of the incident* should at last be laid before the public."

Watson told as much of the truth as could be allowed in 1904. Now here's the rest of the story.

III

I was holed up at 221B, which Mycroft and my landlady Mrs. Hudson (the only non-criminals who knew I was alive) kept ready for me. Moriarty's henchmen were on my trail, so I had to lay low. I was at breakfast when footsteps made me reach for the gun I kept close by.

When I heard the prearranged tap that Mrs. Hudson used to

---

stamp he imprinted in the seal of his letter instead of the double eagle one might have expected him to use, Wilhelm was not yet Kaiser when he penned his sabre-rattling note. Mycroft says the lion device may have reminded him of the Scots, a folk whose truculent attitude toward the British crown evidently delighted the Prussian prince.

declare her identity before bustling in, I relaxed. She entered, her honest face turned down in an anxious frown.

"Mr. Holmes, there's a woman downstairs who won't go away. She insists on seeing you."

"But my dear Mrs. Hudson—!"

"I *told* her," she said, casting her eyes to the ceiling, 'Everybody knows poor Mr. Holmes was dashed to pieces at the bottom of that waterfall in Switzerland,' but she claims to know better."

"Indeed? What's she like?"

"She's a lady, a lovely one, at that. Here's her card."

I stared sternly. "Why did you bring this to me? Now she must conclude that someone is indeed in the house."

"I had no choice, sir. I insisted that she leave, but she said that if she did, she'd go straight to the newspapers and say she knows for a fact you're still alive."

I inspected the card in my hand. "Lady Hilda Trelawney Hope. Hmm. A familiar name . . . possibly an ominous one."

Mrs. Hudson's breath caught. "Ominous, Mr. Holmes?"

I held a finger to my lips to forestall further conversation. "Shh. If my ears do not deceive me, Mrs. H., the dame's afoot." I raised my voice and revolver. "Come in, madam. Slowly."

Without so much as a curtsy, she swept into the room and promptly sat down by the window, just as she'd done the first time she visited my chambers six years earlier. As she composed herself, I conceded that even a man unmoved by distaff charms could not help but appreciate Lady Hilda Trelawney Hope. Though I personally prefer a wider angle to the chin, the blush of her features suffused her delicate skin and her wide eyes sparkled. The morning was heating up, yet she clutched a cloak about her as she sat in a halo of morning light, one gloved hand holding a folded copy of the *Daily Gazette*.

When I saw what it was, I winced. That week, the London press had been chockful of a mystery known as "The Man with the

Watches," a bizarre business that has no bearing whatever on the second stain case. I mention it because a few days earlier the *Daily Gazette* printed the letter of some amateur sleuth who had the audacity to compose a solution to the puzzle and sign it "Sherlock Holmes."

I indicated the newspaper. "Was *this* the instrument that convinced you I was not dead?"

She nodded. "It was indeed the vehicle that suggested the possibility. But if you did not wish to be found out, sir, why on earth did you write it?"

"I didn't. You have some experience of my abilities. Do you really believe I could have penned such ineffable twaddle?"

"At any rate, it brought me to your door."

"Yes," I groaned. "I wonder who'll be next."

Mrs. Hudson, who was dithering near a window overlooking Baker Street, suddenly exclaimed, "Mr. Holmes, I believe I can answer that."

"Eh?" I joined her at the window, looked down and saw a man emerging from a cab. "Good Lord! What is *he* doing here?!"

"Is it my husband?" Lady Hilda's voice trembled.

"It's my brother Mycroft. Something important brings him."

"How can you tell?"

"His life's one of inflexible routine. He goes nowhere except his rooms in Pall Mall, his office in Whitehall and his club, which he visits punctually daily from 4:45 to 7:40 P.M. If the Greenwich observatory ever breaks down, the world can set its clocks by the orbit of planet Mycroft."

My visitor started for the door, but I forestalled her.

"If you go back down, you're going to bump into him. Wait in my bedroom. For the sake of propriety, my landlady will keep you company, won't you, Mrs. Hudson?"

"We're going directly," she said, steering Lady Hilda into the next room.

IV

"Madam, I have heard of you," Mycroft declared.

Casting a doubtful glance at me, Lady Hilda returned to her seat by the window. She waited till Mrs. Hudson left before addressing my brother. "And what could you possibly have heard, Mr. Holmes?"

Instead of answering her, Mycroft turned to me. "A strange coincidence, Sherlock . . . I came here specifically to ask you about this woman. How comes it that she's here, visiting a dead man?"

"That preposterous letter in the *Gazette* led her straight to me."

"A letter planted by a Moriarty alumnus to smoke you out."

Lady Hilda cut in. "Mr. Holmes, you specifically came here to discuss *me?* I demand to know what you claim to have heard!"

"Very well." Mycroft inclined his head half an inch, his version of a nod. "I am aware that you frequent the casinos of Monte Noire."

"How is that any of your business, sir?"

"My responsibilities at Whitehall are both fiscal and advisory. Your extravagances at the gaming tables are a source of concern."

"Of concern to whom, sir?"

"To the government."

She trembled with indignation. "My private life has no national bearing whatever."

Was this the same woman who recently quaked at the prospect of her husband arriving? Obviously, she was trying to tough it out with Mycroft, which I could have told her was a waste of time.

My brother took in a peck of air and let it out again. "Surely, madam, you are not that naive. Your husband, the Right Honourable Trelawney Hope, holds a vital position in Her Majesty's government. He is a likely candidate for political advancement. The success of his role with the administration, as well as all future prospects, depends on a reputation unsullied by incident or scandal."

"Which you impute *I* might bring upon him?"

"Precisely."

She sat perfectly still for a moment, then shifted forward as if about to rise. "Since you are so well informed about me," she said crisply, "I wonder that your sources have not also revealed that I am remarkably expert when I play at vingt-et-un."

Mycroft waggled a finger. "You misunderstand my drift. Normally, your gambling penchant would merely rate a cautionary mark in your husband's dossier. What troubles me and, by extension, Her Majesty's government, is the compulsion that forces you to win large sums which pass swiftly through your dainty hands. Would you care to define it?"

She bit her lip, but said nothing.

Mycroft glanced at me, read my expression and nodded. "Madam," he said, "you may not realize that you have us at a disadvantage. If you promise not to inform a soul, not even your husband, that Sherlock is alive and in London, I vow to keep mum concerning what you have to tell us, provided it poses no imminent threat to national security."

"Mr. Holmes," she replied with a catch in her voice somewhere between a gasp and a sob, "that's the trouble . . . I fear it may."

I put in my oar. "Is this what compelled you to seek my counsel?"

"It is."

For a few seconds, Mycroft's lips worked in and out, then he turned over the broad palm of his right hand. "Here's my proposition. Suppose I tell you what I know already. You may then be in a better position to judge what else appropriately may be divulged. Agreed?"

Lady Hilda nodded.

"Very well. I know you're being blackmailed by a foreign agent. I don't know what hold he has over you, but I have a vague suspicion."

"Specifically, sir?"

"Fact number one," he said, aiming his forefinger at the ceiling. "Six years ago, the former Premier of Britain, together with your husband in his official capacity as Secretary for European Affairs, paid a secret visit to my brother. What happened at that meeting I do not know, but it was my duty to record the draught drawn on the Exchequer to recompense Sherlock for his services. It was for a hefty amount." He pointed a second finger skyward. "Fact two. Soon afterward, a British operative planted in the employ of a foreign agent named Adolphus Zecchino informed Her Majesty that Zecchino had begun to extort large sums of money from you. I think it probable that these two incidents involving your family are linked to one another."

"They were indeed connected," Lady Hilda admitted, "but I am ignorant of what transpired at that meeting between my husband and the Premier and your brother." She spoke to me. "Six years ago, Mr. Holmes, you could but hint at the significance of that occasion. I hope you now are at liberty to discuss it."

I replied, "Only in the most general terms. But may I infer from this that you wish me to share what I know with my brother?"

She said yes. I scrutinized her to be sure she was solid with it before turning to Mycroft and explaining that, though wholly devoted to her husband, before her marriage to Trelawney Hope she had written another man an impassioned letter that she later came to fear might compromise her in the eyes of her mate.

"I presume," said Mycroft, "that adolescent love-note constitutes the hold which the agent Adolphus Zecchino has on you, madam?"

"It's more complicated, Mr. Holmes," she murmured, looking to me to continue my briefing.

"The love-note," I told him, "came into the possession of the spy, Eduardo Lucas. You remember him?"

"His wife stabbed him to death. The second stain case, right?"

"Yes. Lucas threatened to show Lady Hilda's note to her husband unless she stole a letter from his locked dispatch-box."

"And did she?"

Bowing her head in sorrow, she answered the question herself. "I procured an impression of my husband's key. A duplicate was cut. It enabled me to pilfer the paper whose description was furnished to me. But do not judge me too harshly, Mr. Holmes. When I learned of the damage the missing letter might do to my husband's career, I got it back again, as your brother will surely attest."

I verified Lady Hilda's story. Mycroft's eyes widened. "But how the deuce did you manage to get it back from that scoundrel Lucas?"

"I knew where he'd hidden it. On the night he died, when I exchanged the document I stole for my own incriminating letter, I saw him roll back a corner of the rug and stow the purloined paper in a secret recess underneath. Just then, Mme. Fournaye charged in and accused the two of us of having an affair. First they shouted, then they struggled with one another. Her shrieks alarmed me. Fearing recognition, I ran away." She trembled with remembered shock. "Next morning I read that the dreadful woman had stabbed Eduardo to death. I returned to the scene and distracted the constable on duty long enough to fetch the missing paper from the hideaway under the carpet."

Mycroft regarded me cynically. "And for this *you* took credit and accepted a princely sum, though wisely refusing the knighthood."

Lady Hilda defended me. "You wrong your brother. Had he not intervened, I would have burned the government's letter."

"Good God, madam, why?" His eyes goggled like a boiled fish.

"Besides the fact that it caused so much misery, I saw no way to return it to my husband without confessing my guilt. But your brother not only deduced that I'd retrieved it, he devised a means by which I was able to put it back undetected amongst my husband's papers."

"I trust that justifies my recompense," I said with a touch of asperity. "Anyway, that's basically the story. Any questions?"

"Several," Mycroft replied. "I always suspected you were mixed up in that second stain business. Lestrade told reporters that some time after the murder, the carpet in Lucas's office had been moved because the bloodstain on the floor didn't coincide with the smear on the rug. I couldn't imagine Lestrade figuring that out for himself."

"He didn't. I pointed it out to him."

"He never told the press the significance of that second stain."

"Because he never knew what it meant," I said.

"Whereas it led you to the recess and ultimately Lady Hilda."

"Yes. Next question?"

Mycroft turned to my client. "Did you read the paper you stole?"

"Certainly not, Mr. Holmes!" she exclaimed, sitting bolt upright. "What manner of woman do you think I am?"

"That is what I am endeavouring to discover. Sherlock, did you?"

I said no. "I was told that in it a certain foreigner ruffled by our colonial developments recorded his feelings in terms so inflammatory that if made public, dire consequences would ensue."

Mycroft wrote a name on a slip of paper and handed it to me.

"Precisely," I said, inspecting it.

Mycroft asked, "How did Lucas learn this letter existed?"

"He planted a spy in my husband's office," said Lady Hilda.

My brother pressed his fingertips together. "A final question, madam. Since Lucas returned the amorous note that put you in his power, what threat does this new nemesis, Zecchino, hold over you?"

"My nemesis, as you so aptly call him, was the mastermind

behind my original theft. He meant to purchase the document from Eduardo on behalf of Britain's enemies. After that horrible night when Mme. Fournaye slew him, Zecchino made contact with me—"

"And revealed," Mycroft interposed, "that the incriminating letter Lucas returned to you was a forgery?"

"Yes. Zecchino possesses the original. How did you know?"

My brother and I exchanged glances. "Lady Hilda," I replied, "the conclusion is elementary."

"Gentlemen," she said, "till now his demands have been solely fiscal, but the day I long feared is at hand. He has ordered me to filch another secret document from my husband."

Mycroft coughed portentously. "And have you done so?"

"I have not. Rather than place my husband's career in jeopardy again, I would sooner face exposure."

"How did Zecchino react when you told him that?"

"By threatening me with a far worse consequence. Mr. Holmes, he says he'll tell that dreadful woman who I am and where to find me."

"What woman do you mean?" I asked. "Surely not Mme. Fournaye?"

"The same. Recall that on that fateful night six years ago she mistook me for Eduardo's lover and slaughtered him."

"But this fiery woman was apprehended by the police," I declared.

"Yes," said Lady Hope, "but she is no longer in prison."

"That is true." Mycroft rose and walked over to my guest, for him a major effort. Looking down at her, he continued, "As I recall, Mme. Fournaye was declared criminally insane for stabbing her husband. If what I heard is true, she positively butchered him."

"Please don't talk about it." Lady Hilda shivered. "Yes, the woman is mad. She is an inmate of Rièges asylum near Paris."

"Then Zecchino's threat is toothless."

"But, Mr. Holmes, he claims he has the power to free her.

How I do not know, but I take him at his word. He is a terrible man . . . *terrible.*" She began to weep.

Mycroft, who seldom speaks at length while standing, positively detests women's tears. Yet he lingered at her side a moment longer. "Madam, your face is woefully pale. I am concerned for your health."

"My heart may be sick, Mr. Holmes, but my body is not at risk. I am, however, with child."

V

Lady Hilda was trundled off with mutual promises extracted: of her, that she would tell no one, not even her husband, that I was still alive; of us, that the Brothers Holmes would take swift action to protect her from the threats of the spy Zecchino.

Mrs. Hudson replenished my brother's beer and withdrew. Mycroft sat in an oversized chair and rumbled, "Bad business, Sherlock. Worse than I imagined."

"Is it permissible to tell me the particulars?"

Mycroft pursed his lips and thought it over for a few seconds before replying. I knew that he was reviewing things at lightning speed in his great brain. I was tempted to do the same, but he was privy to data I did not have, and it would have been a waste of time. At length he spoke. "Rather than a direct answer, let me remind you that last year London was visited by that same potentate who penned the first letter Lady Hilda was forced to steal."

No need for him to say more. What informed Englishman was not aware of the stormclouds gathering over Africa? It was tempting to mention Cameroons, but I did not wish to put my brother on the spot. "Mycroft," I said instead, "is there a particular document Zecchino wishes her to steal?"

He sighed profoundly. "I wish I could say yes. If there were a single instrument to safeguard, it would be simple enough to beef up security, but in the past few years, there has been a huge exchange of sensitive matter, any of which in the wrong hands might precipitate an international crisis. I shall immediately take action on this front, but Lady Hilda, after all, is but one of Zecchino's puppets."

"And yet, we must also protect her from him." Mycroft grunted, which I assumed signified assent. "What's our next step? Shall I unbeard this lion in his den?"

"We cannot oppose him head-on. He's too powerful."

"Rubbish. You said practically the same thing about Moriarty."

"And look how close you came to death!"

I waved my hand impatiently. "Now look, Mycroft, this woman specifically sought *my* aid."

His broad frame quivered in semblance of a chuckle. "If Watson only knew what an incurable romantic you are."

I ignored the jibe. "I can't sit by and do nothing."

"You shan't. I intend going to send you on a bit of an errand . . ."

VI

From past experience, I knew Mycroft's idea of "a bit of an errand" might be as trivial as purchasing blacking from a dingy shop in Murray Street. But this time it meant a trip to France and a sleepy little village some fifteen miles northeast of Paris.

Rièges, which lends its name to the mental institution on its outskirts, is pitched on the lower slope of a bosky prominence. Its rail platform leads to a single rutted street in whose squat grey inn I stowed my gear. An hour after my late morning arrival, I followed the same dusty road as it rambled past patches of corn and ramshackle farms toward the clinic where Mme. Fournaye was locked away.

Thanks to my brother, I bore a letter of introduction from Sir Henry J. Pettycloch, one of Edinburgh's leading medical authorities, that established my identity as Edwin A. Vollmer, M.D., a physician with special training in the treatment of violent disorders of the brain. It was in this guise that I was received by Dr. Raoul Johnnee, superintendent of the asylum at Rièges.

Perusing and returning my letter, he squinted curiously at me through his pince-nez. Crinkling his forehead and stroking a pepper-and-salt goatee, he purred, "M'sieur, are you aware that you resemble the late illustrious detective Sherlock Holmes?"

"Zut, alors," I exclaimed, smiting my forehead gallicly, "this curse plagues me in England, but here, too, in my homeland?" The rest of our opening amenities passed wholly in French, a language I'm fluent in, thanks to my maternal relatives, the Vernets.

"But to business," he remarked presently. "You are fortunate to have arrived today of all days to observe Madame Fournaye."

"Ah? Why so?"

"She is about to be examined by no less an authority than Fritz von Waldbaum. You have heard of him, of course?"

"Certainly. In Edinburgh, we regard him as Europe's preeminent specialist on the criminal mind. He lives in Poland, does he not?"

Dr. Johnnee nodded. "He and his assistant arrived from Dantzig a short time ago. Come . . . we shall observe him at work."

He led me up steep wooden stairs to a plastery canal that circled the inner partition of the building's central cavity. As we threaded our way around a peculiar series of shallow stalls that divided the inside wall into compartments, I peered everywhere, trying to assess the condition of security at Rièges. Could the intriguer Zecchino, with his formidable financial resources, find a way to free Mme. Fournaye from her earthwork prison? What I saw did not reassure me. The locks were rusty; the walls of limestone. Determined hirelings could break into the clinic and snatch the madwoman. Then again, force might not be necessary. It was too soon to tell if Dr. Johnnee was corruptible, but his staff's white jackets were frayed, with more loops than buttons; they might well be assailable.

My host held up his hand and we stopped walking. "We are just above the cells of the violent ward," he said. "One enters them from the other side of the asylum."

"What's the purpose of this place, then?"

A feline smile. "Our modest facilities are not without a degree of ingenuity. You are aware that patients who know they are being observed frequently behave less characteristically than when they trust they are alone. Now behold!" he exclaimed, sliding an oblong panel of the inner wall into a recess. He beckoned me to step forward.

Doing as he bade me, I perceived a polished surface where the panel had just been. Peering through it, I saw a padded cell several feet below and a dusky woman muttering to herself as she crouched on a straw cot. I recognized Mme. Fournaye, Eduardo Lucas's Creole wife. In her cupped hands she clutched a crumpled square of cloth.

Her cell door opened and two men entered. Mme. Fournaye squeezed the fabric into one fist and pressed it to her chest. Our high angle of vantage revealed the newcomer's hats, but not their faces. My companion identified the larger man as "your great colleague from Dantzig."

Von Waldbaum addressed the patient. She raised her head, but instead of looking at him, seemed to stare straight up at us.

I took a step backward. "Can't she see us?"

"No," my companion said. "On her side, this spot high on the wall appears to be covered by a painting of a waterfall."

I shuddered. Waterfalls make me nervous.

VII

I sat in a stuffy antechamber outside Dr. Johnnee's office on the ground floor waiting for my host to return with the specialist from Dantzig. As I sipped coffee laced with armagnac (the latter an imposition of my assumed nationality), I considered how best to deal with von Waldbaum. My own practical experience of the workings of the criminal mind is considerable, yet I knew the wisest policy would be to adopt an ingratiating manner with the Polish expert. But after eavesdropping for nearly an hour on his "treatment" of Mme. Fournaye, I felt neither sympathy nor respect for the man or his methods; thus I argued with myself over the degree of sycophancy I must needs adopt.

But then Dr. Johnnee returned with his guests and I got a shock that topsy-turveyed my intentions; to use a term indigenous to the Balkans, the sum total of my fawning over von Waldbaum came to *bupkis*.

Standing in the doorway, the superintendent of Rièges identified me to his esteemed colleague and stood aside as Fritz von Waldbaum, splendiferous in crushed velvet trousers, burgundy waistcoat, ruffled cream shirt and gleaming black opera pumps, loomed into view. His pug nose, smooth cheeks and jug-handle ears reminded me of some huge porker trained to prance on two legs, an impression intensified by the taut dome of his bullet-bald head. The specialist deigned to press my hand limply in jewel-infested fingers. Releasing me, he waggled a plump forepaw in the direction of his assistant, just then entering the room. "Permit me to introduce my student, Monsieur Guillaume . . . like you, an expatriate Frenchman."

I stuck out my hand to shake Guillaume's, then our eyes met and we recognized each other. Von Waldbaum's "student" was in reality Henri-Guillaume Dubuque, prefect of the Paris police. For an instant twice the length of eternity, I froze. The gendarme, rapidly twisting his wide-mouthed gape into a thin-lipped parody of a smile, grasped my hand and pumped life back into both of us.

His was the greater jolt, of course. Dubuque's unheralded appearance merely startled me, but I was supposed to be dead. His silence, at least, proved that neither one of us wanted to strip away our masks. As we exchanged amenities, I wondered if the policeman's real business at Rièges might be similar to mine.

But it was no time to discuss it. Dubuque assumed a deferential stance behind von Waldbaum, whose grandiose throat-clearing implied it was his prerogative to dominate the conversation. He smiled at me benignantly and said, "Doctor Vollmer, our host informs me that you were privileged to monitor my recent session with Mme. Fournaye. I trust you found my example instructive?"

"Most instructive."

"Please be good enough to tell my student what you learned."

I'm not sure which irritated me more, his smug presumption that I'd witnessed something of enormous value, or the condescending tone in which he couched his command. Nevertheless, I hesitated, until I caught Dubuque's stifled smirk and realized that, willingly or unawares, von Waldbaum was just his pawn. Would it matter, then, if I truly spoke my mind? I decided to risk it.

"Monsieur Guillaume," I told the disguised prefect, "if I am permitted to examine this patient, I shall take considerable pains *not* to emulate your mentor."

To my great astonishment, the specialist nodded his head and grinned. "Excellent, Vollmer, excellent! There is only one von Waldbaum. Who could possibly imitate him?"

"Or want to?" I retorted. "One of you is quite enough."

Bowing without a trace of irony, the ass thanked me! I marveled at his obtuseness, but remember, von Waldbaum was the first modern psychiatrist I'd ever met. I've since learned that impregnable ego is endemic to the profession: an occupational *hubris* directly analogous to the stock-in-trade of confidence men, evangelists and ninnyhammers.

"And now, monsieur," the ninnyhammer continued, "tell me if you have formed a theory concerning Mme. Fournaye's malady?"

"Yes. Based upon three observations I made—"

Von Waldbaum interrupted. "Only *three?*"

"Un deux trois," I said, mentally counting past that point. "But of course *your* profound insight into the workings of the criminal mind will enable you to interpret even such a paucity of clues with your inimitable éclat . . ."

"But of course, monsieur! Tell us your three little things."

Dubuque cocked an eyebrow, amused. Dr. Johnnee, who by then I'd written off as a toady, at least was no fool. Catching the true tenor of my challenge, he glanced back and forth anxiously between me and his pompous Dantzig authority.

I touched the tip of my forefinger. "The first little thing is that several times during the examination, she muttered, 'revenge.' " I tapped my ring finger. "Second, she invariably refers to herself in the third person. She said, 'Fournaye, elle est mauvaise,' instead of *Je suis mauvais.' "* My middle digit rose to pose my third point when von Waldbaum's paw paddled the air as a signal to pause.

"But these are signs of the selfsame condition," he declared. "The patient had passion sufficient to murder her husband, but cannot grapple with the guilt. Her mind rejects it in the only way possible—by withdrawing from close association with herself."

"But what about her threats? Whom does she want to kill?"

His piggy eyes widened. "She is bent on suicide! I should think that is, how shall I say . . . obvious?"

"Is it? She's obviously obsessed with avenging Lucas's death, but in my opinion, she wants to kill Mme. Fournaye—"

"But that's what he just said!" Dr. Johnnee exclaimed.

I shook my head. "Gentlemen, you may regard her as suicidal. I think she's plotting murder."

The glance Dr. Johnnee and von Waldbaum exchanged suggested they both thought Rièges was about to admit a new patient.

For the first time since we were introduced, my colleague Dubuque entered the conversation. "I think I see what our Edinburgh friend is getting at. The patient has convinced herself that she is no longer Mme. Fournaye. Thus she diverts anger at her own crime to a mythical woman whom she blames for slaughtering her husband, *n'est-ce pas?"*

"That's my theory." If I was correct, Zecchino somehow knew the truth and had based his blackmail threat upon it. If my client refused to do his bidding, he'd spirit away the madwoman from Rièges and tell her where to find "Mme. Fournaye" . . . in other words, Lady Hilda.

Von Waldbaum was earnestly whispering to Dr. Johnnee, whose bearded chin bobbed up and down in agreement. Slapping the Frenchman's shoulder, the porcine Pole approached me.

"I congratulate you, Doctor Vollmer, on your accurate assessment. I was testing you before, of course, but I was about to express the identical view of the case to Raoul here."

His temerity struck me speechless. I stared at him with the wary fascination of one who discovers some new breed of slug.

"I have recommended," von Waldbaum said magnanimously, "that you be accorded the courtesy of examining her yourself."

"Indeed? In your presence, I presume?"

"Not at all," he demurred. "Monsieur Guillaume and I must return to the inn to work up our report. We take our leave of you now."

I was tempted to quote Hamlet's famed parting shot, but "Monsieur Guillaume" spoke first. "Perhaps you'll join us later in the bistro?"

"Perhaps." I knew it was a command, not an invitation.

With a polite nod, Dubuque started out, but von Waldbaum paused in the doorway. In a cheerfully offhand manner, he said, "Ahh! I nearly forgot. You mentioned a . . . ah . . . third observation?"

The parasite wanted to bleed me dry. I shrugged. "A trifle, no doubt. What is the scrap of cloth Mme. Fournaye clutches in her fist?"

"A mere trifle," he agreed. "When one's life is reduced to the confines of a tiny room, it is not uncommon for a patient to ascribe enormous value to some simple object, be it cup, chair, or patch of linen . . . veritably transmuting it into an icon."

"I see. Have you examined her particular bit of holy cloth?"

"She would never willingly surrender it, and it would be too traumatic to take it from her."

"We could sedate her and have a look," Dr. Johnnee suggested.

I stiffened. "I trust you have not done that in the past?"

Dubuque heard my question and stepped back into the room as the superintendent of Rièges denied "any prior knowledge of Mme. Fournaye's unimportant little totem. I never noticed this cloth before today. I merely suggested sedation to satisfy Doctor Vollmer's curiosity . . ."

But Johnnee seemed crestfallen when I refused the needle.

VIII

I wasn't taken in by von Waldbaum's charade. He saw me as a rival. Patting my head in public was a set-up for knifing me in the back professionally.

My suspicions were confirmed when Johnnee guided me to the violent ward and turned me over to a lieutenant, excusing himself because of "pressing business with another patient." It was clear where my host's loyalties lay.

As I entered Mme. Fournaye's cell, I repressed an urge to wave hello to the flock of Poloniuses hiding behind the waterfall portrait. But I had a better way to frustrate them. The acoustics in their spyhole were far from ideal. Let them think I didn't know they were there. I'd speak too softly for them to hear.

When I saw Mme. Fournaye's tragic countenance, I relegated the eavesdroppers to the back of my mind. The smoky light of murder did not fill her eyes, as I'd been led to expect. As she looked up at me, I saw they welled with tears.

"Mme. Fournaye?"

She murmured, *"Elle est mauvaise* (she is bad)," the same sorrowful reply I'd heard earlier when von Waldbaum questioned her.

"Who told you that?"

"Tout le monde." (Everyone.)

"But what do *you* think of . . ." Instead of saying "Mme. Fournaye," I changed my mind and substituted, ". . . yourself?"

"N'importe." (It doesn't matter.)

That's what I had to work with. Before I could hope to learn whether Zecchino had already approached her, I must overcome her present disorientation somehow. I thought of an obvious trick. Would it work, or was she too far gone to reach?

I knelt beside her and told my secret. I said I knew she was Mme. Fournaye, and meant to prove her innocence. I had to repeat the lie twice before she responded. But respond she did! I'd triggered a veritable floodgate of emotion. She spoke of her undying passion for Eduardo Lucas with an eloquence I never wish to hear again. She catalogued with infinite detail her late husband's abuses and mental cruelties, and reeled off the intimate facts of his habitual infidelities. She revealed her horror, watching him die that night she caught him with "that awful woman." (Here her delusion resurfaced and she referred to her as Mme. Fournaye.)

This was the opportunity I'd sought to engineer. Focusing on the murder's aftermath. I told her I was on the trail of "the real killer" and only needed *her* help to bring the culprit to justice.

Her tear-streaked face shone with sudden hope, but the light flickered and died. "Monsieur, what help can I be? I am nothing."

"You are the victim of an international criminal named Adolphus Zecchino. Have you heard of him?"

"But yes. He said he was my friend."

"Where did you meet him?"

A bleak smile and a rational reply: "Have I a choice of salons in which to entertain?"

"He came here? When?"

"Yesterday? Last week? Every day is yesterday to me."

"Do you recall what transpired?"

"Yes, but . . ." She cast a furtive glance over her shoulder, then murmured, "I think they are listening to us."

"Who?"

"I don't know. I see no one, but sometimes I hear a sniff, a cough . . . unless . . ." Here she shuddered. "Unless I *am* going mad."

It was a tough call. I decided to tell her the truth. "Madame, if you remember who you *really* are, I promise that you won't go mad. Yes, they *are* listening. That's why I keep my voice down. I suggest you do the same. Now tell me about Zecchino. What did he say to you?"

"That he was my friend. That he would help me."

"In what way?"

To my surprise, she pressed the scrap of linen that von Waldbaum called her "icon" into my hand and closed my fingers on it. "He gave me this and said to keep it safe."

"Did he explain what it was for?"

"He said it will enable us to capture Mme. Fournaye."

"Madame, I tell you again that *you* are that personage."

"Non! Non! She murdered my husband! Everyone says so. That is why you must help me punish her!"

It was no use. One moment she was rational, the next she slipped back into fantasy. She couldn't face up to her crime, and it would have been cruelty to make her. I pitied Mme. Fournaye. Sometimes even a criminal rates a modicum of sympathy.

Anyway, I'd gotten what I came for, so I told her goodbye. As I prepared to pass through the cell door, she raised her eyes and voice.

"Return to me soon!" she implored.

The superintendent intercepted me at the front gate. "I hope your session with the patient was rewarding?"

"Indeed. She gave me a gift." I showed him the linen scrap.

"Merveilleux!"

"I shall keep it as a memento of the day I worked alongside the great Fritz von Waldbaum!"

"But, Doctor Vollmer," Johnnee demanded, gesturing with his pince-nez, "what could you possibly have said to Mme. Fournaye to establish such a measure of trust in so short a time?"

"M'sieur," I said, patting his shoulder conspiratorially, "I have you to thank for that. You gave me the idea . . ."

"I did?" He tugged at his goatee. "What was it?"

"But what else?" I paused for dramatic effect. "That I am Sherlock Holmes."

IX

Mutually pledging our secrecy, Dubuque and I swapped facts and opinions over strong coffee at *La Trique au d'huit*, the sole bistro in Rièges. As I'd suspected, von Waldbaum was an unwitting accomplice to whom Dubuque had been introduced with a letter similar to the one I employed on Johnnee.

When our business was over, I accepted Dubuque's invitation to ride to Paris with him. En route, I prepared a detailed report in code to Mycroft. When we reached the French capital, the police chief courteously arranged to have it telegraphed immediately to London.

Here's a small piece of it.

. . . told D. as much of my mission as I could safely divulge. Otherwise, I couldn't ask my next question.

SH: So what brought you to Rièges?

D: We've heard . . . things.

SH: What things?

D: I am not at liberty to say.

When I pressed him further, D. reluctantly mentioned rumours of patient abuses at the asylum, which he'd been appointed to look into. The caution he employed suggests Johnee has informants in the town.

D: And what was *your* business at Rièges?

SH: The level or lack of security.

D: Did you know a major contributor to the upkeep of the asylum is English? Or rather . . . he lives in London.

SH: Can you tell me his name?

D: *Non*. And I knew it *front and back like the alphabet . . .*

I got it. The alphabet runs from "ah to zed." *Conclusion:* "Ah Zed" can remove Mme. F. from the asylum whenever he wants to.

D. thinks Mme. F. already may have "escaped," I mean for a limited time in the past. He believes she may have committed a series of Parisian copycat Jack the Ripper murders. Implication: Z. held a dress rehearsal, briefly springing her to find out if he could indeed count on her services as a killer.

D.'s theory may be ominously confirmed by the fabric scrap. It was torn from a larger piece of material, and has a circular splotch on it that could be blood. If so, I will have to surrender it to D., but I want to examine it at home before I do.

X

I sent my brother a second telegram as soon as I got back:

ARRIVE LONDON AFTERNOON STOP SEE CLIENT STOP THEN AHZED (from) ROXTON★

Advance notice of my coming might alarm Lady Hilda, so I went straight to Whitehall Terrace, arriving in the late afternoon. Upon entering the residence of the European secretary, I inquired after the lady of the house and was shown into the morning-room.

"Mister . . . uh, Lord Roxton!" She kept her voice low. Her forehead was lined with worry. "Once before I chided you for

---

★*Roxton* is one of the aliases Holmes adopted during the period he pretended to be dead. See: Kaye, M., *The Histrionic Holmes* in ibid., *The Game Is Afoot* (St. Martin's Press, 1994)—jaf visiting me in my husband's house . . . and yet I confess I'm relieved you're here. This matter's about to come to a head."

"I suspected it would. That's why I came in person."

Peering into the corridor to make sure we weren't overheard, Lady Hilda shut the door, an action she never would have performed under normal circumstances. "Mr. Holmes," she said in an urgent undertone, "I've been given an ultimatum. I must deliver up the paper he wants this very night, or suffer the consequences."

"Zecchino told you this in person?"

"No. I tried to arrange a meeting in order to forestall him, but I was told he's been out of the country."

That confirmed Mme. Fournaye's timetable, but I didn't want to mention her. Lady Hilda was already upset; I feared additional stress might compromise her pregnancy. Still, I had to ask one question . . .

"Please don't take offense at what I'm about to say. Have you removed the document Zecchino wants from your husband's dispatch-box?"

Her reply was almost inaudible. "Yes."

"And your husband hasn't missed it?"

"No." She wrung her hands. "He was suddenly sent abroad on business he could not discuss with me."

I detected my brother's hand in this. Trelawney Hope's mission had two purposes: to caution England's partners to beef up security over written materials relating to certain international pacts, and also to send him away from home till the threat that hung over his wife (of which he knew nothing) could be removed for good and all.

"Bring me the paper you took," I told Lady Hilda. "I'll go in your place and deal with Zecchino myself."

Excusing herself, she soon returned with a sealed packet, which she handed to me. "This is a great risk, Mr. Holmes!"

"Less than you think. Mycroft's had time to defuse the threat of this particular document. Apparently, Zecchino doesn't know that. By the way," I added, withdrawing Mme. Fournaye's tattered cloth from my pocket, "do you know what this represents?"

Her face, already pale, went white. She reeled. I led her to a divan, got water from the sideboard and guided the glass to her lips. She gulped it down, then clutched my hand. "Where did you get that?"

"From Mme. Fournaye. She claims Zecchino gave it to her. What is it? You obviously recognize it."

"I saw it that night."

"What night?"

"The night she killed her husband." Lady Hilda trembled. "It's the dress she wore."

XI

Adolphus Zecchino told Lady Hilda to meet him in a public park across from his townhouse in Templeton Square. This simplified my approach. Inside, he might have refused to see me, but in the open, I was on the spy before he knew it. Hailing him, I revealed my mission.

"I wasn't expecting a deputy," he snarled.

"All the same, you've got one. Return my client's correspondence and you'll get your document."

"Let me see it first."

I withdrew a corner of it from my coat, but quickly thrust it back when he lunged. Feinting to one side, I stuck my hand inside my jacket pocket. "Steady there! Don't force me to shoot."

Like wary pugilists, we studied one another. The master spy had a forehead that sloped up and up to a dome fringed with thin faded hair. There was something reptilian about my late archenemy Moriarty, but Zecchino was a shark. Watching him in the lamp-light's cool evening glare, I conceived that his lashless cobalt eyes might easily intimidate a cobra. But refusing to be cowed, I glared back at him.

"So the Great Detective is still alive," he murmured softly. "This isn't the first time you've crossed me, you know."

"It probably won't be the last."

"Ah, but the future is *so* uncertain, Mister Holmes." Zecchino smiled; a remarkably unsettling spectacle. "But tonight, fate decrees we work together, so shall we proceed with our swap?"

"You haven't shown me Lady Hilda's letters yet."

"Come inside and I'll get them for you."

"I'll wait right here. Bring the originals this time!"

"They're in my safe. Follow me."

I kept my gaze and aim steady. "I prefer dealing with you in public. I have no idea who might be lurking inside your house—"

A woman's scream split the air, followed by a crash.

"My God!" Zecchino exclaimed, "That came from *my* house!" He started across the square at a fast clip.

I dashed past him and barred the front door.

"Get out of my way, Holmes!"

"Give me the key!" I demanded, drawing my gun. With a blistering curse, he put it in my outstretched palm. Waving him back a step, I opened the door, entered and turned the latch, locking Zecchino out.

I trotted down a hallway, peered into a parlour heavy with the hothouse reek of orchids, and saw a woman struggling to free herself from an armchair, to which she'd been tied with a bell-pull.

"Help me!" Lady Hilda cried. "I've been kidnapped!"

I rushed to untie her, but suddenly heard footsteps in the hall and the click of the front door. I spun round, pistol cocked, afraid I'd walked into an ambush . . .

A gentleman I hadn't seen in years entered the room. "Mr. 'olmes," he requested politely, "would you mind lowering your weapon?"

Gun still pointed, I stared, amazed, at Inspector Lestrade, of Scotland Yard. "Don't tell me you're on Zecchino's payroll!"

"Mr. 'olmes," he growled good-naturedly, "you know me better!"

I lowered my pistol. "Then I suggest you untie Lady Hilda. She is the wife of Trelawney Hope, the European secretary. Adolphus Zecchino, a foreign agent whose house we're in, has obviously kidnapped her!"

Lestrade gave me an oddly affectionate smile. "Well, there's a first time for everything! This time, Mr. 'olmes, your version don't jibe with the facts. But it's a real pleasure to see you're not dead!"

"What facts, man?"

"First of all, I caught Lady H. breaking into the 'ouse through a back window." With an unlit cigar, the inspector pointed to a large knife lying on the carpet. "Secondly, that was in her possession. You heard the racket she made when I asked her to surrender it."

I turned to my client, who was still trussed up in the chair. "Are you mad? Did you intend to use that knife on Zecchino?"

"Of course she meant to," said a familiar voice, "the same way she murdered Eduardo Lucas." My brother Mycroft, followed by a tight-jawed Adolphus Zecchino, entered the room.

XII

Depositing his substantial bulk in the largest armchair he could find, Mycroft laced his fingers over his middle and waited while Zecchino chose a red seat beside a table laden with pots of Vanda suavis and Miltonias in full bloom. Lestrade and I, on our feet, bracketed the yellow chair where Lady Hilda fidgeted in her bindings.

"She's in a family way, you know," Mycroft told the inspector. "I think you'd better release her."

Lestrade apologized effusively and untied her. Regardless of her crime, she was, after all, still the Duke of Belminster's daughter.

Lady Hilda rose and shrilly confronted Mycroft. "Mr. Holmes, your reprehensible behaviour shall not go unpunished!"

"Pfui! A gambler with no cards resorts to bluff." He glanced at Lestrade. "Inspector, I prefer eyes on my own level. Would you persuade her ladyship to take her seat?"

The light arm of the law rested on her shoulder and she sat.

Meanwhile, Zecchino, staring at the knife on the carpet, said, "I actually thought I'd be safe meeting her outside in the park."

"Don't talk to me!" Lady Hilda snapped.

"I'm not," Zecchino said, turning to Mycroft. "You know more about this than I'd imagined."

"Obviously. Otherwise, this interview would not be taking place."

They stared at one another, but kept their mouths shut. This was more than mere protocol, this was pure bullheaded stubbornness.

I broke their stalemate by speaking. "I assume you're saying that Lady Hilda killed Lucas to stop him from further blackmailing her?"

"Sherlock," my brother sighed, "despite your genius, you're still a novice when it comes to understanding women. Certainly she wanted to end the blackmailing, but that's just the tip of the iceberg . . . or perhaps a volcano is a better image for this smouldering business."

"Are you suggesting that I've been unfaithful to my husband?" the lady exclaimed. "I love him with all my heart!"

"Perhaps, madam," said Mycroft, "but at any rate, I'm not accusing you of infidelity. Before you were married, you and Eduardo Lucas had a brief, torrid affair. The letters you have vainly tried to recover were originally sent to him, were they not?"

She didn't answer, so Mycroft spoke to Zecchino. "I ask you, sir, to produce this immensely troublesome correspondence."

The spy stared at him. "What makes you think I've got it?"

"Does the fact she meant to kill you for it jog your memory?"

"You did me a favour intercepting her," Zecchino admitted, "but this is business. If I give you the letters, what do I get in return?"

"Your freedom, sir."

"Freedom to do what?"

"To go elsewhere. France, perhaps . . ."

"Why should I?"

"If you stay in England, you will be prosecuted as a black-mailer."

"Mr. Holmes, you can't prove a thing."

"I think I can, but even if I'm wrong, sir, the publicity will severely compromise your future effectiveness as an agent."

The shark bared his teeth. "I'll risk it, Fatso."

Mycroft addressed Lestrade. "Inspector, be so good as to summon our special guest." He asked it blandly enough, but I knew Fatso was angry from the way his fingertip traced tiny circles on his thigh.

Lestrade went to the archway and waved his hand. A tall, good-looking man with white hair entered the room and acknowledged Mycroft.

Zecchino jumped up. "Who let you in?"

"She did," he answered. "Not that she knew it."

"What are you doing here?"

"Mr. Holmes invited me to this party." With that, he went to the sideboard and helped himself to a small glass of brandy.

"Permit me to introduce Mr. Maturin," said Mycroft. "Sherlock, did you bring the scrap of fabric you described in your telegram?"

I took it out and gave it to him. He, in turn, handed it to Mr. Maturin, who studied it carefully.

"Yes," the newcomer nodded. "It looks just like the dress Mr. Zecchino hired me to bring him the day after his crony Lucas died."

With a gasp, Lady Hilda bounded to her feet. Mycroft waved her to keep still. Zecchino couldn't be silenced, though. He raged at Maturin, "I paid you to shut your mouth!"

"I don't keep swinish secrets." He sipped the spy's brandy. "Mr. Holmes, should I say where I got the dress, and in what manner?"

"That won't be necessary."

"Won't it?" Zecchino roared. "If my secrets are forfeit, so are Lady Hilda's—and so are yours, 'Mr. Maturin!' And who's going to take a thief's word against mine? I say he's lying, Holmes!"

Mycroft exhaled a bushel of air. "Omit the dramatics, sir. Fournaye went mad after witnessing her husband's murder. You spoke with her and realized the woman she'd seen was Lady Hilda. You hired Mr. Maturin to find evidence. He found the bloodstained dress she'd worn crumpled in her closet. A few days ago, you tore off a swatch and left it with Mme. Fournaye to prime her for the time when she either frightened Lady Hilda into stealing for you, or killed her."

"You still can't prove anything. Where's the dress now?"

Maturin stepped through the arch and immediately returned, carrying the garment. "The other evening, while you were in France, I dropped in and found it in a horsehair trunk."

He showed me the place where it had been torn. The patch fit.

XIII

Late that night, Mycroft and I shared a cab. We agreed that my recent activities had attracted altogether too much attention, and until Professor Moriarty's surviving henchmen (with whom we suspected Zecchino was affiliated) could be neutralized, I would do well to absent myself a while longer from England. Fortunately, I had a long-standing invitation from one of our maternal cousins to avail myself of the research facilities of a laboratory he supervised in the south of France.

"Excellent," said Mycroft. "On the way, you can visit Paris and apprise Dubuque of the true facts of the case. I hope something can be done to alleviate Madame Fournaye's suffering."

"She'll probably never recover from the shock of witnessing her husband's murder. But her needs at least will be better tended elsewhere than at Rièges."

"Whose staff, I suspect, soon will undergo change."

"I hope so. And now, my dear Mycroft, permit me to congratulate you upon the brilliant intuition that led you to uncover the truth."

"Intuition?" my brother repeated. "I *beg* your pardon?"

"You had neither witness nor evidence to suspect Lady Hilda."

"Lady Hilda provided three distinct reasons to suspect her."

"Three?" I felt a belated twinge of sympathy for von Waldbaum.

"On the morning we first interviewed Lady Hilda, you must recall how she swept across the room and seated herself with her back to the window, a deliberate maneuver to have the light behind her."

"Certainly I noticed! She didn't wish us to read her expression."

"And what did that suggest to you, Sherlock?"

"Vanity's *frou-frou.*"

"As I remarked earlier, the mind and heart of Woman is a book you've browsed imperfectly. Admittedly, to borrow Gilbert's phrase, her choice of seat might mean 'little, or nothing, or much.' That's why I stood near her and spoke of Lucas's murder. She paled visibly. That was my second clue."

"Due, perhaps, to her condition of expectant motherhood."

"Perhaps. But in conjunction with my other reasons—"

"One of which you have not disclosed."

"The most telling of the three, Sherlock. We live in an age characterized and often stultified by a bewildering nicety of formal titles. Even close friends, such as you and Watson, invariably address one another by their last names. The other morning, Lady Hilda solely referred to her spouse as 'my husband,' yet three times, and in the most suggestive of contexts, called her late lover Lucas 'Eduardo.' "

"I see. And now, what's going to happen to her?"

A weary sigh from the depths of Mycroft's chest. "That's going to be a rather ugly job, I'm afraid. Lestrade, at least, is prepared for the governmental ramifications of the situation . . ."

"You're not suggesting a cover-up?"

"If this business becomes public, not only will Trelawney Hope's career be ruined, but the integrity of Britain's European policy for the past six years will be submitted to the most intense scrutiny. Add to that the pitiful plight of the ailing Duke of Belminster, who only hopes to live long enough to set eyes on his future grandchild."

"But she destroyed one man and nearly killed another!"

Mycroft's lips twitched in ironical amusement. "A boon to England, wouldn't you say, ridding us of Lucas? As for Adolphus Zecchino, I debated with myself whether to apprehend her after . . . but that, I fear, would have been too much for Lestrade."

"And for me! Society cannot possibly condone murder!"

Venting another hugely jaded sigh, my brother said, "Be thankful, lad, that you don't occupy a high post in government."

XIV

So that's the third stain deal, or it's still the second if you count the ones on Lucas's floor and the rug that got moved as the same.

Hilda presented her husband with a son, then mysteriously retired from society. Trelawney Hope left office soon thereafter, grief-struck at the sudden mental collapse of his wife.

In France, police intervention plus sudden financial failure closed Rièges. Mme. Fournaye was taken in by an aunt, who nursed her back to health. But the Creole widow never remarried.

The pseudonymous Mr. Maturin was a casualty of the Boer War. He died saving the life of his best friend, a reformed burglar.

Watson learned most of the above facts years later. But he accompanied me in 1903 on a visit to New York when I succumbed to curiosity and vanity and took in a performance of Mr. William Gillette's at the Garrick Theatre on West 35th Street.*

---

*Watson's transcriber did not make this up. Gillette really performed that year at that theatre, at that address.—jaf

As we entered the lobby at the end of the show, I felt a tug at my sleeve. Turning, I found myself faced by the great gammony features and figure of Fritz von Waldbaum, who, still unaware of my true identity, hailed me as Dr. Vollmer. We spoke for a time, and I'm afraid that what I told him spoiled his evening out.

As the Dantzig specialist quitted our company, Watson pointed out a tall gentleman about to enter a cab.

"Holmes, do you know that fellow? A second ago, I saw him give you the most dreadful look."

The cab door closed, but not before I glimpsed the high forehead and predatory eyes of Adolphus Zecchino.

I identified him to Watson, who asked if he'd settled in America.

"That's what Mycroft led me to believe."

"Is that why we're really here, Holmes?"

"Not at all, my good fellow. Seeing him is mere coincidence."

"But oughtn't we to do something?"

I shook my head. "In the words of America's own Benjamin Franklin, this continent has spawned a new breed . . . rougher, simpler, more violent. If 'Ah Zed' puts down American roots, he may find the wolf at his door. In the long run, Watson, good wins and always shall. And now, shall we sup at Lüchow's? I've an appetite for a hearty steak, some berried Caesar salad and champagne galore."

"Make that champagne for one," Watson demurred. "There's only one possible complement for fare such as you describe, Holmes."

"What's that?"

"A quantity of excellent stout."

Contributors Notes

JOHN GREGORY BETANCOURT is head of Wildside Press, publishes the trade magazine *Horror,* and is a partner with Marvin Kaye of Bleak House, a new publishing firm affiliated with *Weird Tales* magazine. He has written many short stories and novels, including *Johnny Zed, The Blind Archer* and *Rememory.*

TERRY MCGARRY works for *The New Yorker,* has written a number of dark fantasy tales, including "Cadenza," "Loophole" and "Red Heart" and was a 1992 runner-up for the Gryphon Award.

HENRY SLESAR won the Mystery Writers of America's Edgar for *The Gray Flannel Shroud* and television's Emmy award for his former position as head writer of the long-running daytime drama, *The Edge of Night.* His prolific writing career includes over five hundred short stories, of which approximately one-third are science-fantasy, a novel adapted into film as *Twenty Million Miles to Earth,* and scripts for *The Man from U.N.C.L.E.*

MORGAN LLYWELYN lives in Ireland, where she writes a series of acclaimed best-selling historical fantasy novels, including *Bard, The Horse Goddess, Lion of Ireland* and *The Elementals. The Earth Is Made of Stardust . . . ,* a collection of her short stories, will be published soon by Bleak House.

PETER CANNON is no stranger to literary parody. His earlier volume, *Scream for Jeeves,* cross-pollinated several H. P. Lovecraft stories with P. G. Wodehouse's style, while his novel, *Pulptime,* is subtitled "the Singular Adventure of Sherlock Holmes, H. P. Lovecraft, and the Kalem Club, As if Narrated by Frank Belknap Long, Jr." A native Californian, Mr. Cannon grew up in Massachusetts and now resides in New York, where he is a freelance editor.

Craig Shaw Gardner writes both horror and hilarious fantasy, notably a series of Arabian Nights spoofs and the rib-tickling "Ebenezum" sorcery novels. His earlier Sherlock Holmes redaction, "The Sinister Cheesecake" (ascribed to Damon Runyon) appeared in *The Game Is Afoot* (St. Martin's Press, 1994).

Darrell Schweitzer is a prolific fantasist, erstwhile editor of *Weird Tales* magazine and one of science-fantasy's most recondite scholars and collectors. His fiction appears regularly in Guild-America (Doubleday) anthologies. His controversial earlier Sherlock Holmes tale, "The Adventure of the Death-Fetch," was published in *The Game Is Afoot* (St. Martin's Press, 1994).

Roberta Rogow is a New Jersey children's librarian who contributes to the *Merovingen Nights* anthologies and science-fantasy periodicals. Paragon published her *Futurespeak: A Fan's Guide to the Language of Science Fiction*. Her earlier Sherlock Holmes story, "Our American Cousins," appeared in *The Game Is Afoot* and was dramatized and performed off-off-Broadway by The Open Book theatre company.

Paula Volsky is one of America's most accomplished fantasists. Her epic novels, startlingly literate cross-pollinations of Jane Austen and Jack Vance, with a soupçon of Shakespeare thrown in for good measure, include *The Wolf of Winter, Illusion, The Luck of Relian Kru* and the forthcoming *The Gates of Twilight*.

Mike (Michael D.) Resnick is a popular science-fantasy novelist whose novels include *The Goddess of Ganymede, Pursuit on Ganymede,* both patterned on Edgar Rice Burroughs, and *Redbeard.* He also compiled the *Official Guide to Fantasy Literature* for collectors.

Richard A. Lupoff won a Hugo early in his career for *Xero,* a fan periodical which he coedited with his wife, and several years later collaborated with the late Don Thompson on an excellent and popular survey of comic books, *All in Color for a Dime.* Author of two highly regarded studies of Edgar Rice Burroughs, he has written a wide variety of fiction, including science-fantasy, mysteries and parody.

CAROLE BUGGÉ is a New York comedy improviser and teacher, playwright-composer, poet and short story writer. She never read "Dead Yellow Women," a Dashiell Hammett story whose plot resembles parts of "The Madness of Colonel Warburton." ("Maybe I channeled Hammett," Carole quipped.) Her earlier Holmes pastiche, "The Strange Case of the Tongue-Tied Tenor," appeared in *The Game Is Afoot,* and was dramatized and performed in New York by The Open Book theatre company.

EDWARD D. HOCH is one of the world's most mind-bogglingly prolific genre writers. Every issue of *Ellery Queen's Mystery Magazine* since May 1973 has contained one or more stories by Ed, including the Jeffrey Rand cryptography puzzles, the semi-supernatural Simon Ark mysteries, the New England-based Dr. Sam Hawthorne series and the wonderful Nick Velvet stories, about a thief who only steals things without value. "The Theft of the Persian Slipper," a Nick Velvet tale with a Holmesian theme, appeared in *The Game Is Afoot.*

WILLIAM L. DEANDREA is a mystery novelist (*Killed in the Ratings, The Hog Murders,* etc.), a regular critic and columnist for *The Armchair Detective* and a devotee and scholar of "the two finest detectives in the English language, Sherlock Holmes and Nero Wolfe."

MARVIN KAYE's fourteen novels include *Fantastique, The Incredible Umbrella,* the scholarly mystery *Bullets for Macbeth* and six other detective puzzles. He edits a series of anthologies for Doubleday, The Fireside Theatre and St. Martin's Press, is adjunct professor of creative writing at New York University, is a former Edgar judge and former chairman of judges of the Nero Award for best American mystery novels. He is cofounder and artistic director of New York's twenty-year-old professional readers theatre ensemble, The Open Book.

Acknowledgments

BY J. ADRIAN FILLMORE, G. AD.

Here we are backstage, where it is permissible to whisper the name of the great British writer, ARTHUR CONAN DOYLE (1859–1930), who wrote many excellent novels and short stories himself, yet still found time to serve as Dr. John H. Watson's literary agent.

Behind the scenes, we confess the dating of the tales in this volume was a headache. Watson was often imprecise, contradictory, at times downright obfuscatory. Scholars wrangle over the year, month, day of the week and even the hour that various cases occurred; they debate how long Dr. Watson was married and to whom, and the problem of sorting out Holmes's whereabouts during The Great Hiatus drove the editor to drink (to be fair, reading criticism by Harold C. Schonberg has the same effect). I have done my best to conform the dating of the individual pieces to those promulgated by the late William S. Baring-Gould in *The Annotated Holmes*: a source, however, that some Holmes buffs quibble with, but then most of them quarrel with *all* sources. Thus, individual contributors are not to blame for dating errors or misjudgments that may have crept in. If you discover one, be sure to bring it to my attention (not Mr. Kaye's). I may be reached c/o Parker College, English Department, College Heights PA 16801.★

★St. Martin's Press advises me that Mr. Fillmore's check for his participation in this book has not been cashed. The scholar appears to have taken an extended and rather sudden sabbatical.—mk